Brigid stabbed out an arm, pointing ahead

The figure was a statue, standing in erect position. At least fifteen feet tall, it represented a humanoid creature with a slender build draped in robes. The features were sharp, the domed head disproportionately large and hairless. The eyes were huge, slanted and fathomless.

The stone figure pointed toward the farther, shadow-shrouded end of the cavern.

"Somebody lived down here," Kane muttered.

Brigid nodded thoughtfully. "A long, long time ago."

Kane suddenly tugged Brigid to a stop. "Are you sure nobody's lived down here for a long, long time?"

Nettled by the hint of sarcasm in his tone, she followed his gaze downward.

In the fine rock dust on the cavern floor, they saw a fresh, clear print of a small foot with six delicate toes.

Other titles in this series:

JAMES AXLER

OUTLANDERS™

ICEBLOOD

A GOLD EAGLE BOOK FROM

WORLDWIDE®

TORONTO • NEW YORK • LONDON
AMSTERDAM • PARIS • SYDNEY • HAMBURG
STOCKHOLM • ATHENS • TOKYO • MILAN
MADRID • WARSAW • BUDAPEST • AUCKLAND

First edition December 1998
ISBN 0-373-63820-5

ICEBLOOD

Special thanks to Mark Ellis for his contribution to the
Outlanders concept, developed for Gold Eagle Books.

When Man's blood is of the broth of ice,
    his life is measured by a wanton throw of the dice;
In the midnight hours he broods in a lonely state,
    with spirit dead and desolate.

                       —Justin Geoffrey

The Road to Outlands—
From Secret Government Files to the Future

Almost two hundred years after the global holocaust, Kane, a former Magistrate of Cobaltville, often thought the world had been lucky to survive at all after a nuclear device detonated in the Russian embassy in Washington, D.C. The aftermath—forever known as skydark—reshaped continents and turned civilization into ashes.

Nearly depopulated, America became the Deathlands—poisoned by radiation, home to chaos and mutated life forms. Feudal rule reappeared in the form of baronies, while remote outposts clung to a brutish existence.

What eventually helped shape this wasteland were the redoubts, the secret preholocaust military installations with stores of weapons, and the home of gateways, the locational matter-transfer facilities. Some of the redoubts hid clues that had once fed wild theories of government cover-ups and alien visitations.

Rearmed from redoubt stockpiles, the barons consolidated their power and reclaimed technology for the villes. Their power, supported by some invisible authority, extended beyond their fortified walls to what was now called the Outlands. It was here that the rootstock of humanity survived, living with hellzones and chemical storms, hounded by Magistrates.

In the villes, rigid laws were enforced—to atone for the sins of the past and prepare the way for a better future. That was the barons' public credo and their right-to-rule.

Kane, along with friend and fellow Magistrate Grant, had upheld that claim until a fateful Outlands expedition. A displaced piece of technology...a question to a keeper of the archives...a vague clue about alien masters—and their world shifted radically. Suddenly, Brigid Baptiste, the archivist, faced summary execution, and

Grant a quick termination. For Kane there was forgiveness if he pledged his unquestioning allegiance to Baron Cobalt and his unknown masters and abandoned his friends.

But that allegiance would make him support a mysterious and alien power and deny loyalty and friends. Then what else was there?

Kane had been brought up solely to serve the ville. Brigid's only link with her family was her mother's red-gold hair, green eyes and supple form. Grant's clues to his lineage were his ebony skin and powerful physique. But Domi, she of the white hair, was an Outlander pressed into sexual servitude in Cobaltville. She at least knew her roots and was a reminder to the exiles that the outcasts belonged in the human family.

Parents, friends, community—the very rootedness of humanity was denied. With no continuity, there was no forward momentum to the future. And that was the crux—when Kane began to wonder if there *was* a future.

For Kane, it wouldn't do. So the only way was out—way, way out.

After their escape, they found shelter at the forgotten Cerberus redoubt headed by Lakesh, a scientist, Cobaltville's head archivist, and secret opponent of the barons.

With their past turned into a lie, their future threatened, only one thing was left to give meaning to the outcasts. The hunger for freedom, the will to resist the hostile influences. And perhaps, by opposing, end them.

Prologue

The Byang-thang Plateau, northwest Tibet

Clots of frozen blood glittered like rubies dropped from a broken necklace. They stretched back over the hard-packed snow as far as Grigori Zakat could see, swallowed by the shadows cast by the titanic peaks of the Cherga Mountains.

His booted feet had barely left their imprints on the hoarfrost overlaying the crust of snow, but the drops of blood left an unmistakable trail in crimson for his pursuers.

Zakat stumbled, a rushing wave of dizziness engulfing him. He sank down to the snow, supporting himself by his left arm, keeping his right hand pressed tightly against the pressure bandage taped over the throbbing wound beneath his ribs. Blood oozed around the edges.

He shook his head and remembered he had only one pursuer now, and that was death itself. Boro Orolok and his Mongol clan-brothers were at least a thousand miles behind him and could no longer threaten him with their *bundhi* daggers.

Zakat didn't know what had turned the followers of the Tushe Gun against the Russian garrison in the Black Gobi, but he suspected the three Americans

who had accompanied Colonel Sverdlovosk were
somehow responsible. He didn't know what had happened to his superior officer, either, but whatever influence the colonel exerted over Orolok's clan had
come to an obvious and decisive end.

Zakat slowly pushed himself to his feet, despising
the tremor in his legs, silently enduring the wave of
vertigo. He refused to voice a cry of pain as the raw
lips of his wound pulled and stretched. He was more
than just a major in the Internal Security Network or
even an operative of District Twelve—he was an ordained Khlysty priest and he knew pain was only of
the body and could thus be controlled.

He began walking again, concentrating on placing
one foot ahead of the other. He had no destination in
mind; he wanted only to put as much distance as possible between himself and the wreckage of the
Tu-114 cargo plane.

Zakat wasn't sure how much time had elapsed
since the huge aircraft had crashed onto the mountain
plateau. He could remember only the snowcapped
peaks coming up fast, then a splintering shock, a
grinding, relentless screech of rupturing metal. Something fell on him and knocked him unconscious.

The sound of crackling flames, the stench of burning oil and scorched flesh woke him. His back was
hot, and he looked around to see flames filling the
interior of the ship. Fortunately the fuel tank was
nearly drained so it didn't explode, but oil and other
flammable lubricants were aflame. The fire was intense enough to consume the bodies of the two troopers in the passenger compartment.

Not bothering to examine Kuryadin, slumped over

in the pilot's chair with a razor-edged fragment of the foreport embedded in his throat, Zakat unbuckled the safety harness and climbed out through the port, heedless of the lacerations he received. He cut himself several times in the process.

The broken-backed aircraft was afire from the wings back, so even if there were useful items in cargo, he couldn't reach them. He staggered away, his body a screaming mass of agony, but the most pain radiated out from the stab wound in his midsection. He stumbled across the frozen snow and forced himself to continue for hours upon hours.

The air, though bitingly cold, was quiet and still. So far, his heavy topcoat, fleece-lined gloves and insulated boots had kept him from freezing. He knew, however, that once the sun dropped behind the distant peaks, the temperature would plummet. He would have to find shelter or perish of exposure. Even the superhuman vitality granted to him by his faith had its limits.

He recalled the details of the martyrdom of Saint Rasputin, how he had survived poison, multiple gunshot wounds, blows to the head and near drowning. At last, he had succumbed to the freezing temperature of the waters in Moika canal.

Zakat fumbled beneath his blood-stiffened woolen shirt to finger the token of his faith hanging from a thong around his neck. He touched the tiny wooden phallus and caressed the stylized crystal testicles affixed to it.

The emblem symbolized Rasputin's penis, cut off by one of his assassins, then recovered and preserved in a velvet container by his devoted followers. Upon his initiation into the priesthood, Zakat had been permitted to glimpse but not touch the blackened, desiccated holy relic.

As he staggered onward, Zakat mouthed Rasputin's last words, "I will not die. *I will not die!*"

He continued whispering the mantra in an under-the-breath singsong as he had been taught. Even someone near him wouldn't be able to understand the hymn hissing from his lips.

No one, not even his superior officers, suspected he was a Khlysty priest. The few members of his sect who held high posts in the Russian government had helped him to dodge the rigorous background checks prior to his assignment to District Twelve, the ultra-secret arm of the Internal Security Network.

Zakat was his Khlysty name not his birth name, but no one questioned it, even though it meant "twilight." The few people who had glimpsed the pattern of wealed, raised scars on his back, the result of numerous flagellation rituals, had kept their curiosity in check. In the Internal Security Network, it was considered bad form to question a comrade, and even quite dangerous to make personal inquiries of an officer. It hinted at ambition. Primarily because he didn't appear to be ambitious, Grigori Zakat had advanced rapidly as a District Twelve officer under the command of Sverdlovosk.

Zakat went to great lengths to present the image of an aesthete, an effete intellectual who wrote charming verse for his own amusement in his off hours. Tall and slender, with a high pale forehead beneath sleek black hair and a languid manner, he didn't look as if he entertained any ambitions more taxing than rising by noon.

But of course he did. He couldn't be a Khlysty priest otherwise. He approached the obstacles to his ambition differently than other men. His approach relied on an offhand comment made to a superior officer regarding rivals, the discreet planting of black market contraband among their possessions or, if they were particularly impressionable, a campaign of subtle suggestions that they were being treated unfairly, passed over for advancement. When his competitors filed their complaints, they tended to cither disappear or be reduced in rank, and Zakat easily stepped into the power vacuum.

He had achieved the rank of major less than a year ago, after he arranged matters to make General Stovoski believe he had been seduced by his middle-aged, oversexed wife. Zakat managed to smile at the memory of Stovoski's face when the general stumbled into the parlor to find his wife kneeling before him, clawing at his trousers, oblivious to his pious protests.

The stupid cow of a woman, her brain saturated with vodka, had been childishly easy to manipulate, never realizing that the strength of Zakat's will had overwhelmed hers. And if his mind was exceptionally strong, his body complemented it. None of his comrades or even the surprisingly perceptive Sverdlovosk knew he had the strength in his delicate-appearing hands to throttle a man to death, something he had done as part of the ordination ceremony.

Much of his Khlysty training revolved around camouflage, infiltration and deception. Through years of long practice, he could make his gray eyes reflect nothing but a mild, dull disinterest in his surroundings.

His eyes glinted now with flinty sparks of a fierce determination not to die on this desolate waste. He knew he could survive a long time without food, sustained only by his faith and the power of his convictions.

"I will not die," he chanted. *"I will not die!"*

He trudged on, the terrain steepening gradually. Sometime toward late afternoon—he guessed it was late afternoon, since his wrist chron had been damaged in the crash—clouds thickened over the face of the sun.

At first he was grateful because the cloud cover reduced not only the glare from the hoarfrost but also the chances of contracting snow-blindness. Then a wind sprang up and slashed at him with icy talons.

Sleet began slicing across the rocky plain, turning his surroundings to formless, misty shapes. Zakat squinted against the stinging ice particles and kept moving, uncomfortably aware he could be only a few steps from a bottomless crevasse. The blood on his clothing froze hard as a sheathing of metal.

Tearing a strip from the lining of his greatcoat, he tied it around his eyes so his lids wouldn't freeze together. The driving sleet rendered him almost blind anyway.

He forced himself to concentrate only on what lay ahead, to plod through the swirling curtain of white. His body lost all sensation, even pain, numb to anything other than putting one foot in front of the other. Then, he put one foot in empty air.

Fanning his arms, Zakat plummeted straight down, lips clamping tight over the scream forcing its way up his throat. He didn't fall far or long before his plunge turned into a head-over-heels tumble, his body plowing through banked snow like the prow of a ship. His thrashing descent ended, and he lay motionless, breathing shallowly through his nostrils.

He continued to lie there, noting how pleasantly warm his limbs began to feel. That spreading warmth galvanized him into a floundering rush to hands and knees. He knew he was freezing to death, with the subzero wind wailing around him like the sound of distant violins.

The fall had dislodged his blindfold, so he experimentally opened one eye. For a moment, he saw nothing but white and wondered if he was snow-blind, despite his precautions. A strong gust of wind ripped a part in the sleet curtain, and he saw the dark bulk of the monastery.

Buildings reared above him, constructed so closely together they appeared to be pushing one another off the cliff. A courtyard barely a hundred feet squared was jammed between the monastery storehouse and a mountain wall. The roofs of the buildings looked of Chinese design, but the architecture was careless and crude.

Struggling erect, he forced his legs to carry him toward the entrance between two tall bastions of snow-covered rock. He no longer felt his feet at all.

A figure wearing a soiled yellow cloak and a red cowl materialized between the two rocks. With a prayer wheel spinning in his right hand and a brass bell clanging in his left, the monk shouted a warning into the courtyard behind him, then a challenge to Zakat.

The Russian smiled humorlessly. The monk probably thought he was an earthbound Dre, a malign messenger of death that figured prominently in Tibetan legend. He lifted his left hand and gestured to the monk. His right closed around the butt of the Tokarev holstered at his waist.

The monk's eyes narrowed to barely perceptible slits in his face as Zakat approached him, palm outward to show he was unarmed. The monk's eyes focused on his left hand. With a long-legged bound, Zakat sprang to the small man, planting the short barrel of his Tokarev pistol against the monk's jaw. He didn't speak, assuming the monk understood his actions.

The bell and the prayer wheel flew in opposite directions. The bell gave a final, feeble chime when it struck the frost-encrusted flagstones. Gathering a fistful of soiled robe in his left hand, Zakat pushed the monk ahead of him through the monastery's gate, into the courtyard.

As he entered, he heard the bellowing of a great brass horn and a clangor of bells from the walls. A small man in yellow robes emerged from a door on the far side of the courtyard. Worked in yellow thread on the breast of his black tunic was a swastika running to the left, the symbol of the Bon-po religious order. Like most Bon shamans, he was starkly dressed. Beneath a dark leather turban, his black hair was tied back with a clip made of a human finger bone. Oddly pale, finely textured skin stretched tight over prominent cheekbones and brow arches. Behind the round, steel-rimmed lenses of thick spectacles, his huge, fathomless eyes glittered like those of a raptorial bird.

A bloodred baldric extended across his torso from left shoulder to right hip. A coiled whip hung from it. Tucked into the baldric was a short, curving *ram dao* sacrificial sword. The oak hilt was extravagantly designed with ivory and gold inlays.

The Bon-po priest was followed out the door by a group of six excited men. Their red armbands and soot-blackened faces marked them as Dob-Dobs, the monkish soldiery. In their sashes, they carried iron cudgels shaped like oversize door keys. Rawhide thongs were looped through the handles, and already several of the Dob-Dobs were whirling them overhead. When released, the cudgels struck with deadly, bone-breaking force.

Zakat only briefly considered triggering his pistol. Perhaps he could kill three of the monks, maybe four, but he saw no point to it. Either the Dob-Dobs would crush his skull with their crude weapons or he would perish out on the plateau. He released the monk and stood motionless, angry shouts filling his ears. His head throbbed in rhythm to the gibbering cacophony.

The black-turbaned man gracefully stepped through the howling Dob-Dobs, and Zakat was struck by his fluid, danceresque movements. His jet-black gaze swept over Zakat, then focused on him, staring unblinkingly through the lenses of his spectacles. His almost inhumanly large eyes widened, his lips moved and a whispering, altered voice came forth.

Zakat met that stare, transfixed, unable to tear his gaze away. Although his Khlysty training revolved around a form of psionics, of imposing the force of one will upon the other, he knew the black-turbaned man was a master. With a distant sense of dread, he realized the Bon-po shaman was invoking the *angkur,* the powerful one-pointedness of thought, and directing a blade of *tsal* energy into his mind. He felt it as a sensation of a cold, caressing cobweb brushing his brain.

If he hadn't been exhausted and weak from blood loss, Zakat knew he stood a good chance of deflecting that blade, even turning it on its wielder. As it was, he could only stand as the shaman's eyes filled his field of vision, then his mind. He tried to erect a barrier around his thoughts, visualizing an impenetrable brick wall.

A ghost of a smile creased the shaman's thin lips, and the edges of Zakat's vision blackened. The insubstantial cobweb ensnared his mind, capturing his dreams, his desires and most secret yearnings like a fisherman would net a school of fish. He felt the black-turbaned man examining them as they wriggled and thrashed.

Then, for an instant that felt like a chain of interlocking eternities, his mind meshed with the shaman's. A tsunami of raw, naked ambition crashed over him, the undertow dragging his conscious mind into dark, cold depths. Suddenly, Zakat felt trapped, his spirit locked forever with a black yet somehow shining stone, its facets cut to form a trapezohedron.

The sleet-blurred sun seemed to reel in the sky. Zakat was only dimly aware of falling, first to his knees, then on his face, stretching out on the snow-encrusted flagstones. Right before he sank into the warm embrace of unconsciousness, he heard a deep voice bellowing commands. He didn't respond to it, assuming he was delirious.

The language the voice spoke was Russian.

"EASY," the voice whispered. "Easy."

Grigori Zakat grunted and opened his eyes. He was a little dismayed by how much effort it required and even more dismayed when he saw nothing but a dark, blurred shape looming over him. Still the shape spoke in a language he knew.

Clearing a throat that felt as though it were lined with gravel, he managed to husk out, "Russian. I thought I dreamed hearing it."

A deep, slightly mocking laugh boomed from the shape, and the rich odor of wine wafted into his nostrils. "Perhaps you are dreaming still, no? Perhaps you are freezing to death out on the plateau. The mind plays cruel tricks on the dying."

Zakat blinked several times, and the laughing shape slowly resolved into a more or less human outline. A big man beamed down at him. Although burly, with a massive belly straining at a blue-and-gold satin tunic, he didn't look fat. A thick gray beard spilled over his chest, and his small brown eyes, bagged by flesh pouches, twinkled with amusement.

Squinting around the small stone-walled chamber lit by torches sputtering in sconces, Zakat became aware of the overpowering smell of rancid yak butter drifting in from the corridor. The only decoration in the room was provided by a hanging tapestry, covered with geometric forms. The central one, worked in black thread, appeared to be a trapezohedron.

"Where am I?" he asked.

"Directly above the center of the Earth," the bearded man replied. He unsuccessfully swallowed a belch. "Tibet. You are enjoying the hospitality of the Trasilunpo lamasery. I am the high lama here. My name is Dorjieff."

The name rang a distant chord of recognition in Zakat's memory, but it was so faint he didn't care to seek it out. He shifted on the hard cot, and flares of pain blazed all over his body. Lifting his trembling hands in front of his eyes, he saw they were swathed in bandages, soaked with a foul-smelling unguent.

"Frostbite," Dorjieff said. "I believe you'll recover without the loss of any extremities."

Lifting the blanket, Zakat saw his naked body was covered with blue contusions and raw abrasions. Many windings of bandages encircled his midsection. He kept his expression blank, even when he noticed that his Khlysty emblem was no longer around his neck.

"You were blessed, all things considered," continued Dorjieff. He pinched the air with a forefinger and thumb. "That sword thrust missed your vitals by *this* much. I was able to suture the wound without complications. Internal bleeding was slight. You'll bear a rather unsightly scar, I fear."

"You are a doctor?"

Dorjieff shrugged. "Necessity has forced me to act in many roles during my life."

"How long have I been here?"

"Your second day draws to a close." Dorjieff's hair-rimmed lips quirked in a smile as he added, "Father Twilight."

Zakat did not react. He only gazed up at the bearded man with a mild question in his eyes. Like a street conjurer performing before an audience of urchins, Dorjieff made exaggerated passes through the air with his hands. When he opened his left hand, the tiny wooden phallus dangled by its thong from his forefinger, the crystal testicles reflecting the torchlight.

"A Khlysty cross," Dorjieff murmured. "I was under the impression the sect was outlawed in the motherland, much like the Skotpsis."

Zakat couldn't disguise his distaste at the comparison. Skotpsis were among the most ancient of Russian sects, true enough, and savagely persecuted. An all-male cult, its followers paradoxically swore fealty to the pagan goddess Cybele. The primary expression of their worship was the surgical removal of their penises and testicles.

Dorjieff noticed his sour expression and chuckled. "I did not mean to insult you. I was under the impression the Skotpsis were a breakaway group of the Khlystys."

"A common misapprehension," Zakat murmured.

"I understand that Khlystys practice a so-called communal sin," Dorjieff said. "An indiscriminate sexual orgy among the male and female apostles. A ceremony difficult to participate in if the males have had their tools put away."

Dorjieff's gentle smile disappeared. "However, what is not a misapprehension, common or otherwise, is that for an officer of the ISN to be a Khlysty priest is more than a conflict of interest—it is a firing-squad offense."

As much as he wanted to, Zakat did not reach up to take the talisman. In a low voice, he said, "We are far from the motherland."

Dorjieff gusted out a sigh overlaid with the smell of wine and dropped the emblem onto Zakat's chest. "And from District Twelve."

Zakat covered his astonishment by hiking himself up on his elbows and slipping the thong over his head. "You are now a Buddhist?"

The bearded man shrugged noncommittally. "As I said, necessity has forced me into many roles. Soldier, doctor, holy man. Guardian."

Zakat was puzzled by the remark, but he didn't question the man. Swinging his legs over the edge of the cot, he tried to sit up, but his head swam dizzily. Dorjieff put a hand under his elbow and steadied him until he had planted both feet firmly on a woven-reed floor mat.

"I took the liberty of looking at your identification papers and orders," Dorjieff said. "That is how I know your name and your affiliation with District Twelve. Or at least, the name you currently use. I suppose you have played many roles with just as many affiliations."

As the vertigo ebbed, Zakat saw the torchlight reflected in a pinpoint from a ring on the middle finger of Dorjieff's left hand. Made of thick, hammered brass, in its setting was a single stone, cut in a confusing geometric pattern. It took him a moment to recognize it as a trapezohedron.

"How do you know of District Twelve?" Zakat asked.

Dorjieff combed a hand through his beard, smiling

crookedly. "Many years ago, I was an operative. I was dispatched here to establish an intelligence network in the Himalayas, just in case our old friends, the Chinese, tried to reclaim Tibet."

His smile became a broad grin. "You might say I went native. I found higher rewards here than any Mother Russia could offer. My intelligence network is still intact. A sherpa brought to me the tale of your aircraft crash. And of its one survivor, struggling through twenty miles of rugged snowfields in subzero temperatures. An endurance born of your Khlysty training?"

Zakat nodded. "The power of the mind controlling the limitations of the flesh."

"You intrigue me, Father. We may perhaps be of some use to each other. Tsong-ka-po, the lama who founded the Trasilunpo order many centuries ago, made a prophecy associated with a man much like you."

That piqued Zakat's interest, and he lifted his head to stare into Dorjieff's eyes, searching for indications of deception. He saw only a glaze from imbibing too much wine. He didn't stare long, as two figures appeared in the arched doorway on the far side of the cell.

One was a diminutive girl of perhaps sixteen years, wearing the black shirt and baggy red trousers of a Tibetan peasant, her glossy black hair intricately braided on both sides of her head. Even in the dim light, Zakat noticed her firm breasts swelling beneath the coarsely spun fabric. The other figure was a man, not much taller than she.

Glancing over his shoulder, Dorjieff said, "Come

in, Trai. Gyatso, our visitor appears to have recovered from your ministrations.''

The black-turbaned Bon-po shaman stepped into the room, a thick yellow robe folded over one arm. The girl held a pair of sandals. Her black almond eyes were cast downward. Gyatso fixed an unblinking stare on Zakat as he approached him.

Zakat tried to meet it.

Dorjieff chuckled softly, and said, ''The secret of Bon training consists of developing a power of concentration surpassing even that of men like yourself, who are the most gifted in psychic respects.''

Dorjieff turned to Gyatso. ''This is Father Zakat,'' Dorjieff told him genially. ''He will be staying with us for a little while.''

Gyatso nodded. ''Yes, Tsyansis Khan-po.''

Trai placed the sandals on the floor mat and, not raising her eyes, backed out of the room, head bowed. Gyatso laid the robe on the foot of the cot. His fingers were exceptionally, almost inhumanly long, the middle ones nearly the length of Zakat's entire hand.

As he shouldered into the robe, Zakat said quietly, ''I know a little of this dialect, Dorjieff. Tsyansis Khan-po translates as 'the king of fear.' A title you assumed or earned?''

Dorjieff shrugged negligently. ''A bit of both over the years. The question of the moment is what to do with you.''

He belched loudly, and Zakat caught the swift, disgusted glance Gyatso flicked toward Dorjieff.

Standing up, knotting a sash around the robe and stepping into the sandals, Zakat chose his words carefully. "You might look at me as a fellow expatriate seeking asylum."

Dorjieff threw back his head and laughed. "This lamasery is not a sanctuary. It is more of an embassy...or a guard post. If it had not been for Gyatso's intervention, the Dob-Dobs would have slain you on the spot."

Zakat glanced quickly at Gyatso and once more experienced the sensation of a cold cobweb wisping over his mind. "Why did you intervene?"

Dorjieff stated, "He is a priest, like ourselves, but of the old Bon-po religion. He is also an emissary, a hereditary ambassador. Therefore, his whims are given a certain deference."

Zakat eyed the slightly built, bespectacled man. "Emissary from what nation?"

"A group of nations, actually, known by different names in different ages."

Dorjieff seemed inclined to continue, but when Gyatso cast him an unblinking stare, he coughed self-consciously. "You will learn more," the bearded man said, "or you will not. The decision is not mine."

Zakat steeled himself and fixed his eyes on Gyatso. When he felt the caressing mind touch, he didn't flinch or blink. In a soft, lilting whisper, he inquired, "Is the decision yours, my myopic friend?"

As if mocking him, Gyatso answered in the same tone, "You owe your life to me, Father Zakat. Do you pay your debts?"

Zakat allowed a smile to slowly crease his lips. "Always," he answered. "And sometimes, with a great deal of interest."

Gyatso nodded. "Then we have much in common. And much to share."

Chapter 1

Five months later

Kane lowered the compact set of binoculars and hissed out a slow, disgusted breath. "Now, isn't *this* just what we need."

"What do you mean?" asked Brigid Baptiste.

Wordlessly, Kane handed her the binoculars. She elbowed closer to the crest of the ridge and peered through the eyepieces, adjusting the focus to accommodate her own slightly astigmatic vision. The microbinoculars' 8×21 magnifying power brought the details of the distant Indian village to crystal clarity.

The settlement of tepees, looking like upside-down cones, were arranged in two loose circles, one surrounding the other. She caught the faint whiff of wood smoke. To one side of the village, she saw a herd of hobbled horses and on the other were wooden racks upon which animal hides were stretched. Women in fringed buckskin smocks labored over the frameworks, scraping away fur from the hides.

"The camp of the Sioux and the Cheyenne," Brigid said. "So what? We knew they were here."

"Look a little to your left," Kane directed grimly.

As she complied, she heard a faint yell from the outer perimeter of the lodges. In a clear area, she saw bare-chested men cavorting around a tall wooden pole. Their long black hair was bedecked with sprays of colorful feathers, and their bodies were painted a variety of bright hues and confusing patterns. They canted their heads back so they could stare at the round object topping the pole. She couldn't quite make out whether the object was a stone or part of the pole itself.

"Some kind of ceremony," Brigid commented, unconsciously lowering her voice.

"Keep looking."

Brigid did as he said. After a moment, the cluster of men around the pole separated, and her breath caught in her throat. Auerbach lay staked to the ground, his legs spread-eagled, his wrists bound tightly to the base of the pole. A pyramid of dry twigs rose from the juncture of his naked thighs. She saw how sweat glistened on his face, how his eyes were wide with terror. On the pale skin of his bare right shoulder spread a great blue-black bruise.

Sweeping the binoculars in a slow scan over the village, Brigid tried to make a head count, but the people milled about among the tepees.

"I don't see Rouch anywhere," Brigid murmured, lowering the binoculars. "I wish I knew if that was good or bad."

Kane sighed, running an impatient hand through his dark hair. "Why break with tradition? Let's assume it's bad."

She imitated his sigh. "What do you want to do?"

Kane began inching backward from the top of the knoll. "What I want to do is turn around and go back to Cerberus. But I know I'll end up doing what I *don't* want to do.''

Brigid paused a moment before following him, loath to give up the springtime sun driving the last of the early-morning chill from her body. She tried to enjoy the warm air, rich with the smell of new growth. Under other circumstances, she would have enjoyed the two-day hike from the foothills of the Bitterroot Range. She liked being outdoors, away from the sepulchral silences and cold vanadium confines of the Cerberus redoubt. But neither she, Kane nor Grant was on a nature hike.

She joined Kane and Grant at the bottom of the slope. ''Just like we suspected,'' Kane said to him. ''The Indians have them. They're working up to roast Auerbach's chestnuts.''

Grant winced, then his dark face contorted in a scowl of angry frustration. ''How many of the opposition?''

''I couldn't get a clear idea,'' Brigid said. ''But if you're asking whether they outnumber us—they definitely do, by at least a five-to-one margin. And that's a conservative estimate.''

''What's new about that? We're always outnumbered.'' A very tall, very broad-shouldered man, Grant's heavy brows knitted, shadowing his dark eyes. A down-sweeping mustache showed jet-black against the coffee brown of his skin. His heavy-jawed face was set in a perpetual scowl. Impatiently, he tugged up the collar of his black, calf-length coat.

Brigid shrugged. She didn't deny Grant's statement but said, ''We don't know if Auerbach and Rouch might have offended the Indians, broken one of their taboos. We should practice a little diplomacy first. They're our nearest neighbors, after all.''

She was a tall, full-breasted and long-limbed woman, and Brigid Baptiste's willowy figure reflected an unusual strength without detracting from her undeniable femininity. An unruly mane of long, red-gold hair spilled over her shoulders, framing a smoothly sculpted face with a rosy complexion dusted lightly with freckles across her nose and cheeks. There was a softness in her features that bespoke a deep wellspring of compassion, yet a hint of iron resolve was there, too. The color of emeralds glittered in her big, feline-slanted eyes.

Kane glanced toward her, a wry smile playing over his lips. ''I don't think what they're doing to Auerbach is part of a 'welcome to the neighborhood' routine.''

An inch over six feet, he was not as tall or as broad as Grant, but every line of his supple, compact body was hard and stripped of excess flesh. He looked like a warrior—from the hawklike set of his head on the corded neck, to the square shoulders and the lean hips and long legs. Kane was built with the savage economy of a gray wolf. His high-planed face, normally clean shaved, bristled with a couple days' worth of beard stubble. Though his mouth held a smile, his narrowed gray blue eyes were alert and cold.

''Anybody got a suggestion of how to play this?'' Grant asked dourly.

After a thoughtful moment, Kane replied, ''I think you should stay put, be our ace on the line.''

Out of the pocket of his dark tan overcoat, he withdrew his trans-comm. Thumbing up the cover of the

palm-sized radiophone, he pressed a key. "I'll keep
the frequency open. Monitor my channel."

The range of the comm devices was generally limited to a mile, but in open country, in clear weather,
contact could be established at two miles.

Clipping it to the underside lapel of his coat, he
continued, "Another option is just to leave Auerbach
and Rouch where they are. It'd be simpler all the way
around."

"Safer, too," Grant rumbled. "For all we know,
it's how the Indians deal with slaggers."

Brigid knew they weren't serious, so she didn't respond to their comments. Still, it was a reminder that
Grant and Kane had spent their entire adult lives as
killers—superbly trained Magistrates, bearing not
only the legal license to pass final judgment on slaggers, or lawbreakers, but the moral sanction, as well.

She couldn't deny their anger was justifiable. Four
days ago, Auerbach had volunteered to make the trek
from the mountain plateau housing the Cerberus redoubt to the foothills to perform routine maintenance
on a motion sensor on the road. The only pass to the
plateau had been blocked several months ago by a
C-4 triggered avalanche, and the old blacktop highway remained completely impassable by vehicles.

Auerbach served the redoubt as a medical aide, not
as a tech, and his eagerness to jockey a Land Rover
down the treacherous path to perform a mechanical
task had struck everyone as odd, particularly Kane.
The fact that Beth-Li Rouch was willing to accompany him seemed even stranger, but no one questioned it. Kane figured they were entitled to their
whims, assuming they were suffering from redoubt

fever, chafing at being cooped up inside the installation now that spring had arrived.

The journey from the plateau to the foothills usually required several hours, so Auerbach and Rouch weren't expected to return until late the following day. When it drew to a close, with no sign of them, no one in the redoubt was overly concerned. The signals transmitted by their subcutaneous biolink transponders showed no indications of stress. The transponder, a nonharmful radioactive chemical that bound itself to the glucose in the blood and a middle layer of epidermis, transmitted heart rate, brain-wave patterns, respiration and blood count. The signal was relayed by a Comsat satellite to the Cerberus redoubt and could be employed as a tracking device.

The telemetry showed that Auerbach and Rouch had left the foothills, crossing the tableland on foot, for reasons that none of the redoubt's personnel could fathom or even guess at. They had far exceeded the range of the trans-comms, so Kane, Brigid and Grant commandeered the Sandcat fast-attack vehicle and set off in pursuit.

They discovered the Land Rover parked at the edge of the rockfall. Grant found their trail in the grassy plains, which left no choice but to track them on foot. The only settlement within a hundred miles of the Bitterroot Range was a small one consisting of Amerindians. After the nukecaust, many of the surviving Plains tribes had reasserted their ancient claims over ancestral lands, and the group of Sioux and Cheyenne had done the same with this region of Montana. The atomic megacull had been a blessing to most Native peoples, the "purification" of prophecy.

The Indians never ventured into the Bitterroot Range, or the Darks, as they had been called for over a century. They attributed a sinister, superstitious significance to the mountains' deeply shadowed ravines and grim, gray peaks.

The nearest the tribesmen had come to the range was on the same day the pass had been blocked, when they were pursuing a roamer band that had attacked their village and carried off captives. One of the Indian warriors had glimpsed Kane, and so it was assumed they knew this part of Montana harbored other human beings.

After a day of trailing Rouch and Auerbach across the grasslands, Grant, Brigid and Kane came across the prints of unshod horses around the cold ashes of a campfire. The conclusion was inescapable, though they were able to take a small comfort in the lack of blood or signs of a serious struggle. They'd followed the trail to the Indian village, where Auerbach—and Rouch, presumably—were held captive.

Kneeling beside his backpack, Kane reached into a pouch and removed a small M-60 gren.

Uneasily, Brigid said, ''Do you think you'll need that?''

''I haven't thought that far ahead,'' he answered curtly. ''Do you think you can speak their lingo well enough so I won't have to?''

She paused a moment, thinking. Some months before, she had found a Lakota-to-English dictionary in the Cerberus database. Due to her eidetic memory, she had no problem recalling what she had read, but the Siouxan language relied on tones, as well as phonemes, and she had only once heard it spoken.

She murmured, *"Hota Wanagi."*

Kane straightened up, squinting at her quizzically. "What?"

"Hota Wanagi," she repeated. "That's what the warrior who shot Le Loup Garou called you, remember?"

Kane did and his lips quirked in a mirthless smile. "Gray Ghost, right?"

Brigid nodded. "Right. Maybe he'll remember you."

Kane doubted that very much, recollecting how he had been coated from head to toe with gray rock dust during the knife duel with the roamer chieftain, Le Loup Garou.

"He saved your life," said Grant. "Maybe he's a man of some standing in the village."

Kane pocketed the gren. "Maybe. But more than likely, he was concentrating on chilling Le Loup, not on saving me."

"He saw you fighting him," Brigid argued. "It's not much of an ace, but it's the only one we have to play."

Kane grinned at her use of the slang she had picked up over the eight months of her association with him and Grant. Because of her precise manner of speaking, it sounded incongruous.

He inspected his Sin Eater, holstered at his right forearm beneath the sleeve of his coat. He tested the spring-release mechanism by tensing his wrist tendons. The handblaster leaped into his hand, the butt unfolding and slapping into his palm.

Less than fourteen inches in length at full extension, the Sin Eater featured a magazine that carried twenty 9 mm rounds. When not in use, the stock folded over the top of the weapon, lying along the frame, reducing its holstered length to ten inches. The forearm holster was equipped with sensitive actuators that controlled a flexible cable in the holster and snapped the weapon smoothly into the hand, the stock unfolding in the same motion. Ingeniously designed to fire immediately upon contact with the index finger, the Sin Eater had no trigger guard or safety. Since the gun fired upon touching the crooked finger, Kane took pains to keep his finger straight and outstretched.

Brow slightly furrowed, Brigid watched as Kane pushed the blaster back into its holster, adjusting his coat sleeve. Then she unslung the mini-Uzi from her shoulder and placed it next to her pack.

"What are you doing?" demanded Grant.

She shrugged. "If we want the Indians to believe we mean them no harm, it's best we don't stroll into their village weighed down with musketry."

She opened her jacket, showing a flat, razor-keen knife in a sheath stitched to the lining. "I'll have this."

Grant lifted an eyebrow. "Domi's idea, right?"

She only nodded. Domi, the outlander girl, was a wellspring of sneaky inventiveness. At Lakesh's request, she had stayed behind at the redoubt, in case she had to rescue the three of them.

"If she was here," Grant continued, "she could flank the settlement."

Brigid refrained from mentioning that Domi had expressed an extreme dislike of Beth-Li Rouch, and more than likely wouldn't put herself in jeopardy to rescue a woman she despised.

Kane buttoned up his coat, wishing it were his Magistrate-issue Kevlar-weave garment, a twin to the one Grant wore. He had abandoned his own protective garment a few months before when he was forced to take a swim in the Irish Sea.

Eyeing the position of the sun, he announced, "Well, if they're going to take our scalps, we might as well give them the chance while it's still daylight."

Grant took out his trans-comm and keyed in the frequency of Kane's unit. He put one finger to his nose in the wry one-percent salute as they started off around the knoll. It was gesture reserved for those undertakings with a very small chance of success. Kane deliberately didn't return the salute, not calculating the odds at such a low number.

Before following him, Brigid spared a moment to glance back at the distant gray peaks of the Bitterroot Range shouldering up from the horizon. Clouds wreathed them, and snow still patched some areas. Winter lingered a very long time at such high altitudes.

Kane walked with a self-assured, long-legged stride, and Brigid's swift, almost mannish gait helped her keep pace with him. They walked directly toward the jumble of tepees, noting a lack of sentries on the perimeter.

They didn't speak as they walked, but the closer they came to the village, the more Brigid sensed a change in Kane. With every step, he slipped deeper into his Magistrate's persona, walking heel-to-toe as he entered a potential killzone, his passage barely rustling the high grasses. He moved swiftly, as gracefully as a wraith. His long months as an exile had not dulled the edge of his instincts.

Kane observed wryly, "I guess everybody is too occupied with Auerbach's cookout to post guards."

Brigid repressed a shudder. "Where do you think Beth-Li is?"

Kane's shoulders moved beneath his coat in a shrug.

"Maybe she got away," Brigid suggested.

After a moment of thoughtful silence, Kane replied, "Maybe. She's resourceful. Probably more so than Auerbach."

"So I've been told." Try as she might, Brigid couldn't blunt the edge of sarcasm in her voice.

Kane detected it, cast her a swift slit-eyed glare, but said nothing. Brigid regretted the comment, but she doubted Kane had been seriously stung by it. She knew more about Beth-Li Rouch and Auerbach's relationship than he did, but she kept that knowledge to herself.

They reached the outer perimeter of tepees before they were seen. A yelping outcry arose, and the onlookers clustered around the pole whirled, then several men surged forward. They wore buckskin leggings and breechclouts with feathers in their long braided hair. Paint distorted their coppery faces into fearsome masks. They shouted angrily.

Brigid hesitated, but Kane side-mouthed, "Keep walking. Brazen it out."

Into the trans-comm, he whispered, "We're about to make contact."

Grant's filtered voice responded, "Acknowledged. Moving up."

The warriors rocked to a halt and started whooping. He saw no blasters, only knives and tomahawks, though one beefy man carried a long lance. Kane guessed they were yelling of what they were going to do to the interlopers and he figured it was just as well he didn't understand their language.

Chapter 2

The man with the lance swaggered toward them, his gait almost a provocative strut. Painted vermilion stripes crisscrossed his blunt-jawed face.

Brigid and Kane continued walking, doing their best to keep their expressions composed.

Shaking the lance, the warrior howled, *"Hoppo, wasicun! Hoppo!"*

"I think he's telling us to go away," Brigid whispered.

Kane didn't reply. Instead, he swiftly assessed the man's broad chest and heavily muscled arms. He looked to be strong, more than capable of hurling the lance right through either one of them. His jet-black eyes darted back and forth between the two people, then fixed on Kane.

With a shrill cry, he rushed at Kane, swinging the butt of the lance in a whistling arc toward his face.

Without breaking stride, Kane lifted his hands, crossed his wrists and caught the end of the wooden shaft between them. Grasping it tightly, he pivoted, thrust out his hip and tossed the warrior over it. The man crashed full-length onto the ground with a thud everyone heard.

Kane released the lance and it dropped across the warrior's lap. As the warrior struggled dizzily to a sitting position, Brigid stamped down sharply on the steel head and the shaft jumped up, connecting sharply with the underside of his chin. Wood cracked loudly against bone, and the warrior fell over onto his back.

Instantly, Brigid and Kane were at the hub of a wheel of enraged people, many of them with knives in their fists. They shouted and pointed their blades, closing in. Kane readied his hand to receive the Sin Eater, but Brigid raised her arms and shouted, *"Mita kuye cola! Hota Wanagi!"*

The enraged outcries dropped to a mutter, but the Indians didn't lower their blades. A man's voice said forcefully, *"Hota Wanagi?"*

A warrior shouldered his way through the throng. He had strong Amerindian features, wide cheekbones with yellow lightning bolts painted on them and shiny black hair plaited in two braids that fell almost to his waist. Behind his right ear, a single feather dangled, as white as one of the cirrus clouds overhead.

He wore a loose vest of smoked leather and a pair of boot moccasins. Around his waist was a heavy, brass-studded belt that carried, in loops, a knife, a set of pliers and a polished chunk of turquoise. His erect carriage exuded a quiet dignity.

Narrow, burning eyes bored deeply into Kane's. *"Hota Wanagi.* Gray Ghost. I didn't recognize you."

Both Brigid and Kane were surprised into speechlessness for a long moment. The man's English was flawless and unaccented.

Kane nodded to him politely. "I'm good deal cleaner now, Chief."

"I'm not a chief. My name is Sky Dog, a shaman, what you *wasicun* would call a medicine man."

In a respectful tone, Brigid announced, "I am Baptiste. This is Kane. We're here for our friends."

Sky Dog shrugged. "Your friends are trespassers." He pointed to the object topping the pole. "And so was he, as you might recall."

Kane gave the skull an expressionless stare, as if he only looked at it to be polite. He recognized the scraggly beard and shriveled features of Le Loup Garou.

"Our friends aren't roamers," he said. "You know that."

Sky Dog nodded, smiling thinly. "I know it. But my people are just poor, ignorant redskins. They can't tell the difference between all the varied pedigrees of *wasicun*. Even I have trouble."

Kane ignored the sarcasm in the man's tone. He looked past him toward Auerbach, who stared at him with a panicky, pleading light in his eyes. Although tremblings shook his body, they didn't dislodge the heap of tinder at his groin. He called out hoarsely, "I've told them over and over that we meant them no harm, but they don't care!"

Brigid asked calmly, "Why is that?"

Sky Dog jabbed an arm toward the distant bulk of the Darks and grimly stated, "We care very much that the mountains shelter *wasicun*. But as long as you stayed up there, we were content to leave you be."

Kane struggled to control his rising impatience. "As we are you. If our people encroached on your territory, it was accidental. It's not like you posted signs."

Sky Dog's lips compressed. "It is enough that we know the boundaries of our land. We don't make allowances for ignorance. Nor do you, or you would not have blocked the only pass to the mountains."

Kane took a deep breath and exhaled it slowly. Gazing intently into Sky Dog's eyes, he said quietly, "For the trespass, I offer my apologies. I promise it will never happen again."

Sky Dog's mouth stretched in a mocking smile, but he made no reply.

"But," continued Kane, "we will not leave without our people. If you force me, we'll fight for them. Much blood will be spilled. Ours and yours."

Eyebrows knitting together, Sky Dog asked in a low tone, "You threaten us, Gray Ghost?"

"I make promises," Kane retorted sincerely. "If you insist on holding our people, torturing them, then I'll view you as no different than Le Loup Garou and his roamers. Enemies to be chilled."

Sky Dog stared unblinkingly, his eyes locked on Kane's. Kane stared back. By slow degrees, he began tensing his wrist tendons. Then, with a laugh, Sky Dog ended the eye-wrestling contest. He wheeled around, pointing to Auerbach and shouting at the onlookers.

Several of the men glowered at him, one warrior snapping out a stream of harsh, angry consonants. Sky Dog raised his voice, pointing again to Auerbach, then to Kane.

Squinting in concentration, Brigid murmured, "He's telling them to release Auerbach into Gray Ghost's custody, that you are a mighty warrior and a friend. A couple of his people don't think much of it."

Kane nodded. "I figured that out myself." He casually glanced over his shoulder, wondering which declivity in the rolling plain hid Grant.

After a minute of loud shouting and gesticulating on Sky Dog's part, the warriors bent over Auerbach and began cutting through the rawhide thongs binding him to the pole and stakes. The man Kane had hip-tossed cast sullen sidelong glances in his direction, gripping his lance so tightly his knuckles stood out like knobs on his hand.

Auerbach arose hastily, the pile of twigs clattering from his crotch. Rubbing his wrists, gasping in relief, he joined Brigid and Kane. She considerately averted her eyes from his nakedness.

"Thank you," he stammered, "thank you."

Gruffly, Kane demanded, "Where's Rouch?"

Auerbach's fearful eyes flitted around, then settled on the scowling face of the Indian with the lance. "Ask him. His name is Standing Bear."

Kane directed his question to Sky Dog. "Where is the woman?"

The shaman fluttered a dismissive hand through the air. "She stays. Standing Bear claims her as his own. He won her."

Kane faced the bare-chested warrior and said, "Tell him he can't keep her. She's one of us, so she goes with us."

Sky Dog spoke briefly to Standing Bear. The man shook his head with a great deal of vehemence, black tresses whipping around his face. Furious words burst from his lips, accompanied by frequent gestures with the lance.

After a few moments, Sky Dog cut off Standing Bear's oration with a sharp command. Turning to Kane, he said, "Little Willow—the woman—will stay. Standing Bear fought the red-haired man for her and won. He finds mounting her very pleasant because of her enthusiasm."

Auerbach uttered a noise of outrage. Sky Dog continued, "Standing Bear says that if she is your woman, you should not have let her leave your lodge with the red-haired one. She must be dissatisfied with you."

Kane gritted his teeth and was about to say she wasn't his woman. But he thought better of it and instead declared, "The woman goes with us. That is all there is to it."

Sky Dog cast Standing Bear a sideways glance, then stepped closer to Kane. In a conspiratorial whisper, he said, "Gray Ghost, Standing Bear is intractable on this subject. He will not even trade for her, even if you had ten ponies to barter with. If you try to take Little Willow from him, you'll have to fight the entire village. Me included, just so I can keep face."

He paused, then asked, "Is one woman worth it? She's seems very lazy and argumentative to me. Standing Bear may tire of her eventually and let her go."

Kane's mind raced over a series of options, alternatives and courses of action.

Brigid asked, "What if she doesn't want to stay?

You'll hold her against her will as a captive? Like the roamers?''

Sky Dog obviously felt uncomfortable by being questioned by a woman, a *wasicun* woman at that. Slowly, as if begrudging each syllable, he answered, ''If Little Willow wishes to go with you, that is one thing. We are not slavers. But Standing Bear will oppose it and will fight for her.''

He smiled again, hooking a thumb toward Auerbach. ''I must point out that he fought Standing Bear for Little Willow. He was about to pay the ultimate penalty for his defeat when you arrived.''

Auerbach's hands, clasped over his groin, tightened reflexively.

Kane said, ''Bring out the woman. If she wants to stay with you, that's fine.''

Sky Dog called out to a teenage girl, who turned and rushed into the village. Auerbach muttered bleakly, ''She won't want to stay now that you're here, Kane.''

He narrowed his eyes. ''What do you mean?''

Unsuccessfully swallowing a shamed sigh, Auerbach replied, ''I think this whole deal was part of Beth-Li's plan.''

''Plan?'' repeated Brigid sharply. ''Explain.''

Auerbach opened his mouth, but nothing came out except another weary sigh. Faintly, he muttered, ''I was a stupe. A triple-dipped stupe.''

He had no opportunity to say anything more. The girl returned, trailed by a small, slender woman wearing a fringed smock of bleached doeskin. At first glance, Kane took her for one of the Indian women. Her almond eyes and long hair were no lighter in shade, but her skin was ivory-colored and smooth. Her cheekbones weren't as prominent, but her lips were full and pouting. The smock did nothing to conceal the curvaceous figure beneath. She stared at Kane in a way uncharacteristically bold for an Indian woman.

"Took you long enough," Rouch declared. "I've about had my limit of sour berries and boiled venison." She nodded in Standing Bear's direction. "Not to mention that overstimulated idiot."

Standing Bear, not understanding her words, responded to her nod by stepping up beside her and placing a possessive hand on her shoulder. Rouch glanced at him contemptuously. "See what I mean? Dirty savage."

Sky Dog's lips curled in a silent snarl.

Coldly, Kane asked, "I'm told you belong to that 'dirty savage.' Do you want to stay or leave?"

Rouch's Asian features twisted in a mask of disgust, as if she were scandalized by the mere suggestion. "Do you honestly think I want to stay in this pesthole? Get me out of here."

Brigid said tightly, "It's not that simple."

Rouch flung Standing Bear's hand from her shoulder and made a motion to join Kane. Grasping her roughly by the upper arm, Standing Bear yanked her back, grunting a word in Lakota.

"See?" Brigid asked.

The disgust in Rouch's face instantly became fear. To Kane, she said beseechingly, "Get me out of here—get me away from him!"

Refusing to acknowledge her stricken features and

fearful tone, he said flatly, "Auerbach mentioned something about a plan. I want to hear it."

Rouch cast her eyes downward as if she were deeply embarrassed, but Brigid received the distinct impression it was exaggerated, if not feigned completely. She didn't trust Rouch, and her wariness stemmed from more than just jealousy; Rouch had, with Lakesh's blessing, tried to seduce Kane. And she'd wasted no time sharing her affections since then, if Auerbach's admission was true.

Tugging at the fringe on her dress, Rouch said in a halting whisper, "It wasn't a plan, not really. An idea…I was angry with you…I'm sorry."

Her words trailed off, then she said, "I didn't expect to run across these savages."

Sky Dog broke in harshly, "You refer to us as savages one more time, I'll lodge-pole you, Standing Bear and these others notwithstanding."

Kane wasn't sure what lodge-poling consisted of, but he guessed it wasn't pleasant. To the shaman, he said, "She wants to leave. Tell Standing Bear that."

"I will, but it won't make any difference."

Sky Dog spoke tersely, briefly to the warrior, and rage glinted in the man's dark eyes. He thrust Rouch behind him, looked Kane up and down, hawked up from deep in his throat and spit a glob of saliva at his feet. He grated, *"Zuya."*

Sky Dog rolled his eyes. "It's what I expected. You'll have to fight him for her. In my opinion, she's not worth the effort. Leave her here. Standing Bear is bound to get tired of her and her disrespectful mouth sooner than later."

Kane said nothing for a tense tick of time. Brigid

breathed, "I'm leaning toward taking Sky Dog's advice."

So did Kane. He knew he could chill Standing Bear in his tracks, and with Grant as his ace, they stood a decent—not necessarily good—chance of escaping with Rouch. He saw no firearms among the warriors, not even the home-forged muzzle loaders they might have taken from the roamers.

But if he opted for a firefight, a state of war would exist between the tribesmen and the handful of Cerberus exiles. When and if the forces of the villes arrived looking for them, the Indians would eagerly talk all about the dishonorable *wasicun* hiding in the Darks.

Tactically, employing violence to retrieve Rouch might be sound. Diplomatically, it would be a disaster from which nothing could ever be salvaged.

Kane started to speak, but hesitated when he noted the triumphant smirk appearing on Standing Bear's face. Fighting for or leaving Rouch behind was now more than a choice; it had become a challenge. Kane realized if he backed down, knuckled under, he would be branded a coward, not worthy of respect. If he or any of the Cerberus people traveled across the Indian's country again, the warriors would view them as targets.

"Kane!" Rouch's cry was full of desperation, of quivering terror.

Into the trans-comm, Kane muttered, *"Merde."*

He knew Grant would instantly understand the code word, signifying the current situation could be compared to excrement and that he was to stand by.

Kane began to turn away. Standing Bear's patronizing chuckle triggered a hot flash of anger within him, and he spun around on his heel. He struck the warrior across the face with his open right hand. Weighted by the holstered Sin Eater, the impact of the blow cracked like a whip and Standing Bear reeled, almost bowling Rouch off her feet.

Recovering his balance, the warrior stared at Kane in shocked disbelief, the paint designs on his face smeared by the slap. Howling in fury, he lunged forward. Several other men did the same, echoing his cry.

Sky Dog placed himself in front of Kane, speaking curtly and incisively. The men halted, muttering and glaring. The shaman faced Kane, eyes questioning but amused. ''You've thought this course of action all the way through?''

''Only the ramifications of not taking it,'' Kane replied.

Sky Dog shook his head, laugh lines deepening around his squinting eyes. ''I'm just an ignorant savage. I don't know big *wasicun* words like that.''

He smiled in rueful resignation. ''But I know a couple of small *wasicun* words—like, 'you're fucked, dude.' ''

Chapter 3

The Indians formed a giant circle out on the open floor of the plain. In the center of the circle, a post had been driven into the ground. Rouch stood tethered to it by a length of leather slip-knotted around her right wrist. The wind caught her hair, making it stream behind her like an ebony banner.

Auerbach, once his clothes had been returned to him, had become a bit more talkative, but not cheerful. As he walked with Brigid and Kane toward Sky Dog, he said quickly, "They're doing it just like with me yesterday. Hope you last longer than I did. Not that it makes any difference. The fucking Indians don't play fair—"

"Shut up," growled Kane. "This is their country, and they make the rules."

Auerbach fell silent and dropped back a pace. Sky Dog and Standing Bear stood with two snorting ponies. The animals wore no saddles, only rope halters with a single rein attached to them.

Kane eyed both horses as he approached, studying their withers, their legs, their chests. Though one was dappled and the other a bay, they appeared matched in general size and physical condition. He looked around at the grinning warriors encircling the field in a solid wall of flesh and steel.

Brigid whispered, "I think you'd better call Grant. This isn't just a trial by combat—it's a contest of horsemanship."

"I've ridden horses," he retorted tersely.

She looked at him suspiciously. "For what—all of thirty seconds in Mongolia? You told me you were bucked off."

Kane mentally kicked himself for ever telling her about the incident. He admired horses, but his fondness for them was tempered by his lack of personal contact with them. Bred in Cobaltville, he was accustomed to horses that were dray animals, docile to the point of being comatose. His single experience with a high-spirited steed was during his escape from Kharo-Khoto, when his stolen mount had helped him flee, true enough, but more by accident than design.

He stopped before Sky Dog. The shaman held a pair of rawhide-wrapped wooden staffs, five feet long with the ends curved like blunt-tipped fishhooks.

"You will each take a horse and start at opposite sides of the field," Sky Dog stated in English. Kane figured the smirking Standing Bear didn't need instructions. "You will be armed with the coup sticks. To win, you must remain on the field. The man who rides from the field, is forced from it or unhorsed forfeits the contest. The man who releases Little Willow wins her."

"Sounds simple enough," Kane commented.

Sky Dog chuckled and nodded in Auerbach's direction. "That's what he thought. He learned otherwise."

Kane took a staff, hefting it experimentally. Made

of lightweight but sturdy wood, it felt easy to wield, but Kane didn't think it was much of a weapon.

Standing Bear snatched the other staff, twirled it deftly in one hand, tossed it high in the air and caught the butt end on the palm of his other hand. He balanced it there, staring at Kane with a mocking smile. A wave of appreciative laughter rippled among the onlookers.

Kane pretended not to hear it. He asked, "Which is my mount?"

The shaman pulled the bay pony forward. Taking the rope rein, Kane looked into the horse's brown eyes, searching for any signs of a nasty or tricky disposition. Stroking its muzzle, he murmured, "I don't want to ride you any more than you want me to ride you. If you're going to get mad at a human being, get mad at Standing Bear."

The pony snorted and pawed at the ground.

The eager Indians voiced high-pitched ululating cries. Standing Bear nimbly vaulted onto his horse's back, grasping the coup stick in his right hand and looping the rein lightly around his left wrist.

Kane mounted the bay, grateful that the animal didn't shy away from him. He considered stripping off his coat, but decided to keep it on since it concealed his Sin Eater. If matters turned ugly, he wasn't about to fend off Standing Bear or his friends with a stick of wood, rules of conduct be damned. He was a veteran hard-contact Mag—rules wouldn't come between him and survival.

He caught Brigid's eye, and she extended the index finger of her right hand and brought it smartly to her nose. Gravely, Kane returned the one-percent salute. This time, he figured the odds were correct.

The two men kicked their ponies' flanks and trotted out onto the field. Kane watched how Standing Bear guided his horse with the pressure of his knees and heels. He did his best to emulate it. The bay obeyed, even though he jounced painfully on the animal's spine. Without a saddle or even a blanket, it was about as comfortable as riding a fence rail.

He looked toward Rouch, standing at the post. She had her eyes on him, and though her dark eyes shone with fear, they glittered with another emotion—a thrill, an excited anticipation.

She had worn a similar look a month before when she learned he knifed a swampie to death during a mission to the bayous of Louisiana. A cold sickness sprang up in the pit of his belly.

Sky Dog shouted, *"Oh-oohey!"*

Before the echoes of the cry had faded, Standing Bear heeled his pony around and galloped straight at Kane, holding the coup stick like a jousting lance. Kane pressed with his knees, and his pony obediently jumped out of the path.

Standing Bear rode past, almost to the edge of the ring of onlookers. He reined sharply, and his pony reared up on its hind legs. He brought the animal around without its forelegs touching the ground. The crowd shouted its approval. Standing Bear acknowledged the cheers with an arrogant toss of his head.

Kane couldn't help but marvel at the warrior's expertise. He was less a man on horseback than a centaur, the mythical half human, half beast. Standing Bear charged again, riding around Kane in lightning-swift gambados and curvets, swinging his coup stick like a reaper's scythe.

Leaning forward, then backward, Kane barely avoided being struck and hooked. The pony responded to an involuntary squeeze of his knees. It turned and slammed into Standing Bear's mount, drawing an angry whinny from it.

The horse staggered, and Standing Bear swayed on its back. The Indians shouted in approbation, as if Kane's maneuver had been intentional. For a moment, the two animals snapped at each other, then whirled apart. Standing Bear galloped up the field, recovering his balance.

Straightening up, ignoring the spasm of pain in his testicles, Kane patted the bay's neck. "Good boy," he whispered, even though he didn't know if the horse was male or female.

He glanced toward Rouch, still standing tethered. Their eyes met briefly, and he saw her expression of excitement was being supplanted by one of arousal.

Standing Bear thundered back toward him like a sinew-and-muscle typhoon, his long hair whipping around his head. He shrilled the Lakota war cry, *"Hoka-hey!"*

The horses ran at each other, circled, then hurtled around the field, Standing Bear's pony snapping viciously at the bay's rump. Kane's pony shrilled in anger and launched several back-kicks, which nearly unseated him. But the grip of his heels and knees to the rib-slatted sides of the animal was like an iron vise, and his fingers laced about the rein tightly.

Standing Bear flailed at him with his coup stick, and he parried the blows with a loud, castanet-like clacking of wood against wood. One of the blows got through his guard and cracked smartly on his collarbone. Kane tapped with his heels, and the pony lunged away, Standing Bear following closely.

Pounding hooves tore up great clods of turf, and grit and gravel sprayed about. Twice Kane was almost forced from his steed's back by blows from Standing Bear's coup stick. He countered by catching the crook of his opponent's staff, and tried to pull the warrior down.

Standing Bear went with the pull, leaning close and slapping the bay hard on its rump, screaming, *"Dho!"*

Kane had no idea what the word meant, but his pony evidently understood. It exploded beneath him, rearing and bucking. He felt himself slipping off its back and he had no choice but to drop his coup stick and use both hands to grip the rein and the animal's mane.

Standing Bear kept pace, racing by his side, lashing out at him with the wooden staff, raining hard blows on his hip and shoulder.

Pulling hard on the rope rein, Kane managed to slow his pony. Standing Bear rode past and whirled around, his painted face split by a wide grin. His eyes blazed with glee as he kicked his horse into another thundering charge.

Kane knew the obvious option was to turn his pony and allow Standing Bear to pursue him around the field again, but that tactic would only delay the inevitable—and provide more amusement for the Indians. Out of the many things in his life he hated, being pursued, forced into the role of prey, topped the list.

It didn't come naturally to him. Also, his arms and shoulders throbbed from the coup-stick blows, and a deep, boring pain radiated out from his crotch into his upper thighs.

Leaning forward, he murmured into the bay's ear, "Screw this."

He reined the pony to a complete halt and slid off its back, sending it trotting away with a slap and a shout. He faced Standing Bear on wide-braced legs, listening to the astonished cries of the onlookers. As the distance rapidly narrowed between the two men, Kane shucked out of his coat, not caring if his Sin Eater was seen. He stood motionless, waiting.

An instant of uncertainty flickered across Standing Bear's paint-masked face, but his warrior's blood beat too hot for him to spare any time wondering what the *wasicun* might have planned. A high-pitched, warbling scream issued from his throat.

When Standing Bear was less than two yards away, Kane flung his coat out toward the horse's head, roaring wordlessly at the top of his voice. The warrior's steed was well trained in the game of combat, but it was still only a horse. It reacted instantly to the flapping, wind-belled coat by digging in its rear hooves and lurching to one side.

With a gargling cry, Standing Bear catapulted forward, over his horse's head, and slammed face-first to the ground. Kane sidestepped to avoid his rolling body. All the oxygen in the man's lungs exploded out in an agonized whoof.

The warrior's pony galloped off, and the assembled Indians raised a great shout. Kane picked up Standing

Bear's coup stick and held it over his head in a gesture of victory.

Standing Bear writhed on the ground, mouth opening and closing as he tried to drag in enough air to move his limbs and get him back on his feet. Green grass stains blended with his red face paint. He managed to push himself over onto his back, and Kane planted the blunt end of the staff against his breastbone, pressing hard.

"Stay down, asshole," he snapped, knowing full well the warrior couldn't understand his words. He touched his holstered Sin Eater suggestively. "Stay down for a minute or stay down permanently."

Standing Bear glared first at him, then at the weapon, and comprehension slowly dawned in his eyes. He stayed down. Angling the coup stick over a shoulder, Kane stepped back a few feet, then turned and strode toward Rouch.

Her face was jubilant, her eyes shining like pieces of wet obsidian. "You did it." Her voice was a happy whisper. "You won me!"

Kane said nothing as he reached over and unknotted the tether around her wrist with a single theatrical jerk. The Indians rushed onto the field, waving their arms and shouting. They didn't sound pleased.

Rouch paid them no attention. She was too busy embracing Kane tightly, face tilted up toward his, lips parted. "Oh, Kane!"

Roughly, he disengaged himself. "Keep your mouth shut. We're not out of this yet."

Taking her right hand, he raised it as the angry Indians approached. He didn't see either Brigid or

Auerbach among the crowd. Into the trans-comm, he whispered, "Grant?"

"Still here," came the tense response. "I'm watching."

"Keep doing it."

A pair of grim-faced warriors helped Standing Bear to his unsteady feet. Kane saw one of them surreptitiously slip a bone-handled knife into the man's palm. Standing Bear glanced at it, then broke from the crowd and raced at Kane, knife upraised.

Sky Dog's loud, commanding voice brought Standing Bear to a halt a split second before Kane unleathered his Sin Eater.

The shaman approached Kane and Rouch. He looked from one to the other dispassionately. "The contest is over. You have lost."

"I don't think so," Kane said quietly.

Sky Dog shook his head. "You violated the rules, my friend."

"I jumped off my pony intentionally," replied Kane. "I unhorsed Standing Bear and released the woman."

Pursing his lips, Sky Dog said lowly, "Gray Ghost, I am in sympathy with you. You showed great cunning. Yet this was not a contest of cunning, but of skill."

Kane sighed heavily, wearily. He beckoned the shaman to step closer. Eyebrows crooked quizzically, Sky Dog did so and Kane whispered, "This was a rigged contest, and you know it. This was the second time in my life I've been on horseback. We weren't evenly matched."

"True," the man admitted.

"The only way to win a rigged game is to change the rules. Only you can determine whether or not the new rules apply. I suggest—with all respect—that you do so."

Suspiciously, Sky Dog demanded, "Why? You may have a blaster, but you're only one man."

Kane smiled slightly, without humor. "That's where you're wrong and where I'm guilty of a little bit of rigging myself."

Sky Dog's eyes widened, then narrowed. "Just how wrong and how guilty are you?"

"Only a little on both counts. But that little bit can turn into a whole lot of bloodshed. It's up to you."

Sky Dog chuckled, but it sounded forced. "Why do I think this is a *wasicun* bluff?"

Kane shrugged. "A natural assumption. I'd make it myself, if I were in your place. But in this case, it would be a fatal mistake."

Sky Dog glanced over toward Standing Bear, who scowled in fury at Kane. "If I decide in your favor, it will be a great dishonor to Standing Bear. I doubt he'll stand for it—pun intended."

Kane thought a moment, and stated quietly, "I'll apologize to him and offer him compensation. How will that be?"

Sky Dog nodded. "Since Little Willow doesn't want to stay anyway, he might accept your apology. But his idea of compensation might be more than you're willing to pay."

"What do you mean?"

"You'll have to ask him."

Sky Dog walked toward Standing Bear, raising conciliatory hands. Rouch began to speak, but Kane shushed her into silence. Into the trans-comm, he said, "Stand by."

Sky Dog spoke earnestly to Standing Bear for nearly a minute. By degrees, the warrior's posture began to relax, and the wrathful flames in his eyes dimmed, though they didn't gutter out altogether.

At length, Standing Bear grunted a few words, nodded shortly and Sky Dog gestured for Kane to step forward. He faced the warrior as he spoke in a hurried, grim cadence. Sky Dog translated.

"'I accept you have won Little Willow, though not by fair means. However, since she does not wish to stay with me, it would be wrong of me to keep her against her will. But first a price must be paid. I must buy back my honor before I allow you take her. Do you understand?'"

Kane nodded, shifting his eyes over to Sky Dog. "Tell him I regret what happened, that I am sorry."

Sky Dog repeated Kane's words. Standing Bear's lips curved slightly, either in a smile or a moue of distaste. He muttered a question.

"'Will you pay the price for my honor?'" Sky Dog translated.

Kane hesitated, then nodded.

Like the head of a snake with a razor tongue, the knife in Standing Bear's hand flashed up and out.

Chapter 4

The point of the knife inscribed a slanting gash on Kane's left cheek. Standing Bear manipulated the knife so deftly and swiftly, Kane had no opportunity to recoil.

As he clapped his left hand over the blood trickling from the cut, the Sin Eater sprang reflexively into the palm of his right. It required a conscious effort of will to keep his finger from pressing the trigger.

The Indians in the immediate vicinity cried out in astonishment at the magical appearance of the blaster in the *wasicun*'s hand. Kane surveyed their ruddy, disconcerted faces, baring his teeth, index finger quivering over the trigger. The old Magistrate's pride, the righteous rage fountained up within him. He grappled with the mad urge to chill the lesser breeds who dared to scorn one of the baron's chosen.

After a long, tense moment of internal struggle, he barely managed to tamp down the volcanic fury. Staring unblinkingly into Standing Bear's eyes, he made a deliberately slow show of pushing the Sin Eater back into its holster.

Standing Bear didn't seem intimidated or impressed. He made a pompous-sounding announcement, then hurled the knife to the ground, where it struck point first. Sky Dog said, "Standing Bear has put the mark of the *unktomi shunkaha* on you...the trickster wolf. From now on, if any our people encounter you, they will know you are cunning like the wolf and just as mean.''

Voice pitched low to disguise his anger, Kane said, "Tell Standing Bear I accept the mark. Tell him also that he has no idea how close he came to being marked himself...right between the eyes.''

Sky Dog chuckled. "He knows. I think he also knows it takes an honorable man to offer up some of his own honor to buy back that of another.''

Standing Bear thrust out his right hand. Kane's eyes flicked from it to the warrior's impassive face. Then he gripped the man's forearm tightly. Standing Bear uttered another imperious proclamation.

"Take Little Willow," Sky Dog translated. "But treat her better from now on. If she returns to me, I will not let her go again.''

Kane only nodded, feeling blood trickle down his face and along the side of his neck. The wound stung sharply, but he gave no indication of noticing the pain. Absently, he worried about scarring, but since his body already bore so many, he figured one more wouldn't make much difference.

Standing Bear released his grip, teeth flashing in a broad, slightly mocking grin. He looked past Kane toward Rouch, touched his groin and made a comical frown of disappointment. Rouch averted her gaze. The warrior swaggered into the crowd, and his companions made a path for him, laughing and patting his back.

Kane didn't realize how much tension he had bottled up until Standing Bear walked away. He released his breath in a prolonged sigh of relief and said into the trans-comm, "Situation green. Stand down."

"Standing down." Grant's response came not from the trans-comm but from his right and behind him.

As he heard the words, Kane became aware of a commotion in the onlookers. He whirled around and saw Grant stalking toward him, scowling ferociously at the Indians, who stepped back fearfully. With his dark coat wrapped tightly around him, accentuating his exceptionally broad shoulders, Grant presented the picture of death's black agent. Even Sky Dog's face expressed apprehension. Auerbach and Brigid moved out of the crowd to flank Kane.

"So," said Sky Dog, "you weren't running a *wasicun* bluff after all. Is this the only man lying in wait?"

Kane answered curtly, "You'll understand if I decline to tell you."

"You don't trust us?" Sky Dog challenged.

Kane gingerly touched the shallow cut on his cheek, looked at the blood shining wetly on his fingertips and demanded sarcastically, "Hell, why wouldn't I? You've shown us such wonderful hospitality so far."

The shaman only shrugged.

Grant gave Rouch and Auerbach an appraising stare and inquired mildly, "Are we ready to go home?"

"I am," Rouch declared firmly.

Brigid swept a cold glare over her. Rouch boldly met it, tilting her head at a defiant angle.

Slowly, Sky Dog said, "I would like to know more about your people, about your settlement in the Darks. And why Magistrates are up there."

Kane kept his uneasy surprise from registering on his face. "You recognized my blaster."

"They're called Sin Eaters, as I recall. Which ville are you from?"

Auerbach blurted in angry fear, "We're not telling you anything!"

Without looking at him, Kane intoned, "I'm getting awfully sick of telling you to shut up, Auerbach." Addressing Sky Dog, he asked bluntly, "Why?"

"It may be that we could be of some help to each other. Although you must keep your secrets and we must keep ours, together we may find ourselves engaged in a mutually beneficial situation one day."

Kane weighed the man's words, assessing their sincerity. He stated, "We've already revealed some of our secrets simply by being here. Let's have an exchange. A secret traded for a secret. By my estimation, you owe us about five or six."

Sky Dog smiled slyly. "Actually, that's far more than we have. We only keep one. But it's big."

"How so?" asked Grant.

"Have you wondered why my people have settled so close to the mountains they fear harbor evil spirits?"

"I haven't, no," Kane admitted.

"I have, yes," announced Brigid crisply.

Kane cast her an annoyed, questioning glance.

"Just because I never mentioned it doesn't mean I never wondered," she said a bit defensively. To Sky Dog, she declared, "I've examined the predark maps of this region. The topography hasn't altered all that much since the nukecaust. Only a few miles away is a better water supply and richer grazing land for your animals.''

She gestured to the open terrain around them. ''This area isn't substandard, but you could do better.''

Sky Dog looked at her with a new respect. ''I can see I should not have judged you by the same standards I applied to Little Willow.''

Rouch's shoulders stiffened, and Kane did his best to repress a grin. Grant just barely managed to turn a chuckle into a throat-clearing sound.

Sky Dog asked, ''Gray Ghost, I will trade you a secret, if you promise to keep it as such. I will show you and only you.''

Kane shook his head. ''No deal.'' He nodded toward Brigid and Grant. ''They have to share in it. I can't exclude them.''

''You're not their chief?''

Brigid snapped, ''We have no chief.'' She paused, then amended her declaration. ''We do, sort of. But Kane isn't it.''

Sky Dog pursed his lips contemplatively. ''Will you all make the same promise of secrecy?''

Grant and Brigid nodded.

''Very well.'' Sky Dog pointed to Rouch and Auerbach. ''Go to your lodges. Your possessions will be returned to you. Wait until we return.''

Auerbach opened to his mouth to voice a protest, but subsided when Kane gave him a warning glare.

The shaman gestured. ''You three will come with me.''

He marched away.

Grant, Kane and Brigid exchanged brief glances, then fell into step behind him.

SKY DOG GUIDED THEM away from the village, toward a line of trees sprouting from the plain floor. Shadowy humps of ridges interrupted the flat terrain. The shaman spoke little as he led Brigid, Kane and Grant toward them. "What you will see is our secret and the source of my people's fear of the Darks," he said cryptically.

They crossed a crumbling strip of blacktop road, the ancient two-lane highway that had once twisted its way up through the Bitterroot Range. Aspens, pines and high grasses grew in a tangle on the other side of it.

At the bottom of a shallow slope, a tall tripod shape, like a tepee without its hide coverings, rose from the ground. Colorful feathers decorated the wooden struts and fluttered in the breeze. Unidentifiable bits of rusty metal dangled from rawhide thongs. Hanging from the point where the main braces intersected was a brown human skull with the jawbone missing. As they passed it, they saw a bullet hole perforating its right side. Almost the entire left side of the cranium had been shot away.

Kane asked, "What's this? A warning or a signpost?"

"A bit of both," said Sky Dog. "It has been there for generations. Maintaining it is part of my spiritual responsibilities."

"The skull has been there for a very long time," Brigid observed.

"Four generations at least," Sky Dog agreed. "It

once sat on the shoulders of a *wasicun* interloper. According to legend, after killing many of our warriors, he shot himself rather than fall into my people's hands. He fought bravely, but took the coward's path in the end.''

"What would have happened if he'd surrendered?" Grant inquired.

"Death by slow torture, probably," the shaman answered.

"In that case," said Kane, "I'd say he showed good sense, not cowardice."

Sky Dog's response to Kane's opinion was a shrug, as if the matter was of little importance.

The four people strode deeper into the wood. Kane realized that no birds sang from the boughs of the trees, and tension began knotting in his stomach. He didn't suspect the shaman was leading them into a trap. Killing them would have been much easier back in the village, if that were his intent. He and Baptiste exchanged uneasy glances. The shade under the towering trees deepened almost to dusk, and anything could be hiding in the shadows.

Sky Dog showed no apprehension as he walked a more or less straight route through the closely growing trees along a faint path that none of them would have noticed as such if they hadn't been following him. Kane estimated they had walked some seventy yards from the roadbed when Sky Dog came to a halt.

At first glance, they stood in a very small, crescent-shaped clearing, with a tall tangle of bushes, shrubs and foliage making up the inner curve. Kane's eyes picked out tree stumps protruding only a few inches above the ground.

Sky Dog gestured. "My people's secret."

Brigid, Grant and Kane followed the man's gesture and saw only the snarl of overgrowth. Sky Dog stepped to it, thrust his arms into the tangled vines and leaves and pulled. He lifted away a large section of a carefully camouflaged shelter made of cross-braced tree limbs interlaced with grasses, weeds and shrubs. The forepart came away in three large pieces. Inside they saw the outline of a long, bulky shape which at first glance was unrecognizable.

Sky Dog waved them over as he stepped inside the shelter. A huge vehicle lay nestled within. The armor plate sheathing the chassis was rust pitted, but they saw how its dark hull bristled with machine-gun blisters and rocket pods, and was perforated by weapons ports. It crouched on flat metal tracks, like a petrified prehistoric beast of prey.

Grant recognized it first. "An old mobile army command post," he announced, trying not to sound impressed. "Predark model, but modified and re-tooled into a war wag."

Kane's eyes gave it a slow inspection. He gauged its length at around forty feet and its weight at about fifty tons. The fixed, double-thickness steel plates showed deep scoring in places, where armor-piercing rounds had almost penetrated. The juggernaut had seen a lot of action in its day.

He moved to the front, standing on his toes to peer into the cockpit. Since it was eight feet off the ground, all he saw was the bottom portion of a dusty, cracked windscreen. "Is it operational?"

Sky Dog shrugged. "I don't know about the weapons. The wag itself has been out of fuel for a very long time, since my grandfather's day or before.''

''Where did you find it?'' Brigid asked.

The shaman swept a hand in the general direction of the Bitterroot Range. ''According to tribal history, it was found at the foothills. *Wasicun* invaders were inside of it. One group, led by a one-eyed man, went to the plateau of the fog. They never returned.''

''Plateau of the fog?'' Grant repeated skeptically. ''What's that?''

''Our legends speak of a plateau in the Darks cloaked in fog...a mist which killed, rending men apart as if with claws and fangs.''

Sky Dog rapped the hull of the vehicle. ''The second group of invaders rode in the belly of this steel beast. It carried them down the mountain, then it stopped to move no more. When the *wasicun* left it, my people fell on them. The machine was hauled here and hidden, lest other *wasicun* try to breathe new life into it.''

Kane walked to the rear and opened a hatch, the rust-stiff hinges and springs squealing loudly. ''Do you mind if we look inside?''

''I brought you here so you could do so,'' Sky Dog replied.

Kane, Grant and Brigid clambered aboard. The stale air within carried a faint whiff of cordite mixed with the odor of fuel and grease. They moved down the narrow, grate-floored passageway, checking the tiny, cramped sleeping quarters. In one of them, Brigid found a thick notebook. Its plastic covers were torn, and leaves of paper fell out of it. Empty cargo compartments took up most of the interior space. Inside of small side alcoves, they found and inspected the weapons emplacements.

The four-barrel 12.7 mm machine guns were in poor shape, all the moving parts frozen by neglect and time. Grant commented, "Nothing that a couple of days of oiling, cleaning and sanding couldn't fix."

They found sealed crates of many different calibers of ammo and even a few LAW rockets. There were a number of empty gun racks bolted to the walls. In the control compartment, they inspected the instrument panels and were impressed by the array of panels, dials, screens and circuit breakers.

Grant grunted in disapproval, stooping over to inspect the underside of a panel. "The controls were originally designed to be linked by computers. Looks like whoever found this thing bypassed them, rerouting all the circuits to manual-override boards."

Kane nodded, standing between the gimballed driver's and codriver's chairs. He bent down to gaze out the windscreen. The thick bulletproof glass bore ancient starring patterns from projectiles. "This is a hell of a lot of firepower for the Indians to have."

"It's a hell of a lot of firepower for anybody to have," Brigid murmured, pushing past Kane to sit down in the driver's seat. Absently, she thumbed through the notebook.

"What've you got there, Baptiste?" he asked.

"Looks like a log. Nothing much in it but handwritten fuel-consumption reports, weapons and repair status. Here's the only thing of a personal nature."

She handed him a square of coarse wood-pulp paper. The edges were frayed, and it was stained with machine oil and the bottom half bore a smear that looked like either dried ketchup or blood. The hand-printed words on it were faded to almost illegibility. Kane had to lean toward the light peeping in through the port in order to read it.

Hi, Ryan.
If you're reading this, then it means I'm dead. This rad cancer's been eating my guts for months, and I know there's no stopping it. So this is me saying goodbye and the best of luck. If it goes the way I hope, I'll just walk away one night so don't you blasted come after me. Please. That's the Trader talking and not ordering, Ryan, old friend. We've been some places and done some good and bad things. Now it's done. That's all. I thank you for watching my back for so many years. You and J.B. watch out for each other.

There was no signature. Kane handed it back to her.

"Mean anything?" she asked.

"Any reason why it should?"

Brigid's lips curved slightly in a patronizing smile. "You're familiar with the *Wyeth Codex*, aren't you?"

"I've heard you and Lakesh mention it enough."

Though Kane's comment was studiedly dismissive, he knew the memoirs of Dr. Mildred Wyeth were indirectly responsible for Brigid's exile from Cobaltville. Some thirty years before, a junior archivist in Ragnarville had found an old computer disk containing the journal of Mildred Winona Wyeth, a specialist in cryogenics. She had entered a hospital in late 2000 for minor surgery, but an idiosyncratic reaction to the anesthetic left her in a coma, with her vital signs sinking fast. To save her life, the predark whitecoats had cryonically frozen her.

After her revival nearly a century later, she joined Ryan Cawdor and his band of warriors. Although the *Wyeth Codex,* as her journal came to be called, contained recollections of adventures and wanderings, it dealt in the main with her observations, speculations and theories about the environmental conditions of postnukecaust America.

She also delved deeply into the Totality Concept and its profusion of different yet interconnected subdivisions. The many spin-off experiments were applied to an eclectic combination of disciplines, most of them theoretical—artificial intelligence, hyperdimensional physics, genetics and new energy sources. In her journal, she maintained that the technology simply did not exist to have created all of the Totality Concept's many wonders—unless it had originated from somewhere, and someone else.

Despite her exceptional intelligence, and education, Wyeth had no inkling of the true nature of the Totality Concept's experiments, but a number of her extrapolations that they were linked to the nukecaust came very close to the truth.

In the decades following its discovery, the *Wyeth Codex* had been downloaded, copied and disseminated like a virus through the Historical Divisions of the entire ville network.

That particular virus had infected Brigid one morning nearly two years ago, when she found a disk containing the *Codex* at her workstation in the Cobaltville archives. After reading and committing it to memory, she had never been the same woman again.

Brigid declared, "Dr. Wyeth wrote that Cawdor and her lover, J. B. Dix, spent years as members of an organization which traveled the Deathlands, salvaging and dealing in predark artifacts. The leader of the organization went by the name of Trader. So this machine has a certain amount of historical significance attached to it."

Due to her archivist's training, Brigid tried to fit just about everything, no matter how trivial, into a niche in history. Although the exploits of Cawdor, Dix and his band of warriors were still celebrated in folklore and songs in some outland areas, Kane viewed them as just names from the wild old days before baronies were established. He recalled from his Magistrate indoctrination classes that because of the resistance organized by Cawdor, the full institution of the Program of Unification was delayed by several years.

"We know that Cawdor penetrated Cerberus and used the mat-trans unit there," continued Brigid. "So I calculate that this war wag has been here for approximately a hundred years."

Grant pushed himself erect from beneath the instrument board. "All things considered, a pretty good job of jury-rigging. It's not in too bad a shape, given all the time that's passed."

"But it's useless to us," Sky Dog declared. He had entered the vehicle on soundless moccasined feet. "There is no life in it."

"What happened to the handblasters?" Grant asked. "Looks like there were a lot of them."

"My people took them, of course. They are hidden in another place, close by our village."

"Do you have ammo for them?" inquired Kane.

Sky Dog hesitated before shaking his head. "No. What little the invaders had was used on my people long ago."

A sudden suspicion made Kane slit his eyes. "That's one of the reasons Le Loup Garou and his roamers attacked you, isn't it? To get the blasters? He'd heard about them."

Sky Dog sighed sadly. "I fear so. Such a secret can't be kept for so many years among so many people without a few rumors leaking out here and there."

Grant experimentally flicked a switch on a console. Like he expected, nothing happened. "You've got a real prize here, Sky Dog."

The shaman nodded. "I realize that, even if most of my people don't. They still believe it to be a thing of evil, a metal monster symbolizing all the old *wasicun* oppression."

Lowering his voice as if he were afraid he would be overheard and accused of heresy, he added, "But the fact remains if this metal monster had been operational, the roamers would have never been able to attack us and carry off our women and children."

Brigid asked, "You showed us this thing so we can make it operational again?"

"The thought crossed my mind." He pointed to Kane's trans-comm unit. "You have predark tech at your command, wags of your own. And weapons."

"Why should we fix this thing for you?" Kane challenged. "What's in it for us?"

"A simple answer," Sky Dog replied smoothly.

"You're all hiding from something up there in the Darks, else you would be living in the villes among your own kind. Nor would you have sealed the pass. Certainly not to keep us or a few roamers out."

Sky Dog looked expectantly from Grant to Kane to Brigid, waiting for either a comment or a denial. When neither was forthcoming, he continued, "I propose an alliance between my people and yours. Provide us with the means to restore life to this machine, train me how to operate it and give us ammunition for the blasters we have hidden. We will be your first line of defense against the enemies seeking you."

He fell silent, folding his arms over his chest. Kane smiled wryly. "You're not asking for much, are you?"

"What if we refuse?" Grant demanded. "Will you have us chilled, now that we know your tribe's great secret?"

Sky Dog made a sound of derision. "Of course not. I already promised you safe passage. Besides, if you do not return to the plateau, more of your people will come. If there's one thing of which I'm positive, it's that where there are a few *wasicun,* more will follow." His lips twisted in a cryptic smile. "And they probably won't be as well mannered as you three."

Kane matched Sky Dog's smile. "What would keep us from returning with more *wasicun* and simply taking this wag from you?"

"Nothing really," the shaman answered mildly. "Except your sense of honor, the same one I saw when you fought Le Loup Garou and wiped out his followers when you could have made it easier on yourself and let him pass."

"Not to mention that you shot Le Loup Garou with an arrow and saved my life."

Sky Dog's smile widened. "I wondered how long it would take you to bring that up."

"Now that I have," Kane said, "I suppose you expect me to repay the debt by agreeing to your proposal."

Sky Dog shrugged. "Follow your conscience, Gray Ghost. Do whatever your heart tells you to do."

Impatiently, Grant said, "Even if we go along with you, it'll take time. We'll have to send techs and mechs to your village. How do we know your people won't invite them to the same kind of wienie roast you planned for Auerbach?"

"My people look to me as expert on *wasicun* ways since I've lived among them." Sky Dog rolled up his right sleeve and thrust out his forearm. Just below the elbow joint was the faded pucker of an old scar. "I lived in Cobaltville until I was fifteen. After my father died, my mother and my sister and brother and I were cast out. A Magistrate used a knife to remove my ID chip so I could never return."

ID chips were tiny pieces of silicon injected subcutaneously into all ville residents, and the chips responded positively to scanners at checkpoints.

"My mother, my sister and my brother wandered for a long time," continued Sky Dog. "My sister was murdered by a roamer gang, my mother died of rad poisoning when we crossed a hellzone. Eventually, my brother and I ended up here. The tribe took us in, sheltered us, accepted us. You shouldn't wonder that I place their welfare at such a high priority."

Kane didn't wonder, but he couldn't help but speculate about Lakesh's reaction if he accepted Sky Dog's proposal without discussing it with him first. He could easily imagine the blizzard of objections and invective storming from the old man's mouth.

"Something amuses you?" Sky Dog frowned slightly.

Kane realized he was smiling. "Yeah, but nothing to do with what you just said."

He turned toward Brigid and Grant. "What do you think?"

Grant rumbled musingly, "Strategically, what Sky Dog says makes sense. We'd sure as hell have the element of surprise if and when Mags come calling."

Uneasily, Brigid said, "I agree with it in principle. But we should talk this over with our…" She paused, groping for the right euphemism. "Our council of chiefs."

Sky Dog lifted a wry eyebrow. "And do you beat tom-toms and dance around a fire up there in the Darks before you reach a decision?"

Kane laughed. "Only after our animal sacrifices." He put out his hand to Sky Dog. "Deal. My instincts say you can be trusted, though they've been wrong before."

Sky Dog did not hesitate to clasp his hand. "So have mine."

"Good. Then we both know where we stand."

Releasing his grip, Kane moved out of the control compartment, walking toward the rear hatch. "It'll take a few days for us to return, to put together what we need and send some people back."

Sky Dog chuckled. "This monster has waited

nearly a century to live again. A little while longer won't make much of a difference.''

They left the compartment and the vehicle. While Grant helped Sky Dog restore the camouflage, Brigid took Kane aside.

''You should have consulted Lakesh before making a unilateral decision like this,'' she said severely.

''And have him back-burner the issue for a month or year?'' he countered. ''At this point, we can't afford to have anyone but allies at our doorstep.''

''What if he overrules your promise?'' Brigid asked, lines of worry creasing her forehead. ''Then the Indians will think we've broken our word to them and be on the watch for us every time we leave the redoubt.''

Kane nodded sagely. ''Now you're getting it.''

Realization of Kane's reasoning dawned in her eyes. ''You've boxed Lakesh into a corner. Now he'll have no choice but to abide by your decision.''

''Exactly. Besides, he's always been concerned about our relationship with the Indians. We've just reached our first diplomatic accord with them. He may squawk that the decision was made without his input, but overall he should be satisfied with it.''

''And what do you tell Sky Dog when he starts asking questions about Cerberus, about what we're doing there and why?''

''We'll tell him what he needs to know,'' Kane answered. ''I think he's trustworthy.''

Brigid wet her lips nervously. ''Assuming, of course, your instincts are sound this time.''

Kane tentatively touched the knife cut on his cheek.

It was already scabbing over. ''Sky Dog is worried
about the same thing, Baptiste.''

"A balance of distrust,'' she acknowledged quietly.
''Diplomacy in its purest form.''

Chapter 5

By the time they returned to the village, the sun hung a bare handsbreadth above the horizon. At Sky Dog's invitation, they decided to spend the night. After the shaman left them to arrange sleeping quarters, they returned to the knoll to retrieve their packs.

Brigid treated Kane's cut with materials from the first-aid kit. He stood stoically as she cleaned and applied stinging antiseptic to it.

"Superficial," she said, eyeing it critically. "It doesn't need stitches, but you may have a scar."

She started to spray liquid bandage over it, but Kane said, "That stuff itches. Leave it."

As they walked back to the Indian village, Grant asked, "How do we deal with Rouch and Auerbach? Do we take them back as deserters or as captives freed from bondage?"

"That depends on whether they really intended to desert," Brigid answered. "Either way, poor Auerbach was duped by Rouch."

Kane snorted. "You say that because you know he's got the hards for you, Baptiste."

She shot him an icy glare. "And we're all aware of what Rouch has for you, aren't we? She said she was angry with you. It's no mystery about what."

Kane opened his mouth to voice a profane rebuke,

then closed it, clamping his jaws tight, his lips compressing in an angry line. He saw no purpose in arguing with Baptiste on the matter of him and Beth-Li Rouch.

Rouch was the newest arrival among the exiles in Cerberus, only a few months out of Sharpeville. Lakesh had arranged for her exile to fulfill a specific function among the men in Cerberus, but he had made it quite clear that Kane was the primary focus of his—and Rouch's—project to expand the little colony.

Her function had yet to be fulfilled, and Kane couldn't help but suspect that Rouch's interrupted cross-country trip had been designed to draw his attention. Auerbach had certainly implied as much.

Uneasily, Grant suggested, "Whatever the reason and whoever is at fault, we need to get to the bottom of it before we start back for Cerberus. If they're not willing to go back with us, we can't just turn them loose on the plains."

Neither Brigid nor Kane needed him to explain. The possibility that Rouch and Auerbach intended to betray the redoubt to their enemies was remote, but could not be discounted completely. One of the reasons behind the injection of the biolink transponders was to monitor the whereabouts of the exiles.

Kane blew out an exasperated sigh. The cut on his face twinged, and he cursed in irritation. "All we can do is question them. If their stories don't match up, or if they stink..." He let his words trail off.

"Then what do we do?" Brigid demanded. "March them out at dawn and execute them?"

Grant grimaced. "Something like that, maybe. Except I won't get up that early."

Brigid didn't smile at the rejoinder. "We don't have the right to do that," she objected fiercely. "Both of you have said there are no loyalty oaths to Cerberus as reasons for doing what you want to do."

"We never put Cerberus at risk," Kane grated. He gestured to the collection of dwellings around them. "These people may be in jeopardy, too. And I don't see how it will benefit anyone to return a couple of traitors to the redoubt and hold them as prisoners forever. We already have one resident captive. We don't need a couple more."

Brigid didn't respond to his reference to Balam, the entity confined in a holding cell for over three years. She declared, "We're making a lot of assumptions. Let's just ask Rouch and Auerbach what the hell they were up to before we start assembling a termination squad."

"Fine," said Kane. "But let me and Grant talk to Auerbach. You'll be too soft on him."

"And I'll question Rouch," Brigid snapped, "woman to woman. I can guarantee I won't be too soft on her."

They sought out Sky Dog, who directed them to the lodges occupied by Rouch and Auerbach. Grant and Kane fetched Auerbach, taking him outside and away from the village proper. The smell of roasting meat wafted to them from a cooking fire, a sharp reminder to Kane how long it had been since he had eaten anything other than the tasteless ration packs.

Auerbach quickly and almost gratefully responded to Kane's questions. His tale was so simple and simple-minded, neither Grant nor Kane doubted its veracity, though they wondered about his sanity. How-

ever, they were relieved they didn't have to employ
the interrogation techniques they had learned as Cobaltville Magistrates, most of which relied on the
physical abuse of a suspect.

Auerbach claimed he had volunteered to check the
proximity sensors simply to escape the claustrophobic
confines of the redoubt for a little while. He was as
surprised as everyone else when Beth-Li Rouch expressed the desire to go with him. Surprised and
pleased.

Ducking his head, Auerbach cast his eyes down
and started to say something, then broke off, his
words trailing off into inaudible mumbles.

"Well?" prodded Grant. "Finish it."

Auerbach tried to look at Kane, but evidently found
the ground less intimidating. He was a big man, about
Kane's height, but built along heavier lines. Strength-
wise, they were probably evenly matched. The main
difference between them lay in background—Kane
was a blooded killer, while Auerbach wasn't and so
he feared him.

"You may not like what I'm going to say," he
muttered.

"As if I'm delighted with everything else that's
happened in the last couple of days," retorted Kane.
"Spit it out."

Clearing his throat, Auerbach nervously shifted his
weight from foot to foot. His voice was barely above
a shamed whisper. "I've had, ah, relations with Beth-
Li. Only once, about a month ago. I hoped she wanted
to pick up where we left off."

Kane stared at him gravely, stone-faced. "Go on."

"It was her idea to strike out cross-country. Just

for fun, she said. For the hell of it. When I told her everybody back at Cerberus would be worried, she said that was the idea. She was going to go with or without me, so I went with her.''

Grant shook his head in exasperated disbelief. "You two had no destination in mind at all?"

Auerbach fidgeted. "No. Beth-Li claimed that we were doing a recce, you know, for the redoubt. On our second night out, we were captured by the Indians. I guess they saw our campfire.''

"You guess," echoed Kane, voice cold with sarcasm. "On flatlands like this, you're lucky Baron Cobalt didn't spot your fire.''

Auerbach swallowed hard. "I already said I was a stupe."

"A triple-dipped stupe," Grant reminded him.

Auerbach acknowledged the reminder with a jerky nod. "They came on us so fast, we didn't have time to use our blasters. Standing Bear led the party. Sky Dog wasn't with them, so we couldn't talk, understand each other's languages. On the march to the village, Beth-Li tried to make friends with Standing Bear. By the time we got here, he decided he wanted to be more than friends.''

Auerbach's brows knitted in anger and resentment. "When I met Sky Dog, he told me Standing Bear had claimed Beth-Li as his property. He named her Little Willow because of the moves she made. You pretty much know the rest of it.''

Grant hissed out an obscenity. "You opposed Standing Bear's claim and ended up dueling him for Rouch.''

Auerbach shrugged. "I don't have to tell you that I lost."

Kane ran a frustrated hand through his hair. "This is just idiotic enough to be true. Earlier you said something about a plan. Explain."

Auerbach shrugged again. "Just a suspicion. I think she was testing you, Kane, to see if you'd be the one to come after her." He finally managed to meet Kane's gaze. "I guess you passed it. You not only came after her—you won her from Standing Bear."

"I would have come after any member of Cerberus if they'd gone missing," Kane replied dourly.

"Yeah, maybe, but you wouldn't have fought to win me. Whatever Beth-Li was trying to prove, whoever she was trying to prove it to, I guess she succeeded."

Face twisting in self-loathing, Auerbach dry-scrubbed his red bristle cut with furious fingers. "What are you waiting for? Kick my ass all the way back to the Darks. I'd do it myself, but I'd take pity on me."

"You deserve worse," growled Grant. "And you'll probably get it. From your own conscience."

He eyed Kane quizzically. "Unless you think he needs a blaster-whipping on top of it."

Kane presented the impression of seriously pondering the notion. At length, he said, "Right now, I'm too hungry to waste my time denting his skull. After we find something to eat and after we hear Baptiste's report on what Rouch had to say, I may reconsider."

BETH-LI ROUCH REELED, stumbling the width of the lodge. Only the drum-tight hide walls kept her from falling. The sharp echoes of the slap reverberated inside the tepee.

"I asked you a civil question," Brigid said grimly, resisting the impulse to shake her stinging right hand. "'Fuck off' isn't a civil answer."

Beth-Li touched her reddening cheek. A glint of fear, then anger appeared in her dark eyes. She had yet to change out of the white doeskin smock, and as her face darkened in fury she looked more like an Indian maiden than before.

"How dare you?" she demanded. "Who the hell do you think you are? You've got no right to ask me anything!"

Brigid took a slow, threatening step toward her. "I'm assuming the right and you'll answer me—what were you and Auerbach up to?"

Rouch clenched her fists, then her teeth. "I don't have to tell you anything. You have no authority over me."

"Maybe not in Cerberus. But here, it's just you, me and the walls."

Full lips writhing as if she were going to spit, Rouch demanded, "Get Kane in here. I'll answer his questions, not yours."

Brigid struggled to bottle up the anger the young woman's sneering attitude invoked in her. "This was all about Kane, wasn't it? You duped Auerbach into going with you so Kane might think you two were running off together. But you didn't plan on meeting the Indians or becoming Standing Bear's Little Willow."

Rouch uttered a derisive laugh. "You think you're a genius, don't you?"

"I don't need to be a genius to figure out this stupe scam of yours, Beth-Li. It's so transparent it wouldn't fool a child. And it didn't fool Kane."

Rouch planted her fists on her hips. "He came after me, didn't he? He fought another man for me. That's the important thing, not whether he was fooled."

With a sense of shock, Brigid recognized the emotions boiling within her as jealousy, with a strong undercurrent of humiliation. For a moment, her throat thickened and she couldn't speak.

"Kane won me," Rouch continued. "You don't know what that really means to a man, a warrior like him, do you? No, it's too primal for you to figure out. You're all intellect, sterile and cold." She paused, her smile widening as she added, "And barren."

Brigid groped for a response, first contemplating denying it, then despite herself demanding, "How do you know that?"

Rouch waved a dismissive hand through the air. "I was briefed on everybody in the redoubt."

"By Lakesh?"

"Who else?" Rouch retorted impatiently. "He brought me there. Face it, Baptiste—your profile and Kane's simply don't match up. They never did, not even before your...accident."

Brigid narrowed her eyes, to keep Rouch from seeing the tears suddenly springing to them. Only a couple of months before, she had learned she was infertile, due to exposure to an unknown wavelength of radiation in the Black Gobi. She had suffered chromosomal damage, but to what extent and to what degree of permanency was still undetermined. Although Lakesh knew, as did DeFore, the redoubt's resident medic, Brigid had yet to speak of it to Kane. Finding out that Beth-Li Rouch was privy to her condition not only angered her, but it also grieved her deeply.

"I know Lakesh asked you to stand aside so Kane and I could bond," Rouch went on acidly, "but you didn't. I had to make my own plans. You left me no choice."

Forcing a note of calm into her voice, Brigid asked, "Are you saying this charade of yours—running away, nearly getting Auerbach maimed, putting Kane at risk—*is* my fault?"

Rouch's lips pursed. "I'm saying that since you refused to cooperate with the breeding program, adjustments had to be made. I made them."

"And part of those adjustments included duping poor Auerbach? You had this in mind for a while, didn't you, when you first seduced him? You used him."

Rouch shook her head in mock pity. "How can a woman who's supposed to be so intelligent be so naive? Of course I used him. Everybody gets used. Fact of life, Baptiste."

"What if Standing Bear had seriously injured Kane—or killed him? What would that have done to your adjustments?"

Rouch's perfect teeth flashed in a grin. "I would've adjusted to that. My life here wouldn't have been too bad. More primitive than I care for, but I already led Standing Bear around by his cock. I'm an adaptable girl."

"So I've been told," Brigid said with undisguised

contempt. "That's why you were brought into the redoubt."

Beth-Li Rouch wasn't offended by the observation. Agreeably, she said, "One of the reasons, anyway. Besides, I knew Kane wouldn't let that stupe savage beat him—not with me as the prize."

Brigid's anger slowly faded, replaced by a weary resignation. She wanted to sit down, but the notion of doing so in front of Rouch repulsed her. The dark-haired woman noticed the change in her posture and attitude.

"You think you know Kane," she declared. "But you don't, not really. Underneath it all, he's just as savage as Standing Bear. You're wasting your time trying to convince yourself that he's anything other that what he is—a coldhearted killer, all iron and ice. Think about all the people he's chilled, all the throats he's cut. You two could never have a future. Deep down, you know it."

Brigid turned away, running her fingers through her tangled red-gold mane. Rouch softened her tone, striving to sound reasonable, if not sympathetic. "I told you before I don't care if you screw him. But stop standing in the way of the program. Let me carry his seed, bear his children. Stop fighting me. There's no way you can win. Trust me on that."

Brigid glanced back over her shoulder. "Are you threatening me?"

Rouch angled a cryptic eyebrow. "More or less. You don't want me as an enemy, Baptiste. Not only do I have Lakesh backing me up—I won't fight fair. I'll get you out of the way one way or the other."

She took a deep breath and whispered fiercely, *"Stop fighting me!"*

Thrusting aside the triangular piece of hide serving as the door flap, Brigid said flatly, "I'm tired of fighting period, let alone you, Beth-Li."

Chapter 6

Brigid stepped out into the cool air of early evening. She looked up at the vast canopy of sky, at the fiery colors of sunset tracing the horizon. The gray blue tint of the high sky reminded her of Kane's eyes—a little cold perhaps, but with a hint of passion burning behind them.

Following a burst of laughter, she found Kane, Grant and Auerbach sitting cross-legged around a cook fire with half a dozen warriors. A rabbit turned slowly on a spit over the flames.

Kane talked animatedly, using elaborate hand gestures. Sky Dog translated, and the Indians responded with grins and appreciative laughter. Even Grant's normally truculent expression had softened into a smile of enjoyment. Only Auerbach looked uncomfortable, eyeing the fire apprehensively, no doubt imagining the flames dancing on his groin.

Brigid drew near enough to overhear Kane's account of shooting down a Deathbird during their escape from Cobaltville. She vividly remembered how the chopper had pursued their old rattletrap Sandcat as Domi desperately tried to avoid the .50-caliber bullets and rockets.

She had no problem recollecting the terror she felt, the almost suffocating sense of doom. Judging by

Kane's bright eyes and laughing tones, the ground-to-air duel had been a lark, a grand, exhilarating adventure. The Indians apparently felt the same way, although Standing Bear's face wore a skeptical expression.

Savage warriors all, she thought bleakly. Although she stood only a few yards away from the cluster of men, she felt separated from Kane by a distance that could not be measured. At that moment, she might as well have been looking at a complete stranger.

She couldn't help but wonder what the Indians' reactions would be if Kane provided all the details of their flight, the truth behind it, or at least the truth as they understood it.

Even after all this time, Brigid still couldn't fully accept what she had learned about the nukecaust, or about the Archon Directorate. Until eight months ago, neither Kane, Grant nor Brigid had even the vaguest inkling of the existence of the Archons, let alone the fact that they had influenced the course of history for thousands of years.

On the face of it, Kane seemed the least likely to have stumbled over the evidence of their shadowy existence and presence in human affairs. After all, he and Grant had served for many years as Magistrates, enforcers of the ville laws and baronial prerogative.

All Magistrates followed a patrilineal tradition, assuming the duties and positions of their fathers before them. They didn't have given names, but instead took the surname of the father, as though the first Magistrate to bear the name were the same man as the last.

As Magistrates, the courses their lives followed had been charted before their births. They were destined to live, fight and die, usually violently, as they fulfilled their oaths to impose order upon chaos, obeyed the edicts of the barons who ruthlessly stamped out any sign of rebellion.

The steady course of Kane's life was interrupted by what seemed a simple enough Mag raid. A slagger named Reeth was smuggling outlanders into Cobaltville with bogus ID chips. Their squad's mission was to flash-blast the Mesa Verde slaghole and serve a termination warrant on Reeth.

The simple op turned ugly when Kane realized Reeth's operation was too big, too well equipped for a small-time slagger to pull off. His armament and tech were state-of-the-art, and he even had a computer system, a piece of hardware that was usually reserved for the ultra-elite administrators of Cobaltville.

The Mags' commanding officer, Salvo, served the termination warrant before Reeth could be questioned, but not before Kane saw a strange device the slagger called a gateway. Due to his dislike of Salvo and his rising suspicions, Kane palmed a computer disk.

Back at Cobaltville, Kane found the disk was specially encrypted, designed to defy normal unlocking procedures. Instead of shrugging the matter off, he was consumed by the mystery posed by the disk.

He sought out Brigid Baptiste, a high-ranking archivist in the Historical Division. Despite the common misconception, archivists were not bookish, bespectacled pedants. They were primarily data-entry techs, albeit with high-security clearances. Midgrade archivists like Brigid were editors.

Her primary duty was not to record predark history,

but to revise, rewrite and oftentimes completely disguise it on behalf of the ruling elite. Like Kane and Grant, she had believed the responsibility for the nukecaust and its subsequent horrors lay with humankind as a whole. For many years, she had never questioned that article of faith.

As she rose up the ranks, promoted mainly through attrition, she was allowed greater access to secret predark records. Though these were heavily edited, she came across references to something called the Totality Concept, to devices called gateways, to projects bearing the code names of Cerberus and Chronos.

Then one day, over a year before, she was covertly contacted by a secret, faceless group calling itself the Preservationists. Over the following few months, she slowly understood that the Preservationists were archivists like herself, scattered throughout the network of nine villes. They were devoted to preserving past knowledge, to piecing together the unrevised history of not only the predark, but also the post holocaust world.

Whoever the Preservationists were, they had anticipated her initial skepticism and apprehension. To show their good faith, she found an unfamiliar disk in her work area one morning. On the disk was the *Wyeth Codex*, and that began her secret association with the Preservationists.

Though Kane could not have known it, Brigid Baptiste was the perfect person for him to have contacted. She was able to unlock the disk he'd retrieved from Reeth's slaghole, and the digital data held far more questions than answers.

Her curiosity aroused, Brigid didn't devote much

time to contemplating the consequences of delving into top secret historical files. The results of her illegal research yielded frightening revelations about the Totality Concept, the Cerberus mat-trans network and the Archon Directorate, which seemed to have been involved in manipulating the course of human history.

Unbeknownst to either Kane or Brigid, Salvo had placed both of them under surveillance. While Brigid was charged with sedition, being a Preservationist and illegally delving into the database, Kane was taken before a tribunal presided over by none other than Baron Cobalt himself.

The baron told him that since the end of World War II, elements within the American, Russian and British governments concealed their covert contacts with a mysterious race of entities known as the Archons. The Archons had a standard operating procedure that they had employed for thousands of years: they established a privileged class dependent upon them, and that elite class in turn controlled the masses of humanity for the Archons.

Kane was further informed that his father was a member of the Trust, and therefore he must accept the tradition, the honor offered to him. Like his father, he would be a member of the elite that ruled society in secret. Other members of the Trust included high officers from all the divisions, including old Lakesh. Henceforth, like them, he would be working for the evolution of humankind.

Though Kane accepted the offer and even agreed when Salvo told him that Brigid Baptiste must be executed, he didn't believe a word of what Baron Cobalt and the other members of the Trust had told him. Nor was he about to allow Brigid Baptiste to be executed because of his own impulsive curiosity.

After he rescued the archivist, Kane, Grant and Brigid fled Cobaltville, aided by Domi, the outlander girl who'd been forced to work as a sex slave for Cobaltville Pit boss Guana Teague.

Though pursued by Magistrates, they managed to make it to the mat-trans gateway at Mesa Verde and transport themselves elsewhere. When they arrived in Redoubt Bravo, once the base for the Cerberus Project, Lakesh was waiting for them with the group of exiles he'd assembled from other villes.

There, Lakesh told them of his history, his great age, and filled in the gaps in their knowledge. He was, in fact, one of the original people who had worked on the Totality Concept projects, specifically Overproject Whisper, which included Chronos and Cerberus. Shortly after the nukecaust, he spent over a hundred years in cryogenic stasis in an installation known as the Anthill Complex before he was revived to help the Archon Directorate's plans for humanity reach fruition. He told them how the nukecaust was not supposed to have happened, but the misuse of the Totality Concept projects caused a probability-wave dysfunction.

Horrified, Kane, Brigid and Grant demanded to know why the Archons would allow such cataclysmic events to occur. Lakesh detailed the long-range genetic-engineering program in which all nonessential humans were to be reduced to an expendable minority, existing only to be exploited as slave labor and as providers of genetic material. Lakesh described the

Hybrid Dynasty to them, telling them that the previous three generations of barons were human-Archon hybrids under the control of the Archon Directorate.

None of them were convinced by Lakesh's explanation, particularly Kane, until they were introduced to a permanent guest of Cerberus—an Archon named Balam. The creature triggered a primal, xenophobic response in all of them. It communicated telepathically, and according to Lakesh, its mind was somehow linked with all its fellow Archons on a very subtle, unconscious level.

When Lakesh then showed them Nightmare Alley, which offered overwhelming horrific proof of advanced genetic experiments performed by the Archon Directorate, the evidence was undeniable.

Active opposition to the Archon Directorate and the ville network was their only option, since all of them had been reclassified as outlanders. Nonpersons, they could never return to Cobaltville and had been the focus of numerous search parties. Exile had become their way of life.

Brigid's thoughts returned to the present as Kane lifted his hands, index fingers outstretched and made rapid stuttering noises, imitating the reports of autoblasters. In midstutter, he suddenly glanced up and saw Brigid standing there.

His sound effects trailed off, and he said to Sky Dog, "I'll be back in a minute."

As he rose, the warriors groaned in disappointment. "Grant can finish it," Kane said with a grin. "He was there, too."

"Right," Grant drawled. "In my version, *I'll* be the hero."

Kane joined Brigid, taking her by the elbow and guided her away from the fire. "Sorry," she said. "I didn't mean to interrupt the story hour."

He chuckled. "Diplomacy again. These guys judge your worth by how daring you are. I embellished a little, but they expect that."

Brigid gazed up into his face. The knife cut on his cheek was a bright red line, like a streak of war paint. "You're enjoying this, aren't you?"

"It beats sitting around Cerberus waiting for Lakesh to concoct another crisis that only we can deal with."

Brigid didn't reply.

"Did Beth-Li tell you why she and Auerbach did this?"

"Yes. She was trying to get your attention. She took Auerbach along as a pack mule and to make you jealous."

He stood silently even after Brigid had completed the story. "Well?" she prompted.

Kane knuckled his eyes. "Fits with what Auerbach said." He heaved a deep sigh. "Something is going to have be done with Rouch. She's becoming a menace."

"I agree."

"Any suggestions?"

"Cooperate," answered Brigid quietly.

Dropping his hands from his eyes, Kane stared at her incredulously.

"Don't look so astonished," she said crossly. "There's no point to this game any longer. It's getting dangerous, not much different than the macho game you played with Salvo."

At the mention of his mortal enemy and genetic twin, whose driving passion in life was to humiliate and control him, the incredulity in Kane's eyes gave way to anger.

"You're psychoanalyzing again," he snapped. "You know how I hate that, Baptiste."

"Hate it or not, you'd better accept it. You don't find Beth-Li repulsive. The only reason you've been so stubborn is because Lakesh created the project. You don't like the idea of being controlled."

Kane glanced away and cleared his throat. "That's not the only reason, Baptiste. You know that."

She nodded. "Probably not. The other reasons are all mixed up in you—guilt over my exile, feeling responsible for ruining my life, turning me into an outlander. You know that's not true, Kane. Lakesh had already set me up when he slipped me the *Wyeth Codex* anonymously. He had already planned to bring me into Cerberus. You just bumped up his timetable. I would've been part of Cerberus by now even if you hadn't involved yourself."

Pushing out a deep breath, Brigid said, "You spent most of your life taking orders and you'll be damned if you'll obey this one, even if all you have to do is make love to a beautiful woman and impregnate her."

Kane uttered a mirthless chuckle and kicked at a loose stone. "It's nice that everything I do is so simple and transparent."

Brigid shook her head in annoyance. "I'm tired of dealing with this, Kane, of being dragged into a triangle, of talking around it. I'm barren, all right? The radiation I was exposed to in Mongolia damaged my reproductive system, maybe inflicted irreparable harm to my chromosomal structure.''

Kane didn't look at her. His gaze was fixed on a faraway point in the lengthening shadows.

"You knew, didn't you?" Brigid demanded.

"Rouch made a comment about it a while back," he answered faintly. "So I asked Lakesh. I figured you'd tell me when you were ready.''

The two people stood in silence as twilight deepened around them.

"Thank you for respecting my privacy," Brigid said after a few moments.

"Is your condition permanent?''

"I don't know. DeFore doesn't know, either. She wants to begin a regimen of biochemical therapy, but there hasn't been enough time.

"Now you know, Kane. There's no reason to oppose the program out of misplaced loyalty to me. I promised Lakesh I wouldn't interfere and I'm as good as my word.''

She made a move to step around him, but Kane laid a gentle hand on her arm. *"Anam-chara."*

She stiffened, but not to pull away from his touch. Nor did she turn to face him. Both of them had learned the old Gaelic term, which meant "soul friend," during the mission to Ireland. Morrigan, the beautiful, sightless telepath had told Brigid that she and Kane were *anam-chara*s, but she had never found out where he had picked up the word. She decided to ask him.

"Did Morrigan teach you that, what it meant?''

"Yes, and other things I never told you about.''

She repressed a shiver, but it was not due to the

gusting breeze. In a voice barely above a whisper, she asked, "Like what?"

Kane didn't respond for such a long time she wondered if he had heard her. Then in a low, almost embarrassed voice, he said, "You saw Morrigan kiss me on the deck of the *Cromwell.*"

"I don't know about that. I know I saw you kissing each other."

Kane uttered a soft, irritated sound. "Whatever. She said you would forgive me because you're my *anam-chara.* I told her there was nothing to forgive because there was nothing between you and me."

Kane took a breath, then said in a rush of words, "Morrigan said there was much between us, much we had to forgive, much we had to understand. Much to live through. And then she said, 'Always together.'"

Brigid didn't move, but she asked, "Did you believe her?"

"I didn't know what to believe, Baptiste. I guess I'm scared to believe it."

"Why?"

He didn't answer and Brigid knew why. Both of them remembered the mat-trans jump to Russia, which had gone very, very wrong. Both of them had suffered from extreme jump sickness, the primary symptoms of which were nausea and frighteningly vivid hallucinations.

But in that instance, they had shared the same hallucination or revelation—that Brigid and Kane were somehow joined by spiritual chains, linked to each other and the same destiny.

Kane was more pragmatic and literal-minded than

Brigid, so the concept that their souls had been together for a thousand years or more seemed so unbelievable he feared to consciously examine it. However, he didn't believe in coincidence, either, so the fact they had shared the same hallucination—or revelation—couldn't be ascribed only to jump sickness.

"Why?" she asked again.

He groped for a response that sounded reasonable, but couldn't find one. "Because it might be true."

Carefully, Brigid disengaged herself from his hand, turned and looked levelly into his face. She felt a jolt when she saw the genuine pain, longing and confusion in his eyes. She knew it was only a dim reflection of her own.

"Believe what you want to," she said in a low voice. "But believe it because you feel it. Don't worry about how I enter into it. In the grand scheme of things, we don't owe one another anything. You don't need my permission to participate in Lakesh's plan. You never did, even if Beth-Li thinks otherwise. One thing I don't need is another enemy."

"What makes you say that?"

"Beth-Li told me she'd get me out of the way one way or the other. Like you said, at this point we can't afford to have anyone but allies at our doorstep. Go to Beth-Li or don't go, but remove me from the decision."

With that, Brigid walked away from him. She skirted the cooking fire, then wended her way between the tepees.

Kane watched until her figure was swallowed up by the creeping shadows of dusk. He stood for a long time, despising the painful heaviness in his chest and the quivering in his belly. Then, turning on his heel, he marched through the village.

Beth-Li didn't look surprised when he pushed his way into her lodge. She had changed from the fringed smock to her khakis and greeted him with a knowing smile.

"You talked to Baptiste?" she inquired, gliding toward him on bare feet.

He nodded.

"Good. It took a little doing, but I think she finally saw reason. Is she stepping aside?"

"Yes." Kane bit out the word.

Rouch sidled up against him, sliding one arm around his waist. Her other hand caressed his thigh, then her fingernails dug through the fabric of his trousers, lightly gripping his manhood. She stood on tiptoes, moist lips parting, her dark eyes bright with desire.

"I haven't thanked you yet for rescuing me from that stinking savage," she whispered. "Let me do it now."

Gently, Kane cupped her rounded cheeks between his hands, bending his head to nuzzle the side of his face, touching her delicate earlobe with the tip of his tongue. She leaned her body into his, breathing, "Kane…"

Into her ear, he whispered, "Beth-Li…if you ever threaten Baptiste again, I'll chill you."

His hands clamped cruelly tight on her face, trapping it between them, squeezing her features, distorting her full lips. Drawing back his head, he glared into her eyes, all the desire washed out of them by sudden tears of pain.

Between clenched teeth, voice so thick with fury it sounded like an animal's guttural growl, he said, "I'll break your beautiful little neck."

He gave her head a hard little jerk to the left, dragging an aspirated cry from her. "As easy as that, Beth-Li."

Kane stared at her for a few more seconds, then pushed her aside and stepped out of the lodge. Releasing his breath in a prolonged hiss, he glanced up at the first stars of the evening. He wished he could be up there among them, far and remote from humanity. At that moment, he wished he were anywhere else, even the Tartarus Pits of Cobaltville. At least life there, though brutal, was simple.

He started walking back toward the cooking fire. On the one hand, he regretted terrorizing Beth-Li. On the other hand, he regretted not simply snapping her neck instead of telling her about it. All he had actually accomplished was to make another enemy, but he was used to that.

Chapter 7

Grigori Zakat stood on the open balcony, gazing down into the shadow-streaked valley below as light swiftly drained from the sky. The thin air at such a high altitude rendered the transition from day to night startlingly short and abrupt. Only a brief period of twilight marked the demarcation between sunset and nightfall.

Spring took a long time to arrive on the Byangthang Plateau, and the dry, almost rarefied air was still frigid. Zakat figured his chest was a shade larger from breathing it these past five months.

His wounds had healed completely. Trai's daily application of herbal poultices and tinctures quickly repaired the tissue damage caused by frostbite. The only reminder of his stab wound was a faint scar high on his belly.

Although Zakat had fully recovered, he kept that fact from Dorjieff and the other monks. Only Trai and Gyatso knew he had regained his strength and powers. He had made them his confidants, although Gyatso was more than that. The shaman had sought out Zakat, not the other way around.

Trai was different. She had been ridiculously easy to seduce, pathetically grateful for a man who treated her as something resembling a human being and not as a bipedal mule or as an outlet for lust. Although only a peasant, she was far brighter than she appeared, despite her illiteracy. She was also passionate, an aspect of her personality Zakat recognized and manipulated.

Gyatso had told him not to concern himself with the other monks, especially the Dob-Dobs. They were distrustful of him, but they feared the power of the black shaman even more. Zakat's mission was to ingratiate himself with Dorjieff.

He touched the wood-and-crystal phallus beneath his robe and began his breathing exercise, deepening and regulating his respiration, opening his chakra points in order to receive the summons from Gyatso. Every night for the past month, he stood at the balcony, preparing his mind for Gyatso's signal that all was in readiness. Night after night, he waited, but the signal had not come. He never questioned the Bonpo shaman. Infinite patience was one of the prime articles of Khlysty faith.

After all, Saint Rasputin had not been accepted by the family of the czar overnight. He had waited, performing trivial miracles to earn first the czarina's trust, then her bed.

It always amused Zakat to think about the haughty Alexandra submitting to the unkempt holy man from western Siberia. Rumors of her affair with Rasputin had been one of the triggers for the October Revolution, when the starving Russian masses finally understood that the royal family were flesh and blood, not gods and goddesses.

Of course, those rumors led to Rasputin's assassination by royal retainers, but he had accomplished his mission nevertheless. In Khlysty texts, it was known as the power of causitry—persuasion and seduction to achieve an objective.

Texts, he thought. Zakat remembered prowling the lamasery late at night and how, in a rear vestry, he found ceiling-high shelves sagging beneath the weight of hundreds of crumbling scrolls. Most of them were Buddhist doctrines, but a very few bore odd, unidentifiable cryptograms. There were drawings of geometric shapes such as trapezohedrons, polyhedrons and eye-confusing spiral patterns.

A cold breeze gusted up from below, ruffling Zakat's hair, grown long during his stay in the Trasilunpo lamasery. He pushed a windblown strand back from his high forehead, once more surprised by the wide streak of white that extended from his hairline over the crown of his head to the nape of his neck. Though Zakat possessed no real vanity to speak of, he was a little disconcerted when he noticed the change. He assumed it was an outward manifestation of his physical sufferings out on the plateau. Sometimes, he suspected it was due to Gyatso's assault of *tsal* energy, but either way, he didn't worry about it.

Compared to the journey upon which he and the shaman were prepared to embark, the change in his hair color meant less than a sparrow's tears. He closed his eyes, tightening his long fingers around the balcony's rail, visualizing again the images Gyatso had imparted to him of the vault beneath the lamasery, the "center of the Earth," as Dorjieff had said.

Dorjieff had lived in Tibet for over twenty years, spending the first five of them crushing bandit bands, ragtag revolutionaries and Chinese expeditionary forces. The brutality and utter ruthlessness he employed had earned him the title of Tsyansis Khan-po, the king of fear. But over the course of the past decade and a half, Dorjieff had himself been ruled by fear.

Zakat smiled thinly, recollecting how Dorjieff had been pathetically grateful to have a fellow countryman as first a patient, then as a guest. He still retained a few tatters of patriotism and, when drunk, which was often, would sing the old motherland songs—songs that had ceased to have any meaning nearly two centuries ago when the terrible fire had swept over the face of the planet.

Whatever past accomplishments had earned him a high rank in District Twelve had been drowned in a sea of wine and self-indulgence years before. The king of fear was now a fat, pompous drunkard and, by way of Gyatso's thinking, an utter coward.

Zakat didn't completely agree with that assessment. Cowards were not admitted into District Twelve, and if Dorjieff was fearful of the power pent-up in the vault, it was born of a need to protect Mother Russia and what remained of humanity.

Zakat cared little for Mother Russia and even less for the masses of humankind. The primary reason he had volunteered for duty in the Black Gobi was the opportunity to seize the power that had so obsessed the late Colonel Piotr Sverdlovosk. He had never learned the source of that obsession, but Gyatso claimed whatever was buried in the ruins of Kharo-Khoto was nothing compared to what lay in the subterranean vault.

After five months, Grigori Zakat still wasn't certain

what Gyatso truly represented. The Bon-po religion in which he held high status predated Tibet's conversion to Buddhism by five hundred years. Buddhists sought to exterminate the Bon-po exponents, decrying it as an occult sect that followed the left-hand path of black sorcery, and accusing it of practicing rituals that required human flesh and blood.

He and Gyatso shared a common link there, both adepts and adherents of outlawed religions, both forced to conceal their beliefs and faith.

But Gyatso was something other than a priest, and Zakat was not sure what. Dorjieff had referred to him as an emissary, but had never expanded on the comment. Gyatso dropped only the broadest of hints, promising that all would be revealed once the vault was taken.

The strange, almost empathic bond Zakat shared with the Bon-po shaman did not allow him to receive actual thought images, only emotional resonances. Always those emotions swirled with determination, touched with anger and a sense of betrayal.

Why Gyatso felt that Dorjieff had broken faith with him was never made clear to Zakat, but he entertained his own suspicions. The old Russian had promised to deliver something to Gyatso—an object, a symbol, a birthright—and then reneged. Whatever the object actually was, Zakat always received the confusing impression of a dark, yet somehow shining trapezohedron.

Suddenly, a cold cobweb seemed to lightly stroke his mind, then creep down the base of his spine. The touch instantly vanished, leaving the imprint of a single word: *Now.*

Zakat left the balcony, closing and double-latching the door to cut off even the most unlikely means of escape. He strode through the sleep-stilled halls of the lamasery, his yak-skin boots making only the faintest whisper of sound on the stone floor. The cold gray corridor was lit by pine-knot torches sputtering in wall brackets. The overpowering stench of resin and wood smoke had sunk deep into the stonework.

He walked through the assembly hall, keeping close to the bare wall. The roof beams overhead were exquisitely adorned with images of saints and demons. At the right side of the room was a low table at which a dozen lamas sat murmuring over ancient Buddhist texts hand printed on parchment. A monk lifted his face from the scroll and scowled at the intrusion, but said nothing.

Zakat passed through a narrow doorway on the far side of the chamber and into a short stretch of hallway. Turning a corner, he heard a pained, feminine cry and he knew just where to find Dorjieff.

He walked down the gloomy corridor to the closed door at the far end of it. Grasping the handle, he turned it and carefully shouldered the door open.

He saw Trai's fragile frame bent half over the top of an ornately carved oaken desk. Her trousers had been torn away and lay wadded up on the floor. The face she turned toward Zakat showed the first swellings of a welt. Tears glistened on her cheeks.

Dorjieff stood grunting behind her, grasping her buttocks. Though he still wore his silken tunic, his pants were down about his pale hairy legs. On his bearded, drunken face was a dreamy expression.

It took his wine-addled senses a moment to register

Zakat's presence. Gazing blearily in his direction, he belched and burbled, "Comrade…be with you in a moment…just a moment…."

Trai uttered a faint cry of helpless rage. Zakat strode toward Dorjieff, giving his right wrist a little shake. The bone-handled knife dropped from his belled sleeve into his palm.

Reaching over with his left hand, he grasped Dorjieff's beard and yanked. The big man had no choice but to stumble in Zakat's direction or have his beard pulled out by the roots. A bellow of pain and rage started up his throat. His foam-flecked lips writhed.

Zakat pressed the flat of the blade against his lips, stifling the cry. The cutting edge sliced into the thick flange of flesh between his nostrils. A thin film of bright red blood sheeted over Dorjieff's face. He gasped, coughing and choking as it sprayed up his nasal passages.

Dorjieff staggered back, clapping his hands to his face, his pants dropping around his ankles. He sat down heavily on the floor, a squeal of shock bursting from his mouth, crimson spraying out in a fine mist.

Trai pushed herself up from the desk, groping for her trousers, but blinded by her tears, she collapsed sobbing against Zakat. He put a comforting arm around her quaking shoulders.

Dorjieff gaped up at Zakat in total incredulity, then with a mounting rage. He managed to sputter, "You Khlysty scum bastard, I'll have you scourged, your skin peeled off, toss you naked and blind out onto the plateau! You're nothing but a filthy *khampa!*"

Mildly, Zakat said, "I am not one of the diseased

robbers you drove from this land when you truly were Tsyansis Khan-po. Things have changed.''

Dorjieff's bloody face contorted in shame, then fury. At the top of his lungs, he roared, ''Gyatso! *Gyatso!*''

Zakat didn't hear or see the Bon-po shaman enter the room. The bio-psionic field in the chamber shifted ever so slightly and subtly, and Gyatso stood flanking Zakat.

Blowing scarlet drops from his lips, Dorjieff blurted, ''Gyatso, this man is a viper in our midst. He endangers our pact. Deal with him.''

The black-turbaned man didn't blink or even appear to breathe.

Fear began to shine in Dorjieff's eyes. ''Gyatso! Deal with him!''

Gyatso inclined his head toward Zakat. ''Shall we proceed, Tsyansis Khan-po?''

Dorjieff's mouth dropped open, his labored breathing inflating tiny blood bubbles on his lips. His stricken eyes flickered back and forth between the two men. Terror swallowed up the disbelief. Twice he tried to speak before managing to stammer, ''You betrayed me? Gyatso? *Me?*''

''You betrayed yourself,'' the slightly built man replied in a silky whisper. ''Or rather, your fear betrayed you when you allowed it to reign over you. When that happened, you abdicated your title.''

Zakat cocked his head to one side, beaming down into Dorjieff's red-smeared face. ''The king is dead, Dorjieff. Long live the king.''

He gestured with the knife. ''On your feet. You still have a service to perform to your monarch.''

Dorjieff didn't move, staring glassy-eyed, still grappling with the words spoken by Gyatso. Blood clung to the matted hair of his beard in gummy strands.

Zakat's lips tightened, and he gently pushed Trai aside, transferring the knife to his left hand. He reached inside his robe with his right and withdrew the stubby Tokarev automatic. He loudly cycled a round into the chamber.

Not aiming the pistol, he said, "I won't kill you, old man. But I'll trim that peg of yours for the entertainment of Trai, even though it's a small target."

The threat brought Dorjieff around, and he made a convulsive movement to pull up his pants and conceal his wilted organ. Groaning, he lumbered to his feet, swaying from side to side. Zakat pointed with the Tokarev toward the door. "Take us."

"Take you?" he repeated in a dead voice. "What are you talking about? Take you where?"

Zakat grinned. "Directly beneath the center of the Earth. To the vault."

"The vault where the stone is kept," Gyatso said. "The stone."

The terror of those two words flooded Dorjieff's face. He echoed, "The stone?"

"The stone of Sirius," Zakat said. "The stone of Allah, of Solomon, the stone of the Eight Immortals." He dropped his voice to a whisper. "The key to Agartha. The Chintamani Stone."

Chapter 8

With the utterance of the name, Dorjieff's nerve broke. He turned and attempted to dash across the room, tugging desperately at his pants.

Zakat didn't shoot at him. "Gyatso," he stated, his tone chillingly neutral.

There was a splitting, echoing snap, and a plaited length of oiled leather looped like a streak of fire around Dorjieff's ankles. The man fell heavily, face first, to the stone floor. The air went out of his lungs with an agonized grunt.

The man was too frightened to be outraged over the assault to his dignity. He allowed himself to be dragged to his feet by Zakat, then stood motionless as Gyatso uncoiled the whip from his throbbing ankles and hooked it on his belt.

As Dorjieff shambled to the door like a sleepwalker, Zakat turned to Trai. "Stay here until I send for you."

She ducked her head, adoration shining out of her wet black eyes. "As you wish, Tsyansis Khan-po."

Gyatso and Zakat manhandled Dorjieff out into the narrow hallway, pushing him around several sharp curves. The corridor broadened, and at its end stood an immense granite door with a dragon carved in bas-relief coiled across it. Torches in wall sconces flared smokily on either side of it.

With slitted eyes, Zakat studied the recessed lintel, the threshold and the fluted jambs.

"Open this."

Dorjieff's tongue touched his blood-coated lips. "If I do not?"

"Then you will die, as will every monk and serving boy in the monastery."

Dorjieff stepped to the door. He pushed at the stone moulding in a certain place, and a small square of stone flipped open. Beneath it was a small hole, its sharp angles showing it was man-made. Raising his right fist, the bearded man pressed the stone of his ring into it. A loud metallic click echoed in the corridor, as of a hinged spring snapping open.

Very slowly, the heavy slab of stone swung inward at the top. It was precisely balanced on pivots oiled with animal fat. The opening beyond was very dark, shrouded with musty-smelling shadows.

"Lead the way." Zakat prodded the bearded man with the short barrel of the Tokarev.

For a moment, Dorjieff didn't move. "The time is not nigh. The prophecies have not been fulfilled."

"So you have been saying for years," Gyatso said. "The fact that a new Tsyansis Khan-po has arrived proves the time is indeed nigh."

In a low, scholarly tone, Zakat stated, "From Milarepa's *Hundred Thousand Songs for the Wise*— 'That which is held within the heart of the aged king of the East will be taken by the new king fallen from the Western skies.'"

In a hollow, whispery voice, Gyatso said, "And did he not fall from the skies?"

When Dorjieff didn't reply, the black-turbaned man spun him around and pushed him into the gloom beyond the portal. The firelight from the corridor barely penetrated into the murk. Dorjieff walked slowly along the passageway past walls covered with silken, painted *thang-ka*, faded tapestries depicting the lives of various lamas and Buddhas.

With Grigori Zakat digging the bore of the pistol into his left kidney, Dorjieff descended crude stairs hewed out of rock. Ahead and below glowed a dim aurora. The stairway ended in a bowl-shaped chamber. The light shone from a dozen animal-tallow candles in brackets around the curving rock walls.

Drawn on the cavern floor with colored powders was a large *kyilkhor* diagram, a triangular form designed to ensnare Dre, messengers of death. Dorjieff carefully stepped around it. Zakat deliberately scuffled his feet through the intricate lines.

On either side of the cavern, two life-size effigies crafted out of stone faced each other. The statue of a cherubic-faced man squatted cross-legged in the Buddhist attitude of meditation. The image was of Tsong-ka-po, founder of the Trasilunpo monastic order.

The other statue was of a ten-armed monstrosity, wearing a diadem of grinning human skulls above a leering, tusked face. It was Heruka, one of the many wrathful manifestations of the Buddha.

Hanging between the pair of stone effigies was a number of wilted but brilliantly colored tapestries, all bearing twisting *kyilkhor* geometric designs. Gathering a handful of fabric in his right hand, Zakat jerked hard, ripping it loose from the crossbar. The ancient cloth tore easily, and dust puffed up around it in a cloud. In an alcove beyond, a bank of electronic equipment followed the horseshoe shape of the stone walls. Lights flickered on consoles, and the faint hum of power units sounded like a swarm of distant insects.

In the center of the cavern stood a six-sided chamber, all the walls of the same glassy, translucent substance. They had a murky, purplish tint.

The color of twilight, Zakat thought with a half smile.

He turned to face Dorjieff, whose knees had acquired a definite wobble. "A quantum-interphase matter-transfer inducer, part of the old Szvezda Project. The only aspect of the American Totality Concept fully shared with the Soviet Union."

Dorjieff was beyond surprise, but he asked, "How did you know that?"

"How do you think?" Zakat snapped contemptuously. "Have you become so besotted you've forgotten the prime directive of District Twelve, why it was organized over twenty years ago?"

Dorjieff did not answer. With a sleeve, he dabbed gingerly at the blood still flowing over his lips.

"The primary function of District Twelve is to secure any and all predark technology, particularly that related to the Totality Concept," Zakat recited flatly. "Though its parameters have expanded somewhat over the last decade, that was its initial operational protocol. Officially, you may have been dispatched here to keep your eye on China, but you were actually following up on a fragment of damned data. Is that not so?''

Dorjieff blinked in surprise. ''Damned data'' was a coded reference to predark intel of the highest security classification, less than fact but more than rumor.

''Answer me.''

Dorjieff nodded. ''Yes.''

Zakat gestured with the Tokarev. ''Show us what that data led you to.''

Dorjieff slowly shuffled past the statue of Heruka. Hidden behind its broad base and draped with a shroud of black cloth rose a stone pillar some four feet in height. The bearded man tugged away the cloth, sending up a scattering of dust motes.

The pillar was covered on each side with crudely incised, bizarre faces. The faces were humanoid, but with oversize, hairless craniums, huge, upslanting, pupil-less eyes and tiny slits for mouths. Eight of the faces were arrayed around the perimeter of the pedestal.

Atop the pillar rested a box of hammered silver, its hinged lid thrown back. The box was lined by a dusty layer of red silk. Inside was an asymmetrical shape, a dark spherical object six inches around.

Both Gyatso and Zakat stepped to the pedestal and stared at the ovoid within the box. It was a nearly black polyhedron, with purplish striated highlights and many flat, pitted surfaces, like the facets of a crystal. It didn't touch the bottom of the box, but hung suspended by eight delicate silver wires extending from the container's inner walls.

Zakat noticed the fascination the stone exerted

upon the Bon-po shaman. A smile tugged at the corners of his lipless mouth, and his eyes glittered with an emotion Zakat couldn't identify.

"This is the stone intended to impose order on chaos," said Zakat flatly. "And to hold forth a key to the arcana of the Eight Immortals of Agartha."

"Yes," Dorjieff confirmed.

"This is but a fragment of a larger piece, cut and broken ages ago. It was originally a trapezohedron, was it not?"

"Yes."

"Other than the piece once kept in the Ka'aba of Mecca, this is the largest fragment in the world."

"Yes."

"And there is one other, smaller piece somewhere."

"Yes."

"Where?"

Dorjieff wagged his head, bullishly, from side to side. "That I do not know."

"What do you know?"

Dorjieff bowed his head, his voice a wheezing rasp. "I came to this lamasery in search of something else. I found the stone. And far, far more."

Very slowly, as if his tongue were suddenly heavy as lead, Dorjieff continued, "I was privy to damned data which I'm sure was withheld from you. Some twenty years ago, District Twelve was much smaller, comprising only a handful of officers. A discovery was made among our predark intelligence archives, and District Twelve expanded its duties beyond counterintelligence and parochial concerns."

Zakat bristled at the implication he knew less about

the inner workings of his organization than a fat drunkard. Scornfully, he said, ''Speak then of this discovery.''

''There is a force, a power, if you will, whose entire purpose is to subjugate humanity, regardless of nationality. It is very likely they orchestrated the nukecaust, and they may have been responsible for much of Mother Russia's tortured history.''

Dorjieff started to point to the metal box, but dropped his hand. Beseechingly, he said, ''Comrade, you must understand. I found more than a key, I found an object of power that transcended my orders, overruled my oath to my country and District Twelve. I stayed here to safeguard it, to stand sentry so it could never be used against us.''

''Patriotism is a very thin covering for your own avarice,'' Zakat sneered.

Dorjieff straightened, his shoulders stiffening, as he tried to draw the tatters of his dignity around him like a cloak. ''I speak not of patriotism, but of responsibility for what is left of the human race.'' He nodded toward Gyatso, adding contemptuously, ''That hellspawn is driven by avarice, by worse than avarice. I knew it the moment he arrived here last year.''

Gyatso said softly, ''I came here to claim my birthright, to hold within my hands the legacy of Agartha. I am the descendant of the Maha Chohan, the ambassador of the nation of Agartha. All this was foretold by prophecy.''

Dorjieff snorted, blowing tiny blood droplets. He winced in pain. ''A nation you have never seen, Gyatso, one that is more myth than reality. And what little reality may be attached to it is something we should not interact with.''

"Why conceal a key which unlocks no door?" Gyatso's question sounded as sharp as the crack of his whip. "Why stand guard over the gates to a kingdom of myth?"

Dorjieff did not answer.

Zakat's smile became a chuckle. "You're a very clever dissembler, old man. You should have been a Khlysty priest. Whether Agartha—the Valley of the Eight Immortals—exists or not, this stone certainly does.''

He lowered his voice to a mock-conspiratorial whisper. "And why is this lamasery equipped with a mat-trans unit, a gateway? It had to have been installed before the nuclear holocaust.''

Dorjieff still said nothing.

"That is why you came here," continued Zakat. "That was the piece of damned data you uncovered. You wanted to learn why this machine from Szvezda had been placed here and to find out if it still worked. Following up on rumors of a Chinese incursion was only secondary to your mission.''

He paused for a tiny tick of time and declared, "I'm not asking you, old man. You needn't say anything. Your stubborn silence gives assent.''

Dorjieff's shoulders sloped in resignation. Bitterly, he said, "You've got it all figured out, don't you? Yes, old Szvezda documents indicated a gateway here, but not the reason for it. I tortured the abbot here for the information, but either he didn't know or he refused to tell me.

"I cannot be sure if the gateway was placed here

by our countrymen or others, but my suspicion is that its installation was meant as an escape hatch for either the guardian of the stone—or its rightful owner, if such a one exists."

Gyatso announced coldly, "He stands before you."

Dorjieff forced a derisive laugh. "You're a complete fool, Gyatso. If the stone is a key, it is also like a bomb waiting for a detonator. As you pointed out, some of its facets are missing. It may be incomplete, but it is by no means inert."

"How do you know that?" Zakat demanded.

Dorjieff dragged in a shuddery breath. "Many years ago, I was foolishly arrogant as you. I dared to touch it. Knowledge of its true nature flooded into my mind. I was illuminated."

"No," Zakat corrected snidely, "you were terrified."

"Terror can be a form of illumination. The terror of finally realizing that what man knows about reality is nothing compared to what he doesn't know—or what he may never know. Damned data indeed."

Dorjieff's bushy eyebrows drew together as he glared at Zakat. "This lamasery was built at least six hundred years ago, a continuation of other lamaseries that had existed here for thousands of years. Its sole purpose is to house the stone, to keep it segregated from the other fragments scattered across the world."

"To keep it from being restored to a full trapezohedron?" Zakat inquired.

"To keep the gates of Agartha forever locked?" demanded Gyatso.

"Yes, on both counts. Though there is far more to it than that."

"You believe the stone is a thing of evil?" the shaman challenged.

Dorjieff shook his head. "It is not evil, but it is not good, either. Those are human concepts and the stone is much older than humanity. In its original form, the stone was fashioned by a prehuman race known in various cultures as the Nagas, the Annunaki, the Na Fferyllt. It was believed to be a spiritual accelerator, used to advance the intelligences and perceptions of the first primitive human beings."

Dorjieff swept his arms around the cavern. "As humanity climbed up the ladder of evolution, the stone was treasured by them, worshiped. It crossed strange lands and seas that no longer exist, it sank with Atlantis and was recovered by the forerunners of the Egyptians. It rested in an underground crypt between the paws of the Sphinx before the Flood. It was found aeons later, split by priests and scattered across the Earth."

"Why?" demanded Gyatso. "If it is not a thing of evil, then why hide it from the sight of man?"

"Because it is a window on Agartha—on the black, forbidden things which no one has ever heard of, not even in whispers. You think Agartha is a magical, fabulous kingdom? No, it is a repository of secrets and the seat of five hundred thousand years of man's hidden history."

Zakat glanced toward the purple-tinted walls of the gateway chamber. "The mat-trans must lead to the other facets of the stone."

"Perhaps," replied Dorjieff. "Perhaps not. The device's destination codes are locked on a specific point and have probably been for two hundred years or more. Where that point might be, if it exists any longer, is something I do not know or care to know.''

Zakat chuckled. ''And there lies the divide between us.''

Dorjieff made a rumbling sound deep in his chest. ''The stone must be not be made whole again. If you understand what *I* understand, you would flee shrieking from this place, back to the nest of perverts you call a religion.''

''And what do you understand?''

''Assume there are people who have been trained to transcend the accepted laws of physics, who wield wild powers that are called—for lack of a better term—magical. Also assume there are ancient objects and places of otherworldly power that these people can access, using their energies as means of control and as weapons.''

''And you're saying,'' ventured Zakat, ''that the black stone is such a weapon?''

''I am saying that the forces flowing through it can be used as such. The forces flow through it unto like a tide. If a tide goes in two directions at once, you have a catastrophe that threatens not only the body, but the soul. The human spirit. That is what I safeguard, not this chunk of rock.''

Zakat gestured negligently with the Tokarev. ''You are a true martyr, old man, though I doubt Trai would testify you are fixated on safeguarding her spirit.''

Dorjieff's face darkened in anger. ''You understand nothing of the true nature of the stone.''

Zakat smiled mockingly. ''I believe I understand enough.''

Dorjieff's lips drew away from his red-filmed teeth

in a snarling grin. "Then do what I did, if you have the courage. Touch the stone," he taunted.

The smile fled from Zakat's face. He did not move.

"You are afraid," said Dorjieff, a note of triumph evident in his voice. "Not that I blame you for it, but how do you intend to command the forces flowing through it if you fear to touch it?"

Zakat wheeled defiantly toward the pedestal. He extended his left hand toward the open box, keeping the Tokarev in his right pointed at Dorjieff. He caught Gyatso's eye, who looked at him uncertainly.

"My faith," he said, more to reassure Gyatso than to challenge Dorjieff, "will protect me."

Dorjieff gusted out a laugh. "That we will see."

Zakat thrust out his hand, his fingers brushing the surface of the black stone. He felt a distinct tingling rushing up his hand, into his wrist, up his arm. He closed his eyes for a second. When he opened them again, he experienced a vertiginous sensation of seeing in two worlds at once—the world of the senses, and the inner world of the black stone.

With his eyes, he saw Gyatso and the box and the cavern.

In the other world, he saw leagues of endless desert sprouting with black monoliths soaring heavenward. He saw towers and walls in the depths of the Earth, an infinite gulf of darkness, of swirling patterns of force locked forever in a symbiotic contest of order against chaos.

A sudden riot of emotion-fraught images exploded in his mind, triggering a terror so wild it was almost ecstasy, and he became aware of a mindless chittering, as of countless voices murmuring at once.

Zakat felt he was being examined, not by the stone, but by observers that used the black polyhedron as a form of sight more acute than the physical.

A jagged skyline appeared in his mind's eye, in which the hulks of buildings reared from a debris-scattered terrain like broken tombstones. Two monoliths, each at least a hundred feet high, rose from the high tumbles of twisted metal and shattered concrete. The dark windows gaped between tangles of creeping vegetation, but astonishingly, shards of glass still glinted here and there. For a dizzy instant, Zakat felt as if he plummeted through the shockscape of ruins, passing around and over the wilderness of rubble.

Then an animal's snouted face snarled into his, a shocking pink tongue protruding from between great yellow fangs. The brownish silver-tipped fur looked matted and mangy, and Zakat realized it was not the face of a living bear, but an example of the taxidermist's art.

His perspective seemed to broaden, and the bear's face receded. He saw a vast room, almost a man-made cavern. In niches behind shattered glass were elks, elephants, rhinoceros, wolves and other extinct species frozen in eternal postures of stalking or pacing.

Zakat felt a persistent tug. Rather than resist it, he traveled down a broad staircase, past a monstrous, pale blue shape tilting down from the ceiling at a ninety-degree angle. He could not identify it, though its sleek bulk and dimensions reminded him of a wingless Tu-114 fuselage.

At the same time, he became aware of a rhythmic vibration, like the beating of an unimaginably gigantic heart. He found himself floating through a forest of stone, like a geologist's dream. He passed glittering geodes, clusters of the crystals the size of washtubs, mineral formations of all sizes and shapes.

Hidden somewhere among them he felt the pulsing of energy, black yet bright, beckoning him with a siren song of seduction, whispering to him of power and of the price he must pay—

He blinked, snatching his hand back, almost but not quite giving voice to a cry of primal panic.

Dorjieff laughed. "Come now, Comrade. You barely tickled it. Grasp it as I did, hold it within your hand so you may see and feel what I did. And understand."

Zakat despised the shiver that shook his shoulders as he turned to face Dorjieff. "Like I said, I understand enough."

"And like I said, you know nothing," Dorjieff retorted.

"You have nothing more to say, old man," replied Zakat. "You seem to have a problem accepting that. Your position here has been usurped."

With a speed surprising for a man of such bulk and age, Dorjieff lunged forward. All the memories of his training hadn't been drowned in wine, and with two lightning-swift moves, he disarmed Zakat.

Swinging the barrel of the automatic in short half arcs to cover first Gyatso, then Zakat, then Gyatso again, he growled, "You'll die first, you half-breed hell-spawn. As for you, Father Twilight, I will use you for the same kind of target practice you proposed for me. But my hand is not as steady, nor are my eyes as clear as they once were. There will be many near misses. You'll have to be patient with me."

Zakat only smiled. "I am exceedingly patient, Dor-jieff. Get on with it."

Dorjieff aimed the pistol at Gyatso, his finger tight-ened around the trigger, but he did not fire. The gun, his hand and his entire forearm began to tremble, locked in a muscle spasm. He looked in stunned ag-ony at Gyatso, who gazed unblinkingly, serenely at him.

Softly, Zakat said, "What was it you said to me about this half-breed hell-spawn's power? Oh, yes, 'The secret of Bon training consists of developing a power of concentration surpassing even that of men like yourself, who are the most gifted in psychic re-spects.'"

The sweat of effort beaded on Dorjieff's forehead and streamed into his eyes. He did not, could not blink them. In a crooning whisper, Zakat continued, "I will allow you a limited freedom of movement. You may turn your wrist and lift your arm. Point the gun at your face, won't you?"

Groaning, his entire body shuddering with the strain, Dorjieff did as Zakat requested.

"Very good, thank you. Now, if you will please open your mouth and place the barrel inside of it...?"

A keening wail of terror issued from Dorjieff's lips, but he obeyed, his arm trembling. His mouth gaped wide as he inserted the short barrel of the Tokarev, and his lower teeth rattled against the metal trigger guard.

Affectionately, as if he were speaking to a lover, Zakat whispered, "Will you please pull the trigger? If you pull it, all of this ends."

Dorjieff's hand convulsed. The Tokarev made a

popping sound, like the bursting of a balloon in another room. A tiny twist of smoke puffed from his open mouth, followed a microinstant later by a gushing torrent of scarlet. He staggered, limbs flailing, the pistol clattering to the floor.

Dorjieff hit the ground on his back, fingers and feet twitching. He uttered only a liquidy burble before his body stilled.

Zakat turned away, ruefully rubbing the aching spot on the center of his forehead. He knew that without Gyatso's mind augmenting his own force of will, he wouldn't have been able to induce Dorjieff to commit suicide. The old bastard had not lost all of the strength that had earned him the title of Tsyansis Khan-po.

Gyatso nodded, approving the manner in which Dorjieff had been dispatched. "And now?" he asked.

Grigori Zakat reached out and snapped down the lid of the box. It moved easily on its oiled hinges and closed over the stone, the hasp sliding and snapping into the lock. At that sharp click, Gyatso jumped, a sudden fear visible on his face.

Somehow, Zakat knew it was the first time in the memory of the lamasery that the box had been closed. He was suddenly conscious of a formless presence in the cavern—a presence not in the rock walls, but beyond them.

It was a sense of a faraway inhuman intelligence that had instantly become aware of what he had done. Zakat saw nothing, heard nothing, yet he felt a powerful surging of an icy energy. The aura of the cavern was suddenly oppressive, the very air throbbing with menace.

Zakat kept his left hand on the silver lid of the box

as he half turned to face Gyatso. "Now we plan and make our final assessment."

Gyatso cocked his head slightly to one side. "Assessment? I do not understand."

"Of the price we must pay for power." Zakat laughed as he turned to glance at Dorjieff's corpse. "It may be more appropriate to say the price we must persuade others to pay."

Chapter 9

Three a.m., Lakesh thought sourly. The midnight of the human soul, when the blood trickles at low tide and the heart beats slowly. He remembered reading that more people with terminal illnesses died at three o'clock in the morning than at any other time.

Lakesh rarely slept more than five hours out of twenty-four, so he often found himself alone in the central control complex of the Cerberus redoubt.

He stared reproachfully over the rims of his spectacles at the image of a slavering black hound filling the monitor screen in front of him. Three snarling heads grew out of a single corded neck, their jaws wide open, blood and fire gushing between great fangs. Because the security cameras transmitted in black-and-white and shades of gray, he couldn't see the garish colors of the large illustration on the wall. He'd seen the crimson eyes and yellow fangs enough times over the years, as well as the word written in exaggerated Gothic script beneath it: Cerberus.

Like everything else in the redoubt, the image of the three-headed hound had weathered the nukecaust, the skydark and all the catastrophes that followed.

Built near the close of the twentieth century, the Cerberus installation was a masterpiece of impenetrability. The trilevel, thirty-acre facility was equipped with radiation shielding, and an elaborate system of heat-sensing warning devices, night-vision vid cameras and motion-trigger alarms surrounded the plateau that concealed it.

Lakesh looked up from the canine heads snarling still and frozen on the screen to the huge Mercator-relief map of the world sprawling across the expanse of the facing wall. Pinpoints of light shone steadily in almost every country, connected by a thin, glowing pattern of lines. They represented the Cerberus network, the locations of all functioning gateway units across the planet.

The installation had been built as the seat of the Cerberus process, a subdivision of Overproject Whisper, which in turn had been a primary component of the Totality Concept. At its height, the redoubt had housed well over a hundred people. Now it was full of shadowed corridors, empty rooms and sepulchral silences, a sanctuary for thirteen human beings. There was one other, a fourteenth, but for him—or it, Lakesh was never quite certain—Cerberus was a prison.

Actually, all the redoubts linked to the Totality Concept became prisons after January 19, 2001. That was why Lakesh hadn't opposed the proposal that he be placed in cryonic stasis. Nor was he the only volunteer among the personnel in the Mount Rushmore installation. The resources of the vast facility were already strained, and it had suffered unforeseen damage during the nukecaust. Some measures had to be taken to preserve the command post.

Constructed inside of Mount Rushmore, to serve as both the central Continuity of Government seat, as well as the coordinating station for the Totality Concept redoubts, the so-called Anthill became more of a tomb every day.

Very few of the contingency plans worked, especially after the desperate military personnel remaining in other installations began to arrive by mat-trans unit. After a few months, there were just too many people to support and the jump lines were blocked so no one else could find refuge from the horrors of the rad-blasted landscape.

Life in the Anthill became an endless interlocking chain of crises, one after the other, coming so fast they seemed to trip over each other. The Overproject Excalibur genetic experiments soured, essential machinery broke down, radiation leaked in, the nuclear winter disrupted not only the local ecosystems, but also all those across America. Lakesh remembered wishing he had refused the evacuation order and stayed behind in Cerberus, known also as Redoubt Bravo.

Lakesh shook his head, trying to drive away the memories. There was no point in dredging them up. When he was resurrected fifty years ago, the handful of people remaining in the Anthill complex didn't even remember those days. Only the present and the future mattered, and essential to those were the Archon Directorate's edicts to rebuild the world in a new image.

The final stage of that rebuilding, the Program of Unification, was well under way when Lakesh was awakened. The rallying cry of Unity Through Action had already spread across the length and breadth of the Deathlands by word of mouth and proof of deed. The long forgotten trust in any form of government had been reawakened by the offer of a solution to the constant states of hardship and fear—join the Unification Program sponsored by the barons and never know want or fear again. Of course, any concept of liberty had to be forgotten in the exchange.

Not every human was invited to partake of the bounty of the barons. Only the best of the best were allowed full citizenship. The caste distinctions were based primarily on eugenics. Everyone selected to live in the villes, to serve in the divisions, met a strict set of genetic criteria that had been established before the nukecaust. The original drafters of the Unification Program had in their possession the findings of Overproject Excalibur's Human Genome Project, as well as actual in vitro biological samples. In the vernacular of the time, it was known as purity control.

After the Program of Unification was established, the in vitro egg cells were developed to embryos. Through ectogenesis techniques, fetal development outside of the body eliminated the role of the mother until after birth. The ancient social patterns that connected mother, father and child were broken, a break that was a crucial aspect of the Unification Program. For the program to succeed, the existence of the family as a unit of procreation—and therefore as a social unit—had to be eliminated.

Sometimes, a particular gene carrying a desirable trait was grafted to an unrelated egg, or an undesirable gene removed. Despite many failures, when there was a success, it was replicated over and over, occasionally with variations.

Kane was one such success, developed secretly by Lakesh. At the thought of him, the furrows in Lakesh's forehead deepened into ruts. He knew he shouldn't worry about Kane, or Grant and Brigid. Too many times in the past, Lakesh had forced himself to accept their deaths, only to see them reappear alive, if not completely whole. They seemed to lead exceptionally charmed lives, but like any other resource, luck had a way of running out.

In his more metaphysical moments, he viewed the three of them as a trinity, the human counterparts of the heads of Cerberus, each one symbolizing different yet related aspects of the soul.

It always surprised and comforted him that such contrasting personalities worked so well together. Even Domi, the least disciplined of the redoubt's staff, displayed a remarkable resourcefulness. But there were two residents of Cerberus who didn't quite mesh with the other parts of the efficient machine Lakesh dreamed of constructing.

One of them was Beth-Li Rouch. Initially, she seemed to be the perfect candidate for his plan to expand their sanctuary into a colony. She was certainly beautiful, young and vital. After Lakesh selected her from the personnel records of Sharpeville, he put into motion a variation of the ploy he had used on Brigid Baptiste, Donald Bry and Robert Wegmann: he framed them for crimes against their respective villes.

Lakesh knew it was a cruel, heartless plan with a barely acceptable risk factor, but it was the only way to spirit them out of their villes, turn them against the barons, make them feel indebted to him.

Beth-Li was the only exile he had chosen not for technical knowledge or expertise, but solely because her genetic records indicated that she and Kane would produce perfect offspring, superior in every way.

He had eliminated the other women in Cerberus for a number of reasons. DeFore, though healthy, had a family history of diabetes. Domi was a genetic question mark due to her upbringing in the Outlands, close to hot spots and hellzones, and he didn't need to conduct medical tests to ascertain if she possessed undesirable traits. Her albinism was the most obvious indicator.

Brigid Baptiste of course had a splendid pedigree, as he had reason to know. However, even if she hadn't suffered the accident in Mongolia, Lakesh would not have wanted her to breed with Kane —or anyone, for that matter. Her gifts were unique, far too valuable to have them diverted by pregnancy and motherhood.

It continued to dismay and distress him how Kane opposed his plan to impregnate Beth-Li. Only recently had his resistance become overt. Before that, his refusal to cooperate had been known in predark psychological terminology as passive-aggressive behavior. Therefore, Lakesh had been pleased when Kane volunteered to go in search of Beth-Li and Auerbach.

When the young woman first proposed the scheme to him, Lakesh had been extremely doubtful it would work, and duping poor Auerbach seemed exceptionally coldhearted. But Beth-Li convincingly argued that the harmless deception would prove Kane's feelings for her one way or the other. At length, Lakesh had been persuaded and gave his grudging approval.

Unfortunately, he couldn't object to Brigid's participation in the subsequent search party without arousing suspicion. Kane had never fully trusted him anyway, particularly after he learned about Lakesh's covert involvement in his upbringing. Lately, even Brigid had expressed skepticism about his plan to create a colony.

He ran a hand through his hair, which was the color and texture of ash. Her doubt had disappointed him. Kane, despite his high intelligence, tended to view situations in black-and-white, no doubt a carryover from his life as a Magistrate.

Brigid on the other hand, could swiftly meld thesis, antithesis into a synthesis of diverse, sometimes contradictory concepts. Or at least, she had been capable of that until Kane's simplistic approach to life's vagaries infected her.

The breeding program was a stopgap measure anyway. Lakesh had feverishly held on to the hope that the path to reversing the postnukecaust horrors lay in reversing the probability-wave dysfunction triggered by Operation Chronos in the late twentieth century.

It had proved to be a hope so vain, so futile that he could not think of a word in the several languages he spoke fluently to describe it. The very fabric of space-time itself had been deliberately folded, time squared to prevent any change made in the past from affecting the present.

Lakesh never spoke of his profound despair over the failure of the Omega Path program to anyone. Outwardly, he adopted a cheery demeanor, but inwardly he often wished he was still deep in cryo-sleep, blissfully unaware of what the world had become. His wellspring of hope had run dry, the bucket filled only with the dry dust of defeat.

More than once over the past couple of months, he railed at himself to accept the inevitable, to live out the rest of his life among the Cerberus exiles, taking what joy he could find. With the replacement parts surgically bequeathed to him upon his resurrection in the Anthill, he might have another twenty years of life, thirty if he took care of himself.

But he knew Cerberus couldn't remain hidden for that long. In rare, maniacally optimistic moments, he calculated that the redoubt could be concealed for two years. In his more common, pessimistic moments, he figured it would be fortunate to escape discovery for another six months.

Despite the fresh memory of the tortures inflicted upon him before escaping from Cobaltville, Lakesh couldn't repress a smile at the irony. Salvo had been convinced of the existence of the underground resistance movement called the Preservationists. But the group was an utter fiction, a straw adversary crafted for the barons to fear and chase after, while his true insurrectionist work proceeded elsewhere. Lakesh had learned the techniques of mis- and disinformation many, many years ago while working as Project Cerberus overseer for the Totality Concept.

Salvo had believed that Lakesh was a Preservationist and that he had recruited Kane into their traitorous rank and file. When Baron Cobalt had charged Salvo with the responsibility of apprehending Kane by any means necessary, he presumed those means included the abduction and torture of Lakesh, one of the baron's favorites.

Kane, Grant, Domi and DeFore had rescued Lakesh and taken him back to Cerberus, but in the process increased the odds the redoubt would be found. Although the installation was listed on all ville records as utterly inoperable, and the Cerberus mat-trans unit was slightly out of phase to prevent detection, Lakesh extrapolated that Baron Cobalt would leave no redoubt unopened in his search for him, conducting a hands-on, physical search of every redoubt. Other than rescuing Lakesh, his trusted adviser, from the grasp of people he believed to be murderous insurgents, Baron Cobalt's monumental vanity and ego were at stake. Kane had twice humiliated the baron, and that was two times too many for a creature who perceived himself as semidivine.

Despite recent efforts to lay false trails in other redoubts, Lakesh knew the search would eventually narrow to the plateau in the Bitterroots. His options were limited. If he returned to Cobaltville with a tale of having escaped the Preservationists, he feared the baron's suspicions would turn to him. Even if the baron pretended to believe him, he would certainly mistrust him.

Too many things had happened since the rescue. Kane had mortally wounded Baron Sharpe, and Brigid was suspected of assassinating Baron Ragnar. Baron Cobalt would never accept that a doddering old pedant had managed to wriggle out of the clutches of such ruthless revolutionaries.

Another option, often discussed but never implemented, was to relay ransom demands to Baron Cobalt for Lakesh's safe return. There had not been

enough time over the past couple of months to work
out the fiendishly complicated details of such a plan.

Lakesh took off his thick-lensed spectacles with the
hearing aid attached to the right earpiece, and mas-
saged the bridge of his nose. Everything seemed complicated lately, even getting a decent night's sleep.

Tapping a button on the keyboard, he transferred
the vid network to another camera, one trained on a
stretch of empty corridor and the door leading to
Balam's confinement facility. The creature behind the
electronically locked door couldn't be considered as
a member of the redoubt. He—or it—was a prisoner,
a specimen to be studied, not that more than three
years of observation had provided any useful data beyond what had been theorized in the twentieth century.

A sudden flicker of movement on the screen commanded his attention, dragging his thoughts back
from the past. Squinting, Lakesh fumbled for his eyeglasses, seating them on his face. He stared at the
figure on the screen first in surprise, then with a growing alarm.

Banks, the warder of Balam, shuffled down the corridor. That in itself would not have been an unusual
sight except it was 3:30 a.m. and the youthful black
man was clad only in his underwear.

As he came closer to the vid lens, Lakesh noticed
how his normally trim blocked hair was pushed out
of shape on the right side and how his characteristi-
cally bright, alert eyes were almost closed, surrounded
by puffy bags.

Obviously, Banks had just risen, awakened from a
deep slumber. Lakesh expected him to stop before the

door leading to the confinement area, punch in the code and enter. The young man's sense of responsibility toward the imprisoned entity always amused and bemused him. He hadn't been selected for the assignment because of his compassion, but because he possessed the psychic strength to block Balam's telepathic influence.

Lakesh assumed that after three years of looking after Balam, of preparing his cattle blood and chemical nourishment, Banks looked at him as something of a pet. Lakesh had never cautioned him about adopting that attitude, inasmuch as no one else in the redoubt could stand to be in Balam's presence for more than a couple of minutes.

Dread rose in Lakesh as Banks passed the door and continued on down the dully gleaming vanadium-alloy corridor. He lifted his bare feet scarcely an eighth of an inch above the floor. He walked out of range of the vid camera.

Lakesh realized there could only be two places for him to be going—the main sec door or the control complex in which he sat. He doubted Banks had the overpowering urge to step outside for a breath of fresh, predawn air, especially in his underwear. The temperature on the plateau, despite the springtime warmth below, hovered only a degree or two above freezing.

Lakesh swiveled his chair around as Banks appeared in the doorway, looking at him dully from beneath half-closed eyelids. Swiftly inspecting his slack-jawed face, Lakesh wondered if the young man was sleepwalking.

Softening his normally reedy voice, Lakesh said, "Good morning, Banks. What gets you up so early?"

Banks remained standing in the doorway, listing slightly from side to side. A half hiss, half whisper passed his lips like steam escaping from a valve. *"Kayyy-nuh."*

Icy fingers tapped the buttons of Lakesh's spine. "What?"

Banks drew in a soft breath and expelled it in another hiss. "Kayyy-nuh. Where...is...Kayyy-nuh?"

The timbre of his voice sounded utterly flat, totally devoid of any emotion whatsoever, which matched the blank expression on Banks's face. Despite his growing apprehension, Lakesh maintained a quiet, level voice. "Do you mean Kane?"

"Where?" came the rustling question.

"He's not here, Banks. You know that."

Lakesh wet his suddenly dry lips and inquired conversationally, "Why do you ask?"

Banks's eyelids drooped lower. "Must Kane speak. Must stone warn. Must warn about."

Lakesh listened, feeling the short hairs on the nape of his neck tingle and lift. Banks spoke slowly, as if he were feeling his away around verbal communication, not quite grasping the rules of grammar and syntax.

With a surge of both fright and fascination, Lakesh used the armrests of his chair to lever himself to his feet. He blurted, "Balam! *You're Balam!*"

Chapter 10

Banks didn't react, the blank expression remaining steady. "Kane only. Tell must Kane. Danger in stone. He go. He stop. Only Kayyy-nuh."

The last word stretched out like taffy from between Banks's slack lips. His knees buckled, and his lean body sagged and would have collapsed had he not fallen against the door frame. Lakesh rushed around the computer station and caught him, manhandling him into a chair.

Banks shivered uncontrollably, hugging himself. He lifted his head, looking around in bewilderment, eyes blinking rapidly. They focused on Lakesh. "What's going on? What am I doing here?"

He made a move to rise from the chair, but Lakesh pushed him back gently. Soothingly, he said, "Settle down. You were sleepwalking."

Banks raised questioning eyebrows. "Me? I've never sleepwalked in my life."

"There's a first time for everything," Lakesh replied inanely. "What's the last thing you remember?"

"Going to bed," Banks retorted impatiently.

"No dreams that you recall?"

Lines of concentration crossed the young man's forehead. "Not a dream exactly. I remember waking up for a second, thinking there was a bird in my room. Then I went back to sleep. That must have been hours ago.''

Lakesh struggled to keep his voice steady. "What kind of bird?''

Banks frowned. "A big one...not an eagle...all gray feathers. I think it was an owl. Yeah, a great big owl, flying right at my head. Staring at me.''

His shoulders shook in a shudder. "I remember waking up. Or at least, I *think* I remember waking up.''

"What do you remember most about the owl?''

Banks's expression went vacant. "Its eyes. It had great big black eyes. Huge and slanting. But owls don't have black slanting eyes, do they?''

"Ornithology isn't my field,'' answered Lakesh, "but no, I don't think they do.''

He waited a moment before inquiring, "By any chance, did the owl's eyes remind you of Balam's?''

Banks chewed his lower lip, then ducked his head. His "Yeah'' carried a note of anxious realization.

Banks knew almost as much as Lakesh did about Balam and the race he represented, which was very little. The biological studies performed back when the Archons were referred to as PTEs—Pan Terrestrial Entities—were frustratingly incomplete.

At first, the entities were classified as EBEs—Extraterrestrial Biological Entities—but that designation was later amended, since it may have been premature if not erroneous. When everything known about the Archons was distilled down to its basic components, all the scientific minds devoted to the subject could agree on only one thing—they knew very little.

Autopsies performed on bodies recovered in the New Mexico desert in the 1940s proved they were composed of the same basic biological matter as humans, although their blood was of the rare Rh type. They were erect-standing bipeds, with disproportionately long arms and oversize craniums.

The possibility that they originated on another planet was only that, a possibility. Certainly the Archons had never made such a claim, but they never disputed it, either. Nor did they object to being called Archons. The term derived from ancient Gnostic beliefs referring to a parahuman force devoted to imprisoning the spark of the divine in the human soul. Recently, Lakesh began to suspect that an Archon race as such did not exist any longer.

No clear-cut answers about the Archon Directorate had ever presented themselves. Only its agenda was not open to conjecture; it had been the same for thousands of years. Historically, they made alliances with certain individuals or governments, who in turn reaped the benefits of power and wealth. Following this pattern, the Archons made their advanced technology available to the American military in order to fully develop the Totality Concept. It was the use of that technology, without a full understanding of it, that brought on the nuclear holocaust of 2001.

The apocalypse fit well with Archon strategy. After a century, with the destruction of social structures and severe depopulation, the Archons allied themselves with the nine most powerful barons. They distributed predark technology and helped to establish the ville political system, all to consolidate their power over Earth and its disenfranchised, spiritually beaten human inhabitants.

The goal of unifying the world, with all nonessential and nonproductive humans eliminated or hybridized, was so close to completion there was no point in wondering what the Archons actually were.

Lakesh was no closer to solving the enigma than his ancestors had been thousands of years before when they wrote the *Mahabharta* and the *Ramayana,* which described the coming of the "Sons of the Moon and the Sun" in flying machines called *vimana*s.

He had once believed the solution to both the riddle of the Archons and humanity's mysterious origins lay in ancient religious codices. Now he had come to accept that he could not penetrate a conspiracy of secrecy that had been maintained for twenty thousand years or more.

The few surviving sacred texts contained only hints, inferences passed down from generation to generation, not actual answers. Millennia-old documents that might have held the truth had crumbled into dust or were deliberately destroyed.

Or perhaps no clear-cut truth existed.

Perhaps the so-called Archon Directorate was simply part of humankind's existence, forever and always, not a curse, not a blessing, not a friend or a foe.

Lakesh had seen his first representative of the Archons in the Dulce installation, in the early 1990s. Although he watched the entity for less than a minute, lately he had begun to wonder if that Archon might not have been Balam himself. On their mission to Russia, Brigid, Kane and Grant had learned about the discovery of a creature sealed within a cryonic-stasis canister at the site of the Tunguska disaster. According to their source, he had lain buried for over three decades, until the end of World War II. He was revived, spending several years as a guest of the Soviets before being traded to the West. His name was Balam.

On the British Isles, the self-proclaimed Lord Strongbow confided to them that in the performance of his duties as a liaison officer between the Totality Concept's Mission Snowbird and Project Sigma, he dealt directly with a representative of the Archons, a creature called Balam.

Obviously, Balam had acted as something of a liaison officer himself, an emissary of the Archon Directive throughout the latter half of the twentieth century. In light of that information, Lakesh was working on the hypothesis that Balam might be the only and perhaps last Archon on Earth.

And if Balam was indeed the last of his kind, then there was no Archon Directorate, just like there was no real group called the Preservationists.

Lakesh suppressed a curse. At three o'clock in the morning, all sorts of bleak concepts occurred to him.

However, one empirically proved element about the Archons was their great psionic abilities. Each of the entities was connected to the others through some hyperspatial filaments of mind energy, similar to the collective consciousness of certain insect species. Judging by Balam's distressed reaction when Baron Ragnar was murdered, those filaments even included the hybrids, the Directorate's plenipotentiaries on Earth.

Banks said slowly, "According to the abduction literature you had me study, one of the hallmarks of Archon telepathic contact and control was the mental transmission of a terrestrial animal with unusually large dark eyes."

Lakesh nodded. "Using an owl is a classic."

Voice quivering, Banks stated, "Balam took me over. Possessed me."

"Another term might be *channeled,*" Lakesh suggested. "You were asleep, your mental defenses down. We've always wondered about the extent of Balam's psionic abilities—now we know a bit more."

"Why do this to me, after all these years?"

Lakesh tugged at his long nose absently. "The first question is easy to answer. You've been in close proximity with Balam every day for the past three and a half years. He probably knows your thought processes better than anyone else's in the redoubt... perhaps better than any other human being's on Earth. It was child's play for him to insinuate himself into your sleeping mind."

Almost unconsciously, Lakesh began to pace back and forth in front of Banks. "As for why now, he never had a reason before. Through you, he made an effort to initiate communication, something the little bastard has never done."

"Communication?" echoed Banks. "With you?"

Lakesh shook his head. "Oddly, no. With Kane. That's who you—he—asked for."

"How come he didn't know Kane is gone? I knew it."

"Balam didn't, which indicates his psionic manipulation of you was superficial. Which also indicates his abilities have definite limits."

Banks didn't look particularly relieved to hear that. Doubtfully, he said, "So either he can't go very deep or he didn't need to."

His eyes narrowed. "But why ask for Kane? If there's anyone in the redoubt who would pay hard jack for the privilege of breaking Balam's neck, it's Kane."

"True, but Kane is also the only person who ever shook up Balam enough for him to deviate from his patented speech about how superior he and his kind are."

Banks nodded, recollecting his astonishment when Lakesh informed him of the telepathic exchange between Kane and Balam a couple of months before. *Humanity must have a purpose,* Balam had said. *And only a single vision can give it purpose...your race was dying of despair. Your race had lost its passion to live and to create. We unified you.*

"Obviously," Lakesh continued, "something agitated Balam greatly, similar to when he reacted to the murder of Baron Ragnar."

Banks rose quickly to his feet, ruefully eyeing his state of undress. "I should probably check on him, then."

"I'll do it. He got to you once already. He won't get to me."

"I wasn't expecting it," Banks argued. "I'll have my defenses up now."

"Just the same, you shouldn't expose yourself to

another opportunity. As it is, I'll wager you feel enervated, have a headache and a great thirst.''

Banks glanced toward him in surprise. "The headache is going away. I feel exhausted and I'm parched, though. How'd you know?"

"Standard postabduction symptoms, reported by contactees throughout the twentieth century. You're still too weak to completely screen out Balam's influence if he wants to make a second try at speaking through you.''

They left the control center and walked down the corridor to the door of Balam's facility. Banks eyed it anxiously as Lakesh punched in the six-digit code on the keypad. The confirmation circuit buzzed, and the lock clicked open.

"Sir—" Banks began.

"Don't worry," Lakesh said reassuringly. "Go back to your quarters, get dressed, drink a jug of water. If you feel up to it, come back here."

Banks nodded. "Yes, sir."

Lakesh watched him walk away and turn the corner, then he pushed open the door. He stepped cautiously into the large, low-ceilinged room. He saw computer keyboards and medical monitors on their own individual desks. A control console ran the length of the right-hand wall, the multitude of telltales and readouts glowing green and amber.

Lakesh's nostrils recoiled from the astringent smell of chemicals. The room always smelled vaguely of antiseptic and hot copper as a result of the trestle tables loaded down with glass beakers, Bunsen burners and chemical-filtration systems.

The left wall of the room was constructed of heavy

panes of clear glass, behind which was a deeply recessed room dully lit by an overhead neon strip, glowing a ruddy red. Balam's optic nerves were very sensitive to light levels much above twilight.

Lakesh stepped to the wall and peered in. He saw nothing but the crimson-tinged gloom.

"I know you're awake in there," he announced. "Otherwise, you wouldn't have pulled your ventriloquist act on Banks. You're not Edgar Bergen and he's not Charlie McCarthy. If you have something you want to communicate, then do it straight out."

Lakesh watched the blurred shape, a darkness within a darkness, shift like twisting mist in the hell-hued murk. He was able to catch only a glimpse of the entity's fathomless, tip-tilted eyes and narrow features before Balam erected his hypnotic screen, a telepathic defense that clouded human perceptions and concealed his appearance from the ape kin who held him captive.

When the nonvoice slid into his mind, he expected to sense the same message Balam had been imparting for over three years: *We are old. When your race was wild and bloody and young, we were already ancient. Your tribe has passed, and we are invincible. All of the achievements of man are dust—they are forgotten....*

We stand, we know, we are.

The words were less than rhetoric, more than a threat. It was the arrogant, scornful doctrine of a race so old that the most ancient civilizations on Earth were only a yesterday beside it. The underlying psychological message was always the same, stimulating panic, fear and despair in those exposed to it—you cannot win, we are undefeatable, bow to the inevitable. Surrender.

Instead of words, an image flashed into Lakesh's brain, so vivid it was almost a three-dimensional projection. He saw Kane as Balam had first seen him, nearly a year before, pale eyes glinting with hatred, face twisted by revulsion. A jumbled flood of emotions accompanied the vision of Kane—with fear, anger, respect and overlying it all, an almost desperate sense of need.

"Why do you need Kane?" Lakesh asked aloud, shocked almost into speechlessness.

For a chaotic instant, through Balam's mind he caught a flash of black malignity, an impression of something fearsome in a secret place, now spinning a vast web of great menace.

He realized the entity showed him this deliberately, to impress upon him the urgency of his need. Within Lakesh's mind, a series of separate geometric shapes appeared, then rushed together, interlocking to form first a polyhedron, then a trapezohedron.

The image vanished and Lakesh reeled, lungs laboring for air. Cold sweat filled the furrows on his forehead. For a very long moment, he could only stare, feeling fascination, incredulity and fear warring for dominance within him.

For the first time in over three years, Balam had actually communicated a desire and an emotion other than a cold, arrogant superiority. The creature conveyed a sense of a terrible lurking danger and at the same time requested—no, *pleaded*—for help. And not just anyone's help, but that of Kane, a human who loathed and despised him and everything he represented.

"Kane is not here at present," Lakesh croaked. "I hope he will return shortly. I will bring him to you when he does."

The mist faded, as if sucked back to the far end of the cell. The communication ended as suddenly as it had begun. Lakesh turned away from the glass wall, limbs trembling, but not in reaction to the telepathic exchange. His mind wheeled with conjectures. He couldn't understand what had chipped through Balam's armor and evoked such fear in him he would beg for help from one of the lowly ape kin who held him captive.

On a deep, visceral level, Lakesh knew if the haughty Balam was afraid, then he should be terrified.

And he was.

Chapter 11

Domi punched in 3-5-2 on the keypad next to the vanadium sec door, grasped the lever tightly and pulled it up. Immediately came the whine of buried machinery, the prolonged squeaking hiss of hydraulics and pneumatics. With a grinding rumble, the multiton sec door opened, the massive panels folding aside like an accordion. She had been told that nothing short of an armor-piercing antitank shell could even dent the six-inch-thick slabs of metal.

She squeezed her slight body between the frame and the door and stepped out onto the plateau. The ragged remains of a chain-link fence clanked in the breeze that gusted up over the edge of the precipice. A telemetric communications array, uplinked to the very few reconnaissance satellites still in orbit, was nestled at the top of the mountain peak.

Domi raised her right hand to shield her sensitive ruby eyes from the dazzle of the noonday sun, wincing at the twinge of pain from her shoulder. Less than three months before, a bullet had damaged the joint, and DeFore had replaced it with an artificial ball-and-socket joint. Long, painful weeks of physical therapy followed the reconstructive surgery, but she had regained the full use of her arm in a remarkably short time. DeFore attributed her recuperative powers to her near feral upbringing in the wild hinterlands beyond the villes, where the victim of an injury either made a full recovery or died.

Scarcely topping five feet in height and weighing a hundred pounds, she looked too frail to have been born in the Outlands, the untamed wildernesses beyond the cushioned tyranny of the villes. Her ragged mop of bone white hair framed a piquant, hollow-cheeked face. Her sleeveless red tunic was belted at the waist, which left her porcelain-colored arms and legs bare and accentuated the insolent arrangement of her curves.

The average life expectancy of an outlander was around forty, and the few who reached that age possessed both an animal's cunning and vitality. Domi was nowhere near that age; in fact, she had no true idea of how old she actually was, but she possessed more than her share of wits and vigor.

She didn't miss the short and often brutal life in the Outlands. She had quickly adapted to the comforts offered by the Cerberus redoubt—the soft bed, protection from the often toxic elements and food that was always available, without having to scavenge or kill for it.

Domi had enjoyed similar luxuries during her six months as Guana Teague's sex slave. The man-mountain of flab had been the boss of the Cobaltville Pits and he showered her with gifts. He didn't pamper her, though, since she was forced to satisfy his gross lusts.

Domi rarely dwelled on the past, but she often replayed how she had cut Guana's throat and how the blood had literally rivered from the deep slash in his triple chins. She always smiled in recollection of kicking his monstrous body as it twitched in postmortem spasms.

The only possession she had kept from those months spent in Teaguc's squat was the long, serrated knife that had chilled him.

Beneath her shading hand, she gazed at the mouth of the road opening up on the far side of the plateau. The trans-comm message from Grant had been received only a few minutes ago. She was less interested in learning that Auerbach and Rouch had been found than in hearing Grant's lion growl of a voice announcing their return.

Domi didn't list patience among her virtues, and waiting in Cerberus for the past five and a half days for word had been difficult to endure. The reasons why she had to stay behind in the redoubt were sound, and she tacitly agreed with them. The other exiles were ville-bred academics, and few of them dared to venture very far from the sec door.

If Grant and the others didn't return after seven days, her instructions were to come after them. A journey on foot down the rugged road leading down from Cerberus to the foothills would have been a hardship, but she knew how to live off the land. She also knew how to kill, quickly, efficiently and without remorse.

Faintly, borne on the wind, came the muted roar of laboring engines. Within moments the six-wheeled Hussar Hot Spur Land Rover hove into sight, followed a few seconds later by the armored, tank-treaded Sandcat.

The Sandcat's low-slung, blocky chassis was sup-

ported by a pair of flat, retractable tracks. Its gun tur-
ret, concealed within an armored bubble topside, held
a pair of USMG-73 heavy machine guns. The hull's
armor was composed of a ceramic-armaglass bond,
which served as protection from not only projectiles,
but went opaque when exposed to energy-based
weapons, such as particle-beam emitters.

As the two vehicles rumbled onto the plateau and
toward the redoubt's entrance, she saw Auerbach and
Rouch in the Hotspur. Their faces locked in grim,
unsmiling masks, neither of them seemed to see her.
Domi was forced to step aside to keep her feet from
being run over. She resisted the urge to give them an
obscene gesture as they rolled past.

Through the open ob port of the Sandcat, she saw
Kane behind the wheel. Grant leaned over from the
codriver's seat to call out, "We found 'em." He
spoke loudly in order to be heard over the steady
throb of the 750-horsepower engine.

"Nobody hurt?" Domi called back, walking beside
the vehicle.

"Nothing serious," Kane said. "The usual."

Domi saw the thin, scabbed-over dark red line on
his cheek and grinned. "Yeah, so I see."

Glimpsing Brigid's outline in the rear passenger
compartment, Domi stated, "Lakesh big-time wants
to talk to all of you. Attendance as in mandatory."

Kane eyes flashed. "Good. I big-time want to talk
to him, too."

He drove the Sandcat into the redoubt and braked
as Auerbach stopped the Hotspur long enough for
Rouch to disembark. Grant and Brigid climbed out
while he was stopped, then he followed the Hotspur

down the twenty-foot-wide main corridor to the vehicle depot, adjacent to the armory.

Wegmann waited for them to park the wags in their designated stations, on either side of the fuel pump. He eyed Auerbach sourly as the man climbed out of the Land Rover.

"How was your holiday, Auerbach?" he asked snidely. "I wish I could go off for five days with Rouch—or any woman, for that matter. But no, I've got to hang out here, servicing the air circulators, mopping up grease, fixing toilets. As if I didn't have enough to do, now I've got to service both these wags. Thanks a lot."

"Fuck off, pissant," Auerbach snapped.

Wegmann widened his brown eyes in mock hurt. "I thought you'd come back all fit and rested, but hey, you're just as obnoxious as the day you left. What happened, Auerbach? Rouch wasn't as much fun as you hoped? Or was it the other way around?"

Peeling his lips back from his teeth in a snarl, Auerbach lunged for the much smaller Wegmann. Kane managed to insert himself between the two men. He elbowed Auerbach to one side. "Enough."

The red-haired man strained against Kane for a moment, then stepped back. "I'm not gonna take shit from that little asshole."

"You don't have to," Kane replied. To Wegmann, he said, "It'd be a real wise move for you to apologize before you start servicing the wags. I've got other business to attend to, and I won't be here to protect you."

Wegmann glared, not in the least intimidated by either man. In his mid-thirties, he was no more than five and a half feet tall, weighing maybe 140 pounds. He might look slight physically, but he was a scrapper and a mechanical genius. He also claimed to be a musician.

Heeling around toward the Hotspur, he snapped an insincere "Sorry" over his shoulder.

Kane guided Auerbach out of the depot with a hand pressed against the small of his back. "Go to the dispensary. Have DeFore take a look at that shoulder."

Auerbach nodded glumly, his anger replaced by shame. "I guess I'd better get used to that treatment. I'll be the laughingstock of Cerberus once the story gets around."

"You made a mistake," Kane said, slightly surprised by how sorry he felt for the man at the moment. "A time will come when you can make up for it."

Auerbach nodded again and walked away, head hung low, posture slumped, a defeated and weary man.

Kane entered the armory, pressed the flat toggle switch on the door frame and the overhead fluorescent fixtures blazed with a white, sterile light.

The big square room was stacked nearly to the ceiling with wooden crates and boxes. Many of the crates were stenciled with the legend Property U.S. Army.

Glass-fronted cases lined the four walls. Automatic assault rifles were neatly racked in one, and an open crate beside it was filled with hundreds of rounds of 5.56 mm ammunition. There were many makes and models of subguns, as well as dozens of semiautomatic blasters, complete with holsters and belts. Heavy-assault weaponry occupied the north wall, bazookas, tripod-mounted M-249 machine guns, mortars and rocket launchers.

All the ordnance was of predark manufacture. Caches of matériel had been laid down in hermetically sealed Continuity of Government installations before the nukecaust. Protected from the ravages of the outraged environment, nearly every piece of munitions and hardware was as pristine as the day it rolled off the assembly line. In the far corner, his and Grant's Magistrate body armor rested on metal frameworks, standing like grim black sentinels.

Kane went to a gun case and unstrapped his Sin Eater from his forearm. He felt a distant wonder when he realized he hadn't had to fire a shot or chill anyone on this mission. He had returned to the armory with the same full clip as when he'd left it.

However, he had been tempted to fire a few rounds during the three-day journey back to the foothills. Auerbach was silent and sullen and Rouch responded with spits and snarls whenever Kane or Brigid spoke to her.

He hadn't apprised Brigid of what passed between him and Rouch at the Indian village. If she was mystified by the open hostility Beth-Li directed at both of them over the past couple of days, she didn't comment on it.

Kane repressed a snort as he replaced the grens in their foam-cushioned cases. Life was becoming far too complicated in Cerberus lately, and he laid the blame squarely on Lakesh. The situation with Beth-Li had its amusing aspects, but all the entertainment value was squeezed out of it. He was honest enough with himself to be flattered by the young woman's attentions and intents. No man could be otherwise.

Grant and Domi shared a superficially similar relationship. Domi claimed to be in love with Grant, viewing him as her savior from the chains of servitude forged by Pit boss Guana Teague.

From what Grant said, Domi had saved him when Guana was literally crushing the life out of him. Regardless, Domi had attached herself to Grant and for a time her blatant attempts to bed him made Beth-Li's actions seem cold and standoffish.

Although expressing jealousy of other women, it was obvious Domi loved Grant fiercely. Kane did not know if his friend had ever tired of resisting the albino girl's charms and surrendered to them, but he tended to doubt it. Domi could be sixteen or twenty-six. Grant was pushing forty and if he involved himself with Domi, he said he'd feel twice that.

He had spoken in jest, but Kane suspected the emotional wounds inflicted by his ruined affair with Olivia years ago in Cobaltville had yet to fully heal. Kane had never asked Grant about Olivia. The two men observed an unspoken understanding that it was a forbidden topic.

Kane stepped into the corridor and made for the central control complex. He was sure he would find Lakesh there, but he forged a mental resolution not to be distracted by the old man's crisis of the day. He intended to have a final discussion on the matter of Beth-Li, then inform him of the pact he had struck with Sky Dog. He would not allow anything—no matter how urgent—to interfere with it.

His resolve faltered when he entered the huge

chamber. Brigid and Grant stood over Lakesh at the main computer station, listening with rapt expressions as the old man spoke earnestly, gesturing with his hands.

When Lakesh caught sight of Kane, he waved imperiously. "Didn't Domi give you my message?" he demanded impatiently. "You were to report to me immediately."

Kane increased the length and speed of his stride. He saw Grant glance his way and distinctly heard him mutter "Shit" before discreetly sliding away from Lakesh and Brigid.

Lakesh was too caught up his agitated excitement to take notice of the expression on Kane's face or the icy gleam in his pale eyes. "As I was telling dearest Brigid and friend Grant, something unprecedented happened early this morning—"

Placing his hands on the back of the chair on either side of Lakesh's shoulders, Kane thrust his face down and close to Lakesh's.

"Something unprecedented is about to happen right now," he said in a low, deadly tone. "A sneaky old fart is about to fly across this room with only a boot on his scrawny ass as the propellant."

Lakesh blinked at him from behind the lens of his glasses, completely baffled by Kane's words. Then annoyance replaced the confusion.

"You're angry with me again," he said waspishly. "Nothing new about that. But a situation developed here that is so extraordinary—"

"Nothing new about that, either," Kane interrupted.

"He's not exaggerating, Kane. Hear him out," Brigid urged.

Kane straightened up, scowling down into Lakesh's deeply seamed face. "What is it this time? Have you located a new bunch of freaks to shoot at us? Another space station you want us to visit? Just tell me—we live only to risk our lives for you, you know."

Lakesh wisely chose to overlook the sarcasm. "It has to do with Balam. He asked to speak to you."

Kane was shocked into speechlessness for a long moment. All he could think of to say was a faint "What?"

Swiftly, curtly, Lakesh related his brief communication with Balam and how it had come about through Banks.

"A stone?" rumbled Grant. "What the hell is so dangerous about a stone?"

"Not just a stone, but one in the shape of a trapezohedron." Lakesh used his gnarled fingers to trace a geometric form in the air. "That was the image Balam imparted."

"Does it mean anything to you?" Brigid asked.

"It didn't at first."

"And now?" inquired Kane.

Contemplatively, Lakesh answered, "Certain ancient cultures attached mystical significance to a kind of very rare rock—tektites."

"I thought tektites were meteor fragments," Brigid said.

"That's the standard mineralogist's view, yes. But actually, nobody was ever certain where tektites came from. More than one contained isotopes of untraceable radioactive material and had very unusual magnetic readings.''

"How unusual?" Kane demanded.

"They were antimagnetic, with a polarity capable of suppressing gravity…or affecting the electromagnetic field of the human brain.''

"That still doesn't sound like anything to scare anybody," Grant argued. "If Balam is an anybody.''

Lakesh heaved himself out his chair. "I concur. So let us pay him a visit and settle the question.''

Kane lifted a hand. "Hold on. I'm not about to let that little gray bastard crawl around in my head just so he can tell me about some scary rocks.''

"Kane," Brigid began, "you're missing the point as usual. Whatever Balam wants to talk about, this is the first time he's ever initiated a communication. And he wants you, not Banks—whom he knows best. Not even Lakesh—whom he blames for his captivity. Only you.''

Lakesh's head bobbed in vehement agreement on his wattled neck. "Precisely, friend Kane. This is the kind of breakthrough we've been waiting for, hoping for. Balam is our only direct feed for data about the Directorate.''

"You'll understand if I'm less than honored by his request," he retorted.

Lakesh and Brigid stared at him expectantly.

Kane drew in a slow, thoughtful breath. "How do you know he doesn't want to take me over, make me his slave? Or fry my brain?''

"If he had that ability and intent, he would've done it long ago." Lakesh adopted a reasonable, persuasive tone. "He was only able to gain control of Banks when he was at the deepest stage of sleep and he didn't—or couldn't—read his mind completely. Otherwise, he would've known what Banks knew—that you weren't here.''

Kane cast a questioning glance toward Grant. The broad yoke of the big man's shoulders lifted in a shrug. ''Makes sense to me. Just talking to it—him— is important, even if all he wants is to discuss his rock collection.''

Turning to Brigid, Kane asked, ''What about you, Baptiste? What do you think?''

Surprise that he had solicited her opinion flickered in her eyes. ''I agree with Lakesh and Grant. We've been trying to establish a dialogue for months. I doubt there's much risk involved.''

Grant patted the bulge of his holstered Sin Eater beneath his coat sleeve. ''We'll all go with you. If he gets out of line, I'll shoot through the glass and blow his oversize brains out.''

Lakesh muttered tensely, ''Friend Grant, I don't think such an extreme action will be at all necessary.''

Grant grunted. ''I don't think it, either. But since I'm not sure, the blaster goes with us.''

Chapter 12

Kane peered through the glass wall, seeing only his distorted reflection and dripping beads of condensation. "I'm here, you little prick," he announced. "Show yourself."

Standing in a semicircle behind him, Lakesh, Banks, Grant and Brigid shifted uncomfortably. Banks admonished quietly, "You don't have to insult him."

Kane looked toward him, eyebrows angled quizzically. "You think I'll hurt his feelings? You don't really believe he has any to hurt, do you?"

"I don't know," Danko retorted. "But if he can feel fear, it stands to reason he can feel humiliation. And if he can feel humiliation, he can feel anger—"

The young man's words suddenly blurred into an articulate cry, half alarm, half pain. He staggered back a pace, catching himself on the edge of a trestle table.

Lakesh was instantly at his side. "What is it?"

Simultaneously, Kane became aware of a fluttering movement on the periphery of his vision, behind the glass pane. He whipped his head around, seeing the suggestion of a billowing mist in the far recesses of the cell.

In a groaning voice tight with effort, Banks said, "It's Balam—he wants to speak through me."

With a click and whir, Grant's Sin Eater sprang into his hand. Eyes slitted, he aimed it at the transparent panel, finger hovering over the trigger. Shifting the barrel back and forth, he grated, "I can't see him."

"No!" Banks's voice was an anguished bleat. "No, he's not forcing me. He's asking my permission."

Lakesh put an arm around the technician's shoulders. "It's up to you, Banks. At least he's asking."

A dew of perspiration filmed his forehead. Squeezing his eyes shut, Banks said, "It's not like this morning…he's not trying to take me over, animate me. He's requesting a melding of…of perceptions, of intellectual resources."

Grant looked back and forth from Banks to the cell. A shudder racked Banks's body, and he uttered a faint, strangulated cry. He bowed his head for an instant, then slowly lifted it, pushing himself to his full height. Opening his eyes, he swept everyone in the room with a calm, dispassionate gaze that finally fixed on Kane.

He met the gaze and he felt his flesh prickle as if a thousand microscopic ants marched over his skin. Somehow, he glimpsed Balam's huge, slanted black eyes superimposed over those of Banks.

"Kane," Banks said mildly. "Balam is here with me, speaking with my voice, drawing on my knowledge of language and his familiarity with all of you."

Lakesh, Grant and Brigid drew back from him.

Feeling a little foolish but more than a little enthralled, Kane asked, "What do you want from me?"

"Your intervention."

"In what?" inquired Brigid.

Banks-Balam didn't remove his eyes from Kane's face. "Please, don't distract me. This binary state is difficult to maintain. My mental equilibrium must not be disturbed, or the meld will be lost. I must stay focused."

Brigid frowned at the rebuke, but said nothing more.

"You have often speculated about me and my kind," Banks-Balam stated. "It would not be an exaggeration to say that questions about the so-called Archon Directorate have consumed you."

Kane nodded. "It's not an exaggeration. You have no idea how many times I thought about beating the truth out of you—him."

Banks-Balam returned the nod, graciously inclining his head. "Actually, I *do* have an idea. Somewhere on the order of five hundred separate desires, and twice that many passing whims."

"Then you should be grateful I never acted on them," Kane said harshly.

"Such tactics would have availed you nothing. You would not have learned anything."

"Am I going to learn something now?"

"Yes. You believe that the Archons are all part of a collective hive consciousness, all linked mentally in this fashion."

"That's not true?" Kane inquired.

"As far as your limited perceptions can be expanded, it is true enough. However, if we so-called Archons were truly products of one linked group consciousness, all the individual components would be as mindless and interchangeable as ants and bees. Drones driven only by instinct.''

"If you say so," muttered Kane.

"As in any form of electromagnetic energy exchange, there are broadcasters and receivers. And conductors.''

Lakesh stiffened, eyebrows climbing toward his high hairline, over the rims of his spectacles. He opened his mouth to speak, then closed it again.

Banks-Balam apparently guessed—or sensed—the question he wanted to ask. "No, I am not a conductor. If you will relax, Kane, close your eyes and open your mind, I will show you what the conductor is.''

Kane hesitated, glancing from one face to another. Grant scowled, Brigid looked doubtful and Lakesh smiled encouragingly. With a mental shrug, Kane slowly exhaled and let his lids drop over his eyes. Nothing happened. He was very aware of the electronic sounds from the control console, even his own breathing. He waited for a few seconds and was on the verge of opening his eyes when an image crowded into his mind.

He saw floating geometric patterns, orbiting one another. They rushed together and locked in position to form a black trapezohedron, a stone with glowing striations.

"Do you see it?" came the soft query.

"Yes. A black rock or an ore."

"It is that, yes, but it is far more—or less. It does not fit atomically with any of the tables your science understands. You would be unable to study it because only part of it exists within your concept of matter in space.''

Kane opened his eyes, but disturbingly, the vision of the black yet somehow shining trapezohedron remained fixed in his mind. He saw it vividly every time he blinked.

"It was brought here so long ago that it would far exceed your conception of time."

Kane asked coldly, "Back when our race was wild and bloody and young?"

A slight smile creased Banks-Balam's face at the ironic reference. "Exactly."

"Exactly," repeated Kane impatiently, icily. "Exactly what is it? You called it a conductor. Is it a device disguised as a rock or the other way around?"

"It is both and it is neither. It is a creation, pure matter crafted from scientific principles understood millennia ago, then forgotten. Through it, the pulse-flows of thought energy converge. Through it, the flux lines of possibility, of probability, of eternity, of *alternity* meet."

"Which," Kane said flatly, "tells me absolutely nothing."

As if Kane had not commented, Banks-Balam continued, "It is more than an artifact—it is a key to doors that were sealed aeons ago. They were sealed for a good purpose. Now they may be thrown wide and all the works of man and non-man will be undone. Time and reality are elastic, but they are in delicate balance. When the balance is altered, then changes will come—terrible and permanent."

Kane listened, not to the words themselves but to the sense of urgency and conviction behind them, to the implications of vast dark forces flowing like an inexorable tide—a tide even Balam feared.

''What is it you want me to do?'' he demanded.

Banks-Balam blinked and wiped at the perspiration on his face. A tremor shook his hand. His voice sounded hoarse. ''The meld is weakening. I do not wish to inflict further strain on this vessel of communication. He has always shown me kindness and compassion.''

The remark startled Kane, startled them all, but he snapped, ''Get to it, then.''

''The form in which the stone was crafted was not arbitrary. It served a function. It was altered over the centuries, facets of it removed and scattered across the face of the Earth. Each fragment acts as a lodestone for the others. They will always lead to one another. One of the fragments has been seized by a thief, and will draw the thief to the others. He thinks he has found a prize, a means to power. You must prevent him from reaching his objective, Kane. I trust only you.''

Kane's eyes widened in astonishment. ''Me? You trust *me?*''

Banks-Balam drew trembling fingers over his sweaty brow. His breathing came in short, labored rasps. ''I trust a predator to know what to do against another predator. Fang pitted against claw, blood spilled for blood. Violence met with violence. Your father possessed these same instincts, else I would not be here.

''I know your hatred of me is deep, and I understand how you blame me for what was done to this world, to your race. I am content to accept your hatred and blame, regardless of how misplaced it is. However, if you wish to help this world and your race, you will do as I bid.''

Kane clenched his teeth, then tightened his fists as the memory of his father—frozen forever in cryo-sleep, unaware of the vile uses to which his body was put—drove away the image of the black stone. He took a threatening half step forward, momentary rage blotting out the realization that he could not harm Balam without harming Banks.

It was all very convenient, very strategic.

"Where are these fragments?'' he demanded, pitching his voice low to disguise the vibration of fury in it. "Who is the thief?''

"That will be made clear to you in short order, as the thief attempts to recover the piece in this hemisphere, on this continent.''

"Where is it?''

"The place of the dead animals,'' Banks-Balam replied faintly. "In the Hall of the Frozen Past.''

In angry bafflement, Kane growled, "Talk sense, you little son of a bitch. Where the hell is the Hall of the Frozen Past?''

Banks's body abruptly slumped, his knees buckling. Lakesh and Grant secured grips on the young man's arms and kept him upright. A rattling, protracted gasp tore from his throat, and for a moment he shook so violently it was almost a convulsion.

He managed to get his legs under him and stand up, leaning heavily against the edge of the trestle table. His sweat-damp face glistened in the dim light, and his eyes were dulled by fatigue. He stared around without focusing for a few seconds, then put a hand to the left side of his head, wincing in pain.

"Feels like my brain is about to pop out of my skull." He cleared his throat noisily. "I need a couple of gallons of water to drink, too."

Brigid eyed him keenly. "How much do you remember?"

"All of it. I felt like I was an observer, standing in the wings on the stage of my mind." His lips twitched in an uncertain, wry smile. "I coached Balam whenever he needed help with his lines, when he wasn't sure of the right words. He doesn't care for verbal communication. He thinks it's inefficient."

Kane swung around to stare at the glass-fronted cell, eyes trying to pierce the red gloom. "The little bastard learned fast. The question is, do we believe him?"

"Of course!" Lakesh exclaimed, sounding slightly scandalized. "Why wouldn't we?"

"No reason," Grant said tonelessly. "Except that he's a deceiver, an inhuman manipulator who helped to orchestrate the nukecaust and the death of 99.9 percent of the human race, and that his kind tried to hybridize or enslave the remaining one-tenth of a percent. Other than that, I guess his word is unimpeachable."

Banks pulled away from Grant and Lakesh and half stumbled over to the sink. Ignoring the cup on the countertop, he turned on the faucet and bent over it, allowing the stream of water to flow directly into his mouth. All of them watched as he swallowed and swallowed, drinking mouthful after mouthful. Finally, he pushed himself up, wiping his mouth with the back of his hand. "That's better."

"I suppose," ventured Brigid, "we can try to

cross-reference what Balam said about black stones with the historical records in the database. That might yield some results, give us a better idea of what he was talking about.''

''If he wants my help,'' Kane declared, ''he's going to have to offer something substantial in return.''

''He claimed by helping him, you'd be helping humanity,'' Lakesh argued.

Kane scoffed. ''That old saw.''

Addressing Banks, Brigid asked, ''If your thought processes were melded with Balam's, then you must have sensed what he was feeling and thinking. Was he trying to deceive us?''

Banks shook his head. ''I don't think so. He's legitimately afraid of the black stone. The fear was very close to the surface.''

''Did you pick up anything about the Archons?'' Lakesh nearly quivered with excitement. ''Anything, no matter how trivial?''

Banks frowned in concentration. ''No, not really. Balam has a very regimented, compartmentalized mind, locked into specific channels. I don't know if he was deliberately shielding that information from me or just completely focused on the main topic.''

He inhaled a weary breath. ''I did pick up scraps of feelings, like emotional echoes.'' Nodding toward Kane, he said, ''He has a great respect for you, an admiration almost. And a trust.''

''Anything else?'' Brigid asked.

Banks closed his eyes. In a husky half whisper, he replied, ''Sadness. A deep, terrible sadness.''

Grant snorted. ''I'll bet. For himself.''

Banks shook his head. ''No...for all of us.''

Chapter 13

"Don't you understand, Kane? Humanity is vanishing. Every passing day marks one more step toward our extinction."

Lakesh paced his small office, thin arms locked behind his back. "The hybrids multiply while our own procreation is circumscribed either by the laws of the barons or environmental conditions."

Leaning against the wall, arms folded over his chest, Kane said darkly, "We've had this discussion before."

After shaving, showering and changing into a white bodysuit, the duty uniform of Cerberus personnel, Kane had cornered Lakesh in his lair, determined to settle the issue of the old man's breeding program once and for all.

Lakesh didn't acknowledge Kane's observation. "If we had access to artificial-insemination techniques, if DeFore had the knowledge of how to perform them, if we had prenatal-manipulation technology here, I would have never conceived the plan."

Kane stretched out a leg, blocking Lakesh's pacing path. "You're going to have to *un*conceive it, at least as far as Beth-Li and I are concerned. Have you spoken to her since we got back?"

Lakesh shook his head. "No, nor do I know the

details of where and how you found her and Auerbach." He tilted his head, eyeing the cut on Kane's cheek. "Would my assessment that bloodshed was involved be incorrect?"

"Not at all," Kane answered. "Nor would it be incorrect if you placed the responsibility for it on Beth-Li."

"Explain."

"That's why I'm here."

Crisply, Kane told him everything that had transpired at the Indian settlement, what Auerbach and Rouch had said and the details of Sky Dog's proposal to repair the war wag.

Lakesh's reaction was mixed; while he was angry, he seemed the most incensed about the agreement struck with Sky Dog, but he was intrigued about the war wag.

As Lakesh began to upbraid him for making the pact without consultation, Kane cut him off with a stern voice. "It's done. We have to abide by it now. Let's move on to Beth-Li. Her stunt put all of us at risk, and she threatened Baptiste. She can't be trusted, and you're going to have to do something about her."

"Like what?" challenged Lakesh. "Exile her from exile? Return her to Sharpeville so she can be executed? Lock her up in a holding cell, confine her permanently like Balam?"

"Don't ask me—she's your problem," Kane said flatly. "You brought her here, so you deal with her. How you have the balls to accuse me of making unilateral decisions after what you pulled is beyond me."

"And why you refuse to cooperate is beyond me. I'm not asking you to pull sewer maintenance."

"As corrupt as she is," replied Kane coldly, "you might as well be."

"*Corrupt?*" Lakesh rolled the word on his tongue contemptuously. "Since when did you decide to become a paragon of virtue? She's a splendidly healthy young woman, with remarkable genes, and with the very strong female drive to pass them on. How does that make her corrupt?"

"She's a little more than that. If you weren't blinded by your ego, unable to see your own errors, you'd acknowledge it. Beth-Li is underhanded, self-centered, manipulative and arrogant." Kane slitted his eyes. "Maybe that's why you're so fond of her... kindred spirits, that sort of thing."

Sudden rage glittered in Lakesh's rheumy blue eyes. Kane stared at him, stone-faced.

Then, bit by bit, the anger burning in Lakesh's eyes ebbed away. Kane knew the old man realized there was a good deal of truth in his charges, and being an essentially honest man, he wasted no time on sputtering denials.

Heavily, he admitted, "I don't suppose I'm really much of a manipulator, since you see through all my attempts so easily."

"I've been manipulated since the day I was born—even before I was born. I ought to be able to recognize it by now."

Lakesh winced as if he had been stung. He knew what Kane was alluding to. Some forty years before, when he first determined to build a covert resistance movement against the baronies, he riffled the genetic records to find the qualifications he deemed the most desirable. He used the Archon Directorate's own fixation with purity control against them. By his own confession, he was a physicist cast in the role of an archivist, pretending to be a geneticist, manipulating a political system that was still in a state of flux.

Kane was one such example of that political and genetic manipulation.

Lakesh said quietly, "I have already expressed my remorse about that—and offered my apologies."

"Yet you still want to improve the breed, by any means you think are necessary." Kane blew out a long, weary breath. "I've cooperated with the missions you've concocted because you convinced me of their importance. I'm not convinced of this one. The timing is all wrong, for one thing. Our situation here in Cerberus is too chancy. We could be under a full assault at any time. We don't need to complicate it with pregnancies or infants."

Lakesh sat down behind his tiny desk, propping his chin beneath a hand. "I can't debate you on that, but I maintain you are refusing to understand my point of view," he said, his voice petulant.

"Wrong again, Lakesh," replied Kane. "I understand you're trying to atone for the sins you committed when you were part of the Totality Concept and worked unknowingly for the Archons. I admit I've blamed you for your part in all of it, in the nukecaust, in the formation of the baronies. Maybe that blame is misplaced, maybe it isn't.

"Maybe your own guilt is misplaced. I haven't made up my mind yet. But one thing I'm certain about—you can't buy back all the people who died in the nukecaust and after by turning this redoubt into a breeding farm."

Lakesh grunted softly. "Whether you're right or wrong, I will accept your decision not to participate. Which still leaves us with the question of what to do about Beth-Li."

Kane smiled wryly. "Another place where you're mistaken. It leaves *you*—not 'us'—with the question of what to do."

The intercom on Lakesh's desk buzzed, then Bry's strident voice blared out of it. "Sir, are you there?"

Lakesh poked at the key. "I am. What is it?"

"Activity on the mat-trans network. An anomalous signature—again." Bry's voice held more annoyance than agitation.

"I'll be right there." Lakesh rose from the desk, murmuring, "This is getting to be a rather tedious routine, isn't it?"

Kane didn't answer as he followed him out into the corridor. He presumed the question to be rhetorical. Over the past few months, the sensor link of the Cerberus network had registered an unprecedented volume of mat-trans traffic. Most of it was due to the concerted search for the renegades from Cobaltville, who had, in the space of a few short months, kidnapped a senior archivist, seriously injured one baron and assassinated another.

Lately there had appeared anomalous activities, or signatures of jump lines that couldn't be traced back to their points of origin.

The madly ambitious Sindri had been the first, making an excursion on Earth from his base on the *Parallax Red* space station. After the threat he presented had been neutralized, the ingenious dwarf had sent them, via the Cerberus mat-trans unit, a taunting message that he was still alive and could overcome their security locks. Sindri's theatrical gesture had consequences. Although the Cerberus mat-trans computers analyzed and committed to their memory matrixes the modulation frequency of Sindri's carrier wave, and set up a digital block, if he could overcome one measure, it stood to reason he could overcome another.

Certainly there were any number of unindexed, mass-produced, modular gateway units. After the initial success of the quantum-interphase matter-transfer inducers, the Cerberus redoubt had become something of a factory, turning them out like an assembly line.

Years ago, when Lakesh had used Baron Cobalt's trust in him to covertly reactivate the Cerberus redoubt, he had seen to it that the facility was listed as irretrievably unsalvageable on all ville records. He also had altered the modulations of the mat-trans gateway so the transmissions were untraceable, at least by conventional means. Sindri had proved there were ways of circumventing those precautions, although Lakesh still had no idea of how he managed to do it.

After he entered the control complex, Kane's gaze went automatically to the Mercator-relief map spanning the wall. A yellow pinpoint of light glowed steadily in the northeast region of the United States. Bry, from his station at the main ops console, said, "Manhattan Island, in case you're wondering."

A thin man with rounded shoulders, a headful of coppery curls and a perpetual expression of wide-eyed consternation, Bry acted more or less as Lakesh's scientific apprentice in the intricacies of the mat-trans gateways. "It's not the one in Redoubt Victor, in the South Bronx."

From a computer terminal, Brigid stirred. Kane hadn't seen her when he first entered. "Then it's got to be the one beneath the Twin Towers, the World Trade Center. The only other redoubt in New York State is up in the Adirondacks."

She should know, inasmuch as she had memorized the locations of all the Totality Concept–connected redoubts.

Kane set his teeth against a groan of dismay. The best known hellzone in the continental United States was the long corridor between D.C., New Jersey and Newyork, a vast stretch of rad-rich ruins. Not too long before he had visited the vicinity of Washington Hole, and although miles away from ground zero, he had still undergone a prolonged and unpleasant decam process upon his return to Cerberus.

"No registered origin point?" Lakesh asked briskly.

"No, sir," answered Bry laconically. "Just like the last time."

Bry's drawled reference to the last time made both Kane and Brigid nervous. Lakesh, too, but he hid it well.

"Could it be Sindri again?" Brigid asked, adjusting her wire-framed, rectangular-lensed eyeglasses. Though primarily a means of correcting a minor vision impairment, the spectacles also served as a badge of her former archivist's office.

Lakesh shook his head. "I hope not. We don't need to contend with him again."

"If it is him," Kane said, "and he's still looking

for a place to transplant the Cydonia colony, he'll find Newyork less appealing than Washington Hole. He and his trolls won't stay long. We can leave them be.''

Lakesh's mouth turned down at the corners in a moue Kane couldn't read. Though he was consumed with guilt by his long association with the Totality Concept, his ego was still tied up with his history-making breakthroughs on Project Cerberus. The notion of someone else tinkering with the gateways was an affront to his vanity.

Turning to Brigid, he asked, "What results has the database yielded about Balam's black stone?''

"Too damned many," she replied dryly. "I've compiled the most detailed, most substantiated and least contradictory of the reports into a briefing jacket.''

Slightly surprised, Kane asked, "There was a lot about the black stone in the historical records?''

"Not exactly the historical banks. *Esoteric* may be a more accurate description. Another word might be—'' She trailed off, groping for the right word.

"Crazy?" Kane inquired helpfully.

"That,'' she agreed. "And *scary.''*

"I presumed it would be,'' Lakesh stated tersely, "judging by Balam's attitude. Let's round up Banks and Grant and whoever else wants to be in on this and convene in the cafeteria.''

"I don't want to be in on this,'' muttered Kane. "But I don't think that'll matter much.''

Chapter 14

The Cerberus redoubt had an officially designated briefing room on the third level. It was big and blue-walled, with ten rows of theater-type chairs facing a raised speaking dais and also had a rear-projection screen.

The briefing room was never used except to watch old movies on laser disks in storage. Most of the movies were instructional aids, addressing questions about hygiene, routine maintenance of the nuclear generators and what to do in case of an enemy incursion. The latter was intercut with footage from a film made in the 1980s entitled *Red Dawn,* wherein a group of high-school students waged a guerrilla war against Russian invaders.

Kane found the films *The Day the Earth Stood Still* and *Independence Day* silly, too, but a bit more relevant. He especially enjoyed the scene in *The Day the Earth Stood Still* where a dignified English actor playing an alien reamed out the military for acting foolishly with atomic weapons. He laughed out loud when the alien threatened to turn his invincible sec droid loose on them if they didn't change their ways. He couldn't help but take a bitter pleasure in the irony.

At any rate, since the briefings rarely involved more than a handful of people, they were always convened in the more intimate dining hall. Lakesh, Brigid, Banks, Grant and Kane sat around a table, sharing a pot of coffee. Access to genuine coffee was one of the inarguable benefits of living as an exile in the redoubt. Real coffee had virtually vanished after the skydark, since all of the plantations in South and Central America had been destroyed.

An unsatisfactory synthetic gruel known as "sub" replaced it. Cerberus literally had tons of freeze-dried packages of the authentic article in storage, as well as sugar and powdered milk.

Brigid passed out illustrations, downloaded and printed from the historical database. Most of them depicted uninteresting chunks of dark stone, some of them balanced atop obelisks or resting on altars.

Without preamble, she stated, "Many cultures, separated by time and distance, held certain black stones in a kind of respect, fear or veneration for a number of reasons. Apocryphal religious texts tell of Lucifer coming from the sky bearing a black stone that was then split into fragments and scattered among humanity.

"One ancient South American legend relates that the god Tvira built a temple on an island in Lake Titicaca to hold three holy stones, called the *kala*.

"Similarly, three black stones were venerated by Moslems in the Ka'aba at the great mosque of Mecca. There are several traditions associated with these stones, but all agree they are of celestial origin. Moslems say the stones were white at first, but had the property of absorbing black or sinful thoughts."

Brigid pointed to a black-and-white line-scan photograph depicting a dark octagonal shaft of stone with indecipherable characters spiraling around it, leading up to a small black polyhedron.

"In Hungary," she said, "near the village of Stregoicavar, there was a black monolith that nineteenth-century occultists spoke of as one of the keys."

Banks picked up the illustration, studying it intently. "Keys. The same phrase used by Balam."

"What does it mean?" Grant asked.

"I'm getting to that," replied Brigid. "There were a lot of superstitions regarding the stone and the monolith, especially the assertion that if anyone slept in its vicinity, they would be haunted by monstrous nightmares of another world forever after. There are legends of people who died raving mad because of the visions the stone evoked."

Kane looked at the stone balanced atop the shaft. "The shape I saw was a trapezoid."

"A trapezohedron," Lakesh corrected him. "Evidently, that was the original shape of Lucifer's stone."

"And referred to in many ancient documents as 'the shining trapezohedron,'" Brigid interjected. "Which makes sense, since Lucifer's name is derived from *lux* and *fero*...'bringer or carrier of light.'"

"I thought Lucifer was just another name for the devil," commented Grant.

Lakesh smiled impishly. "In revised mythology, his name became synonymous with Satan. He was actually an angel of Heaven, but a fallen one. Like Prometheus, he was punished because he brought mankind the light of knowledge. Something to which I can relate."

"I'll bet," Kane drawled blandly.

Brigid glanced at him in irritation before declaring, "A number of esoteric and suppressed volumes dating back to the Gnostic tradition mention the original form of the stone as a trapezohedron. An Arab scholar who went by the name of Abdul al-Hazred wrote of it in his eighth century manuscript, *Kitab al-Azif*. Von Junzt alluded to it in his *Unausprechlichen Kulten*, as did the Ponape Scripture and Prinn's *De Vermiis Mysteriis*."

The difficult pronunciations rolled easily off Brigid's tongue, which Kane found more annoying than impressive. Due to her eidetic memory, she could memorize almost anything instantly, even words in foreign languages.

"The most recent mention of the stone," she continued, "is from the 1920s and directly reference the reason why the fragments of the black stone were called keys.

"In Buddhist and Taoist legends, there is the tradition of the Eight Immortals, eight masters who reside in a secret city beneath a mountain range on the Chinese-Tibet border. The city, known as Agartha in some legends and Hsi Wang Mu in others, is possibly underground and has been said by many to be near Lhasa. There have been numerous and dubious reports of explorations of tunnels leading to the city, but the most convincing came from Nicholas Roerich, a Russian artist and mystic.

"During his travels through Asia in the first decade of the twentieth century, Roerich heard of the Eight Immortals and their abode in the mountains. He was told, 'Behind that mountain live holy men who are saving humanity.' A native guide told him of huge

vaults inside the Kun Lun Mountain Range where
treasures had been stored from the beginning of history, and of strange 'gray people' who had emerged
from those rock galleries throughout history.''

Brigid paused to take a sip of coffee, then went on.
''In the 1920s, a high abbot from the Trasilunpo
lamasery entrusted Roerich with a fragment of a
'magical stone from another world,' called in Sanskrit
the Chintamani Stone. Alleged to have come from the
star system of Sirius, ancient Asian chronicles claim
that 'when the Son of the Sun descended upon earth
to teach mankind, there fell from heaven a shield
which bore the power of the world.' Perhaps it was a
meteorite, or possibly an artifact brought by visitors
from another solar system.

''Roerich's wife wrote that the stone possessed a
dark luster, like a dried heart, with four unknown letters. Its radiation was stronger than radium but on a
different frequency.

''Asian legends state the radiation covers a vast
area and influences world events. The main mass of
the stone is kept in 'a tower in the City of the Star-
born.'''

Kane murmured, ''I'm starting not to like the sound
of this.''

Brigid paid his comment no attention. ''According
to ancient chronicles, the stone was sent from Tibet
to King Solomon in Jerusalem, who split the stone
and made a ring out of one piece. Centuries later,
Muhammad took three other fragments to Mecca. A
smaller fragment of the stone was sent with Roerich
to Europe to help aid the establishment of the League
of Nations. With the failure of the league, Roerich

returned the fragment to a Trasilunpo lamasery in Tibet. Supposedly, the thirteenth Dalai Lama decreed the fragments were to be kept in separate places for safekeeping. During Roerich's journey to Tibet, he reported that he saw a flying disk, over two decades before the term 'flying saucer' was coined. He was told by his guide that it was an airship from Agartha, leading them to the hidden city.''

Lakesh looked completely enthralled. ''Did Roerich speculate on the physical composition of the stone?''

Brigid nodded. ''He speculated the stone was a form of moldavite, a magnetic mineral said to be a spiritual accelerator. Also, some historians have stated that a fragment of the Chintamani Stone can act as a homing beacon, leading to the main piece and therefore to the abode of the Eight Immortals.''

''What about the unknown letters inscribed on the stone?'' Banks asked.

''Roerich recognized them as Sanskrit and translated them as reading, 'Through the stars I come. I bring the chalice covered with the shield. Within it is a treasure—the gift of Orion.'''

''And the so-called Eight Immortals?'' Kane inquired. ''What are they supposed to have been—or be, since they're immortal?''

''Roerich asked the same question,'' answered Brigid. ''The abbot told him how the immortals were made of air and clay, formed by Mu Kung, the sovereign of eastern air and Wang Mu, queen of the western air.''

She paused, and with a crooked half smile, added, ''Or if you want a post-Taoist spin on it, they came from a planet in the solar system of Sirius and established a stronghold in Asia to conduct their genetic and hybridizing programs.''

Kane pressed the heels of his hands to the sides of his head. ''I should've known.''

Grant pursed his lips. ''I still don't see how the stone relates to any of this. What's the connection?''

''Roerich's theory about the stone is that it's charged with *shug*s, currents of psychic force. He speculated it resembled an electrical accumulator and may give back, in one way or another, the energy stored within it. For instance, it will increase the spiritual vitality of anyone who touches it, infusing him with knowledge or enhancing psychic abilities that allow him to glimpse Agartha, the Valley of the Immortals.''

Brigid touched her lips with the tip of her tongue and said hesitantly, ''There's something else.''

Kane groaned. ''I *knew* there had to be.''

''I cross-referenced Agartha and came across something else in the database.'' She took a deep breath and declared, ''In 1947, the same year as the Roswell crash, a mysterious man who called himself the Maha Chohan, Regent of the Realm of the Agartha, visited France. Not only did he describe the underground kingdom of Agartha, claiming its origins dated back fifty thousand years, but he made allusions to a system of physics that transcended what the scientists of the day understood.

''He was quoted as saying, 'All the sacred sciences are still preserved in Agartha.' He also hinted that it was more than a city, but a sanctuary for the superior ancestors of humankind.''

"Hmm," Lakesh said meditatively. "So far, it all fits with what little we know of the Archon presence on Earth. If Agartha is a sanctuary for Archons, it is little wonder that Balam became so agitated, particularly if the fragments of the black stone are keys that lead to it."

"Do we have any idea where any of these fragments might be?" asked Banks.

Brigid slid a sheet of paper across the table to him. On it was a photographic reproduction of a dark stone, one side of it smoothly angled and faceted. It rested inside of a glass case, bracketed by other, smaller chunks of rock. A metal plate affixed to the base of the case bore the word Tektites.

She said, "This picture shows part of the permanent mineral exhibit at the Museum of Natural History in Newyork."

She swept an expectant gaze back and forth across the faces of the four men.

"Where the anomalous mat-trans signature registered," Lakesh muttered apprehensively.

Banks, in the same low, anxious tone said, "The Hall of the Frozen Past."

"That's as accurate a description of the museum as I ever heard," Lakesh replied.

Kane tapped the illustration with a forefinger. "You're saying this is a fragment of the Chintamani Stone, Lucifer's stone? The shining trapezohedron?"

Brigid shrugged. "What else could it be? Combined with the gateway materialization in Manhattan, and the clues Balam fed us, the conclusion is fairly obvious."

"Maybe too obvious," Grant rumbled suspiciously.

Banks shot him an accusatory glare. "He wasn't lying. I would have sensed it."

"Then why didn't he just tell us where the fragment could be found?" demanded Kane. "Hall of the Frozen Past, my ass. That could just as easily refer to the cryogenic-suspension facility in Dulce."

"I have a theory about his choice of words," Lakesh ventured.

Grant and Kane snorted disdainfully at the same time.

Lakesh ignored them. "During his communication with us, Balam was limited in his descriptive language by Banks's easily accessible store of knowledge." He addressed the young man. "What do you know about the museum?"

Banks shrugged. "Almost nothing. I've heard of it, I guess, but it's not at the forefront of my mind. I usually get it mixed up with the Smithsonian. All I have are impressions of what it was supposed to be."

"Exactly. Balam more than likely drew on your inchoate impressions, and the closest approximation he could come up with was Hall of the Frozen Dead."

Kane swallowed a mouthful of coffee. "Balam also mentioned a thief. Do you figure that's who made the jump into the Manhattan gateway?"

"I would presume so," Lakesh answered. "On his way to the museum to recover the piece of the stone, drawn by the fragment already in his possession."

Thoughtfully, Grant knuckled his heavy chin. "Best as I recall from old Intel reports, Manhattan Island is a flat zone—not part of any baronial territory. It's supposed to be overrun with slagger gangs and muties. All the bridges are down, so there's no way off it…kind of like a giant, open-air prison. There's no escape from Newyork.''

''Which doesn't make it that much different than your average ville,'' Brigid interjected wryly.

Kane leaned back in his chair, frowning at the picture of the tektites. ''So because Balam suddenly gets a hair up his ass—if he has an ass—we're expected to jump to Manhattan on a rock-collecting expedition?''

Lakesh drummed his fingers on the tabletop. ''Yes, but not simply because he wants us to do it. This is a way to establish a rapport with him, and perhaps to others of his kind.''

''And,'' Grant argued, ''it may be a trap, to get as many of us chilled as he can, reduce the number of the opposition so others of his kind can break him out of here.''

Lakesh nodded grimly. ''There's that possibility, too.''

''I believe Balam is sincere,'' Banks declared vehemently.

Gently, Brigid said, ''Don't take this wrong, but you can't trust your perceptions. He may have altered them.''

''Don't you think I'd know it?'' he argued.

''Not necessarily,'' Kane said. ''You yourself told me that you didn't know the extent of Balam's mental influence on the human mind.''

Lakesh shook his head in weary frustration. ''Regardless of the risks, this is a mission we must undertake, for diplomacy's sake if nothing else. We must try to establish a bond of trust and channel of communication with Balam—not just for our benefit, but for what remains of mankind.''

"Diplomacy?'' repeated Kane skeptically. "With the Archons?''

"How is it any different than the way you dealt with the Indians?'' Lakesh challenged.

"A bond of trust stretches both ways. What if it *is* a trap Balam has laid for us?''

No one spoke for a tense moment, then Banks pushed his chair back noisily from the table. "I'll go if the rest of you are afraid.''

His announcement was hard with conviction.

Kane's eyes flashed with anger, then an amused smile played over his face. "There's a difference between caution and fear, kid. This is a percentage play, calculating the odds, figuring if what we might gain outweighs what we might lose.''

"I think it is,'' Banks stated dogmatically.

"No surprise,'' observed Grant. "But since you don't know a blaster from a blister, you'll stay here.''

Brigid glanced at him in surprise. "You're volunteering?''

Grant nodded. "Under one condition.''

"Which is?'' inquired Lakesh.

"If it's a trap, and if I manage to make it back, I get to chill Balam. As slowly and as painfully as I can.''

Banks squinted toward Grant, trying to ascertain if he was serious.

"Whoever makes it back earns that honor,'' Kane said smoothly. "At least we'll have more to look forward to than another cup of coffee.''

Chapter 15

Lakesh stressed urgency and expediency, so an hour after the briefing, Kane, Grant, Domi and Brigid met him in the ready room adjacent to the central control complex. It held only a long table and the Cerberus gateway chamber.

Enclosed on six sides by eight-foot-tall slabs of brown-tinted armaglass, the Cerberus unit was the first fully operable and completely debugged mat-trans unit constructed after the success of the prototype in the late twentieth century.

All of them understood, in theory, that the mat-trans units required a dizzying number of maddeningly intricate electronic procedures, all occurring within milliseconds of one another, to minimize the margins for error. The actual conversion process was automated for this reason, and was sequenced by an array of computers and microprocessors. Though they accepted at face value that the machines worked, it still seemed like magic to Brigid, Kane and Grant.

Intellectually, they knew the mat-trans energies transformed organic and inorganic matter to digital information, transmitted it through a hyperdimensional quantum path and reassembled it in a receiver unit. Emotionally, the experience felt like a fleeting brush with death, or worse than death. It was non-existence, at least for a nanosecond.

Their first jump, made some eight months ago, from Colorado to Montana, had been marked by nausea, vertigo and headaches, all symptoms of jump sickness. Lakesh had explained that the ill effects were due to the modulation frequency of the carrier wave interfacing with individual metabolisms. It had since been adjusted and refined, but Kane wondered how the few hardy souls who had used the devices after nukecaust could have tolerated the adverse physical effects.

Grant and Kane wore their full suits of Magistrate body armor. Though relatively lightweight, the polycarbonate was sufficiently dense to deflect anything up to and including a .45-caliber projectile. The armor absorbed and redistributed a bullet's kinetic impact, minimizing the chance of hydrostatic shock.

The armor was close-fitting, molded to conform to the biceps, triceps, pectorals and abdomen. The only spot of color anywhere on it was the small, disk-shaped badge of office emblazoned on the left pectoral. In crimson, it depicted stylized, balanced scales of justice, superimposed over a nine-spoked wheel, and symbolized the Magistrate's oath to keep the wheels of justice turning in the nine villes.

Like the armor encasing their bodies, the helmets were made of black polycarbonate, and fitted over the upper half and back of their head, leaving only portions of the mouth and chin exposed.

The slightly concave, red-tinted visor served several functions: it protected the eyes from foreign particles, and the electrochemical polymer was connected to a passive night-sight that intensified ambient light to permit one-color night vision.

The tiny image-enhancer sensor mounted on the forehead of the helmet did not emit detectable rays, though its range was only twenty-five feet, even on a fairly clear night with strong moonlight.

Their Sin Eaters were securely holstered to their right forearms. Attached to their belts by magnetic clips were their close-assault weapons. Chopped-down autoblasters, the Copperheads were barely two feet in length. The magazine held fifteen rounds of 4.85 mm steel-jacketed rounds, which could be fired at a rate of 700 per minute. Even with its optical image intensifier and laser scope, the Copperhead weighed less than eight pounds. The two-stage sound and muzzle-flash arrestors screwed into the blasters' bores suppressed even full-auto reports to mere whispers.

Fourteen-inch combat knives were scabbarded on the sides of their boots. Honed to razor-keen cutting edges, the titanium-jacketed, tungsten-steel blades were blued so as not to reflect light.

Brigid and Domi wore long coats and dark clothing of tough whipcord, with high-laced boots enclosing their feet and calves. A mini-Uzi hung from a strap beneath Brigid's coat, and Domi's Detonics .45 Combat Master was snugged in a shoulder holster. A flat, square case containing medicines and dehydrated foodstuffs lay on the table, next to a small packet of precision tools. Other odds and ends of equipment, like Nighthawk microlights, rad counters and the motion sensor lay scattered on the table.

Lakesh swept all of them with a searching, penetrating gaze. "Are you all aware of what you're to do?"

"Other than making our way to the museum," Brigid said, touching the tool packet, "you want us to remove and return with the Newyork gateway's molecular-imaging scanners."

Lakesh nodded. "As you know, every record of every gateway transit is stored in the scanner's memory banks. We need to download and review them in order to trace the point of origin of our interlopers."

Kane snorted. "They're no more interlopers than we are. I'm more concerned with finding the museum. Manhattan is dark territory, has been since the nukecaust."

"I found a New York City street map in the database," Brigid asserted. "I memorized the shortest route to the museum from the World Trade Center...though I imagine there have been some changes since the map was made and since we were last there."

Lakesh acknowledged her oblique reference to the disastrous time-travel mission with a wan smile. A couple of months before, Brigid and Kane had been temporally phased to December 31, 2000, in a desperate bid to change the future in the past. They had arrived in *a* past, but not *their* past, so any action they undertook had no effect on their present.

"You'll materialize in the same gateway as you did on that occasion," Lakesh said. "Or rather a duplicate of it, so you should have no trouble finding your way around."

He picked up the packet of tools and handed it to

Brigid. "I've already shown you the procedure for removing the scanner's hard disk."

As she stowed it in a coat pocket, he asked, "So we're clear on everything?"

"Except," Grant stated, "the reason for this op. I'm still fuzzy about the importance of this rock."

"That makes two of us," said Kane.

Domi held up three fingers. "Three of us."

Brigid eyed her dourly. "You weren't at the briefing."

Grant tapped his breastplate and hooked a thumb toward Kane. "*We* were and we still can't figure it out. Balam hinted that it was a conductor of some kind, you gave us a history lesson and I'm no closer to understanding the point of this than I was two hours ago."

Brigid smiled wryly. "To be frank, neither can I, not completely. But I remembered something I was shown in Ireland, in the Priory of Awen's citadel—the so-called speaking stone of Cascorach."

Lakesh stiffened in surprise. "You're right. I didn't make the connection."

"It was a dark stone," Brigid continued, "and when touched by Morrigan's mind energy, it activated something like a recording, a psionic message implanted within the designs cut into its surface. Morrigan told me that ancient people knew that certain stones and metals could be charged with a memory, like a storage battery. She also mentioned that quantum theory dealt with such an electromagnetic effect."

Kane nodded. "I remember you telling me about

it. So you suspect this black stone of Balam's is the same thing?''

"It's possible," she replied. "Perhaps it holds all the hidden information about the Archons and that's one reason he's so terrified."

Thoughtfully, Grant said, "And some of that information might be about their weaknesses, their vulnerabilities and he doesn't want us apelings to access it.''

"Exactly," stated Brigid.

"Even if that's true," Kane interposed, "won't we need a psi-mutie like Morrigan to tap into it?"

"Worry about that later," said Domi impatiently, picking up the equipment case, a microlight and a rad counter. "Let's jump."

Grant slipped the motion sensor over his left wrist, and the four people crossed the anteroom and entered the gateway jump chamber. Right above the keypad encoding panel was imprinted the notice Entry Absolutely Forbidden To All But B12 Cleared Personnel. Even after all this time, they still had no idea who the B12 Cleared Personnel were and what had happened to them.

Grant pulled the heavy, brown-tinted armaglass door closed on its counterbalanced hinges. Manufactured in the waning years of the twentieth century, armaglass was a special compound combining the properties of steel and glass. It was used as shielding in jump chambers to confine quantum-energy overspills.

The lock mechanism clicked and triggered the automatic initiator. A familiar yet still slightly unnerving hum began, climbing in pitch to a subsonic whine.

The hexagonal plates on the floor and ceiling exuded a shimmering silvery glow that slowly intensified. A fine, faint mist gathered on the floor plates and drifted down from the ceiling. Thready static discharges crackled in the wispy vapor. Lakesh had explained that the vapor was actually a plasma form, a side effect of the inducer's "quincunx effect"—the nanosecond of time when lower dimensional space was phased into a higher dimension. The mist thickened, curling around to engulf them.

Kane watched the spark-shot fog float before his visor and he closed his eyes. He plunged through a kaleidoscope that constantly shifted into patterns of colors he couldn't name, somersaulting over a never ending series of contrasting textures, hues and shapes.

HE OPENED HIS EYES and saw nothing but mist, but he heard the emitter array beneath the jump platform winding down from a hurricane howl to an electronic whine. Kane didn't move, waiting for the world to stop spinning. The vertigo and nausea slowly seeped away, as did the vapor. He heard his companions stirring around him, taking in shuddery breaths.

Raising his head, he blinked blearily and looked around. Through the transparent armaglass walls, he saw a small chamber with a control console running the length of one wall. To his left, a ten-foot-high passage, walled with dully gleaming metal, led straight ahead.

Carefully, all of them got to their feet. Grant said hoarsely, "This unit has clear walls."

"It's not a redoubt, not exactly," Brigid told him. Lakesh had once said that many of the armaglass walls were color-coded to differentiate all the Totality Concept–related redoubts. Inasmuch as use of the gateways was restricted to a select few personnel, it was fairly easy for them to memorize which color designated what redoubt.

They peered through the wall of the jump chamber. The only light was provided by the red and green blinking telltales on the console. The control room was covered by a carpet of dust. They saw faint imprints of feet in the dust of broken plaster that had fallen from the cracked ceiling. Splits high in the walls showed where the vanadium-alloy shielding had buckled.

"A little less tidy than I remember," Brigid murmured.

Kane chuckled uneasily. He still had difficulty sorting out what had happened when they attempted the temporal dilation on the final day of the twentieth century. They had successfully traversed the time stream, true enough, but they arrived in an alternate past, a probability branch almost but not quite identical to their own.

He experienced a momentary disorientation as he tried to reconcile the fact that this was, yet was not, the same subterranean installation they had visited before.

Extending his left hand, Grant made a sweep with the motion detector. The faintly glowing LCD on its face registered no movement within the radius of its sensor beams.

Taking the point as always, Kane lifted up the door handle and stepped out carefully and quietly into the control room. His companions followed, Domi double-fisting her Combat Master. Brigid swiftly moved toward the master console. Removing the tool kit from her pocket, she spread it open and selected a tiny, almost delicate screwdriver.

"You're sure you know how to do this?" Kane asked.

"I went over it step by step with Lakesh after the last time," she retorted a bit peevishly. "Even if I make a mistake, what's the worst that could happen?"

"You could short out the mat-trans," Grant responded gruffly. "And strand us here."

She shook her head in annoyance. "This is a dedicated system. It has nothing to do with the jump cycles. Domi, come over here and give me some light."

Obligingly, the albino girl stepped over beside her, turning on her small Nighthawk. Grant and Kane moved to the six-foot-tall open doorway to peer into the dark passageway beyond. They activated the image enhancers on their helmets. Even through their night-vision visors, they saw nothing but shadows and dust.

They waited quietly while Brigid kneeled beneath the console, removing the protective plate and making all the necessary disconnections. After ten minutes, she held an ovular disk in her hand, about a quarter of an inch thick.

"Done," she announced, slipping it into her pocket.

"Let's get the rest of this mission over," Grant said in a tense whisper. "Triple red."

They entered the corridor, the amber-colored beams from Brigid's and Domi's microlights illuminating their path. The hallway stretched for a hundred feet then reached a junction, where four passages radiated off like the spokes of a wheel, just as Kane and Brigid remembered. It was a very unsettling sensation, to retrace steps through a place they knew they had never actually visited.

At the mouth of each side-branching corridor, red numbers, one through four, were just visible through the patina of dust. The set of tracks drifted off to the opening on their left. Kane led them to the one to their far right. The passage was short and opened into a reception room furnished with armchairs, a couch, a low table and a coffee machine. A television set supported by a metal framework was positioned in a corner just below the ceiling. All of the items showed their age, speckled with rust and covered with a film of dust.

Kane pointed to a double set of doors. "The elevator. Think it still works?"

Brigid stepped forward. "Only one way to find out."

The elevator doors were opened by a proximity sensor, but it didn't respond when she waved her hand in front of the grit-encrusted control plate. She cleaned it of its accumulation of dust and tried again. The doors slid apart with a grinding creak. The car was large, with verdegris-coated brass handrails, and easily accommodated all four of them.

"Whoever arrived before us may still be wandering around down here," Grant observed. "They didn't find the lift."

As soon as the doors slid shut, the car ascended with ominous groans and shudders. The noise didn't decrease as they rose higher, but the ascent lasted only a handful of seconds. When they squealed to a lurching stop, the doors opened on a large square room. The floor was thickly layered with concrete dust. The walls were black-speckled marble and showed ugly crisscrossing cracks.

A long, horseshoe-shaped console occupied the facing wall, but it was half-buried by fallen stone and metal conduits. An ornate, gilt-faced clock lay on the floor, its glass face shattered, the hands frozen at 12:32. On the right side of the room, a hallway stretched away, lined on both sides with wooden doors. On their left they saw a glass-and-chrome door that led to a murky semidarkness. Though the heavy glass bore cracks, it was still intact.

Kane crept out of the lift, followed by Grant, who swept the motion detector back and forth. Domi and Brigid followed them cautiously. The dust was much thicker here, and they moved slowly to avoid stirring it up any more than necessary. Kane paced over to the door and peered out into what was once an underground parking garage.

Now it was a graveyard for scores of rusting vehicles, almost all of them squashed beneath tons of tumbled rubble. Huge chunks of brick and massive slabs of concrete, bristling with shorn-off reinforcing rods, filled the area within and beyond his range of vision. A cold and bleak daylight filtered in from an opening somewhere.

Putting his shoulder against the door, Kane gave it a shove. The electronically controlled solenoids had long ago been burned out and it opened, though not easily. The bottom of the metal frame dragged loudly against small particles of rock.

Stagnant water lay in algae-scummed pools on the floor, and the cool, dank air tickled their nostrils. Kane started walking toward the source of the light. He saw no sign of habitation, recent or otherwise, and Grant's periodic motion detector sweeps caught nothing, either.

The four people picked a path over the heaps of debris on their way to the light, speaking little. The longer they walked, the more repulsive became the odors; an effluvia of urine, rotting meat and mildew hung over the garage like a shroud. The piles of rubbish rustled when small animals darted into them at their approach.

As they strode beneath a roof overhang, a faint click of stone against stone reached their ears. Domi whirled in the direction they had come, leading with her blaster. Her delicate nostrils flared.

All of them stopped, turning to look where she had her Combat Master pointed. They were more unnerved by her stance, like that of a snow leopardess preparing to pounce.

"Just a loose rock," Grant said quietly.

Domi whispered fiercely, "Not just sound— smell."

She had reverted to the terse, broken mode of speech of the outlander, as she always did when under stress.

Kane and Brigid sniffed the air experimentally. Grant didn't bother, inasmuch as his sense of smell was seriously impaired due to having his nose broken three times in the past.

At first, neither Brigid nor Kane smelled anything more noisome than the blended varieties of stench they had already detected. Then a faint miasma inserted itself into Kane's nostrils, and he realized it was an odor he had encountered twice before in his life.

The first time had been a number of years before, when he and Grant stumbled on a snake pit in a hellzone. The second time was far more recent, when the mutagenically altered Lord Strongbow broke a sweat. The musty reek was the same—the cold, repulsive taint of reptiles.

At the same time the memory registered, the scalie dropped from the ceiling.

Chapter 16

Out of the four of them, only Domi had ever seen a scalie before. Most of the obviously mutated human breeds had been on the road to extinction for a long time. Some, like the swampies, managed to survive, due in part to their isolation. Others, like the once fearsome stickies, had been the target of a concerted campaign of genocide on the part of the villes. Since they tended to congregate in clans and form settlements, they weren't hard to find and exterminate. Scalies, on the other hand, reportedly haunted the shadows, often in the shunned ruins of predark cities, more legend than reality.

As his Sin Eater sprang into his hand, Kane caught only a brief impression of a small yet very broad and squat figure dressed in a collection of rags. The hairless, blunt-featured head was coated in thick, overlapping scales, as were the talon-tipped hands it swept toward Domi. They gripped a foot-long sharpened shard of metal.

She squeezed the trigger of the Combat Master before the scalie had fully regained its balance. The .45-caliber round caught the creature dead center, smashing through the sternum and bursting both lungs. The scalie flailed backward, blood spewing in a liquid banner from its chest, clawlike toenails scrabbling loudly on the concrete floor.

It fell with a wet, slapping sound. The scalie's pendulous lips writhed back over yellow pointed teeth, and a geyser of blood fountained up over them. Its dark-rimmed eyes glittered with hate before it gasped and died.

The booming echoes of the blaster's report rolled throughout the garage. Domi's face twisted into a porcelain mask of revulsion, but she stepped closer to the scalie, drawing a bead on its head.

Grant slapped down the barrel of her blaster, saying, "I think you got him."

Domi swung her head up and around, ruby eyes bright with rage, but she didn't aim at the mutic again. "Reminds me of Guana," she muttered in a guttural voice.

Grant remembered the faint greenish tint of Guana Teague's skin and its odd, faintly scaled pattern. A lot of people had suspected that Guana had a scalie in the family woodpile—hence his nickname. The loathing Domi felt for her former master still ran deep, even after all this time, and Grant didn't blame her for it.

Brigid moved closer to the scalie, inspecting it visually, noting its deep-set eyes and the brachycephalic contours of its skull. She didn't bother suppressing a shiver of repulsion or speculate on what bizarre combination of warped DNA could have created such a mixture of reptile and human.

"Let's keep moving," Kane said. "If we have to face more of those things, I'd rather do it in the open."

Taking the point again, he led them to wide concrete steps stretching upward. Painted on the wall beside them, faded almost to illegibility, were the words Exit To Street Level. The feeble shafts of sunlight angled down the throat of the stairwell.

He easily recalled the last time he climbed these stairs, how he, Brigid and Salvo emerged into a courtyard between the Twin Towers and stared in stunned silence at the majesty of prenuke New York City.

He climbed out into the same courtyard and once more stood dumbfounded. Not, however, at the vista of the thriving metropolis, but rather at its ruins, the hecatomb of a vanished civilization. The fields of devastation stretched almost out of sight. The few structures still recognizable as buildings rose at the skyline, then collapsed with ragged abruptness.

The courtyard itself was buried beneath tons of rubble that had fallen from the ramparts of the two skyscrapers. Tilting his head back, Kane saw that both buildings looked as if they had been broken by titanic blows combining shock and fire. The sky was a canopy of pewter-colored clouds, and what little sunlight pierced them had an unearthly, diffused quality to it.

All four people stood for a moment, silently appraising the panorama of desolation. Consulting her rad counter, Brigid said in a hushed voice, "Green. Whatever kind of explosives caused this destruction had an exceptionally low rad yield. Maybe missiles with short-term 'squeeze' yields."

"Which way?" Kane asked.

She pointed eastward. "That way."

Clambering over massive chunks of concrete, scattered shards of glass and twisted girders of steel, they reached the Avenue of the Americas and began walk-ing. Brigid cryptically warned them to stay away from the black maws of subway-tunnel entrances and open manholes. No one questioned her, assuming she drew on information about Manhattan gleaned from the *Wyeth Codex.*

As they passed through the shadows cast by the shattered monoliths, they heard, far in the distance, a rhythmic thumping, as of a metal drum being pounded repeatedly by a mallet. The sound was too regular to be the product of the wind.

Kane's pointman senses rang an alert, and he cast a grim glance toward Grant. The man's lips tightened beneath his mustache. "I think we've been formally announced."

Gaping rents in the crumbling masonry and the dark windows leered down at them, like monstrously distorted, mocking faces. They strode down the broad avenue, turning onto Columbus. On some of the city blocks, the breadth of rubble was so widespread, they could see no discernible difference between the street and the ruins. The roadbed itself had a ripple pattern to it, a characteristic result of earthquakes triggered by explosive shock waves.

As they reached a corner obscured by a great pile of debris and broken stone, they heard a raucous cho-rus of high-pitched shrieks and squawks. A swarm of small black shapes held aloft by furiously beating wings darted over a pair of bodies sprawled on the ground. They dived and dipped and banked at such a blurring speed, Kane couldn't get a good look at them.

"Scream-wings," Domi declared quietly.

All of them had heard of scream-wings, but like scalies, the bat-winged predators had been relegated to the status of legend. Barely six inches long with a two-foot wingspan, the creatures were equipped with serrated razor teeth, curving claws and whiplike tails. Rare even in the wild old days before the Program of Unification, scream-wings traveled in flocks.

Several of them circled overhead, clutching bloody chunks of flesh in their talons, chewing on them as their leathery wings beat the air.

Domi looked around, then approached the edge of the debris and pulled a rusty length of reinforcing steel from beneath a heap of bricks. As the others watched, mystified, she slowly approached the bodies, swishing the metal rod through the air over her head, producing a deep hum.

Almost at once, the scream-wings stopped screeching and in a black, flapping cloud, flew up and away from the bodies. Although they didn't go far, the flock maintained a safe distance overhead, circling clockwise.

Still whipping the rod around and around, Domi explained, "They're deaf, but they feel vibrations in the air. They think a big bird is down here."

Keeping uneasy eyes on the fluttering, banking scream-wings, Brigid, Grant and Kane strode to the bodies. Though it was partially eaten, they recognized one of the corpses as a scalie. A bullet had punched a small hole in its forehead and a much larger one through the back of its head. A slop of blood and brain matter oozed across the street.

The other body was human enough, the face still unmutilated. A thick metal spike protruded from his chest. His clothing consisted of a short dark jacket, baggy, coarsely woven trousers and boots of animal hide. A heavy iron cudgel, shaped like an oversize, old-fashioned door key hung from a thong about his waist.

Despite the black soot smeared over his round face, Brigid noted the epicanthic fold of the glazed eyes. "An Asian. Maybe a Mongol," she said.

Domi, still wielding the length of steel in a circle over her head, said impatiently, "Let's go. My arm is getting tired."

They moved on down the street. After a few yards, Domi dropped the rod to the ground. Almost immediately, the clot of scream-wings swarmed down and covered the corpses again.

"They managed to find another way out of the installation," Grant commented. "We'll be contending with one blaster at least. Fairly small caliber, I'd judge."

"For some reason," replied Kane, "that doesn't make me feel a whole lot better."

They passed between silent shells of buildings and then into an expanse of tangled overgrowth. High grass and rank weeds sprouted between paving stones that had once been sidewalks. From all sides, foliage crept in, making a snarl of thorns and vines.

"This used to be Central Park," Brigid panted, disengaging her coat from a briar bush.

They struggled through the dense thicket until they reached a deeply furrowed avenue. On the other side was a series of huge pillars, thrusting their jagged, sheared-off pinnacles into the sky. The sprawling complex of buildings was overgrown with vines and creepers, masking the facade and the windows. The edifice was staggering in size, and one whole wing had tumbled into a featureless mass of moss-covered stone.

Mammoth blocks of granite lay in the overgrowth. The statue of a man on horseback, his features obliterated by the passage of centuries and acid rain, rose up from a skein of thorny brush.

Carved on a pediment above a huge arched entranceway, the inscription Knowledge was barely visible. It was bracketed by two other words, but the letters had long ago been erased by the hand of time. Behind a wavering line of crumbling walls, they saw a vast, stained dome.

Brigid pointed to it. "The Hayden Planetarium."

Kane crossed the avenue, moving toward a wide expanse of cracked, grass-grown stone slabs leading up to the archway, flanked by crooked columns. He paused at the dark door, waiting for the others to join him. Grant made a motion-sensor sweep, which registered nothing, and they stepped in.

The foyer led directly into a long, broad hall that ran away until its nether end grew indistinct in the distance. Skylights were set in the lofty, vaulted ceiling, allowing weak sunlight to flow through the broken glass and wire mesh. Dead leaves covered the tiled floor in an ankle-deep layer. Here and there, the marble walls showed blackened soot streaks from ancient cooking fires. Moldering rubbish was heaped in the corners.

Grant and Kane had seen wrack and ruin before in their missions as Magistrates, but nothing like the chaos within the walls of the museum. As they strode down the hall, they beheld the fantastic at every turn. On one side was the heaped clutter of a pharaoh's treasure. On another, through shattered glass, they glimpsed the stuffed remains of animals not seen since before the nukecaust.

A massive heap of huge bones lay on the littered floor, and they were forced to pick their way around them. A huge skull, displaying fangs like six-inch daggers, grinned at them as they walked by. Domi gazed at the scattering of bones apprehensively, noting that just one of the ribs was almost the size of her entire body.

"What kind of animal is that?" she murmured. "Mutie? What kind of animal chilled it, ate it?"

Brigid's chuckle sounded forced. "It's the skeleton of a tyrannosaurus, a carnivorous dinosaur. Whatever killed it has been dead for at least eighty million years, so don't worry that we'll meet up with it."

They passed exhibit after exhibit, the litter of treasures from every possible time, the stuff of myth and legend.

The four people turned into an open archway and traversed yet another broad hall lined on either side by all varieties of animals, faces and bodies frozen forever. Many of the beasts were posed within dioramas that portrayed them in their natural habitats.

Lions crouched, antelope frolicked, elephants lifted their trunks to trumpet, a mountain gorilla rose from African foliage to drum on its chest.

All of them had seen pix at one time or another of most of the animals on display. Brigid in particular retained a vivid memory of the collection of preserved and mounted beasts in the archives of Cobaltville's Historical Division.

Bleakly, Kane thought of the astonishing variety of wildlife that had existed in the world before the nuke-caust, although he had been taught that many species were only years away from extinction before the first bomb detonated.

The mutant descendants of some of these animals had very limited life spans and most, if not all, of these were extinct now, too. He wondered absently if a giant mutie variety of gorilla might not live still in the forested vastness of Africa. He couldn't help but smile at the possibility.

The hall ended at a flight of wide steps that pitched downward into a darkness the illumination provided by the skylights could not reach. A gargantuan, streamlined shape, nearly a hundred feet long, blocked the center of the stairwell. By looking up, they saw the giant fluked tail anchored to a steel cable stretching down from an eyebolt in the ceiling.

"What the hell is this thing?" Grant asked, his eyes running from its blunt snout and up along its pale blue surface.

"A blue whale," Brigid replied. "The largest mammal on Earth—a long time ago."

Kane observed where the cable supports had snapped on the leviathan, so it hung down at a ninety-degree angle. "What must a mutie version of it been like?" he murmured in awe.

With a touch of bitterness, Brigid answered, "I imagine they were extinct before the nukecaust. Maybe they were the lucky ones."

The four people sidled around the whale's sus-

pended body, Kane assuming the point. The image
enhancer mounted above his helmet's visor lit up his
path, amplifying the beams from Brigid's and Domi's
microlights and thus dispelling some of the gloom.

"Where to now?" Domi asked.

"The Morgan Memorial Hall of Minerals and
Gems," Brigid replied. "It's the most likely place in
the museum to find the stone."

They reached the foot of the stairs and waited as
Brigid glanced around, trying to get her bearings.
Suddenly, they were galvanized by a sound ahead of
them, a faint but distinct scraping. Grant and Kane
automatically dropped into crouches, Sin Eaters
aimed at the shadows. The noise came again, this time
overlaid by the jangle of breaking glass.

The two men moved forward, walking heel to toe,
carefully placing their feet so as to not raise rustles
from the debris on the floor. Brigid and Domi followed them, allowing the men's armor to act as a
protective buffer.

As they turned a corner in the corridor, hugging the
wall, they saw a white spike of light piercing the darkness. They could hear the murmur of voices, but
couldn't make out the words.

Ahead of them lay a maze of tables, display cases
and platforms. The sweeping beam of the flashlight
struck brief, glittering highlights from the collection
of stone, gems, geodes and crystals that filled the
large room. They were dizzying in number, of all
shapes, sizes and colors, far too much to absorb in a
single glance.

A man's voice echoed in the shadow-shrouded
semidarkness, an exclamation of excited triumph.

Kane didn't recognize the language, but it sounded familiar.

"Russian," Brigid breathed from behind him. "He said, 'Here, this must be it.'"

Kane knew she spoke Russian, so he wasn't surprised by her translation. He was more surprised that they had encountered Russians. "What the hell are they doing here?" he whispered to no one in particular.

"Evidently, the same as what we're doing," Brigid replied evenly.

Grant grunted softly in disgust. Although he had learned like the rest of them that Russia was only indirectly responsible for the nukecaust, the prejudices of a lifetime weren't easily cast aside.

"So the thief came from Russia," he said slowly. "Not from the Peredelinko unit, or we could have traced the jump line. There must be another unindexed gateway somewhere in the country."

Brigid knew scientists had built on Project Cerberus technology and created their own project called Szvezda, but she didn't mention it. "We can't let them take the stone back to Russia," she stated.

Kane nodded curtly in silent agreement. Their prior visit to that country some five months before had scarcely been a pleasure jaunt. To Grant, he whispered, "Flank 'em. I go right, you go left."

"Right."

They bent over in crouches, bodies tensed. Kane murmured, "Set."

"Go," Grant responded.

The two men moved out into the hall, drawing on their long years of service together and their shared heritage as Magistrates. They crept forward slowly to avoid stepping on pieces of glass, alternating their attention from the floor to the wavering glow of the flashlight.

Kane heard two voices now, exchanging words in Russian. He pictured a squad of AK-toting Internal Security Network troopers wearing dun-colored greatcoats, jodhpurs and fur caps with silver disks pinned to them.

Circling a long display table, Kane duck-walked at an oblique angle toward the mutter of voices. He stopped at its corner, eyes widening behind the visor. He saw four figures standing before the shattered remains of a glass case, and they were nothing like the images his imagination had supplied.

All of them were garbed in shaggy fur coats and vests, high boots laced with colorful strips of cloth. One man was short and rather stout, with a shaved head and swart Asian features smeared with soot. Like the corpse they had found on the street, a crudely fashioned, key-shaped cudgel hung from his waist. He held a flashlight in his right hand.

A woman—a girl, really—stood near him. A bright red scarf was wound about her neck, contrasting sharply with tumbles of glossy black hair. The cast of her eyes, and the fullness of her lips put him in mind of Beth-Li, though this woman wasn't as slender.

A man wearing a high black turban of dark leather spoke in a lilting, whispering voice, and Kane felt a cold hand of fearful recognition stroke his spine. His build was slight, graceful and his face seemed to consist primarily of delicate brow arches, prominent cheekbones and a very long, pointed chin. The large eyes behind the round-framed spectacles were jet-black. Although the eyes were slanted, they didn't possess the Asian epicanthic fold. The fingers loosely holding an AK-47 looked excessively, almost inhumanly long.

Kane did not recognize the turbaned man as an individual, but as a type. Although he was more darkly complexioned than others Kane had seen, Kane was certain the man was a hybrid, a mixture of human and Archon genetic material. He noted the bloodred baldric extending across his torso from left shoulder to right hip and the short, curving sword hanging from it.

The third man commanded most of his attention for a number of reasons. He was a head taller than his companions, topping even the black turban by several inches. His black hair fell to his shoulders and bore a wide streak of white. His lean body was clothed from neck to ankle in a long fur coat.

He stood motionless, holding a chunk of stone resembling onyx in both hands. His deep-set eyes seemed to gleam with lights that floated up slowly through pools of darkness.

His aquiline profile rang a distant chord of familiarity within Kane. He was sure he had seen the man before, but he wasn't sure of when or where.

The man cupped the stone in his hands, head bowed over it, as if he were drinking some liquid force that flowed from it. The turbaned man spoke to him in an impatient, challenging tone.

With one hand, he reached for the black stone, but the Russian checked his movement with harsh, peremptory words. The bespectacled man turned, handing the autorifle to the girl.

In the brief of tick of time between the girl firmly gripping the weapon and the man relinquishing his hold on it, Kane swiftly rose to his feet.

"Freeze!" he roared, using his well-practiced Mag voice at a volume that intimidated malefactors and broke violent momentum. He knew he should have apprised Grant over the helmet comm-link of what he was doing, but there wasn't time.

He bellowed in English, so he wasn't sure if any of the four people would understand him, but they did freeze in midmotion. They stared at the black-armored apparition in silent surmise, and Kane couldn't help but feel impressed by their rigid self-control.

The tall man's lips curved in a smile. In English, with only the slightest trace of an accent, he said, "I am afraid the museum is closed for renovation."

Chapter 17

Kane's eyes swiftly swept his surroundings, searching for Grant. His partner's disgruntled voice filtered through the helmet comm-link into his ear. "I'm not in position. Keep them covered."

The four people continued to regard Kane with a bone-chilling calm. They didn't move, but the Russian asked, "What do you intend to do?"

Kane didn't respond to the question. Instead, he ordered, "Tell the girl to drop the blaster."

The Russian spoke to her in an indecipherable conglomeration of consonants, and she carefully laid the AK down on the floor.

Kane said, "I've seen you somewhere before."

The Russian's eyes flickered with surprise. "I confess your voice has a familiar ring, and since I've only met three Americans in my life, by a process of elimination you must be one of them." He paused for a second, as if ransacking his memory. "You were dressed less formally when I last saw you, but I believe your name is Kane."

Kane's mind provided a silver-disked cap, a greatcoat and gave the man's long locks a shearing. He bit back a curse of surprise. He was one of Colonel Sverdlovosk's District Twelve troopers who had accompanied them on the flight from Russia to the base in Mongolia.

"The colonel didn't make introductions," Kane said. "What's your name?"

The man inclined his head in a short bow. "My name is Grigori Zakat, once a major in the ISN. I now go by the title of Tsyansis Khan-po. As far as I am aware, I am the only survivor of the massacre of the Black Gobi garrison. Do you know Colonel Sverdlovosk's fate?"

"He'd dead." Kane waggled the barrel of his Sin Eater. "I chilled him with this blaster."

Zakat's eyebrows rose as if he were impressed. "Ah. And the Tushe Gun?"

"He'd dead, too," Grant rumbled from behind him, his Sin Eater on a direct line with the back of the Russian's head. "I chilled him with *this* blaster."

Zakat didn't even glance in his direction, nor did his companions. They maintained a steady gaze upon Kane. "Our paths haven't crossed again by mere happenstance."

"Very perceptive," Kane replied. "It appears we have the same goal."

Zakat's lips quirked in a smile. "Which is?"

"That chunk of rock in your hands."

The black-turbaned man said in a sibilant voice, "I represent its true owners. We are returning it to where it belongs."

"Who are you?" Kane demanded.

The man squared his shoulders, raising his chin, cocking his head at a defiant angle. "I am Gyatso Chohan, direct descendant of the Maha Chohan, first ambassador from the nation of Agartha and keeper of the key.''

"And this," Zakat offered mildly, pointing to the woman, "is Trai."

"And the guy in blackface?" Grant asked.

"Shu," replied Zakat.

"Is that a name," Grant growled, "or a sneeze?"

Zakat chuckled. He was the only one who did.

Impatiently, Kane declared, "Ownership issues can be worked out later. Right now I want you to put the rock on the floor and kick it over to me."

"No!" Gyatso's voice hit a high note of outrage. "It is not yours, outlander dog!"

"Calling me an outlander dog when we're in my own country is a pretty piss-poor insult. Do as I say, Zakat."

The Russian did not move, but continued to cup the stone in his hands. "What do you know of this stone? Why do you need it?"

"My business," Kane grated. "Do it and live, Zakat, or don't do it and die. Your choice."

Zakat continued to stare expressionlessly. Kane's finger hovered over the trigger of his pistol, lightly brushing it.

The sound of the shot was an explosive, ear-knocking crack! For an irrational half instant, Kane thought he had unintentionally fired the Sin Eater. He jumped and he heard Grant cursing. Reflexively, his head jerked around to where the sound had come. He recognized the report as made by Domi's Combat Master.

"Kane!" Brigid's trans-comm accurately transmitted her fear into his ear. "We've got company. Has to be scalies."

"How many?" he asked into the transceiver built into the jaw guard of his helmet.

"A lot. At a bare minimum, a dozen. Probably more."

"Hold them off," he told her. "Stand by."

Grant demanded, "What the hell's going on back there?"

"Scalies," Kane replied grimly. "The bastards tracked us here."

Zakat shifted his feet slightly. "We encountered a group of them. Shu's brother Chu was killed. I feared they would lay in wait for us."

Kane didn't respond, mind racing over dozens of plans and discarding most of them.

In a bland, colorless tone, the Russian said, "I submit we have no choice but to agree to a truce, an alliance of convenience—at least until we have dealt with the most immediate threat. As you said, issues of ownership can be worked out later."

Kane examined the man's proposal from several angles and realized it was the only short-term solution that made sense. "Agreed," he stated.

Zakat made two swift motions with his hands. He slid the chunk of rock into a voluminous inner pocket of his coat while simultaneously drawing a stubby Tokarev automatic from his belt. He spoke to Trai, and she bent down to pick up the AK. Shu removed the key-shaped cudgel from his waist, holding it by its leather thong. Gyatso unsheathed his sword with a rasp of steel against leather.

"Stay here with them," Kane said to Grant as he stepped into the murk.

He retraced his path through the display cases and tables, reaching Brigid and Domi at the corner. Both women had their blasters in hand and peered anxiously down the corridor. Faintly, he heard the shuffling of feet, the clatter of claws on the floor.

"Do you know another way out of here?" he asked Brigid.

She shook her head. "I memorized only the way to the Hall of Minerals and Gems."

Kane set his teeth on a groan. "It's a safe bet the scalies know their way around this place. Come on."

Domi and Brigid followed him back to the others. Kane didn't waste time on introductions. He stabbed a hand toward the farthest end of the exhibit hall. "That way."

No one questioned his choice of routes, since it stretched in the opposite direction from the way the scalies had to come. Due to the broken glass carpeting the floor, stealth wasn't an option, but the muties knew where they were anyway.

The hall of minerals ended on a wide transverse corridor, running to the right and to the left. On impulse, Kane chose the right. The glow from the Nighthawks and the flashlight in Shu's hand cast an eerie twilight over the passageway.

Narrow arches opened occasionally on either side, but they kept to the corridor. A worry that they had taken the wrong branch grew in Kane. Though the silence seemed absolute, his pointman's sixth sense told him they were not alone. More than once, passing one of the dark arches, he felt the glare of unseen eyes. He suspected they were being played with, herded into a trap.

Ahead of him in the darkness sounded scuffings and slidings not made by human feet. Gesturing sharply behind him, Kane came to a halt. Far too late, he sensed the rush of bodies. At that second, scalies poured from the doorways on both sides of the corridor behind them, toe claws clicking like castanets, giving tongue to guttural yowls.

Kane instantly realized the mechanics of the trap: while one small group of muties pursued them through the hall of minerals, a far larger group lay waiting in adjacent chambers and ahead of them. He had blithely led everyone right into the ambush.

There wasn't time to make a head count. The scalies rushed like shadows, affording Kane only nightmarish glimpses of them. He raised his Sin Eater and pressed the trigger. Flame wreathed the muzzle, smearing the gloom, casting an unearthly strobing effect on the inhuman faces snarling before him. The corridor became a babel of shouts and screams, punctuated by the stuttering roar of the Sin Eater. He heard Grant open up with his own blaster, and Zakat's Tokarev snapped out steady, hand-clapping bangs.

Bodies slammed into Kane, nearly bowling him off his feet, fetching him up hard against the wall. The quarters were too confined to safely hose bullets around without hitting one of his own people, so he used the Sin Eater as a bludgeon, clubbing away taloned hands clawing for the unprotected portion of his face.

Lit by the Nighthawk microlights, the battle in the

corridor took on an unreal, almost hallucinatory quality.

The scalies were armed with crude spears made of sharpened steel rods, poleaxes and daggers forged from metal shards. They stabbed and thrust at the human interlopers, howling and hissing in liquid fury. Kane felt the impacts on the breastplate of his armor as if multiple fingers poked him repeatedly.

Gyatso swung his short sword in a fast, glittering arc, wheeling on the balls of his feet. The blade slashed through scaled throats, plunged into bellies, withdrew to chop at arms and hands. A keening cry issued from his lips.

Using the wall at his back as a brace, Kane kicked out, sending a scalie sprawling into one of its comrades. Taking advantage of the momentary respite, he shoved the Sin Eater back into its holster and reached down for the combat knife in its boot scabbard. His fingers pressed the quick-release button, and he whipped up the long blade just in time to parry a spear thrusting for his face. His knife whirled down to strike the shoulder of his attacker, gashing the chest and driving the hissing monster back.

The same strategy occurred to Grant when he found himself backed to the wall. He leathered his Sin Eater, drew his knife and leaped to the attack even as a dagger point raked along his ribs. He was no defensive fighter. Even in the teeth of overwhelming odds, Grant always carried the battle to the enemy.

His blade chopped out and dropped a scalie, severing a shoulder, while a whistling backhand stroke sank into the skull of another. The scalies crowded him fiercely, raining blows blindly but hampered by their own numbers and lack of strategy.

Domi was reluctant to holster her Combat Master, but she drew her long serrated knife, the one with which she had cut Guana Teague's throat. She sank the point into an arm. She used the blaster barrel to block blows whistling her way. Metal clashed loudly against metal, blue sparks briefly lighting up the darkness. She moved in a blur of speed, dodging, ducking and sidestepping. She slashed the blade in a flat arc, the point tearing through the tough flesh of a scalie's forehead. It uttered a croak of horror as blood rivered into its eyes. As it lifted its hands to staunch the flow, she drove the knife halfway to the hilt into the side of its throat.

Brigid drew her own blade, a Sykes-Fairbairn commando dagger, but it was slapped down by a thrust from a poleax. The blunt end of the shaft rammed into her stomach, and the air shot from her lungs and tears sprang to her eyes. She allowed herself to fall forward against her assailant, smelling the musty reek of its muscular, scale-covered body. As she fell, she stabbed savagely with the dagger, feeling the point meet a second of resistance before sinking deep into yielding flesh. The howl of surprised pain bursting from the scalie's throat nearly deafened her. Hissing and snapping, her foe fell atop her, bearing her to the floor.

Shu lashed out with the key-shaped cudgel, the heavy iron crashing against a skull and shattering it. The scalie yelped, hands clasped to the bleeding split in its scalp and bone, then fell to the floor and rolled in agony.

He struck another stickie with his iron key, smashing it into the mutie's temple. The creature's blood and brains spattered in its face.

Trai wielded the AK like a quarter-staff, blocking knife thrusts on the wooden stock and driving the butt full into faces, breaking noses and teeth, fighting as savagely as the muties.

Only Grigori Zakat did not resort to a weapon other than his firearm. He squeezed off shot after shot, always striking a scaled target. Kane caught fragmented glimpses of him moving swiftly and skillfully, weaving and dodging all blows that came his way.

A crude knife blade flicked out of the shadows, caught the gun and knocked it from the Russian's hand. Zakat skipped to one side, avoiding the sharp point, and his arms whipped out, trapping a scalie's head between them, one at the neck, the other at the rear of the skull. Zakat performed an odd twisting and sliding dance step. The mushy snapping of bone was easily audible even over the cacophony of grunts and growls. When Zakat's hands relaxed their grip, the scalie sprawled motionless to the floor.

Kane's knife ripped open a belly, but he took a hammer blow across his shoulders, which nearly drove him to his knees. A spearhead jammed hard into his solar plexus. He latched on to a scaled wrist and kicked the mutie's kneecap loose with the metal-reinforced toe of his boot.

Screaming and plucking at its leg, the scalie fell into the path of two muties. All three went down in a tangle of thrashing limbs. As one of them tried to get up, Kane kicked it in the head as hard as he could.

A hand clapped onto the back of his neck, and he whirled, his razor-edge blade slashing in a flat arc.

The shock of impact jarred up his right arm into the shoulder, and a scalie reeled away, hands at its deeply gashed throat, blood bubbles bursting on its lips and squirting from between its fingers. Crimson droplets splashed over Kane's visor, obscuring his vision.

Back and forth, the battle rolled, blades slashing and chopping, scarlet streams spurting, fanged mouths screaming, feet stamping the fallen underfoot.

Finally, the scalies engaged in a reluctant, stubborn retreat, snarling and spitting in rage. The wounded backed away, whining. Many mutie bodies lay on the floor in widening pools of blood. Blood splattered the walls, smeared the floor and almost everybody in the corridor. Only Zakat seemed untouched. With Grant's help, Brigid heaved the heavy body of the dead scalie away and sprang to her feet.

Now that there were fewer muties to crowd around and impede each other, the danger for the humans was greater. There was room for the scalies to throw knives and their crude spears.

One of the withdrawing scalies drew its arm back, but the red kill dot projected from the laser auto-targeter of Grant's Copperhead bloomed on his chest. A ripping triburst stitched holes in its torso, slapping the mutie backward, the knife clanging to the floor.

"Let's go," Kane husked out, starting a shambling run down the corridor. He unlimbered the Copperhead from his belt and stroked the trigger, directing a prolonged burst into the murk ahead of him, not certain if any of the 4.85 mm steel-jacketed rounds found targets. Ricochets whined and buzzed like angry insects.

Guttural voices bellowed behind them, and he heard the others begin sprinting after him, following his lead. Ahead of them glimmered a faint wedge of light, briefly limning the scuttling figures of the fleeing scalies.

Kane palmed away the blood spatters on his visor and increased his speed, not wanting to give the muties time to stage another ambush. He heard a smacking thud behind him and he risked a quick over-the-shoulder glance. Shu stumbled forward, clawing at the three-foot-long rod of rusty metal sprouting between his shoulder blades. He hit the floor heavily on his face, making no attempt to break his fall.

The girl, Trai, slowed her pace a trifle, but Zakat's clipped voice blurted a string of syllables and she began running again, ignoring the impaled Shu.

The wedge of dim light was another archway, and when Kane sprinted under it, he saw four scalies dashing pell-mell for the stairwell that led to the upper level. The corridor branch he had chosen evidently angled around the below-ground floor, ending on the opposite side of the exhibit hall.

Zakat caught up to him. He had taken the AK from Trai and cradled its knife-nicked stock in his arms. "We must not allow the misbegotten lizards to gain the high ground," he panted.

Kane wheezed, "My thoughts exactly."

Zakat triggered the AK as he ran, shifting the barrel in short left-to-right sweeps. Flinders of stone exploded from the stairwell's balustrade, and bullets punched a series of dark holes in the back of one of

the scalies. Flinging up its arms, it staggered for a
few feet before falling facedown at the foot of the
stairway.

Bleating in fear, the other three muties bounded
over the body and took the stairs two at a time. Zakat
and Kane reached the base just as the scalies struggled
to squeeze past the massive head of the blue whale,
forced to climb the steps in single file.

The two men opened up at the same time, the
drumming roar of the AK-47 drowning out the silenced reports of the Copperhead. There was nothing
silent about the reactions of the scalies as the double
hailstorm of lead battered them.

They screamed, jerked, flailed and spasmed. Blood
and brain matter sprayed the sleek surface of the
whale, and its pale blue surface acquired several
punctures from wild bullets.

The trio of muties slammed down on the stone risers and, after a few twitches, made no further movement.

Gusting out a sigh, then inhaling, Kane coughed
from the acrid cordite fumes. He turned to face the
panting Grant, Brigid, Domi, Trai and Gyatso. All
were daubed with liquid crimson, but it was impossible to differentiate scalie blood from their own.

He asked, "Is everyone all right?"

All but Gyatso and Trai responded with affirma-
tives. The girl eased past them to stand beside Zakat,
looking up at him in adoration.

Grant hooked a thumb over his shoulder. "I don't
think we're being followed, but they can always circle
back around through the hall of minerals and come
up behind us again."

Before Kane could respond, Zakat announced, "In that case, I suggest our truce continue until we reach the gateway installation. There may be a mob of the monsters waiting to waylay us on the streets."

Kane nodded tersely. "Only until then."

Zakat started up the steps, but Kane restrained him. "I'll walk point."

The Russian smiled thinly. "As you wish, Comrade."

Kane went first, followed by Zakat and his party. Grant brought up the rear, continually checking their backtrack out of habit. There were no signs or sounds of muties who may have regained their courage.

To get past the whale, Kane had to step on the bullet-riddled corpses of the scalies, and blood squished loudly beneath his feet. Zakat's shoulders heaved in an exaggerated, theatrical shudder as he crossed them, murmuring, "Filthy, wretched things."

At the top of the stairwell, they waited for the others to join them. As Brigid struggled over the bodies, one hand on the whale and the other on the balustrade, Kane said to Zakat, "Since you didn't know what happened to Sverdlovosk, I'm assuming the Mongols weren't answering any of Russia's questions."

"You assume correctly," Zakat replied smoothly.

Then, in an eye-blurring burst of speed and coordination, he whipped up the stock of the AK autorifle, crashing it into the side of Kane's jaw.

Chapter 18

The brain-jarring impact of the unexpected blow caused Kane's surroundings to wink out for an instant.

When they returned, he became aware of two things more or less simultaneously: a sickening pain in his head and the realization he was falling down the stairs, his back bumping violently against the risers. The cut on the tender lining of his cheek filled his mouth with blood.

He heard Brigid cry out a nanosecond before he caromed into her. She clawed out for the balustrade and managed to keep her footing, but Domi wasn't so fortunate. He clipped her ankles with his head and sent her tumbling over the corpses of the scalies. She uttered a piercing shriek of anger and fear as she fell.

Kane heard the staccato stuttering of the AK-47 and he frantically tried to bring his Copperhead to bear. No bullets came near him, however. He heard semimusical twangs, as of giant guitar strings being plucked, then a pair of whiplike cracks.

He had a fragmented glimpse of Zakat, Trai and Gyatso at the head of the stairwell, right before the vast body of the blue whale began a roaring tobogganing slide down the granite steps.

The Russian had shot away the leviathan's few remaining support cables, and it cannonaded down the stairwell like a runaway locomotive. Kane pressed his body tightly against the stone pedestals of the balustrade, and a giant fin missed his head by a finger's width.

The whale rocked slightly from side to side, its pale underbelly bouncing off each riser with nerve-racking screeches. It rumbled past Kane and Brigid, then its snout smashed into the floor below with a hollow thunderclap.

Kane elbowed himself to his feet, glanced toward Brigid to make sure she was all right, then looked down the stairwell. Over the rolling echoes of the crash, he faintly heard a voice lifted in mocking laughter and Zakat calling out, *"Dasvidanya, idiotisch!"*

The passage of the gigantic whale body and its impact had raised flat planes of dust, and Kane didn't see either Domi or Grant. Torn between running up the stairs after Zakat or running down to check on his team, he spit out blood then called, "Grant! Domi!"

For a long moment, he heard nothing. Then, in a voice tight with strain, high and wild with fear, Domi cried, "Help him!"

Spitting out more blood and a curse, Kane lunged down the steps, Brigid on his heels. He followed the streamlined contours of the blue whale and cautiously approached the massive head. Domi, a white wraith in the murk, lifted a tear-wet face and repeated in a forlorn whimper, "Help him."

Icy fingers of fear seized Kane's heart. Domi knelt beside Grant, trying to cradle his head in her lap, which was all that was visible of him beneath the sweeping, furrowed curve of the whale's underjaw.

Grant was in a great deal of pain and as angry as Kane had ever seen him, which probably kept him conscious.

"Do you fucking believe this?" he raged through mashed and bloody lips. "I'm probably the first bastard in three hundred years to be crushed by a whale!"

"You're not crushed," Kane told him, kneeling down, although he had no way of knowing. "Maybe a little compressed."

The preserved carcass of the animal had caught Grant broadside, steamrollering him down the stairs. The weight of the whale had to be gauged in tons and if Grant hadn't been wearing his armor, he most definitely would have been crushed. Only his left arm and his head were free. Domi, on the verge of hysterics, tried to hold him up. Neither Brigid nor Kane had ever witnessed such an emotional reaction in her, not even when she learned the grisly fate of her people in Hell's Canyon some months back.

Out of the corner of his eye, Kane saw Brigid kneading her midsection and grimacing. "You sure you're all right?"

She nodded. "More or less. You?"

Kane gingerly probed the laceration on the inside of his cheek with his tongue. The bleeding seemed to be tapering off, but his facial muscles throbbed fiercely. "More or less."

To Grant, he said, "Don't go anywhere."

He and Brigid hunted through the lower levels for anything they could improvise as a fulcrum. After what seemed like a maddeningly long time, they came across a storage room holding the remains of some long-ago and forgotten construction project: disassembled scaffolding, concrete blocks, sturdy planks and timbers.

They had to make two trips, staggering under the weight of a square timber and several concrete blocks, alert for any sign of scalies who might have lingered.

Balancing the wooden beam on a concrete block, Kane jammed and worked and nudged one end beneath the whale's jaw, as close to Grant as he could manage. Brigid combined her strength and weight with Kane's on the timber. After a long moment of grunting exertion, they were able to lever up the whale's head just far enough for Domi to shove in a concrete block to act as support. Grant swore, wrestled, strained and managed to free his right arm.

"Can you feel your legs?" Brigid asked him, green eyes bright with worry.

"Yeah," he rasped. "They hurt like hell."

"That's a good sign," said Kane.

"I know," Grant snarled. "That's why I'm so goddamn happy at the moment."

Kane stated, "Domi, Baptiste, I'll need you to work the timber while I try to pull him out. Neither one of you are strong enough for that."

They acknowledged his instructions with grim nods. Domi took Kane's place at the fulcrum as he stooped over Grant, securing firm grips on his forearms. Grant clasped him about the wrists.

"I'm going to pull hard," Kane warned. "If it starts to hurt too much, sing out."

He knew Grant wouldn't, even if he experienced

the agony of the damned, but he figured he'd give the man the option.

Kane counted backward from three, bracing his legs, planting his feet solidly. At his shouted "One!" Domi and Brigid hurled their bodies against and over the timber. With a creak of wood and grate of stone, the whale's jaw shifted upward.

Kane catapulted backward. For an eternal moment, he strained against Grant, muscles quivering with tension. Adrenaline surged through him, and with a scraping, slithery sound Grant slid free. Kane saw he used his left leg to kick himself out from under the pinioning weight, so he wasn't paralyzed.

Breath coming in harsh, labored gasps, Grant hiked himself up to a sitting position and took off his helmet. Perspiration sparkled against his dark skin. His lips were swollen and lacerated, but only a cut at the corner of his mouth looked deep enough to require stitches.

Brigid examined his legs as best she could through the polycarbonate sheathing. She guessed the right ankle was broken and suggested removing his boot.

Grant took a sip from the water bottle Domi handed to him and shook his head. "Big neg on that. You'd have to have cut it off. With the metal bracings in it, it's the next best thing to a splint."

He washed down a painkiller, coughed and winced. "Pain in my chest. Hurts when I breathe too deep or swallow."

"Cracked ribs maybe," Kane said. "You got off lucky, though."

"Why is it," Grant asked between clenched teeth, "that whenever I get hurt, you always tell me that?"

Kane tried to grin, despite the pain in his jaw. "I just don't want you to feel sorry for yourself."

Domi dabbed at the blood streaking Grant's chin with a square of gauze taken from the equipment case. "Got to get out of here before sundown. Muties may come back with reinforcements."

Brigid cast an anxious glance up the stairwell. "It won't be easy getting out of here."

"Hell," Kane snapped, "what is?"

She ignored the observation. "One or two of us could make it back to the gateway. Go back to Cerberus and return with DeFore and a stretcher."

"That could take hours," Grant said. "By then, we could be contending with an army of scalies. Let's just go."

With Domi's and Brigid's help, Grant rose to his feet. He draped an arm over Kane's shoulders, leaning into him, balancing on his left foot.

"Just like old times," Kane grunted as Grant sagged into him. "Except you've put on weight since then. I hope I'm in shape for this."

Grant understood the reference to the time a dozen years ago when he had been wounded in the Great Sand Dunes hellzone and Kane had lugged him for days through appallingly rugged terrain.

Sarcastically, he replied, "If it starts to hurt too much, sing out."

Climbing the staircase wasn't quite the ordeal Kane had feared. The risers were broad, not particularly high, and Grant was able to relieve him some of the burden by bracing one arm against the balustrade. Though they staggered and swayed a bit, they managed to make it to the top without falling or stopping for a rest.

They shuffled through the vast exhibit halls. Domi took the point while Brigid walked beside Grant and Kane, steadying them.

"Did the Russian and his crew make off with the rock?" Grant asked.

"Afraid so," Kane answered curtly, boots crunching loudly on shards of glass.

"You should've gone after them," Grant said reproachfully. "I would've been all right."

"Now you tell me," Kane retorted. "Fuck it. If Balam wants that rock so much, he can go after it himself."

By the time they reached the museum entrance, the pewter-colored sky had darkened to the hue of old lead.

"If we're really lucky," Brigid commented dourly, "we'll get back to the installation just as the sun goes down."

They weren't lucky. Fighting through the tangled green hell of Central Park was slow, exhausting work. Thorny vines constantly snared Kane's legs, and twice he nearly tripped and dropped Grant. After they made their way through the park, they were forced to stop and rest for ten minutes.

Despite the pain pill Grant had taken, he winced constantly and was barely able to bite back groans. Brigid and Domi took turns supplementing the support Kane provided for him, although he protested, claiming two blasters were needed to adequately cover the zone. However, only once did they catch sight of a darting, indistinct figure that might have been a scalie. It maintained a safe distance from them. They came across the corpses of Chu and the scalie still lying in the street. The scream-wings had stripped almost all the flesh from them, and it was impossible to tell by the bloody, skeletal carcasses which had been mutie or human.

By the time the jagged tops of the World Trade Center came into view, full night had fallen. Nearly two hours had passed since they left the museum. All four people were too tense and weary to celebrate. The scalie Domi had shot floated in a pool of drying blood in the parking garage.

"About there," she chirped, striving to sound cheerful.

Kane glared at her. His legs wobbled, his jaw throbbed and his shoulders and back ached with a constant, bone-deep pain.

"Another one-percenter to add to our scorecard," Grant husked out faintly. "That's something."

WITHIN MINUTES of rematerializing in the Cerberus jump chamber, Grant was wheeled off in a gurney to the dispensary. Domi ignored all of DeFore's instructions to remain behind. She distrusted the "fat-assed doctor lady," as she referred to DeFore, because she suspected the older woman had designs on Grant.

Lakesh was full of questions, and his seamed face collapsed into a scowl of disappointment and anger when Kane tendered his report.

"So," he said, his reedy voice pitched low, "you got nothing but hurt?"

Brigid removed the imaging scanner's hard disk from her coat pocket and handed it to him. "We can find out where Zakat and his people came from and jumped from, at least.''

Lakesh said nothing, but judging by the set of his lips, he didn't think the disk was much of a prize.

Kane tugged off his helmet and fingered the swelling at his jaw hinge. ''When Balam mentioned a thief, he didn't mention that he was a District Twelve officer. A professional.''

Lakesh peered at him over the rims of his eyeglasses. ''You said he was in the company of Asians?''

''And one hybrid, as far as I could tell.''

Lakesh blinked in surprise. ''A hybrid?''

Brigid nodded. ''I didn't have the chance to get a really good look at him, but he had all the primary physical characteristics.''

''More than that,'' interjected Kane, ''he claimed his name was Gyatso Chohan, direct descendant of the Maha Chohan, the Agarthan ambassador.''

Both Brigid and Lakesh stared at him in astonishment. Brigid was the first to recover sufficiently to speak. ''Then there could be a direct link between the Chintamani Stone, Agartha and the Archon Directorate.''

''Which means,'' Kane declared coldly, ''Balam isn't telling us everything he knows about the stone— which should come as no great surprise.''

Lakesh shook his head in furious negation. ''You don't seriously suspect Balam sent you into a trap, do you?''

''At this point, I seriously suspect everything Balam told us—or didn't tell us, particularly about a hybrid with a connection to this Agartha place.''

"The only way to settle the matter," Brigid said crisply, "is to question Balam. Do you think Banks feels up to another ventriloquism session?"

Kane eyed Brigid's face, which was crusted with speckles of scalie blood. "Whether he is or isn't, I know I don't feel up to it at the moment. We should clean up before we do anything."

Lakesh slapped the hard disk against the palm of one hand. "And I should trace the jump line used by Zakat and his people. Let's meet at Balam's holding facility in an hour or so."

Kane and Brigid crossed the control complex to the main corridor. Since the rad counters registered negligible levels of radiation, they saw no need to visit decam. Kane said to her quietly, "You handled yourself well back there, Baptiste."

Dryly, she replied, "If I hadn't, I'd be dead. Later I'll have a nice case of delayed reactions."

"I'll slap you if you really need it."

She turned a bend in the corridor, heading toward her quarters. "And I'll do the same for you."

Kane went to his own suite of rooms, shucked out of his armor and took a long, hot shower. After pulling on the one-piece white bodysuit, he took ice from his small refrigerator, wrapped it in a towel and applied it to the side of his face. He sat down and tried not to dwell on dark thoughts, but they crowded into his mind. It was always difficult to reconcile the present with the past.

Shortly after skydark, a group of families who had taken measures to survive a nukecaust and its resulting horrors emerged from their shelters, their caves, their refuges. The North American continent was now the Deathlands, but they believed they had inherited it by divine right—they had survived when most others had not.

The families and their descendants spread out and divided the country into little territories, much like old Europe when it had been ruled over by princes and barons. Though the physical world was vastly changed, they were determined to bend it to their wills, to control it and the few people still struggling to live upon it.

At first the families half-jokingly referred to themselves as barons, but as the years crawled by, the title no longer had a fictitious origin. The families instituted a tradition and bestowed upon their descendants the title of baron, and the territories they conquered became baronies. Though these territories offered a certain amount of sanctuary from the anarchy of outlying regions, they also offered little freedom. In the beginning, people retreated into the villes ruled by the barons for protection, then as the decades went by, they remained because they had no choice. Generations of Americans were born into serfdom, slaves in everything but name.

After nearly 150 years of barbarism and anarchy, humankind reorganized, coalescing from the ruins of the predark societal structures. Many of the most powerful, most enduring baronies evolved into city-states, walled fortresses whose influence stretched across the Deathlands for hundreds of miles.

In decades past, the barons had warred against one another, each struggling for control and absolute power over territory. Then they realized that greater rewards were possible if unity was achieved and common purpose exploited.

Territories were redefined, treaties struck among the barons, and the city-states became interconnected points in a continent-spanning network. The Program of Reunification was ratified and ruthlessly imposed. The reconstructed form of government was still basically despotic, but now it was institutionalized and shared by all the formerly independent baronies.

Control of the continent was divided among the nine baronies that survived the long wars over territorial expansion and resources. With this forward step in social engineering came technical advances. Technology, most of it based on predark designs, appeared mysteriously and simultaneously with the beginning of the reunification program. There was much speculation at the time that many previously unknown stockpiles were opened up and their contents distributed evenly among the barons. Though the technologies were restricted for the use of those who held the reins of power, life overall improved for the citizens in and around the villes. To enjoy the bounty offered by the barons, all anyone had to do was to first accept responsibility and then to surrender it.

It had all seemed so simple. Irresponsible humanity had allowed their world to be destroyed by the irresponsible people they had put in charge; therefore humanity would no longer be permitted to have responsibility, even over their own lives. The barons accepted the responsibility, or rather had it ceded to them.

The populations of the villes and the surrounding Outlands cooperated with this tyranny because of a justified fear and an unjustified guilt. For the past eighty years, it had been bred into the people that Judgment Day had arrived and humanity had been rightly punished. The doctrines expressed in ville teachings encouraged humanity to endure a continuous punishment before a utopian age could be ushered in. Because humanity had ruined the world, the punishment was deserved. The doctrines ultimately amounted to extortion—obey and suffer or disobey and die.

The dogma was elegant in its simplicity, and for most of his life, Kane had believed it, had dedicated his life to serving it. Then he stumbled over a few troubling questions, and when he attempted to find the answers, all he discovered were many more troubling questions.

However, the most important question, the guiding mystery of his life was to learn who—or what—was actually responsible for the nukecaust and for implanting these mistaken beliefs in humanity.

Intellectually, he knew all the conditioning was a sham, psychological warfare practiced on a national scale. Dealing emotionally with the realization was a different matter altogether. Breaking away from a lifetime of indoctrination, of believing in certain things in certain ways, sometimes seemed an insurmountable problem.

Conditioning.

Kane turned the word over in his mind a few times, then removed the ice pack. His jaw was numb, but the swelling had been reduced. He left his quarters and walked to the dispensary.

Grant lay on one of the beds within a screened

partition. DeFore hovered over him, elevating his right leg. It was swathed in bandages and encased in a metal splint from instep to knee. An IV drip was attached to a shunt on the inside of his left elbow. Black stitches showed at the corner of his mouth. Domi stood at the head of the bed, crusted blood showing stark against her white face.

"What's the diagnosis?" he asked, attempting a bantering tone.

He had directed the question at Grant, but DeFore answered curtly, "A closed fracture of the tibia and talus bones. A number of strained ligaments, abrasions and some internal bruising."

DeFore, a stocky, buxom woman with bronze skin, ash-blond hair and deep brown eyes, made no secret of her dislike of Kane—or rather, her distrust of him. In her medical opinion, he displayed unstable tendencies and exhibited symptoms of post-traumatic stress syndrome. In the recent past, she had tried to order Kane confined to the redoubt so he could be treated, but she had been overruled.

"And the prognosis?" he inquired, this time asking her directly.

Grant answered before she could. "At least a week flat on my back."

"Could be worse," remarked Kane. "Not everybody who's gone one-on-one with a blue whale got off so lucky."

"I'll chill that scrawny Russkie rat-bastard next time I see him," Domi asserted fiercely. "Big time."

"You'll have to get in line," Grant rumbled.

DeFore finished propping pillows beneath Grant's leg and turned to face Kane, full lips pursed in disapproval. "Thanks for bringing me another casualty, Kane."

"Don't start," Grant said sharply. "This wasn't his fault. Blame Lakesh for buying into Balam's wild-rock chase."

DeFore looked to be on the verge of saying more, but she addressed Domi. "You need to clean up. We don't know that scalie blood might not have toxic bacteria swimming around in it."

Domi glowered at her, but Grant side-mouthed to her, "Do as she says or you'll be on the receiving end of a sponge bath."

The girl reluctantly moved away from the bedside. Grant met Kane's eyes. "You figure what happened was part of Balam's plan to get us chilled?"

"I don't know. I doubt it. I *do* figure he knows more about all of this than he let on. I intend to get the answers out of him."

Grant snorted scornfully. "What makes you think he'll be straight with you the next time?"

Kane showed the edges of his teeth in a hard, humorless grin. "Because next time, I'm making the rules."

Chapter 19

Kane, Banks, Lakesh and Brigid stood before the glass walls of Balam's cell. All eyes were fixed on Kane, and they reflected incredulity and skepticism in equal measure.

"No," Lakesh declared, shaking his head vehemently. "Absolutely not. I forbid it."

Kane bristled at Lakesh's autocratic tone, but he kept his anger in check. "I'm not suggesting this for the hell of it. We've got to try a new approach in dealing with Balam. We all troop in here like we're requesting an audience with a goddamn baron, communicating through a second party while he's safe and smug behind glass. He won't even allow us a good look at him."

"He's a prisoner," Banks protested.

"But he doesn't act like one," Kane countered, "and most of the time he's not treated like one. You in particular treat him like a foreign dignitary or a diplomatic envoy instead of what he really is—an arrogant, conniving, inhuman monster who wants something from us."

Although her expression showed doubt, Brigid said, "You've got a point. The only time we've ever achieved any kind of exchange was when you behaved disrespectfully toward him."

Lakesh squinted toward the cell, swallowing hard. "But to release him after all this time...it's dangerous."

"That's what he's conditioned us to believe," Kane declared. "Psy-war tactics, just like the conditioning perpetrated by the unification program. We know now it was all bullshit, nothing but control mechanisms. That's what I think Balam's standard 'we stand, we know, we are' message is.

"He's been a prisoner here for over three years. That's the hard reality. We can keep him here forever or let him go. We have the power to do that. Not him. Past time we let him in on that fact."

No one spoke, but they eyed each other questioningly, nervously.

"We've got to knock him off his pedestal," Kane argued. "Stop segregating him from the apekin. Prove to him once and for all who is the prisoner and who are the warders. If he wants favors from the warders, then he's got to give something in return. Like the truth."

Brigid clicked her tongue absently against her teeth, swiveling her head to stare at the red gloom within the recesses of the cell.

Contemplatively, she murmured, "You're right. We did what he asked us to do and nearly got killed. If he had told us a hybrid was involved, we could have taken measures."

"Maybe he didn't know a hybrid was involved," Banks protested, though he didn't sound convinced of his own words.

"You told us he had an extreme reaction to Baron Ragnar's assassination," Brigid reminded him. "That proves the existence of a mind-link between Archons and hybrids.''

Banks shrugged. Kane gazed levelly at Lakesh. ''Well?''

The old man sighed and tugged at his long nose. ''I don't know. I simply don't know. I traced the jump line Zakat and his people used. The transit path didn't track back to Russia but originated from an unindexed unit, not part of the Cerberus network.''

''Did you get a fix on the unit?'' Brigid asked.

''Tibet, somewhere in the Himalayas. By cross-referencing the coordinates with the geographical database, it locked in on the Byang-thang Plateau.''

''The Byang-thang Plateau?'' echoed Kane, stumbling over the pronunciation. ''What the hell is there?''

''An old Russian or Chinese military installation, perhaps.''

''Or,'' Brigid ventured, ''the Trasilunpo lamasary I found mentioned in the historical records—the same lamasery where the Chintamani Stone was reputedly sheltered. A modular gateway unit could have been installed there before the nuke.''

Lakesh nodded. ''I considered the same thing. The autosequencer shows a live transit line, so our unit can lock in on it.''

Kane's lips compressed. ''Waste of time.''

Lakesh looked at him quizzically. ''Why so?''

''Because none of us will be following that line unless you agree to release Balam.''

The old man's blue eyes flashed with sparks of anger. ''Blackmail is beneath you, friend Kane.''

''It's not blackmail, it's negotiation. You want

something from me, I want something from Balam, Balam wants something from us. We all get something or nobody gets anything.''

Lakesh scowled ferociously, but Kane maintained a composed, neutral expression. He noticed Brigid doing her best to repress a smile.

Kane guessed the kind of thoughts wheeling through Lakesh's mind. The cooperation among the Cerberus exiles was by agreement; there was no formal oath or vows like those he and Grant had taken upon admission into the Magistrate Division. There was no system of penalties or punishments if cooperation was withheld, nor was there a hard and fast system of government within its vanadium walls.

There were security protocols to be observed, certain assigned duties that had to be performed, but anything other than that was a matter of persuasion and volunteerism. Lakesh really didn't have the power to forbid anyone to do anything, so Kane had him over the proverbial barrel and he wasn't ashamed of it.

Finally, Lakesh spit a wordless utterance of frustrated disgust and gestured toward the control console. ''Do it, Banks. Open the cell.''

Banks opened his mouth as if he were about to protest, closed it and stepped over to the panel. He touched a knob, and the overhead lights dimmed to dusk level. ''We don't want to cause him discomfort.''

''Like hell we don't,'' Kane snapped. ''Bring them up a bit more—not enough so he's blinded, but enough so we can get a good look at him for once.''

Banks hesitated. Dolefully, he said, ''Has it occurred to you that we may be doing exactly what

Balam wants us to do? Maybe he implanted this suggestion in your mind so he can escape."

Kane thought that possibility over for a few seconds. "If the little bastard can get through all of us, out of this locked room and somehow out of the redoubt, then he's more than welcome to escape. Good riddance to a bad alien."

As Banks manipulated the knob again, the lights brightened. He reached out to a row of keys on the console and depressed three of them in a certain sequence. Electronic chimes rang from the vicinity of Balam's cell, then one entire pane slowly rose, sliding into a double-slotted frame. A puff of air wafted out, carrying with it the faint scent of wet cardboard sprinkled lightly with cinnamon and bleach. The mingled odors weren't repulsive, but they were certainly odd.

Facing the open portal, Kane announced loudly, "Recess time, you little hell-spawn. After three and a half years, you should be happy to stretch your legs."

Nothing stirred or shifted within the gloom of the cell. Kane took a threatening step forward. Sharply, he commanded, "Come out or I'll drag you out."

He half expected his mind to be clouded by the quasi-hypnotic mist that Balam projected to mask his true appearance. Instead, he heard a soft footfall, then another and another. A figure loomed in the crimson-hued murk, stepped to the open portal and paused, looking around curiously.

Always before, Kane had received only a fleeting impression of Balam's physical appearance, and then it was overshadowed by an image of his huge, penetrating eyes. He sensed Brigid tensing beside him.

She had seen the mummified remains of an Archon

in the Black Gobi, and both of them had encountered a horde of hybrids at the Dulce installation. They had been shown the preserved corpse of an Annunaki, purportedly the root race of the Archons. There had been a suggestion of the monstrous about all of them.

Balam did not resemble a monstrosity. He reminded Kane of a work of art, as crafted by a minimalist sculptor. He was very short, barely four feet tall, and excessively slender, his body like that of a half-grown boy.

He wore a dark, tight-fitting suit of a nonreflective metallic weave. The one-piece garment covered him from throat to toes, leaving only his hands and head bare.

His high, domed cranium narrowed down to an elongated chin. His skin bore a faint grayish pink cast, stretched drum tight over a structure of facial bones that seemed all cheek and brow, with little in between but two great upslanting eyes like black pools. His nose was vestigial and his small mouth only a tight, lipless slash. Six long, spidery fingers, all nearly the same length, dangled at the ends of his slim arms.

"Polydactyl," Brigid murmured.

"What's that?" asked Kane.

"An extra digit on his hands, probably his feet, too."

Balam stood swaying like a reed before a breeze. Kane had seen the movement before, when the hybrids in Dulce addressed Baron Cobalt. He had guessed it was a form of ritual greeting.

Kane stepped closer, close enough to be aware of Balam as a living creature, smelling his unearthly, musky perfume. He saw the faint rise and fall of respiration and the tiny pores in his finely textured skin.

The huge, tear-shaped dark eyes regarded him, alert but not frightened. Thin membranes with a faint crisscrossing pattern of blue veins veiled them for an instant. Balam breathed, moved, blinked and reacted to his presence.

Kane gestured grandly. "No need to stand on ceremony. Join the apekin in our jungle."

Balam stepped into the room with the same kind of bizarrely beautiful danceresque grace possessed by the hybrids. He didn't seem intimidated, even by the three humans towering over him. He looked around, and his slit of a mouth parted. A sound issued from it, faint, hoarse, but far deeper in timbre than any of them expected.

Balam asked, "Why?"

"SO YOU *CAN* SPEAK," Kane declared, smiling mockingly. "Why were you using Banks here as your mouthpiece?"

One of Balam's bony fingers unfolded, touching the base of his throat. "Difficult," he said in a scratchy, strained whisper. "Structure here different. Verbalizing thoughts difficult."

"Atrophied vocal cords?" Lakesh murmured.

Banks dragged a stool over. "Do you want to sit?"

Balam shook his head. Again he rasped, "Why?"

"Because you're no longer of value as a captive," Kane replied flatly. "Or a hostage. It doesn't seem like the Directorate knows you're here. And if they do know, they don't care."

"You..." Balam paused to cough, a shockingly human sound. "You set me free?"

Kane eyed him coldly. "Not yet. But if we did, where would you go?"

Balam responded to the question with one of his own. "Stone...did you find stone?"

"We found it, but we didn't recover it," Brigid stated. "And here's why."

She launched into a terse, blow-by-blow recounting of the events in New York. Balam's placid, masklike countenance didn't alter. Kane wondered if it could.

"A hybrid was one of the thieves," Kane said. "He claimed descent from the Agarthan ambassador. What do you know about that?"

Balam only blinked.

"This is all tied up with the Archon Directorate, isn't it?" Kane pressed, a note of anger apparent in his voice. "What's it about?"

"You must get stone, Kay-nuh."

"Why must he?" Lakesh asked.

"Key," Balam replied. "Key to all futures. Key to all our destinies."

"*Our* destinies?" Kane repeated derisively. "Humans and Archons share a destiny other than master and slave?"

Balam swallowed hard and painfully. His tissue-thin eyelids dropped over his eyes for a moment, then his fathomless black gaze sought out Banks. He stretched out a beseeching right hand toward him.

"Meld me," he whispered. "So may explain."

"I don't think so," snapped Kane.

"It's my decision," Banks countered. "I'll do it so we can get this over with."

Balam kept his hand out. "Touch. Make meld more strong. Explain more."

At that, Banks's determination wilted a bit, his brow knitting in consternation. But he firmed his lips and stepped forward, reaching with his left hand. Their fingers touched, then intertwined.

"Relax," whispered Balam. "Like before. Empty mind."

Perspiration suddenly sprang to Banks's forehead, then ran down his face in large drops. His lean body quaked in a seizurelike shudder, his sweat-sheened face contorting.

"Banks?" Brigid questioned, putting a hand on his shoulder.

In a barely audible whisper, he said, "Now we may proceed."

Kane saw Balam's lipless mouth move slightly, synchronized with Banks's voice, forming the words he wanted vocalized. The ventriloquist-and-dummy analogy had more foundation than ever before, and it made Kane shiver.

"I was not aware of the new human's presence," Banks-Balam said, voice growing louder and stronger.

Kane quirked an eyebrow, remembering "new human" was Baron Cobalt's choice of euphemisms for the hybrids.

"I sensed only the man you call Zakat because he touched the fragment of the trapezohedron sheltered in the lamasery. He now has two of the pieces, which will lead him to the third and prime facet."

"Which lamasery?" Lakesh demanded.

"You know it as the Trasilunpo in the nation called Tibet."

"You still haven't explained the importance of the stone," challenged Kane. "Or at least why *we* should consider it important."

Banks shifted his gaze toward Lakesh. "*You* know, Mohandas Lakesh Singh. The knowledge is buried within your mind, but you have yet to make the connection."

Lakesh's face acquired a new set of seams. "I see no reason to speak in riddles."

"I described the stone as a creation through which the flux lines of possibility, of probability, of eternity, of *alternity* meet."

Lakesh stared first at Banks, then at Balam in bewilderment. Then his head snapped up, eyebrows crawling above the rims of his glasses, toward his hairline. "The trapezohedron is a point of power, a nontechnological quantum vortex?"

"Vortexes which you once tried to locate and access by technological means."

Brigid demanded, "Are you saying the Chintamani Stone, the trapezohedron is a naturally occurring hyperdimensional vortex point like the one we found in Ireland?"

"It is a key," Banks-Balam stated simply.

Kane thrust his head forward, eyes glittering in predatory anticipation. "A key to the home of the Archons?"

Banks-Balam did not respond for such a long time Kane almost repeated himself. Finally, the soft answer came, "Those you call the Archons cannot be found with any key."

Crossly, Brigid asked, "Why do you keep qualifying every remark about the Archons? What do you call yourselves?"

The word passed the lips of Banks in a rustling whisper. "Humans."

Everyone gaped at Balam in outraged disbelief. Kane snarled, "You're not human, you little son of a bitch. We learned all about you, how you're the result of a cross-breeding program between a reptilian species called the Annunaki and the Tuatha De Danaan—who, though humanoid, weren't human."

The sound that floated from Banks was so unusual, it took them several seconds to recognize it. Balam was forcing Banks to laugh.

"You learned only a small, oversimplified bit of my people's origins, our history, and even that was distorted by myth and legend. But it does not change the fact that the so-called Archons are still human, native to this world.

"Yes, what you believe to be mankind is old, but they were not the first on Earth. My race is far, far older, but it was your folk who so long ago cut the thread that bound us to one another. We had no choice but to draw apart. Far, far apart have we drawn, we who might have shared this world with you but for the slings and swords and spears of your ancestors. We who were not aliens, yet alienated."

Banks-Balam spoke with bitterness, but a note of pride underscored his words. "It is we who gave you the legacy of science and spirit, yet you allowed it to drift into madness."

Kane felt rage building in him, and it required all of his self-control to contain it. "We've heard vari-

ations of this speech before," he said. "We know all
about how your kind raised us from the ape, how
fucking superior you are to us, how you're reducing
us to the ape again. If the stone doesn't lead to the
Archon Directorate, then where can they be found?"

"They cannot be found."

The response came so quickly, Kane felt his nape
hairs prickling with suspicion. "You're lying."

Balam cocked his head at him, a movement that
was reminiscent of a praying mantis trying to figure
out the nature of a new prey. "You have been misled
by your people, trained to think in rigid channels.
They created the Archon Directorate appellation for
the sake of simplicity, to ease clerical chores."

"Are you saying," Brigid ventured haltingly, "that
there is no such thing as the Archon Directorate?"

Banks and Balam shook their heads slightly at the
same time. "This is not the topic of the discussion."

Lakesh suddenly hugged himself, shivering, but not
from fear. His eyes shone with a jubilant light. In a
thrilled whisper, he declared, "The Oz Effect. I was
right. By God, I was right."

"What?" Brigid and Kane demanded in unison.

"A theory I've been toying with. Balam, we know
more about you than you realize. Once there were
many of your kind. You mastered space and hyperdimensional travel aeons ago, probably using the
quantum-pathway technology left by your forebears.
Your people served, either by accident or design and
sometimes both, as the source of myth cycles, religions and secret societies.

"Revelations about your people, our cousins, were
kept hidden for thousands of years. Why? Because

they may have accelerated the spiritual evolution of mankind. But your scientific secrets were doled out piecemeal until humanity's fixation with technology reached critical mass and plunged us into a cataclysm.''

''One of many cataclysms,'' Banks-Balam said softly. ''This last one was the ultimate baptism of fire for humankind to overcome—to forge your spirits in a crucible and have them grow strong or to shatter forever.''

Lakesh acknowledged the observation with a dry chuckle. ''A baptism for your people, as well, wasn't it? A last-ditch solution to the final curtain of extinction.''

The old man took a step forward, bending down, hands on his knees so he could stare unflinching and unblinkingly into Balam's huge eyes. ''Over two hundred years ago, I saw you at the installation in Dulce, New Mexico. Since then, I have learned you acted as the liaison between the American government's Overproject Majestic and the so-called Archon Directorate.

''Before that, you were a guest of the Soviets. They dug you out of the crater at the Tunguska blast where you'd been in cryostasis for thirty-some years when your vessel crashed.''

''What's all that got to do with the home of the Archon Directorate?'' Kane asked, not trying to disguise the angry impatience in his voice.

Lakesh grinned broadly. Without removing his gaze from Balam, he said, ''Friend Kane, dearest Brigid, the Archon Directorate stands before you.''

Chapter 20

Balam's blank face registered no emotion whatsoever, but he jerked his hand free from Banks's grasp as if scalded. The young man gasped, his features squeezing together like a fireplace bellows. He staggered and pressed his fists against his temples, and would have collided with a trestle table if Brigid hadn't caught him.

All of Kane's anger was washed away by icy floodwaters of shock, incredulity and denial. He was too dumbfounded to speak.

Banks steadied himself, massaging the sides of his head. He glared at Balam and said accusingly, "You might have told me you were going to do that."

Lakesh laughed, a harsh sound without mirth. "He might have told us a lot of things."

"Lakesh, you're going to have explain what you mean," Brigid declared.

Lakesh kept his eyes on Balam's. He crooned, "You gave us enough clues to put the puzzle together—I grant you that. Not to mention an equal number of diversions, false trails and pieces that almost fit but didn't quite. But now we know the truth, Balam—you're the only one of your kind. The last Archon, or whatever you prefer to call yourself."

Kane and Brigid were stunned speechless, grappling with the enormous implications of Lakesh's confident assertion.

"The Archon Directorate was protective coloration," he went on, "an art your people were masters of over the long, long track of centuries and civilizations."

Brigid finally found her voice. "You mean the Archon Directorate is only him?" she questioned. "All along, only one of them?"

"At least over the last couple of hundred years." Lakesh's tone held a gloating note. "The Oz Effect, wherein a single, vulnerable entity created the illusion, the myth of an all-powerful force as a means of manipulation and self-protection. My compliments, Balam. Over the last four millennia, you kept the entire human race guessing.

"You allowed us to suspect you were gods, demons, fairies and finally extraterrestrials, always fitting your presence into the current frame of reference. You let us believe you were everything but what you really were—a dying people, racing inexorably to the finish line of extinction.

"That was the reason for the hybridization program, so your people would live on in one form or another, a form you chose. I don't think I'd be too far off the mark to suggest that most, if not every molecule of Archon genetic material in the hybrids derives solely from you.

"Thus, you are both the last of your kind and the father of a new race. A bridge between the old and the new. Hence the reality of the psionic threads supposedly linking all of the so-called Archons to each other and to your half-breed spawn."

Lakesh straightened up swiftly, face flushed, eyes shining brightly. "And for the first time in thousands of years, a race of beings that carry the genetic characteristics of your folk may at last win the game of the survival of the fittest. A contest your people knew they had lost probably twenty thousand years ago."

Kane tried to speak, but he felt numb, dislocated, as if his brain were immersed in soggy cotton wadding. "He—Balam…he's it? He and he alone orchestrated the nukecaust, the unification program, all of it? Just so *his* genes would be the ones in the majority?"

"Every father wants the best opportunities for his children," Lakesh said. "Balam—whether he had hands-on control of events that led up to the nukecaust or not—was simply eliminating the competition. He stacked the deck, and if a few hundred million of us had to die in the process, that was all part of the game."

Kane stared at the fragile creature, recalling all the equally fragile hybrids he had seen. He remembered what Baron Cobalt had told him: "The humanity you know is dead. The new humanity is taking its place. All a matter of natural selection. Nature taking its course…. We are a highly evolved breed, and our numbers are growing…. This is our world now, and nothing can be done to arrest the tide…. Accept our kind as we have accepted *your* kind."

A roaring red madness shredded Kane's soul. He lunged forward, shouldering Lakesh aside, his hands encircled the slim, short column of Balam's throat. His flesh felt slick, but warm with life. Kane snatched

Balam up, swinging his feet clear of the floor. The slender creature weighed no more than a child's doll.

Dimly, he heard Brigid, Banks and Lakesh shouting his name. He squeezed, staring straight into Balam's fathomless eyes, silently daring him to fight for his life. Banks and Brigid latched on to his arms, beating at his wrists, trying to prise his fingers from Balam's neck.

The pain of their blows was drowned in his hatred, so intense it in turn became pain. Kane felt as if his body had turned to steel, and his hate flowed like electrical current out along the line of his vision, pouring into Balam's eyes to shrivel whatever imitation of a soul he possessed.

With appalling suddenness, the expressionless face of Balam dimmed, blurred and all Kane could see were the huge eyes, engulfing everything. First there was an utter blackness, then vague, evanescent shapes wavered within it before taking shape.

Like storm clouds dispersing, the blackness rolled away and Kane saw a huge city of dark stone rising at the base of towering, snowcapped mountain ranges. A massive, round column of white rose from the center of the city, jutting at least three hundred feet into the sky. With a faraway sense of shock, he recognized it as a prototype of the Administrative Monoliths in all of the villes. On a subliminal level, Kane understood the city was more of a symbol, representing many similar settlements scattered over the world.

A thready nonvoice whispered, *This was who we were.*

Kane floated over the buildings, receiving an impression of odd angles and immense green-black blocks. Though the lines of the structures looked simple, they possessed a quality that eluded real comprehension to their size and shape, as if they had been built following architectural principles just slightly apart from those the human brain could absorb.

From the city, silvery disks like polished coins seen edge-on rose and flitted across the sky. Some were very small and delicate, while others were gargantuan spheres, like moons given the power of flight.

Through the streets of the city moved beings cast in the mold of humanity, but they were not human as Kane defined the term. They were dome-skulled, slender creatures, very tall and graceful. Their tranquil eyes were big and opalescent, their flesh tones a pale blue.

Somehow, Kane understood that they were a branch on the mysterious tree of evolution, yet the twigs of humanity sprouted from their bough. In physical appearance, they were as separate and as apart from Balam as humanity was from his Neanderthal progenitors. In spiritual and intellectual development, they were as superior to mankind as a Neanderthal was to an ape.

Kane knew that they existed, much less thrived, as part of a pact between two root races that had warred for possession of Earth. They were a bridge, not only between two races, but flowing within them, mixing with the blood of their nonhuman forebears, was the blood of humanity.

These beings were mortal, though exceptionally long-lived. Like the humanity to which they were genetically connected, they loved and experienced joy and sadness. Their cities were centers of learning, and the citizens didn't suffer from want. They knew no enemies; they had no need to fight for survival. As the end result of a fight for survival between their ancestors, the beings had been born to live on the world of humans and guide them away from the path of war that had nearly destroyed Earth.

Their duty was to keep the ancient secrets of their ancestors alive, yet not propagate the same errors as their forebears, especially in their dealings with mankind, to whom they were inextricably bound.

Humanity was struggling to overcome a global cataclysm, striving again for civilization, and the graceful folk in the cities, the outposts, did what they could to help them rebuild. They insinuated themselves into schools, into political circles, prompting and assisting men into making the right decisions.

They sought out humans of vision, humans with superior traits. They mingled their blood with them, initiated them into their secrets, advised them. On many continents—Mu, Gondawara, Hyberborea, Atlantis—new centers of learning arose, empires and dynasties spread out carrying the seeds of civilization.

The folk had no god, no true deity they worshiped, but they valued a relic, a totem, an oracle. Kane saw it in a vast space. He couldn't see the roof or the walls, but had the impression of an enormous chamber. In front of him, a strange radiance played about an altar made of six sharply cut slabs of stone.

The source of the glow he couldn't see, but on the altar lay a night black, yet shining object. He inspected it from all sides, but its confusing lines looked different from every angle. Its facets were highly polished, and it didn't resemble a stone. It was a sculpture, incorporating much of the same geometric principles as the city itself.

It pulsed with life, yet it wasn't alive. It exuded an immeasurable intelligence, but it wasn't sentient. Kane only vaguely understood its nature. The trapezohedron was the sum-total of all that the root races knew and believed. It was a teacher, a means of communication, a key to parallel casements. Kane wasn't quite certain of what that meant, but it didn't matter. He was only an observer of the panorama of a prosperous, self-satisfied civilization, of the accomplishments of a prideful people who had tamed a savage world.

The trapezohedron wasn't the deity of their civilization, yet it was their heart.

Then, after uncounted years, came the new cataclysms. The magnetic centers shifted, the great glaciers and ice centers at the poles withdrew toward new positions. Vast portions of the ocean floor rose, while equally vast land masses sank beneath the waves. The configuration of the Earth altered.

Convulsions shook mountains and the nights blazed with flame-spouting volcanoes. Earthquakes shook the walls and towers of the city made of green-black stone. Many of the folk died quickly, while others lingered in a state of near death for years. The vast knowledge of their ancestors, the technical achievements bequeathed to them, became their only means of survival.

The survivors consulted the stone, the shining trapezohedron, desperate to find a solution to their tragedy within its black facets. It showed them how to build thresholds to parallel casements. Over the stone appeared what seemed to Kane to be an archway surrounded by fireflies, strung around it in a combination of glimmering colors.

In ages past, the root races had used such thresholds, knowing that Earth was the end of a parallel axis of these casements. Kane only dimly realized what all of it meant, but he understood the basic principles of the mat-trans units were in use, although expanded far beyond linear travel from place to place.

The stone also suggested that they changed themselves with the world, to alter their physiologies. Using ancient techniques, the race transformed itself in order to survive. Muscle tissue became less dense, motor reflexes sharpened, optic capacities broadened. A new range of abilities was developed, which just allowed them to live on a planet whose magnetic fields had changed, whose weather was drastically unpredictable.

Their need for sustenance veered away from the near depleted resources of their environment. They found new means of nourishment other than the ingestion of bulk matter. They had no choice.

The proud, unified race of teachers and artisans degenerated, scattered, a lost tribe skulking in the wilderness. The survivors had no choice but to spread out from the city.

A few of them stayed, trying to adapt, the land changing them before they changed the land. Their physical appearance altered further as they retreated. The changes wrought were subtle, gradual. In adapting themselves to the changing conditions of the planet, they who had been graceful neogods became small, furtive shadow dwellers. Only a handful of the folk remained among the lichen-covered stone walls of their once proud city. The new generations born to them were distortions of what they had been. The weak died before they could produce offspring, and the infant-mortality rate was frightful for a thousand years. They did not leave the ruins to find out how humanity had fared in the aftermath of the changes.

Humankind adapted much faster to the postcatastrophic world, and new generations began to explore, to conquer. They conquered with a vengeance and ruthlessness and spilled oceans of blood. In their explorations, they found their way into the city—men in leather harness, helmets of bronze, bearing bows, spears and swords.

They brought war to the stunted survivors of the catastrophes, viewing them not as their progenitors had, as mentors or semidivine oracles, but as *things*—neither man, beast nor demon, but imbued with characteristics superior and inferior to all three.

Scenes of screaming chaos and confusion filled Kane's mind, bloody sequence following bloody sequence, coming so swiftly they melded into one long tapestry of atrocity, murder and theft. He glimpsed a bearded man working the blade of his sword between the facets of the stone, prying them out, putting them in his cloak and fleeing.

The men pursued the small folk through the vast ruins of their city, slaughtering and butchering until they had no choice but to fight back. The farther they had retreated from the world, the greater had grown their powers in other ways. The humans fled in blind panic, but the folk knew others would inevitably return, perhaps to steal the rest of the trapezohedron.

They had not been defeated, only beaten back. They knew they couldn't hope to defeat humans, but they determined to control them. If nothing else, they still possessed the monumental pride of their race and devotion to the continuity of their people. To accomplish that, they knew they had to retreat even further.

Kane glimpsed a mountain and a cavernlike opening hidden between great boulders. He groped through a long, narrow tunnel built of heavy joined stones. Small worn steps, too small for human feet, led downward out of sight, into clinging blackness. He came to a round, low chamber with a domed ceiling.

In its center, on an altar sat the black stone, incomplete yet still pulsing with power. The small, stunted folk clustered around it, caressing its dark surface with their six-fingered hands, drawing on its wellspring of knowledge, projecting their own experiences into it, using it as a means of broadcasting to any of their brethren who might still live on the face of the world. The message was simple: "We are here. Join us."

A pitifully small few did, descending into the bowels of the Earth to live and plan. One who came was the last of the parent race, still alive and unchanged. The name Lam entered Kane's mind. He rallied his people, becoming a spiritual leader, a general, a mentor. He knew his folk could not stay hidden forever, nor did they care to do so. The human race could not be influenced without interaction.

Under Lam's guidance, he and some of his people ascended again into the world of men, to influence the Phoenicians, the Romans, the Sumerians, the

Egyptians, the Aztecs. Lam was known throughout human historical epochs, but by names such as Osiris, Quetzacoatal, Nyarlthotep, Tsong Kaba and many others.

Lam and his people watched many nations and tongues be born and die, and they were proud that they survived while so many human civilizations did not.

The visions came faster now, images whirling through Kane's mind, then vanishing.

Legends filtered out among holy men about the underground city beneath Asia. It was called many things, Hsi Wang Mu, Bhogavati, Shamballah, Agartha. Myth and yearning built Agartha into a noble and beautiful metropolis with streets paved with mosaics of emeralds, rubies and diamonds. It was, of course, nothing but a refuge for the pitiful remains of a once proud people.

Though their life spans had been reduced over the preceding centuries following the changes, they were still long-lived. But they weakened and died while the human race was still young and virile. Within humans lay their salvation.

As they were themselves the product of genetic manipulation, Lam turned to humankind, first to restore their own flagging vitality, then to carry the seed of his folk onward so it wouldn't vanish.

Most of the bioengineering experiments took place in Asia, and there were many, many failures. Sterility was the common defect in the hybrids birthed in Agartha.

Finally seven hybrids were born who could reproduce. The seed of Lam's once proud race lived, albeit in diluted form. If there were such a thing as pure-blooded hybrids, these seven creations were it. Kane saw them, slender and compact of form, amber skinned, wearing simple draperies, huge eyes displaying wisdom but little passion.

They were attuned to the trapezohedron, the Chintamani Stone. They used it to manipulate the properties of the stolen facets, to lead those humans seeking Agartha away from it.

With Lam as their guide, the seven ventured out into the world, visiting the lamaseries, teaching lessons as their forebears had done. Legends collected around them, and they became known as the Eight Immortals.

But they were not truly immortal, and even long life spans have their limitations. Eventually they died, but not before spreading the concept of Agartha, the mystical community that guided the evolution of humanity. In reality, Agartha was a refuge for Lam's people, drawn there by the beacon of the stone.

In the centuries that followed, Lam and his people continued to interact and influence human affairs, from the economic to the spiritual. They allowed things to happen they could have stopped, or nudged events in another direction. Employing the technology left behind by their forebears, they visited their ancestors' bases on the Moon and the other planets in the solar system.

Balam himself was returning from a mission in space when his vessel malfunctioned and exploded over the Tunguska River region in Siberia. He lay in cryosuspension for over thirty years until discovered and revived by a Russian scientific expedition.

After another accident involving one of their flying vehicles in the late 1940s, an Agarthan emissary was dispatched to war-weary Europe for a twofold purpose: to sprinkle fanciful tales about the hidden city of Agarthans with its perfect beings with diplomatic ties to extraterrestrials, and to make certain the Roswell incident was properly covered up.

The ambassador, who went by the title of the Maha Chohan, was one of the most human appearing of the hybrids, and possessed a glib tongue and pronounced psionic abilities. He was instrumental in negotiating the release of Balam from the Soviets.

By the middle of the twentieth century, the number of Lam and Balam's people had dwindled as humanity's population had exploded. They had inbred the same gene pool too often, replicating it over and over, until the bloodlines had degenerated, and only pale, disease-prone imitations of their people were born.

Now, Balam's nonvoice whispered, *see us as we are.*

Once more, Kane saw the altar room of the trapezohedron, but the chamber had become a catacomb. Around the altar reposed bare bones, the skeletal remains of the seven immortals, hollow eye sockets staring at the roof for eternity.

Lam stood at the altar, eyes wide open and seeming to stare straight into Kane's soul. Within his long fingers rested the cube of dark stone.

Spare him his pitiful immortality, sighed Balam.

WITH A SAVAGE EFFORT, Kane tore his gaze away from the obsidian depths of Balam's eyes, glimpsing for an instant a reflection of his face, drawn in a bestial snarl.

Immediately, his ears rang with shouts, and he felt fists battering at his arms, hands wrenching at his fingers. He released Balam, and the small figure alighted on the floor without a misstep.

Kane allowed himself to be borne backward by Brigid, Banks and Lakesh. Banks cried out angrily, "What the hell are you doing?"

Bewilderment was in the stare Kane cast him. "How long?"

"How long what?" Lakesh demanded, breath coming fast and frantic.

Kane yanked his arm away from Banks's grasp. "How long was I holding Balam?"

"I wouldn't call it holding," Brigid snapped. "You were trying to strangle him."

"I know what I was doing," Kane retorted. He winced as a needle of pain stabbed through the left side of his head. "How long was I doing it?"

Banks scowled. "Only a couple of seconds, thank God. We kept you from getting a good grip on him."

The strangeness of Kane's question finally penetrated Banks's anger, and he looked at him curiously. "Why do you ask that?"

Kane probed his temple with fingers. The pain was already ebbing. "I think I learned more about Balam in those couple of seconds than you learned in the last three years."

Balam stood and blinked calmly at them, completely unperturbed by his brush with violent death.

"He telepathically gave me a history lesson," continued Kane. "He didn't answer all the questions, but he answered a good deal of them."

Brigid, Lakesh and Banks stared at Balam in silent wonder. Kane did, too, and for the first time realized Balam's pride and dignity had foundation.

He said to him quietly, "You never tried to escape because you have no place to go. There's nothing for you in Agartha. Your work is done, you've accomplished the mission to keep your race alive."

He did not ask a question; he made a statement. Balam inclined his head in a nod.

"And you fear that if Zakat returns the facets of the stone to the trapezohedron, he'll accidentally tap into these 'parallel casements' and undo everything you have achieved."

Again came the nod.

"What are parallel casements?" asked Lakesh, sounding mystified and intrigued.

Kane shrugged. "I don't know. Some phenomena associated with the stone. Phenomena that Balam fears."

"Why?" Brigid asked, enthralled yet disturbed.

Kane shook his head, still trying to reconcile the history Balam had imparted with his own hate-fueled prejudices. "He wasn't clear about it."

He forced himself to lock gazes with Balam, mentally comparing the small, pale, big-domed entity with the images of his parent race. It was like seeing a reflection in a distorted mirror, a cruel reminder of what might have been. As his people had risen higher than humanity's aspirations, so they also sank lower than mankind's nightmares.

But for humanity, Kane felt even worse—he had

no sense of the mighty brought low by an indifferent cosmos. Compared to Balam and his people, mankind was always low, not the first lords of Earth at all. They only arrogantly imagined themselves that they were ever really its lords, but older and more enduring races preceded them.

Balam met his gaze dispassionately, but Kane sensed the loneliness and pain radiating from him like an invisible aura. But regardless of his reasons, Balam and his kind had conspired against humanity for uncounted centuries. A natural cataclysm had decimated their civilization, so in turn they had orchestrated an unnatural one to bring mankind in line with their concepts of unity.

He remembered what Balam had said to him: *Humanity must have a purpose, and only a single vision can give it purpose.... We unified you.*

Now he knew part of the reason why, but it didn't erase the sin.

"You unified us, all right," Kane said grimly. "You gave us a purpose—to reclaim our world from those who carry your blood."

Balam whispered, "And yours."

Kane felt the anger build in him again, but it was a weary kind of anger, an afterthought to the bleak realization that the so-called Archon Directorate hadn't really conquered humanity—it had tempted humanity with the tools to conquer itself.

Naked greed, ambition, the thirst for power over others, those were the carrots snapped up gleefully by the decision makers. Yes, in order to survive Balam and his people had tricked mankind into living down to its most base impulses, but always the choice of whether to do so had been man's.

"Kane?" Brigid stared at him keenly, quizzically.

Kane shook himself mentally and said to Balam, "You want our help?"

"*Must* help," Balam corrected.

"We apekin have done enough of your dirty work over the centuries," he declared flatly. "So, whatever must be done, you'd better roll up your sleeves. You're going to be right on the firing line with us."

Chapter 21

Nausea and a blinding headache kept Kane on his back. He was aware of nothing for a long time, except for the blanket of pain and weakness that covered him.

Just how long it was before he opened his eyes he couldn't say. He forced himself to roll over, gathered himself and rose on shaking hands and knees. He squinted at the purple-tinted armaglass walls, feeling the pins-and-needles static discharge from the metal floor plates even through his gloves.

Brigid groaned and stirred.

"Lie still. Sickness go away soon."

The scratchy, whispery voice carried no tones of friendliness, only an appreciation of reality. Kane looked up at Balam standing near the chamber door, his small form swathed by a fleece-lined, hooded parka. The light from the ceiling fixture struck yellow pinpoints in his ebony eyes.

Brigid pushed herself to a sitting position, briefly sinking her teeth into her underlip. "Rough transit," she murmured. "The matter-stream phase lines must not have been in perfect sync."

Kane forced himself erect, stumbling slightly as he stepped on the hem of his coat. "Piece of Russian shit. Should have known what to expect after our jump to Perdelinko.''

Brigid smiled wanly and took Kane's proffered hand, allowing him to hoist her to her feet. The mattrans jump to Russia was always held up as a standard for bad transits, especially by Grant. So, in a way, it was good that he had been physically unable to accompany them.

Kane and Brigid were dressed similarly to when they had jumped to Russia. She wore a long, fur-collared leather coat over a high-necked sweater, whipcord trousers and heavy-treaded boots. The mini-Uzi hung by a strap around her shoulder.

Kane had decided against wearing the armor since their destination was a cold one. He had borrowed Grant's Magistrate-issue coat, since its Kevlar weave not only offered protection from weapons, but was also insulated against all weathers. However, it was a bit too big for him, and the coattails fell nearly to his heels.

The Sin Eater was snugged in its forearm holster beneath the right sleeve, and he wore a gren- and ammo-laden combat harness over his sweater.

Brigid picked up the pack containing emergency medical supplies, concentrated foodstuffs and bottled water. She started to shoulder into it, but Kane said, "Give it to Balam. Let him do his share."

Brigid glanced quickly at the creature. He gazed placidly at her, then extended his hands. She gave him the pack, and he struggled to slip it on. Bending over him, she adjusted the straps, feeling foolishly like a mother helping a child get dressed for school.

She had to forcibly remind herself Balam was as

far from a child as it was possible for even a semi-human to be. After Kane had recounted the details of Balam's telepathic history lesson, she speculated that he might be as old as fifteen hundred years, born around the time the tales of Agartha began circulating throughout Asia.

After snugging the pack straps, she turned on the motion detector and swept it toward the door. No readings registered, so she nodded tersely to Kane.

Stepping to the door, Kane grasped the handle, lifting and turning it. Lock solenoids clicked open loudly, and he toed open the door, a few inches at a time. Through the armaglass, he saw dimly what lay beyond.

The jump chamber nestled inside an alcove with a bank of electronic equipment curving in a horseshoe shape along the stone walls. Like Kane had expected, lights flashed on consoles and he heard the faint hum of power units.

Past the bank of electronics, he saw what he didn't expect. Two life-size statues faced each other, one with ten arms and a demonic face, and the other a likeness of a cherubic man squatting cross-legged on a stone block.

Blended with a musty, dusty odor, another stench permeated the rock-walled vault, one Kane had smelled many times in his life but never grown accustomed to. He saw a humped shape covered by a black cloth behind the ten-armed statue. Striding over to it, he snatched the fabric away.

The bearded face of a man gaped up at him. His face was layered by a thin crusting of blood that had stiffened and discolored his beard. A brownish puddle surrounded his head. His eyes possessed the opaque film of a corpse in the first stages of decomposition. Brigid and Balam came closer, although Balam seemed disinterested.

"Shot through the mouth at close range," Kane said quietly. "Three, maybe four days ago."

Balam padded over to a stone pillar nearly as tall as he was. He fingered the pedestal topping it. The surface bore a vague square outline, as if something that had rested there for many years had been removed.

"Here was stone," he said.

Kane glanced toward him, noting how the pillar was covered on each side with crudely incised faces. The eight faces were humanoid, but with oversize hairless craniums, huge, upslanting, pupil-less eyes and tiny slits for mouths. They were stylized representations of Balam's own face.

Kane looked around at the vault, sensing its vast age. Only the gateway unit and its control systems struck a discordant note in the overall atmosphere of antiquity. "Why is there a mat-trans unit here?"

Brigid shrugged. "Any number of reasons. If this is a Szvezda unit, then it may have been installed here so Russian intelligence could keep their eye on Red China. If Szvezda was anything like Cerberus, then all military or government officials had to do was say they needed a unit for security reasons."

"I have a feeling there was more to it than that," Kane replied, glancing sharply at Balam. "Am I right?"

Balam didn't answer. He moved toward the shadowy, far end of the bowl-shaped vault. After a moment, Kane and Brigid followed him. In the eight hours since his communication with Balam, Kane's natural suspicion had risen. Despite the information Balam had imparted, Kane wasn't convinced that he had been given the truth, or if he had, that he'd been given the whole truth.

When he presented his uncertainties to Lakesh, the old man had said sadly, "As a species, perhaps we can retain a semblance of sanity only by *not* understanding our frightfully shaky position in the scheme of things."

Kane grudgingly admitted that possibility, but he also didn't believe that Balam had withheld certain truths simply to spare his fragile human brain.

They followed Balam up a flight of stone steps and into a passageway with walls covered by silken, hand-painted tapestries. They came out into a corridor, through an open door crafted from granite. Kane barely glanced at the ornate dragon bas-relief carved over it. His pointman's instincts rang an alert, and the Sin Eater filled his hand.

Balam turned to the left. The corridor narrowed, turning and bending sharply several times. They passed several closed doors, but Kane heard no sound from behind any of them, so he didn't bother to see where they might lead.

Turning a corner, he heard a faint humming from behind him. He whirled and saw a shaved-headed, black-faced man spinning a key-shaped cudgel over his head by a leather thong. Before he could press the trigger of the Sin Eater, the heavy metal bludgeon snapped out.

Kane shifted position, slamming into Brigid with a

shoulder, and the key crashed loudly against the wall, passing through the space that had, a microsecond before, been occupied by his head. The cudgel struck sparks from the stone, chipping out a finger-sized splinter.

As Kane aligned his red-robed form with the bore of the Sin Eater, Brigid shouted, "Don't!"

The man yanked back on the thong, the key clattering on the flagstoned floor. Kane lunged in the same direction. He stamped down on the cudgel, and the man stumbled, the length of rawhide slithering from his grasp. Kane swept the barrel of the blaster across the base of his skull.

Kane didn't put all of his strength into the blow, assuming Brigid not only wanted him alive but conscious so he could be questioned. With a grunt, the shaved-headed man fell to his hands and knees.

Gathering a fistful of soiled robe in his left hand, Kane wrestled him to his feet. The man's small eyes blinked back tears of pain, and he looked at Kane dazedly. Brigid came forward, putting questions to him in a halting, singsong language that sounded like utter gibberish to Kane.

The man didn't reply, his soot-smeared features settling into a stubborn mask. Annoyed, Brigid said, "I don't know if I speak Tibetan with such an accent he doesn't understand or if he's just being uncooperative."

Kane shoved him against the wall. "Is he a priest?"

"A warrior monk, a Dob-Dob. The lamasery's version of a sec man. Traditionally, Dob-Dobs are drawn from the ranks of condemned criminals."

"Slaggers with religion," muttered Kane, planting the bore of his Sin Eater under the monk's chin and forcing his head back. "Tell him we offer him the chance to join a new religion—the Holy Order of Talk or Die."

"That's pretty much the first thing I said to him," Brigid retorted. "He doesn't fear death."

At the periphery of her vision, she noticed Balam edging closer. He pulled back the hood of his parka. The Dob-Dob's eyes darted toward him, then widened as far as the epicanthic folds would allow. A high-pitched yammering burst from his lips, and a jet of urine streamed down and collected in a noxious pool at his feet. His body was consumed with shudders, then seemed to turn to melted wax and flow down to the floor.

Mystified, Kane allowed him to sink down, watching him press his forehead against the flagstones, hearing him speak rapidly in an aspirated voice. Then he realized the Dob-Dob's reaction to the sight of Balam didn't stem necessarily from terror, but from an awe so intense it was almost ecstasy.

Kane stepped to Brigid's side. "What the hell is he saying?"

She narrowed her eyes in concentration. "It's a dialect, Sanskrit words mixed with Tibetan. A prayer language, I think. He believes Balam is one of the eight immortals."

Bleakly Kane thought that Balam very well could be.

Balam dammed the flood of words by interjecting questions in the same babbling tongue.

The Dob-Dob responded quickly, face still pressed

against the flagstones. Kane experienced a wave of disgust at the way the man abased himself, wallowing in his own waste. He saw him as a symbol of what Balam's folk had been trying to achieve with humanity for thousands of years. In place of knowledge, they implanted superstition, and in place of truth, fear.

Balam spoke again, and the Dob-Dob ceased gibbering. Turning to Kane and Brigid, he said, "The thief we seek departed this place at dawn."

Kane demanded suspiciously, "That's all he said?"

"He prayed to the eight kings who walk in the sky and thanked me for leaving the illuminated abode of Agartha to speak to him. He also begged forgiveness for failing to protect the stone as this sect had been charged with doing."

Balam's voice grew strained, and his last words were so faint and hoarse they had difficulty understanding him.

"How did the thief leave here?" Brigid asked.

Balam tapped the prostrate Dob-Dob on the top of his head until he reluctantly lifted his face. Tears cut runnels through the black soot smeared over his cheeks. Balam pointed to Brigid and whispered a few words.

The monk slowly climbed to his feet and bowed deeply, respectfully toward her. Brigid asked him questions in Tibetan, and the man responded promptly.

After a couple of minutes, she said to Kane, "They left on horseback. Tsyansis Khan-po, as he calls Zakat, carried a metal box. Gyatso, the girl and another Dob-Dob by the name of Yal went with him. He claims he was corrupted."

Recalling how he used the term to describe Beth-Li Rouch, Kane echoed, "Corrupted? How?"

"Leng—that's his name—wasn't really clear on that. He calls Zakat and Gyatso *dugpa*s, or black magicians who can reflect their images on weaklings. I take that to mean they have the ability to impose their wills on others."

"Since Gyatso is hybrid, I'm not surprised. But what about Zakat? Is he a psi-mutie?"

The only breed of human mutant that had increased dramatically since skydark was the so-called psimutie—otherwise normal in appearance, they possessed advanced extrasensory and precognitive mind powers.

"It's possible," she admitted. "But not everybody in the lamasery was corrupted. My guess is that Zakat and Gyatso, working in tandem, were able to zero in on the most impressionable minds. Maybe their powers were augmented by the stone."

Kane glanced toward Balam. "Is that likely?"

Balam nodded once.

"Do you know where they're going?"

Balam nodded again, evidently wishing to save his voice.

"And can it be reached overland?"

Balam nodded once more, then turned away. To Brigid, Kane said, "Ask Leng if he can provide transportation for the immortal and his party so the thieves can be caught."

Brigid did as he directed and after Leng replied, she said, "Yes, and we're more than welcome to them."

They followed Leng along the hallway, through

several large chambers and out into a courtyard. A bitter wind whistled over the walls. The sun sank behind far-off mountain peaks that looked like gray shadows. The cold, rarefied air made their lungs ache with the effort of breathing.

"We're going to have to wait until sunrise," Kane said. "Ask Leng to show us around."

Other than Leng, there appeared to be only a few people in the lamasery. Most of the monks and other Dob-Dobs had fled after the murder of the high lama, whom Zakat had not only killed but whose title, the king of fear, he had appropriated. They had left his body where it fell, too frightened to enter the vault of the stone.

Leng showed them around the monastery and to its library, which was underneath the main building. The majority of the manuscripts were scrolls as much as fifty feet long; others were sheets of ancient parchment tied between wooden blocks.

Brigid looked at the shelves, entranced. "There are enough ancient manuscripts here to keep a hundred translators busy for a lifetime—but there's probably not five people alive who could read the script."

Kane nodded toward Balam. "I'll bet he could."

Balam didn't confirm or deny the observation.

Leng led them back upstairs and served them an unsatisfactory meal of yak butter, grain porridge and a bitter green tea. Both Kane and Brigid were a bit surprised to see Balam consume it, apparently with relish as if he considered it a delicacy.

Unaccustomed to the thin air, Brigid and Kane tired quickly. After eating, they both did their best to stifle yawns. Leng escorted all three of them to a cell. Kane glanced out the solitary window and saw a view of snow-clad peaks. Looking down, he saw a sheer drop of at least a thousand feet.

Leng built a fire in the stone hearth in the middle of the floor, and since there was no chimney, they had to keep the wooden shutters of the window open to allow the smoke to escape.

The temperature dropped quickly after the sun went down, and they tried to find a balance between asphyxiating and freezing. The cell came furnished with only one cot, and Leng made it obvious that it was reserved for Balam. He did fetch piles of quilts and fur robes for Kane and Brigid to burrow in. To conserve body heat, they lay together. In order to breathe, they lay near the window. Balam simply draped himself in a number of blankets and quilts and apparently dropped off to sleep as soon as he lay down.

Quietly, Kane asked Brigid, "What was the word Leng used for Zakat and Gyatso? *Dugpas*?"

"Yes," she replied. "Gyatso is a practitioner of the old Bon religion. They're thought to cultivate evil for evil's sake. Supposedly, they're hypnotists and just as keen on getting control of humanity as, for instance, Balam's people were."

Kane shivered. He was too cold and tired to listen to another history lesson. The acrid smoke of tamarisk roots smoldering in the hearth made his throat feel raw and abraded.

"If Gyatso truly considers himself the Agarthan ambassador," Brigid continued drowsily, "he's in one deep psychological quandary."

"How so?"

"As a Bon-po shaman, he is as much Agartha's

enemy as the law of gravity is the enemy of people who think they can fly.''

Kane found the simile funny due to his oxygen-starved brain. He couldn't help but laugh. Brigid's teeth chattered, and she snuggled close to him, resting her head on his shoulder. ''I'm glad somebody finds something amusing about this.''

''An hour from now, after I suffocate, I probably won't.''

He briefly wondered how she would react if he kissed her, but decided not to risk it. Balam's presence in the room was a definite ardor-squasher. He drifted off into a surprisingly deep and thankfully dreamless sleep.

He awoke at dawn, when the first rays of daybreak shafted in through the window. He felt stiff and sticky, as he always did after sleeping in his clothes. He was also very cold and thirsty. Brigid awoke when he pushed himself up, and groaning, she hiked herself to a sitting position.

Balam perched on the foot of the cot, gazing out the window, the golden light of the sun casting amber shadows over his pale flesh, his eyes half-closed. He paid them no attention as they stumbled to their feet, kicking away the quilts and robes.

Balam rasped, ''We go now.''

''We go later,'' Kane stated in harsh tone that brooked no debate. ''After we apekin have attended to a few wake-up traditions. I *do* hope you'll be patient with our primitive customs.''

Balam ignored the words and sarcastic tone in which they had been delivered.

Leng arrived with more bowls of porridge and cups

of tea. He directed Kane and Brigid to a bathroom, which was more of a latrine. They took turns relieving themselves and splashing water on their faces from basins that were filmed with ice. If nothing else, the freezing water helped Kane come to full alertness.

Leng took them outside to a shed where half a dozen sturdy, shaggy ponies were stabled. They all looked very tough, bred in the Tibetan wilderness and used to hardship.

Knowing which horses were the best, Leng carefully selected three. Kane helped him saddle and bridle them. Balam stood apart, watching the process with what seemed like trepidation.

Kane gestured for him to come near the smallest of the animals, and when he did, it squealed and snapped its teeth viciously at him. Kane couldn't help but grin. "He's a good judge of character, at least."

Balam gazed at the pony impassively, and Kane received the distinct impression he had no idea of how to mount it. Putting his hands under Balam's armpits, he swung him up and planted him firmly in the saddle. He held the bridle, restraining the pony until it grew accustomed to the smell and feel of its rider. Kane stroked the animal's neck and crooned soothing words to it until it calmed down.

Leng adjusted the stirrups, and Kane inserted Balam's tiny feet into them. He whispered, "Thank you."

Kane looked at him in surprise, a bit startled by the acknowledgment of help. Biting back a sarcastic rejoinder, he said simply, "My pleasure."

Chapter 22

They rode the trail with one leg dangling over the edge of a precipice and the other scraping against the cliff face. The rock-ribbed slant pitched downward at an ever steepening angle.

Above them were snow-gilded peaks glimmering like powdered diamonds, but the trail beneath them was cast into cold, silent shadow. It wound around and down, ever down, skirting gorges and ravines littered with house-sized boulders.

Since Brigid and Kane assumed Balam knew where he was going, they didn't question him as he took the point. The trail led in only two directions—back and up to the Byang-thang Plateau, and down, ever down.

Around noon, they reached a windswept level place on the path, and Kane pointed out the remains of a cold camp and scatterings of horse dung. After the discovery, his pointman's sense was nervously alert, his eyes scanning crags and outcroppings for any sign of life.

Less than an hour past the campsite, a wind sprang up and began blowing powdery snow in swirling, eye-stinging clouds. The ponies lowered their heads and trudged through it. Balam bowed his head likewise, wrapping the lower portion of his face in a woolen scarf.

For what seemed like a chain of interlocking eternities, they marched through the thickening curtains of snow, which revealed only glimpses of fissures and chasms when the howling wind tore momentary rents in it.

The billowing clouds of snow reduced their range of vision to only a few yards, and the moisture froze on their eyelids. Their faces, hands and legs grew numb, and ears and teeth ached fiercely.

Over the keening wail of the wind, Kane thought he heard the frightened neighing of a pony and he cautiously squinted directly into the wind. He caught only a blurred fragment of Balam's pony disappearing over the edge of the trail.

Reining his own mount in sharply, Kane slid from the saddle. He shouted to Brigid, "Stay there! Something's happened!"

He could barely see her on her horse and he wasn't certain if she heard him, but she remained in the saddle.

Kane made his way slowly to the point where he thought the pony had fallen, the wind setting his coattails to flapping like the wings of an ungainly bird. The snow burned his eyes, so he closed them, dropping to his knees and inching forward, calling for Balam.

He reached the ledge rim and shouted over it, but he scarcely heard his own voice. He started to back away when fingers clutched desperately at his right hand and wrist. Groping down, Kane felt Balam's arm and he pulled him up from the rock knob where he had been dangling.

Balam lay in Kane's arms like a child, trembling

violently and once or twice he tried to speak. Cautiously, Kane worked his way backward until he felt the cliff pressing into his back, and then he sidled over to his horse. He knelt beneath the animal, using it as an unsatisfactory windbreak, and put Balam on his feet. "Are you all right?"

Balam nodded, vein-laced eyelids squeezed shut. He still shivered, and Kane had no way of knowing if it was from fear or cold, but he didn't blame him either way. After spending three and a half years in a twenty-by-twenty cell, Balam was experiencing a very unpleasant reintroduction to the world.

He hoisted him onto the saddle of his pony and led it by the bridle past the point where Balam's mount had plunged into the ravine. He climbed on behind Balam, heeling the pony forward.

The trail entered a gash in the cliff face and descended through a tunnel that had been enlarged out of a natural cave. Sheltered from the merciless lash of the wind, they reined up and dismounted. Now at least they could speak without shouting.

"What happened back there?" asked Brigid, her heavy, disheveled mane of hair glistening with snow, her face reddened by the scouring of wind-driven sleet.

"Balam's horse missed his step," he answered. "Nearly took Balam with him."

"Good thing you were paying attention." She made the comment between chattering teeth.

Balam husked out, "Thank you."

Kane tried to grin derisively, but his lips were too chapped. "My pleasure. How far now?"

Balam made an odd gesture with one hand, languid and diffident. "Not long now."

"You're not sure?" demanded Brigid.

"Long time since I came this way. Landmarks change."

"How long?" Kane inquired.

Balam performed the hand gesture again, and Kane wondered if it was the equivalent of a shrug. "Not sure. Around time when we aborted Norse colonization of the North American continent."

Brigid's eyes widened in astonishment. "That has to be eight or nine hundred years ago."

"Long time," Balam whispered agreeably.

After resting for half an hour, they continued on their way. The storm was gradually blowing itself out, and there were longer lulls between the freezing, gale-force gusts.

The trail led for two miles along a fairly level parapet of basalt until it turned sharply and began to zigzag downward. Kane could see that it was largely hand-hewed and in some places it looked as if demolition charges had done the work. Regardless, the construction work was obviously ancient.

The snow became little more than intermittent flurries the longer and deeper they rode. As sunset approached, the flurries ceased altogether and Kane saw more horse droppings on the path.

The trail flowed seamlessly into relatively flat, stone-littered ground. Balam's slender frame stiffened in the saddle, as though he was excited or apprehensive.

They followed a dry, boulder-filled streambed that wended its way through a sheer-walled ravine. Kane had visited some wild places before, but this piece of Tibet had to be one of the most inaccessible regions on the face of the Earth.

The sky purpled with twilight when they marched out of the ravine into a box canyon. Bulwarks of granite stood like huge tombstones all around them. In the rock face fifty yards beyond the ravine, they saw a black cleft, partially hidden by clumps of tall, dry grass and slabs of limestone.

Balam inclined his head toward it. "There."

"That?" demanded Kane. "That hole in the wall is the door to your magic city of immortals?"

Wriggling impatiently, Balam tried to dismount, so Kane reined the pony to a halt. He jumped to the ground and stood with his eyes fixed on the dark gap. His body swayed slightly, gracefully to and fro like a reed touched by a gentle wind.

It occurred to Kane that Balam might be experiencing a deep emotion, so he said nothing. At the same time it had occurred to him that although he had seen horse manure on the trail, he saw no sign of horses anywhere in the vicinity. The ground was far too hard and stony to take tracks, but he scanned it anyway.

Then he heard the flat cracking snap of a rifle, followed a shaved slice of a second later by a little thump of displaced air next to his left ear.

Kane lunged off the saddle, Sin Eater springing into his hand. Another shot split the heavy silence of the canyon, and the gravel gouted in front of Brigid's pony. It shrilled a frightened cry, rearing up on its hind legs. She managed to kick free of the stirrups and slid over the horse's rump, alighting on her feet. She fumbled to bring her mini-Uzi to bear.

Grigori Zakat's disembodied voice floated on the air, the echoes distorting it as to the direction from which it emanated. "I did not kill you before when I had the chance, Kane. I prefer not to kill you now."

Kane looked wildly around, assuming a combat stance, eyeing every boulder, declivity and decent-sized bush in the zone. "Then why are you shooting at us?"

"To illustrate my preference that you stay alive. I hope you don't hold my actions in the museum against me."

"You hope wrong," Kane replied, crouching down behind his pony, pulling Brigid to him.

A note of laughter twisted through the canyon. It held an odd, high note. "You are the grudge-holding type. I'd hoped you were more emotionally mature than that. How did your friends, the black man and the white girl, fare?"

"They had a whale of a time," answered Kane, ignoring the sour look Brigid cast in his direction. "What do you want?"

"Obviously, the same as you. The Chintamani Stone, the shining trapezohedron. I have two of its facets in my possession, and they have led me here, to Agartha, to the Valley of the Eight Immortals, to claim the primary piece."

"What makes you so sure this is Agartha?"

"Call it intuition. Besides, I have the ancestral ambassador with me. He should know."

"If that's true, what's keeping you from strolling in and taking it?"

Balam behaved not only as if he were oblivious to the gunshots, but to the conversation. He continued to stare at the cleft, body still swaying.

"I intend to wait until morning. Now, however, with you here—by the way, what is wrong with your small friend?—I propose another alliance of convenience. Safety in numbers and all that."

"We've already had an example of your version of a truce, Zakat."

The Russian laughed again. "I understand your point of view is different from mine, but what harm will it do to cooperate? I have you pinned down— you can't go anywhere. It won't cost you anything to go along with me. I know you think I handed you a raw deal in Newyork, but I'll make it up to you. Are you a religious man, Kane?"

Out of all the threats and boasts he expected Zakat to taunt him with, that question took him aback. "I've never thought about it. Why?"

"Because I am. In fact, I am an ordained priest. The deity of my religion is power, and the way one communes with such a god is to recognize and accept one's destiny. We are all agents of it. What is happening now is supposed to happen."

"What are you going to do next?" Kane asked sneeringly. "Read my fortune?"

Zakat laughed again, as if he found the question truly funny. "Once I retrieve the prime piece of the trapezohedron, I can probably do far more than that. My point is, if you obey the law of power, you therefore shall gain more. It is a cumulative effect, known in my religion as causitry."

While Zakat spoke, Kane scanned every inch of the

area. Because of the deceptive echoes, Zakat and his people could be behind them. He felt ridiculously vulnerable, hunkering down behind a shaggy pony. He knew he had been in tighter spots in his life; he just couldn't recall them offhand.

"Therefore," Zakat continued reasonably, "causitry is part of destiny and my actions caused your destiny to interact with mine."

"Oh, shut up," Brigid muttered.

Zakat continued to wax eloquent on subjects metaphysical. Kane listened to the man's blandishments and with a start he realized he was actually considering the man's proposition. He was a masterful persuader. He couldn't help but suspect that the fragments of the stone in his possession were augmenting Zakat's psionic abilities.

Balam suddenly commanded Kane and Brigid's attention. He strode deliberately toward the opening in the cliff wall, unzipping his parka as he did so.

"Tell the midget to stop, Kane," Zakat commanded sharply. "All of us enter together when the time is right."

"Do as he says, Balam," Brigid called.

Balam kept walking, shrugging out of his coat, dropping it on the ground behind him. The rifle cracked again, and a column of dirt spouted less than two feet in front of him. His measured, single-minded stride didn't falter.

Kane watched, completely dumbfounded as Balam began peeling off his dark one-piece garment, stripping naked. He stopped only to step out of the leggings and then continued on, padding over sharp-edged pebbles on bare, six-toed feet.

A voice burst out with a stream of agitated consonants, and black-turbaned Gyatso squeezed out between two boulders. He raced toward Balam, shrieking frenzied words, waving his arms over his head. Zakat bellowed something in Russian, and Kane figured it was an order to stop.

Kane sprinted after Balam, firing a triburst in Gyatso's direction. The light was poor, the man's clothing was dark and he reacted with inhumanly swift reflexes. He bounded straight back, and the 9 mm rounds dug gouges in the dirt and ripped white scars on the rocks behind him.

Two blasters opened up from behind the bulwark of stone, one obviously the Tokarev. The canyon walls magnified the staccato reports. Brigid fired her autoblaster, spraying Zakat's basalt shelter with a hailstorm of lead, driving Gyatso back behind them.

Kane didn't divert his attention from the rocks and so caught only brief glimpse of the darkness of the cleft swallowing Balam's pale body. He continued firing round after round until he reached the gap. It was just wide and high enough for an adult to slip through on all fours. He knew the gap was not a shallow depression but a tunnel. His flesh tingled at the prospect of crawling headfirst into a pitch-dark passageway, but it tingled even more at continuing a firefight with enemies who probably outgunned both Brigid and him and had good cover.

As Brigid joined him, he snapped, "Get in there. I'll cover you."

She looked at the opening fearfully, then flinched as a bullet struck the cliff over her head and sprinkled rock chips in her hair.

Grabbing her by the collar, Kane forced her down in front of the opening. "*Go,* goddammit!"

With a fatalistic shrug, Brigid wriggled into the cleft.

Chapter 23

The rough-edged tunnel narrowed from a four-foot diameter to three within the first yard. The little light peeping in from outside vanished quickly, and Kane stared straight ahead into unfathomable darkness. If not for the sound of Brigid's scuffling on the stone, he wouldn't have known she was there. He resisted the urge to unpocket and turn on his microlight.

The sound of voices from ahead of him was such a surprise he nearly stopped dead. A second later, he realized he had heard the echoes of Grigori Zakat's voice, but he wasn't comforted. He glanced behind him. Outlined against the hazy, irregular opening, he could just barely make out the Russian's head.

He crawled faster and could only pray the tunnel would curve or drop before it occurred to Zakat to open fire into the cleft. He crawled as rapidly into the blackness as his hands and knees could move. His head bumped into knobs, and loose pebbles dug into his knees. His coat might turn a 7.62 mm bullet, but he didn't want to find out.

At the sudden crack of the triggered AK, he dropped flat, hoping Brigid did the same. He heard a soft zing over his head. The whine of a ricochet instantly followed.

He whispered, ''Baptiste, are you all right?''

"More or less," came the pained reply. "I bumped my head."

"Belly crawl or you'll have more than a knot up there."

They wormed forward on their bellies. There came the crack of another shot, and rock chips sifted down on the back of his neck. Kane and Brigid slithered and scraped along. The tunnel narrowed even more, and the walls caught at Kane's shoulders, but he kept clawing and scrabbling onward, sweat stinging his eyes.

The click of a firing-rate selector reverberated throughout the darkness. He knew Zakat had switched from single shot to full-auto.

He heard a frightened cry from Brigid an instant before the tunnel floor vanished under his hands. He dived headlong into a sepia sea. Just as he fell, a stream of bullets tore through the tunnel and passed over his plunging body. They bounced off rock with a series of eerie screams.

Kane wasn't listening. He was too busy clawing at empty air, groping for a handhold. He didn't grope for very long. A breath-robbing crash numbed his body, and he was only dimly aware of tumbling head over heels down a slope. By the time a rock stopped his thrashing descent, the burst of autofire had ceased.

When his senses returned, he found he had fetched up against the base of a boulder in a half-sitting position. He heard a deep groan from Brigid, somewhere nearby.

He thrust his hand into his coat pocket and removed the Nighthawk microlight, flicking it on and shining the amber beam around. Brigid was pushing herself up from the rocky ground, teeth clamped tight on groans of pain.

"Don't ask me if I'm all right," she said lowly. "I'm liable to hit you."

Kane cast the light upward, and it haloed a set of small, worn steps leading downward from the tunnel opening, nearly ten feet above them. Now he knew how Balam had kept from breaking his neck. He heard sounds from the tunnel, scramblings and murmurings.

He forced himself erect, wincing at the flares of pain igniting all over his body. "Can you walk, Baptiste?"

She wobbled to her feet, gingerly dabbing at the blood flowing from a cut on her scalp, right at the hairline. "Guess I have no choice."

Pulling off the glove from his left hand, Kane wetted a forefinger and tested the air currents that swirled around unseen obstacles. He detected a movement of air to their left and, taking Brigid by the hand, began a shambling run in that direction. Chunks of rock clattered at their feet as they threaded their way between outcroppings of granite and basalt. He kept listening for the approach of Zakat and his crew or the sound of their fall when they reached the point where the tunnel opened into empty space.

After a couple of minutes, when the sound had still not come, Kane and Brigid set out along a narrow corridor of stone. Holding the microlight out before him, Kane led the way quickly, occasionally confused by his own writhing shadow.

"Balam didn't have that much of a jump on us,"

he said. "We ought to come across his tracks or something."

Brigid patted her pockets and said grimly, "My Nighthawk is gone. It must have fallen out of my coat when I fell."

Kane nodded, but said nothing. The microlights emitted a powerful beam, and therefore the batteries didn't last very long. Relying only on one source of light in an environment like this didn't do much for his sense of optimism.

The corridor widened and the ceiling grew higher. Irregular stalactites hung from above, and they wended their way around stalagmites thrusting up from the floor. The light beam glinted off mineral deposits embedded in the rough walls—silvery mica, brilliant quartz and soapy limestone. A brooding, unbroken silence bore down on them, like the pressure of a vast, invisible hand. Then they heard the scuff of footfalls.

Cursing under his breath, Kane set off at a trot with Brigid beside him, both of them trying to move as quietly as possible. The passage they walked branched into a Y. They chose the opening on the left, because it had the strongest current of air.

They strode along it for only a short distance, then stopped. The movement of air was almost a breeze, wafting up from below. The cavern floor dropped straight down into utter darkness. Brigid kicked a pebble over the edge and counted quietly. She got to five before they heard it strike far, far below.

Shuddering, Brigid and Kane backed away. They heard the sound of voices and saw the glow of a flashlight, dimly illuminating the branching-off point of the tunnels. They ran noiselessly, on the balls of their feet, toward the Y. They paused a moment at the junction to make sure they couldn't be seen, and then darted into the right-hand shaft. They flattened themselves against the wall. Kane turned off the Nighthawk and double-fisted his Sin Eater. They watched the halo of light grow brighter.

Framed by the aura of two flashlights, Zakat, Trai, Gyatso and a black-faced Dob-Dob—the man Leng had called Yal—appeared at the junction. They looked warily around. If any of the four had taken the tumble out of the tunnel into the cavern, they looked none the worse for it.

Though he knew he was nearly invisible in his black coat, Kane pressed himself harder against the side of the tunnel. He watched Zakat check the air movement with a wet fingertip and, as he and Brigid had done, they turned down the left-hand tunnel.

Kane removed a concussion gren from its clip on his combat harness.

Because of the darkness, Brigid couldn't see what he had done, but she heard the faint clinking of metal. In an alarmed tone, she whispered, "What are you going to do?"

"I hate being chased," he grated.

He soft-shoed back to the junction and heard Zakat and Gyatso speaking in low tones. Peering down the tunnel, he saw they had reached the end. Kane unpinned the gren and lobbed it down the shaft with a gentle, underhanded toss.

Zakat heard it bouncing and silenced Gyatso with a sharp hiss. Kane stepped back swiftly and turned, but he saw the Russian bounding forward with inhuman speed. He kicked the gren like a football, propelling it down the tunnel into the branching-off point, back toward him.

A blaze of light illuminated the junction with a yellow-white glare. The detonation was a brutal thunderclap, which instantly bled into a loud rumble, as if a great wheeled machine were approaching. Bits and pieces of rocks pelted down from overhead, and Kane moved back to the right-hand tunnel, glancing behind him. Chunks of stone fell into the branching-off point of the passageways. Rocks and debris rained down with splintering cracks and crashes. The entire cavern roof seemed to be in motion.

Kane grabbed Brigid by the sleeve and pulled her farther into the shaft as a small rockfall filled the junction with heaps of stone. The floor trembled under their running feet, riven with ugly, spreading cracks.

With an earsplitting roar, an entire section of cavern floor collapsed, plunging downward and carrying Brigid with it. Kane still had a tight grip on her sleeve, and her unsupported weight caused him to fall flat on his stomach.

She dangled at the end of his arm over a void of impenetrable blackness. There was a crack of splitting rock, and her weight abruptly increased. Kane felt himself slipping forward, and he fought to dig the toes of his boots into the hard ground. He heard Brigid's boots groping for purchase.

"Grab me with your other hand," Kane directed through clenched teeth.

Brigid's other hand grasped his forearm, just below the elbow, and Kane was dragged forward a few frightening inches. Straining every muscle in his shoulders, arms and back, he wormed backward, pebbles pressing cruelly into his thighs, groin and chest. He ground the side of his face into grit and dirt. Sweat slid down into his eyes, and his limbs quivered with the strain.

Finally, he lifted Brigid to the level where she was able to swing up a leg over the edge of the rockfall. For a long minute, they lay on the cavern floor, panting and gasping. Finally, Kane pushed himself into a sitting position and turned on the Nighthawk.

When the microlight illuminated Brigid's face, Kane almost wished they were in darkness again. The woman's face was clotted with dried blood from her scalp wound, and her emerald eyes were dulled with fatigue and pain and surrounded by dark rings. Even her curly mane of hair drooped listlessly.

She looked at him and said, "You look terrible."

"Thanks to you," Kane retorted angrily. He scowled at her, then forced a laugh. He stood up slowly, silently enduring the spasms of pain igniting in his back and legs.

"Well," he said after a moment, "Zakat and his crew are behind us, so we can't go back. Balam is somewhere ahead of us. So we have to go out."

"And down," said Brigid gloomily. Gingerly, she stepped forward and peered into the yawning blackness below.

She took a deep breath and inched out onto the ledge, flattening herself against the rock wall, digging the fingers of her hands into the fissures and crevices. After a moment of hard swallowing, Kane stepped out after her, strapping the microlight around his left wrist.

The ledge made a sharp turn to the right after a few steps, and its pitch descended at an increasingly steep angle. Kane and Brigid were forced to edge along it with their hands gripping the wall tightly. Kane wondered how deep beneath the surface they were. He couldn't hazard a guess, but he suspected the ledge beneath their feet wasn't natural. Its smoothness spoke of craftsmanship, though whether it was carved by human hands, he had no way of knowing. Nor did he particularly want to know.

It was slow, laborious work and it was perilous, for ominous cracklings at the lip of the ledge warned that their combined weight might start a slide, sending them both plunging into the blackness.

Kane worried that the batteries of the Nighthawk were dangerously low, but he didn't turn it off. The ledge gradually widened into a true path. Both of them breathed easier when they no longer had to inch sideways, but the dim glow of the microlight diminished their relief. The flashlight offered little more than a firefly halo where the ledge met and joined with a rocky floor.

A faint rumble sounded to their right, and they halted, expecting another downpour of stones. A few seconds of hard listening told them the noise was that of an underground stream or river. Kane was suddenly, sharply aware of how thirsty he was.

They moved along the path, beneath ponderous masses of stone. The Nighthawk abruptly went out. The echoes of Brigid's despairing groan chased each other through the impenetrable blackness.

The two people stopped walking, hearts triphammering within their chests as they stood motionless in the stygian darkness. Kane's breath came in harsh, ragged bursts as he struggled to control his mounting terror. The mission priority was the spur that drove him to start walking again, taking Brigid by one arm and feeling his way along the rough walls. Then, far away, he saw a tiny blue-yellow flicker of light. He pointed it out to Brigid, and they increased their pace. The crunch of their footfalls sent up ghostly reverberations.

The path suddenly debouched into a gloomy underground gallery with walls of black basalt. Stalagmites and outcroppings thrust up from the floor. To both Brigid's and Kane's dismayed surprise, they saw that the source of the ectoplasmic light came from a small square panel of a glassy substance inset in the gallery wall.

Walking over to it, Brigid eyed it curiously, reaching out a tentative hand to touch it. "I've never seen anything like this before."

"I have," declared Kane grimly.

She jerked her hand away and turned to face him. "Where?"

"In the Black Gobi, in the tent of the Tushe Gun. I guess there isn't any need to wonder where he got them...or where this one came from."

Brigid nodded and stepped away from the glowing panel. The self-styled Avenging Lama had made the ancient Mongolian city of Kharo-Khoto his headquarters. Beneath the black city lay an even more ancient structure, a space vessel. The Tushe Gun had looted much Archon technology from it, without understanding what it was.

Softly, Brigid said, "And I guess there's no more need to wonder why Balam was drawn to this place."

They strode through the gallery, accompanied by the ever present echoes of their footsteps. Every few yards, they came across more of the light panels. They provided a weak, unsatisfactory illumination, but they were grateful for them nonetheless.

The gallery narrowed into a crevasse, which they squeezed into, clambering over fallen masses of stone. The splash of rushing water grew louder as the fissure turned to the left. After a few steps, they found themselves standing on a stone shelf a foot or so above the surface of a river. The opposite bank was about seventy feet away, butting up against a wall of basalt.

The water looked black, but Kane rushed to it anyway, lying flat and plunging his head into the icy current. Brigid kneeled beside him, taking off her gloves before cupping handfuls of water to her mouth.

The water had a peculiar tang to it, a sour limestone aftertaste, but they drank their fill anyway, washing away the blood and grime on their faces. When Kane blunted the edge of his thirst, he became aware of a gnawing hunger and he wondered aloud if there were any fish in the stream.

Brigid didn't reply. She peered in the direction of the river's current. "There isn't a path. If the river leads to a way out, we'll have to swim. Or go back."

Kane raked the wet hair out of his eyes. "There's nothing to be gained by that. Zakat and his crew are better armed than we are."

Brigid nodded. "Yeah, but I'm not up to swimming. The river is cold, probably fed by meltwater.

We'd both succumb to hypothermia inside of a couple of minutes."

Kane rose, looking past Brigid to the other side of the stream. Though the light was uncertain, he was sure he saw a long object bobbing on the surface, almost directly across from their position. Leaning against the rock wall, he tugged off his boots, shucked his coat and slid into the water.

"What are you doing?" Brigid demanded.

"Wait and see, Baptiste."

His feet touched the gravelly bottom. The water was shockingly, almost painfully cold, and it took all of his self-control not to curse. He started wading across, moving as quickly as he dared. After a few steps, the icy water lapped at his thighs, then up to his waist. He kept walking, fighting the strong current. A time or two, loose stones turned beneath his feet and he nearly fell.

When he reached the other side, he was gasping and out of breath. From the hips down he was completely numb, but the bobbing shape was what he had hoped it would be. A six-foot-long boat made of bark and laced yak's hide was tethered to a boulder by a length of leather. A wooden pole about ten feet long lay on the bank.

Pulling himself ashore, Kane snatched the tether free and took the pole. Tentatively, he eased into the little boat. The craft sank a bit, the hide-and-bark hull giving a little, but it seemed river worthy.

With pushes of the pole, he propelled the boat across the river. He had difficulty crossing it because of the current, but the pole always touched bottom. When the prow bumped against the opposite bank,

Brigid handed him his boots and coat. She hesitated only a moment before gingerly climbing into it.

Hastily, Kane put on his coat and boots. He shivered as he did so. Taking the pole again, he pushed off and the boat slid out into the river, rocking a bit. He poled the craft so it hugged the right-hand wall, close to the light panels, not voicing the host of new fears assailing him.

He was afraid the river might debouch in a dozen different directions, or lead to a waterfall or that the boat might spring a leak. But after twenty minutes of steady poling, with none of his fears bearing out, he tried to relax. When his strained shoulder muscles couldn't take any more abuse, he turned the task of poling over to Brigid.

Kane sat down while she expertly directed the craft. She said, "This used to be a form of recreation. It was called punting."

"Offhand I can think of a dozen recreational activities I'd rather be doing."

"All with Rouch, I'll bet," she replied with a studied nonchalance.

Kane glowered at her, but didn't respond. Linking his hands behind his aching neck, he inquired, "What do you think, Baptiste?"

"What do I think about what?"

"Is this Agartha, the Valley of the Eight Immortals Zakat is so crazy to reach?"

Brigid pushed her shoulder against the pole. "If it is, it's a far cry from the way the city was described in legend. I haven't seen a speck of gold or a chip of diamond yet. If there ever were Agarthans, they came down here ages ago to die."

Brigid paused, started to say something else, then stopped talking and poling. Kane straightened up. The waterway opened into a huge, vault-walled cavern. It was immense, most of it wrapped in unrelieved darkness. Black masses of rock hung from its jagged roof.

The river narrowed down to a stream, and the current carried the boat beneath an arching formation. A constant sound of splashing beyond it indicated a waterfall.

Brigid pushed the craft toward the nearest bank. She poled them aground on the pebble-strewed shore. They climbed out of the boat and looked around at the city of stalactites and stalagmites rising all around them. Illuminated by dozens of light panels, they saw towers of multicolored limestone disappearing into the darkness overhead, flying buttresses and graceful arches of rock stretching into the shadows.

Kane and Brigid moved forward uncertainly, struggling not to be overcome by awe. Then Brigid stabbed out an arm, pointing ahead. They stopped and stared, surrendering to astonishment.

The figure was a statue, standing in erect position. At least fifteen feet tall, it represented a humanoid creature with a slender, gracile build draped in robes. The features were sharp, the domed head disproportionately large and hairless. The eyes were huge, slanted and fathomless.

The stone figure pointed with one long-fingered hand toward the farther, shadow-shrouded end of the cavern. There was something so strikingly meaningful about the pointing arm and the intent gaze of the big eyes that the statue seemed not crafted out of stone at all, but a living thing petrified by the hand of time.

"Somebody lived down here," Kane muttered.

Brigid nodded thoughtfully. "A long, long time ago."

They started in the direction of the statue's solemnly pointing arm. It led them across the cavern, to a crevasse that yawned at the far end. A worn path was still discernible, and they followed it toward the black opening.

Kane suddenly tugged Brigid to a stop. "Are you sure nobody's lived down here for a long, long time?"

Nettled by the hint of sarcasm in his tone, she followed his gaze downward.

In the fine rock dust on the cavern floor, they saw the clear, fresh print of a small foot with six delicate toes.

Chapter 24

In the wavering glow of the light panel, Kane and Brigid looked at each other, at the footprint, at the solemn statue and back to each other.

"If Balam made this footprint, then he's not too far ahead of us," Kane said, unconsciously lowering his voice to a whisper.

"That print could have been here for ages," replied Brigid. "There's nothing down here to disturb it."

She studied the looming sculpture. "There must have been a migration down through these caves. Balam's people set up that statue as a marker, a guidepost so that they would know the way to follow."

Kane stepped forward. "I think we should do the same thing."

They followed the worn, broad path that led into the cavern and to a fissure at the far end. Another light panel illuminated a very narrow, winding stair hewed out of stone, a route taken by a doom-driven race. The stairs angled steeply into darkness.

When Kane and Brigid started down, they discovered its downward angle was not quite as sharp as they feared. The stairs led to a wide, vault-walled space from which many other fissures radiated. A square light panel shed a feeble glow over one of the cracks.

They didn't speak as they entered the passage, but Kane's mind was in a fever of speculation and conjecture. He understood now why Balam and his kind had such huge eyes, why they were most comfortable in low light levels, why historically they had been slandered as hell-spawn. They had no choice but to shun the light, lurk in the shadows, and early man had viewed them as demons, scuttling up from the bowels of the Earth to practice devilment.

Perhaps the myth of Agartha was a long-range public-relations campaign, to plant in human consciousness the concept of a semidivine race living in a subterranean city, not a horde of inhuman devils.

Kane and Brigid forged their way through a bewildering labyrinth of fissures, galleries and small caves. Every few hundred feet, the path was marked by the blue radiance of a light panel.

They squeezed into another crack in the rock and were plunged into complete darkness. They felt their way for a few minutes, then in the black void ahead of them, Kane saw a filtered, pale blue glow. The scope of the illumination was far wider than one of the light panels.

"Do you see that?" he asked over his shoulder.

"I do," Brigid answered. "Maybe it's a natural phosphorescence given off by fungus and lichens."

Their ears detected a distant, almost inaudible reverberation. The regularity of its throbbing rhythm instantly gave them both the knowledge of its nature.

"Archon power generators," blurted Brigid. "Like the ones we saw in Dulce, and in the spacecraft beneath Kharo-Khoto."

The passage ended on a broad shelf of basalt,

thrusting out over a cavernous space so vast their eyes could only dimly perceive its true proportions. Their first stupefied impression was of an alien underworld, occupying the entire center of the Earth. As their eyes adjusted, they gained a sense of perspective on the vista spread out before them.

From the stone shelf, the ground sloped gently downward toward a collection of structures. The buildings were of black basalt, quarried from the cavern walls, and Kane realized they were built in the same odd architectural style as the surface cities Balam had shown him.

The structures were low to the ground, windowless and some of them sprouted fluted spirals. A tower identical to the Administrative Monoliths, but less than half the height, jutted up from the center of the settlement. Like the villes, the city plan was a wheel, radiating out from the central tower.

The roof of the enormous cavern was tiled with the light panels, every square inch completely covered by them, except for where jagged stalactites thrust down.

The area wasn't quite as gigantic as their first stunned impression, perhaps only half a mile in circumference. They saw and heard no signs of people in the streets, only the rhythmic drone.

"Agartha," Brigid murmured. "Shamballah. Bhogavati. The source of all the myths about underground kingdoms."

Kane swept his gaze over it, mentally comparing it to the visions of the mighty cities Balam had imparted to him. It had a desolate, abandoned look to it, evoking more sadness than awe.

''No one has lived here for a long time,'' he said quietly.

As they walked down the slope, Brigid sniffed the air and detected the faint whiff of ozone. ''The power generators are probably hooked up to an air-circulation system, either recycling the oxygen trapped down here or pumping it in from the surface.''

They approached the city cautiously, alert for any signs of habitation. Brigid gestured with her left hand toward the tower, opening her mouth to point out a detail to Kane. The motion detector on her wrist suddenly emitted a discordant beep. Both of them came to sudden halts.

She raised the LCD to eye level. Three green dots marched across the window in a more or less straight line. At the bottom edge of it, a changing column of digits flickered.

''Three hits,'' she breathed tensely. ''About ten yards ahead of us.''

''Zakat and his people?''

Brigid shook her head. ''If they survived the cave-in, they couldn't have gotten ahead of us.''

The two people stood out in the open, and the only available cover was the nearest building. To reach it, they would have to run in the direction of the approaching contacts.

Kane double-fisted his Sin Eater. ''We've got no choice but the old brazen-it-out strategy.''

Brigid hefted her mini-Uzi, remarking sourly, ''Your favorite.''

They stood stock-still as three figures appeared around the corner of a building. At first glance, they looked like Asians, but when they drew closer, Kane drew in his breath sharply and he sensed Brigid stiffening beside him.

Clothed in flowing garments of a saffron hue, their bodies were short and stocky, and their hairless heads unusually round. Their skins were pale, but with a bluish pallor, perhaps due to the illumination cast by the light panels. They looked like human beings except for two details—their huge, large-pupiled dark eyes and their six-fingered hands and feet.

They didn't appear excited at the sight of Kane and Brigid, almost as if they were a welcoming committee sent to meet them at the city limits.

"Don't make a move," Brigid said. "I don't think they mean us harm."

She held up her right hand, palm outward in the universal sign of peace. The Agarthans—if that was who they were—showed no signs of recognizing it. Their blank expressions didn't alter.

Brigid spoke a few words of Tibetan to them, and still they didn't react. Kane noticed the strange, sluggish uniformity in the way they walked. Alarmed, his finger rested lightly on the trigger of his blaster.

"If they don't stop," he side-mouthed to her, "I'm going to fire a warning shot."

"They don't appear to be armed."

"And they don't appear to be friendly, either."

"Maybe they just don't understand."

As three figures drew closer, Kane suddenly realized why they didn't understand, and his stomach lurched sideways. Not only did the three men appear identical in shape, form and clothing, but also they all wore the same slack-mouthed, vacant expression.

Their staring eyes were dull, and the look they gave
Kane and Brigid was the same one a cow might give
to a passerby. Spittle flecked their lips, and their chins
glistened with drool.

Kane felt a surge of horror and didn't know why.
Mental retardation is pitiable, pathetic, not horrible—
but the three men were.

"Oh, my God," Brigid breathed. "They're idiots."

The triplets halted a few feet in front of them,
gazed at them in impersonal silence, then simultaneously pointed to the tower.

"An invitation," muttered Kane, "or a command?"

"Whatever," Brigid said, "I think we'd better accept. It's where we were going eventually, anyhow."

The Agarthans turned and marched back in the direction they had come, not looking back to see if the
outlanders were following them or not. Kane and Brigid fell into step behind them.

"It'd be nice to know if we're guests or prisoners,"
Kane remarked.

"They probably don't care one way or the other,"
she declared. "They were assigned the task of meeting us, they're fulfilling it and that's all there is to
it."

"Who assigned it?"

Brigid shrugged. "I'm sure we'll find out."

They passed windowless dwellings that reminded
them both more of mausoleums than homes. The
streets were completely deserted, and the silence was
absolute except for the tramping of their feet.

They followed the three men to the base of the
tower, through a low-arched doorway and into a cor-

ridor. The hallway curved around, then abruptly became a flight of stairs—small stairs, exactly like the image Balam had implanted in Kane's mind.

"Seems a little redundant," Brigid commented wryly, carefully balancing herself on the small, irregular risers.

"What does?"

"They live in the cellar of the planet, yet they build another cellar beneath it."

Kane felt too tense to chuckle. A dim light shone below, its radiance peculiar, suggesting an electric arc light as seen through a milky mist. The throbbing drone grew louder as they descended, like the murmur of a far-off crowd.

When the steps ended at another archway, they saw a pair of generators. Twelve feet tall, they resembled two solid black cubes, a slightly smaller one placed atop the larger. The top cube rotated slowly, producing the drone. The odor of ozone was very pronounced.

Past the generator-flanked door, they entered an oval gallery whose walls, floor and ceiling seemed coated by a lacquer of amethyst, reflecting the light cast by flames dancing in a huge bowl brazier.

At the very center of the gallery, in a stone-rimmed depression, stood a stone altar, with a figure behind it. Kane caught his breath. The scene was exactly the same as Balam had shown him. Around the altar reposed bare bones, hollow eye sockets staring into eternity.

Lam stood at the altar, eyes wide open and seeming to stare straight into Kane's soul. Within his long fingers rested the cube of dark stone.

At first glance, the figure appeared to be a life-size statue, crafted with marvelous perfection. The high-boned face exuded a dignified calm, aware of all the immensity of time. The two big eyes were veiled by heavy, shutterlike lids.

Kane forced himself to step closer, heart hammering within his chest, focusing on the black yet somehow shining stone gripped in the six long fingers.

A hoarse, disembodied voice echoed through the gallery. "This is who we are."

BALAM STEPPED from the wavering shadows cast by the flames in the brazier. Like their escort, he wore a simple, draping robe of saffron. He gestured around him with one hand.

"Thousands of years ago was our migration. This is all that remains of the exodus. This is the nest of the Archons you sought in order to destroy. This is the home base of your enemies."

Balam nodded to the three men who stood shoulder to shoulder, eyes and expressions uncomprehending. "They are the last of the original hybrids created here, birthed to command the future. They are the immortal kings sung about in Agarthan legend. They bear the mingled blood of both our peoples."

His whispering voice held no emotion, no heat, but both Brigid and Kane sensed a grief so deep it was almost a despair. "We had no choice but to expand our breeding stock, our gene pool. To purify our impure blood."

Kane could not find words, but Brigid inquired quietly, "More and more genetic irregularities began cropping up, congenital defects became common-place?''

She indicated the triplets with one hand. "They appear to be suffering from a form of myxedema.''

Balam nodded, but did not speak.

Kane tried to dredge up anger, even pity, but all he found within him was a cold, weary resignation. "You misled, tricked and nearly obliterated humanity because of birth defects?''

Balam whispered, "One avoids disease by living in accordance with the laws of health. If not, one is at the mercy of those who spread disease.''

"What's that supposed to mean?'' Kane demanded.

"We set for ourselves the goal of not being affected by the disease spreaders. So we manipulated them to infect their own kind.''

"Disease spreaders,'' Brigid repeated bitterly. "You mean humanity.''

"Humankind had as many opportunities to check the disease, to cure it, to immunize themselves as they did to spread it. The final choice always lay with them. What you know as the Totality Concept could have accelerated man's development. Instead, it was used to accelerate the disease.''

Kane wished he could squeeze the trigger of his blaster and so blot out Balam, but he knew it wouldn't blot out reality.

"You could have had the stars by now,'' Balam continued. "You chose the slag heap instead.''

"We're nothing but savages to you,'' Kane said lowly. "Like you said, you will reign when man is reduced to the ape again. So it's all over, isn't it? The human race has come to an end.''

He didn't expect a response, but if Balam did, he figured he would agree. Instead, Balam husked out, ''Nothing ever ends, Kane.''

Balam stepped down gracefully into the depression, walking among the bones, standing beside the stiff figure with the black stone in its hands.

''This is Lam. My father. Within his hands, he safeguards our forebears' archives, the keys to what might have been and what yet may. His vigil is almost done.''

Brigid frowned. ''Explain.''

Balam's mouth quirked in an imitation of a smile, which was almost as startling as his reply. ''Would you have me explain the workings of one of your primitive aircraft if you did not first have a grounding in all the mechanics of its operations—the laws of friction, aerodynamics, electricity? Do you expect me to explain with a single sentence the nature of the trapezohedron?''

He paused to cough, then stated, ''When my people first determined the course of their future, they consulted the trapezohedron. Through it, they saw all possible futures to which their activities might lead. From the many offered to them, they chose the path that appeared to have the highest ratio of success.''

''What are you saying?'' Brigid asked impatiently. ''That the stone is some kind of computer, extrapolating outcomes from data input into it?''

''It does more than extrapolate. It brings into existence those outcomes.''

Brigid's eyes suddenly brightened. "You're talking about alternate event horizons."

"That is one description," replied Balam. "You experienced something similar recently. Time is energy. A flow of radiation particles your science has named chronons. Chronal radiation permits objects in sync with its frequencies to go up or down. This is the basic underpinning principle of what was called Operation Chronos."

"But we didn't go up or down," Brigid objected. "It was almost as if we went..." She paused, groping for the right word. "Sideways."

"Side-real space, where there are many tangential points lying adjacent to each other."

"Parallel casements," murmured Kane.

Again came the ghost of an appreciative smile. "You remembered."

"But I don't understand what it means."

Balam beckoned to him. "I will provide a small demonstration, so perhaps you may glean a faint comprehension."

Hesitantly, Kane stepped down into the depression, eyeing the motionless figure of Lam apprehensively. "Is he dead?"

Balam said only, "Touch the stone, Kane."

He didn't move. "What will happen?"

"That only you can say. Touch it."

Tentatively, Kane reached out with a forefinger, placing the tip on the cold surface of the black stone so as not to come in contact with the flesh of Lam. He waited for something to happen. Then it did.

Light, sound, vibration and solidity flared up through him, and the circuitry of his nervous system seemed to fuse as awareness and perception multiplied.

He saw himself dying on the street. He leaned against a lamppost with one hand, with the other pressed over his stomach, blood oozing between his fingers. His body wore tight black breeches and high black boots, an ebony uniform jacket with silver piping tight to the chest and shoulders. He saw an insignia patch on the right sleeve, worked in red thread, a thick-walled pyramid enclosing and partially bisected by three elongated but reversed triangles. Small disks topped each one, lending them a resemblance to round-pommeled daggers.

A broad black belt held half a dozen objects sheathed in pouches. Between his feet lay a Sin Eater and a peaked uniform cap.

As Kane watched, he saw himself sag to his knees, toppling sideways and down, sprawling across a cobblestoned gutter. Another figure slid into his frame of vision. It was a tall man, almost cadaverously lean, wearing an identical uniform.

Kane instantly recognized his narrow, sunken-cheeked face with its odd, flat complexion. The dark curved lenses of sunglasses masked his eyes. Before holstering his own Sin Eater, Colonel C. W. Thrush nudged his body with a booted foot.

Kane jerked his hand back, stumbling as if from a blow. Present and future mingled in his mind for an instant of utter chaos. Sounding half-strangled, he gasped, "I saw myself. I was wounded, dying. Is that my future?"

"No," Balam replied. "Your present on a parallel casement. On a lost Earth."

Kane blinked, desperately trying to rid his memory of what he had just seen, snatching for some straws of comprehension. "I don't understand."

"If you seek hard enough, to every question you shall know the answer." He paused, and added cryptically, "There are others who seek answers."

At that moment, Grigori Zakat, Gyatso and Trai stormed in.

Chapter 25

Zakat wielded the AK automatic, his face streaked with blood that trickled from a laceration on the side of his head. Gyatso's turban and spectacles were missing and a bruise purpled his forehead. Only Trai appeared unhurt by the rockfall. Kane assumed Yal had been seriously injured or killed, but he didn't figure on asking about him.

Zakat swept the barrel of the autorifle back and forth in jerky arcs, covering the triplets, then Brigid, then Kane and Balam.

His eyes widened when he saw the figure of Lam and widened even more when he got a good look at Balam. He seemed to be struck speechless, tongue glued to the roof of this mouth.

Gyatso's reaction was similar to when Leng first saw Balam. A torrent of words spilled from his lips and he dropped to his knees, bowing his head. Balam regarded him disdainfully, then coldly turned his back on him.

"Nobody move," croaked Zakat, his face shocking pale beneath its layer of dirt and blood. He had to forcibly wrest his gaze away from Lam and the black stone. "Disarm yourselves."

Kane and Brigid exchanged glances, and Kane

growled, "Screw you. You're the one who's out-gunned."

Zakat laughed, a wild, high tittering with notes of hysteria running through it. "Ah, but I have more targets."

He stepped swiftly behind the triplets, who looked his way disinterestedly. "Who are these cretins?"

"They have the minds of children," Brigid stated with a forced calm. "They're harmless."

"But you force me to use them to prove to you that I am not."

The shot sounded obscenely loud in the gallery, thunderous echoes rolling. The little man in the center arched his back, as if he had received a fierce blow between his shoulder blades. A wet crimson blossom bloomed on the front of his robe, the fabric bursting open in an eruption of blood. He toppled forward into the depression, bones clattering and rattling with the impact.

The other two men clapped their hands over their ears, eyes wide in wonder, drooling mouths each forming an O of wonder.

"You sick bastard!" Brigid shrilled, bringing her Uzi to waist level.

"To save the others," Zakat replied mildly, "all you have to do is disarm."

Kane holstered his Sin Eater, unbuckled it from his forearm and dropped it to the floor. He unscabbarded his boot knife and laid it next to the blaster. Reluctantly, Brigid unslung her Uzi, holding it by the strap. Trai rushed forward, snatching the weapons, frowning uncertainly for a second at the Sin Eater.

"What is it you want?" Kane demanded angrily.

Zakat stepped from behind the Agarthans and nodded toward the kneeling Gyatso. "What he wants."

"Power?" challenged Brigid.

Zakat smiled a pitying smile. "About three hundred years ago, an English novelist wrote, 'We seek power entirely for its own sake. We are not interested in the good of others; we are interested solely in power...the object of power is power.'"

He walked closer to Gyatso, who appeared to be mumbling a prayer. "The power locked up in the stone is the key to achieving that object. It is Gyatso's legacy, his by right of birth."

Balam spoke for the first time since Zakat and his people entered. In his scratchy, whispery voice he said, "He is the end result of many experiments conducted on this continent over a period of many centuries. His only legacy is that he exists at all."

Gyatso's expression slid from one extreme to another—shock, hurt, betrayal and finally outraged anger. Because Balam had spoken in English, he responded in the same language.

"I have heard all the tales about my ancestor, the Maha Chohan. I strengthened my will to find his nation and take my place in it. I did not allow myself to fail at any task, no matter how trivial. I devoted myself to learning the old ways of Agartha. I studied my entire life for this moment. I abase myself before you."

Balam's tone was flat, but it carried a contemptuous undercurrent. "You debase yourself, rather." He nodded toward Zakat. "You are but a foil for that man, and that is the true goal of all your ambition. To be used."

Gyatso sucked in a deep, shuddery breath, then released it in an enraged roar, *"I demand my legacy!"*

Balam gestured diffidently with a six-fingered
hand. "Take it."

Blinking at him in astonishment, Gyatso stammered, "You grant me permission to claim my birthright as the descendent of the Maha Chohan?"

Balam's retort was a whisper. "I grant you nothing."

With a rustle of his coat, Gyatso bounded to his
feet. He stepped down into the depression, pushing
Kane aside. He stopped before the figure of Lam. His
eyes widened until his jet-black irises were completely surrounded by the whites. His lips moved, and
a whispering, altered voice came forth. He spoke
quickly, the syllables tripping over each other so rapidly the words were unintelligible.

Gyatso grasped the stone, first with his left hand,
then his right, covering Lam's fingers with his own.
He bent forward, head touching it. Kane felt his nape
hairs tingling when the man crouched over as if drinking an invisible radiation into his soul.

Then Lam's eyes opened.

For an instant, there was a movement in the air
about him, such as the ripples made in water when a
fish swims close to the surface.

Gyatso's body spasmed violently, writhed and he
threw back his head and howled, a scream ripped
from the roots of his soul. His mouth gaped open, but
no words came out. He croaked a sound of pain and
terror and despair.

His back arched violently, and the sharp cracking
of cartilage and bone seemed to fill the gallery. From

the corners of each bulging eye squeezed droplets of blood. Then those eyes burst in gelatinous, watery sprays. He collapsed onto his back, arms and legs kicking and contorting.

Trai screamed long and loud in horror, and the shriek broke the invisible bonds weighing down the limbs of Brigid and Kane.

Kane sprang out of the depression directly for Zakat. The stunned Russian just managed to catch Kane's streaking movement in time to bring the AK around, but his motion was impeded by the two men standing around him.

Kane changed direction in midleap, diving low, bowling the men off their feet, knocking them into Zakat. All of them went down in tangle of thrashing limbs and hooting calls of confusion and distress.

Simultaneously, Brigid lunged for Trai, who stood and shrieked, hopping up and down in her terror. Because she bore a slight resemblance to Beth-Li, Brigid had no compunction about punching the girl as hard as she could on her rounded chin.

Trai spun almost completely around, stumbling over the kicking legs of the men, and went down, sprawling awkwardly.

Kane crawled over the twins, backfisting the barrel of the AK aside. Zakat's finger closed over the trigger at the same time, and he fired a stuttering burst into the ceiling. Ricochets screamed, and rock chips and fragments sifted down. The bolt of the autorifle snapped loudly against an empty chamber.

Kane gripped the barrel and the stock, throwing his weight downward, pressing the frame against Zakat's throat. The Russian wrenched and heaved for a frenzied instant, straining to keep the rifle from crushing his windpipe.

He flung up his left leg, twisting with surprising agility, slamming the back of his heel against Kane's collarbone and tossing him aside.

Zakat rolled to his feet immediately, giving his right hand a little shake. Kane saw the bone-handled knife with the six-inch blade slide from his sleeve into his palm.

The Russian cast a single, feverish glance in the direction of Gyatso, then spun around and ran.

Kane spared a moment to snatch up his holstered Sin Eater before he raced in pursuit. Brigid called out after him, "He has two facets of the stone, remember."

Kane didn't waste time or breath to tell her he was well aware of that. He stumbled up the small steps, cursing when he banged his knee against a riser. Grigori Zakat was already out of sight, in the corridor above, but his running footfalls echoed back to Kane.

He followed Zakat by sound alone, out of the tower and through the silent streets of the eerily illuminated city. The Russian was amazingly fleet of foot.

As Kane scrambled up the slope that led to the tunnel, he heard faintly, over the sounds of his scrabbling ascent, a swishing hum. The Sin Eater, still in its holster, was torn from his hand by a blow from a key-shaped cudgel. Pain stabbed through his metacarpal bones, into his wrist. He skipped around just as Yal appeared from behind a clump of boulders, snapping the key back into his hand by the leather thong.

Kane rushed him, legs pumping furiously. Yal

swung out with the cudgel again. Kane dodged, felt it smack along his left shoulder and kept running. He delivered his boot full into the Dob-Dob's groin.

Yal uttered a strangulated screech of agony and bent at the middle. Kane drove him half-erect again with a knee to the chin, and his fist flattened his nose, knocking him unconscious.

Retrieving his blaster, Kane noted with a grunt of disgust that the spring-release-cable mechanism in the holster was knocked askew. He knew from past experience it couldn't be repaired quickly or easily, so he raced into the tunnel opening.

He bumped and bounced from wall to wall and when he exited it, he caught just a fragmented glimpse of Zakat darting into one of the side passages. Kane went in after him.

The shaft was narrow, lit by the pale blue astral glow from overhead light panels, which turned complete darkness to twilight. He moved stealthily, somehow sensing that Zakat had stopped running and lay in wait for him.

The Russian's voice drifted through the passageway, from the murk ahead. "Why do you chase me, Kane?"

The unexpected question confused him, threw him off balance. "You have two pieces of the trapezohedron."

"So? Is that a reason to hound me, to murder me? If I give them to you, will you spare my life?"

Kane ignored the query, creeping on down the shaft, trying to make as little noise as possible.

Zakat chuckled, his voice a sepulchral echo. "You don't know the answer to that, do you? You believe you can kill me and suffer no consequences. Such arrogant simplicity."

Kane snorted. "Look who's talking, King of Fear. You murdered a mentally retarded man just to make a point. You think you're free of those consequences?"

"As you said," came Zakat's reply, "I had a point to make. His death was not gratuitous. I was obeying the law of power. All power has its price, whether in blood or dignity. Depending on the market value of the power sought, the price goes up. If you murder me out of revenge, you are squandering spiritual coin. You gain nothing."

"Except," Kane grated, "a crazy dead Russian. I'll settle for that."

The tunnel opened onto a broad, curving sweep of shelf rock. By the feeble glow shed by a light panel over the shaft mouth, Kane saw an outcropping of flint to his left. It was large enough for a man to hide behind.

Cautiously, Kane circled it, glancing over the rim of the ledge, seeing nothing but a pitch-black abyss below. The Russian hadn't concealed himself behind the rock formation, so he paced around the shelf, returning to the edge, wondering if the man had found a way to climb down into the chasm.

A rasping, scraping sound reached him, and he pivoted on his heel just as Grigori Zakat dropped lightly from a shadow-shrouded fissure above the tunnel mouth.

Zakat took a step forward. Kane backed up carefully so as not to slip on a loose stone and plunge over the precipice. He tossed his Sin Eater to one side to keep both hands free. The Russian took another slow, deliberate step, then leaped forward, knife held for a disemboweling thrust.

Kane kicked off the rock shelf and dived for Zakat's groin, but the slender man was ready. His knee came up hard against Kane's head, and at the same time, the edge of the knife slashed down at the base of Kane's skull.

Kane rolled frantically, feeling the dagger sink into the collar of his coat. Only the tough, Kevlar-weave fabric prevented it from biting deep into the back of his neck.

Springing to his feet, he faced Zakat, who now had his back to the abyss, but the Russian had no intention of staying there. Rushing to the attack, he wove a whistling web of steel with the dagger blade held before him. Kane stood his ground, balanced lightly on the balls of his feet, leaning back from the waist, batting Zakat's knife hand aside as the blade menaced his neck and chest.

For a long moment, they exchanged a flurry of knife strokes and hand slaps, the point of the blade missing Kane's midsection and throat by fractional margins, once dragging along the front of his coat.

Grigori Zakat's breath came in labored rasps, and his face darkened in exertion and frustrated fury. He stumbled slightly from the force of one of Kane's open-hand blows against his forearm. As he regained his balance, he lashed out with the knife in a back-swing.

Kane turned with him, locking the man's right wrist under his left arm and heaving up on it with all his upper-body strength. Zakat cried out in pain and jacked up a knee, seeking to pound Kane's testicles, but Kane shifted so the impact was on his upper thigh.

Zakat's free hand darted out, locking around Kane's throat, fingers clamping down like a steel vise. Kane maintained the pressure on the captured arm, and the knife dropped from nerve-numbed fingers, chiming against the stone.

Zakat's hand tightened, and Kane fought for air, blackness closing in on the edges of his consciousness. Releasing the Russian's arm, he lunged backward, at the same time raising both hands above his head. Pivoting violently at the waist, he used the well-developed wing muscle at the base of his shoulder as a fulcrum, prying away Zakat's stranglehold.

The Russian snarled as his hand lost its grip, and he ripped strips of Kane's skin away beneath his long fingernails.

Kane inhaled deeply, repressing the cough reflex. He knew if Zakat had latched on to him with both hands, the man would even now be choking him to death.

Zakat swung at his face with a knotted fist. Kane dodged back and then in, ramming into him with a shoulder, carrying him back to the rim of the ledge, hand full of the man's coattails.

Digging in his heels, feet gouging shallow channels through the scattered pebbles, Zakat pounded his fists into Kane's kidneys, sending waves of pain-induced nausea through him. The Russian wrenched his body back and forth, heaving from side to side as he wriggled out of his coat, slipping away from Kane's rush. Kane tripped over his out-thrust leg and sprawled on his hands and knees within a couple of feet of the shelf lip. He caught a glimpse of the facets of the black stones falling from the coat's pocket and bouncing into the shadows of the outcropping.

Uttering a cry of dismay, Zakat lunged for them, and Kane swept out his legs in a slashing kick, catching the Russian just behind the knees. He fell, half on top of Kane. They thrashed in a limb-flailing whirl, Zakat clawing for Kane's eyes.

Kane stiffened his left wrist, locking the fingers in a half-curled position against the palm, and drove a killing leopard's-paw strike toward the man's face, hoping to crush his nose and propel bone splinters through his sinus cavities and into his brain.

The struggling Zakat lowered his head, and Kane's hand impacted against his skull. Needles of pain lanced up his forearm and into his elbow joint.

Face contorted in a bare-toothed snarl, Zakat punched him in the jaw, bouncing the back of his head against the unyielding surface of the ledge. Little multicolored pinwheels spiraled before Kane's eyes. He thrust up his right leg, pounding the knee into Zakat's rib cage. The Russian grunted, cursed and slid to one side. Kane rolled, bucking the man off of him.

Zakat leaped onto Kane's back, arms quickly curving under and up, hands linking at the back of Kane's neck in a full nelson. Kane's head went down under the relentless pressure of the Russian's arms. With a thrill of horror, he heard the faint creak of vertebrae.

"Not the first time," Zakat grunted breathlessly into his ear, "I have broken a man's neck."

Kane had no reason to doubt it as his face flattened against the unyielding surface of the stone shelf. Zakat used his toes, the balls of his feet to muscle

Kane forward. Sharp-edged pebbles bit into his knees, cut into his hands as he resisted the Russian's efforts to manhandle him off the ledge. Zakat strained against him, trying to snap his neck and propel him into the abyss.

Levering with his arms, bucking with his hips, Kane shoved himself sideways. Zakat twisted to keep from being pinned beneath him. He steadily applied the full nelson, driving Kane's chin against his collarbone.

Clawing up a fistful of grit, Kane thrashed and kicked, getting his hand up behind his head. He mashed and ground the rock particles into Zakat's face, ruthlessly scouring his eyes.

The Russian didn't cry out, but he inhaled sharply, tossing his head, and for an instant the pressure against Kane's neck lessened. In that instant, Kane tightened his body like a bowstring, arching his back, planting both boot soles firmly on the ground and slamming the back of his skull against Zakat's forehead.

The Russian uttered a growl, bearing down again, and Kane head-butted him a second time. The distance was too short for maximum effect, but Zakat's grip loosened even more.

Kane's legs levered like springs, powering him up and over in a somersault, breaking the full nelson. Zakat spit an oath in Russian and flailed around for the knife, fighting to get to his feet at the same time.

Kane made it a full half second before Zakat did, and as the Russian's fingers touched the handle of the dagger, Kane swept his left leg up in a fast, powerful kick. He delivered the metal-reinforced toe of his boot against the underside of the Russian's jaw.

Head snapping back, Zakat fell heavily to the shelf edge, his body dislodging a few loose stones. They clicked as they bounced against the chasm wall, disappearing into the blackness.

Despite glassy eyes, the slender Russian bounded to his feet and launched several roundhouse punches at Kane's face. Kane ducked one fist, blocked the other with a forearm and caught Zakat in the face with a lightning-swift double hammer blow. Blood sprayed from the man's nostrils, and he swayed, clumsily trying to return the punches.

Zakat was deceptively strong, with years of experience as a back-alley fighter, but as Kane evaded the man's fists, he knew he had never stood toe-to-toe with an opponent and fought it out—at least not against an opponent with Kane's training, instincts and reflexes.

Zakat thrust his arms forward, hands seeking another stranglehold. Kane knocked both arms aside with his elbows and whipped his right fist into Zakat's temple. He drove a pile-driver punch deep into the man's belly, fancying he could feel the his backbone press against his knuckles.

The Russian jackknifed at the waist, a strangulated wheeze bursting from his lips. Zakat staggered to one side, boots grating loudly on rock as he fought to keep erect. Measuring him off, Kane bent diagonally at the waist, arcing his left leg up and around in a spinning crescent kick.

The toe of his boot slammed against the side of Zakat's jaw, turning him completely around in his tracks. It was a fast move, deftly delivered, but nothing his Mag martial-arts instructor would have cheered about.

Zakat stumbled, arms windmilling, and he stumbled off the rim of the ledge. He didn't plunge into the darkness. His hands shot out, fingers securing a grip on the stone lip. Kane heard him kicking frantically for a foothold.

Kane stepped to the outcropping, groped around its base for a few seconds and his hands closed over the facets of stone. He moved to the edge of the shelf. Towering over him, Kane gazed down into Grigori Zakat's blood-wet face. Panting, he bared his red-filmed teeth at him in either a grimace or a grin, eyes darting to the two black rocks in Kane's hand.

"You don't dare let me die," he half gasped. "You need me, need my abilities to channel the energies of the stone."

Kane stopped himself from massaging the deep, boring pain at the back of his neck. He rasped, "What makes you think I give a shit?"

Uncertainty flickered in Zakat's pale eyes. "You have the stone, but you don't know how to use it. Its power is useless to you without me."

Kane said nothing, but upon glancing down he saw a small object glinting against the dark rock. Slowly, he eased to one knee and picked up the tiny wooden phallus with the stylized crystal testicles by its leather thong.

Zakat stared at it in hungry shock.

"What about the power of this?" Kane asked in a soft, rustling tone.

With his right hand, Zakat made a grab for the

amulet. He missed it by inches, and the fingers of his left hand slipped. Frantically, he scrabbled to regain his hold. In a high, aspirated voice, he shrieked, "Useless! You'll have a key, but no idea of how to find the lock!"

Zakat's forearms trembled with the strain of resisting the irresistible drag of gravity. His wild eyes followed the pendulum-like movement of the Khlysty cross dangling from Kane's hand.

"You need me!" His scream slashed through the darkness, echoing repeatedly.

Kane dropped the wood-and-crystal emblem between Zakat's hands. "And you need this," he said quietly, flatly. "Use it as a key."

Zakat made a frantic grab for it. After an instant of mad clawing, he snatched it up and then disappeared over the edge of the shelf. He pitched down into the impenetrable blackness, and Kane heard his body slithering against the rock wall, then nothing, not even a scream.

He kneeled at the rim of the ledge, waiting for the faint sound of Grigori Zakat's body striking the floor of Hell. When it didn't come, he slowly pushed himself to his feet. Tension drained out of him, leaving him weak and trembling.

Hefting the fragments of stone in his hand, he tried to sense something special in the way they felt or looked. They appeared to have properties no different from the rocks that surrounded him.

"Doesn't that just figure," he muttered to the abyss. He slipped the rocks into a pocket, then turned and shuffled into the tunnel.

Chapter 26

The first thing Kane heard upon returning to the gallery beneath the tower was a woman weeping piteously. Trai sat on one of the paving stones at the rim of the depression, huddled in a little ball of grief, hugging herself, rocking back and forth. To his surprise, Brigid sat beside her, patting her back, speaking to her soothingly in her own language. They were alone, the bodies of Gyatso and the slain triplet nowhere in sight.

"What's with Zakat's bitch, Baptiste?" he demanded. "She'll have more to cry about once she hears about where he ended up."

Brigid glanced at him reproachfully. "She knows already, somehow. She felt the link she shared with him disappear."

"Good. I wasn't sure if the son of a bitch was dead or not."

"What about you?" she asked.

He rubbed the back of his neck. "Just don't ask me to stand on my head for the next couple of days."

Brigid got to her feet, a hand on Trai's shoulders. "She's just a child, not really to blame. She was a servant in the monastery, and the monks, particularly the high lama, treated her badly. Zakat seduced her with kindness—and probably his psi-abilities."

Kane shrugged disinterestedly. "Where's Balam?"

"Attending to the body of his son."

"His son?" Kane echoed, startled.

"The triplets are his children, born of a human woman nearly four hundred years ago. Like he said, they are the last of their particular breed."

Kane shook his head and covered his eyes for a moment. He tried to loathe Balam again, even tried to pity him, but he could find neither emotion within him.

"Kane."

At the hoarse whisper, he dropped his hand and saw Balam, flanked by the drooling twins, stepping down into the depression. "You recovered the facets of the trapezohedron."

Balam wasn't asking; he was stating. Kane removed them from his pocket and held them out. Balam made no indication he even noticed. He inclined his head toward the ebony cube laced within Lam's fingers.

"Take it and go."

Kane's blood ran cold and his flesh prickled. "And end up like Gyatso? Offhand, Balam, I can think of a hundred easier ways to check out."

"The new human was responsible for his fate. The energy he directed into the stone was strong, but it was of an incompatible frequency. It was deflected, turned inward and it destroyed him. Take the trapezohedron, Kane."

He looked into the face of Lam, eyes closed again in placid contemplation. He stepped down into the depression.

"Kane!" Brigid spoke warningly, fearfully. "What if—?" She bit off the rest of her question.

He replied, "If the 'what if' happens, you know what to do."

He heard the clicking of the overhung firing bolt on her Uzi being drawn back, and he threw Balam a cold, ironic smile. It wasn't returned.

Reaching out, he touched the black rock in Lam's hands, feeling his pulse pound with fear. He tugged gently, experimentally. The trapezohedron came away easily, and without resistance it nestled in Kane's hands.

Almost as soon as it did, the flesh on Lam's face and limbs dried, browned and withered. His eyes collapsed into their sockets, and his body fell, his robe belling up briefly as he joined the skeletal remains around the altar.

Kane froze, the hair lifting from his scalp, his mind filling with primal, nameless terror. He gaped wild-eyed at Balam.

"His vigil is complete. Yours begins."

Kane despised the tremor in his hands and voice. "My vigil for what?"

"To find a way for your people to survive, as mine did."

Kane swallowed with painful effort. His throat felt as if it were lined with sandpaper. "The only way is to displace the barons—you know that."

Balam nodded.

"What do you want in return?"

"Nothing in return. I have returned to the old, old ways of our forebears when we passed on truth rather than burning it."

"But you *did* burn it," Brigid spoke up accusingly.

"To preserve ourselves," Balam replied. "A sacrifice made for an appointed period of time. That time is over. Our blood prevails."

Kane shook his head in frustration. "I don't— Are you *betraying* the barons, blood of your blood?"

"They are blood of your blood, too, Kane. I no more betray them than you do."

"A state of war will exist between our two cultures again," Brigid noted. "Rivers of that mixed blood will be spilled."

"If that is the road chosen," Balam said faintly, "then that is the road chosen. Blood *is* like a river. It flows through tributaries, channels, streams, refreshing and purifying itself during its journey. But sometimes it freezes, and no longer flows. A glacier forms, containing detritus, impurities. The glacier must be dislodged to allow the purifying journey to begin anew."

Quietly, Brigid asked, "And what of you? What will you do?"

Balam stood, swaying slightly, his huge, fathomless and passionless eyes fixed on them. Then he flung up one long, thin arm in an unmistakable gesture, pointing to the entrance to the gallery. "I will do nothing, and you must do what you can. Go."

Then he turned and walked away, trailed by his sons.

For an instant, Kane grappled with the desire to go after him, but he knew there was no point to it. Taking Balam back to Cerberus served no purpose. What Balam actually was, Kane could not know, but a strange, aching sadness came over him as he watched the creature stride gracefully away.

He didn't know why he felt such a vacuum within him; then he realized he was reacting to an absence of hate.

Kane turned toward Brigid, and she saw the confusion, the uncertainty in his eyes. Softly, he asked, "Now what do we do?"

Brigid looked from Kane to Trai and to the black stone nestled between his hands. "We wait for tomorrow."

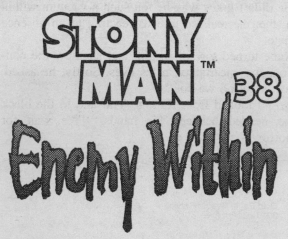

Take
2 explosive books
plus a
mystery bonus
FREE